Critics on Sujata Massey and the Rei Shimura Series

"*The Kizuna Coast* is Sujata Massey's most moving novel in the Rei Shimura mystery series so far. Her and her sleuth's love for Japan and its people is evident in this tale involving the destruction of the earthquake and resulting tsunami in the Tohoku region in 2011. While Rei follows clues to locate her antiques mentor and later investigate a murder, readers get an authentic look at what it was like for survivors and rescue workers days after the devastating disaster. Bravo to Massey's clear-eyed recounting of a recovery that is still ongoing."
—Naomi Hirahara, Edgar-award winning author of *SNAKESKIN SHAMISEN* and *MURDER ON BAMBOO LANE*

"Agatha-winner Massey's engaging tenth mystery to feature antiques dealer and part-time spy Rei... An appealing protagonist and memorable supporting characters blend smoothly with lessons in Hawaiian and Japanese history in a tale sure to win new readers for the series."
—*Publishers Weekly* on *SHIMURA TROUBLE*

"Fans of Sujata Massey's series, starring stylish Japanese antiquities dealer Rei Shimura, are in for a fashion show as well as a mystery... Catching up with Rei is always rewarding."
—*USA Today* on *GIRL IN A BOX*

"Massey builds the bridge between mystery fiction and mainstream women's fiction... A lively, intuitive view of contrasting societies and a young woman trying to find her place in the world."
—*Fort Lauderdale Sun-Sentinel* on *THE TYPHOON LOVER*

"Massey's pungent take on mixed marriages and East-West culture clashes is first-rate."
—*Kirkus Reviews* on *THE PEARL DIVER*

"Combining the legal mystery with Japanese history and antiques is a winning stroke for Ms. Massey. Intricately plotted and filled with Asian lore and customs, this charming love story is spiced with courage and danger."
—*Dallas Morning News* on *THE SAMURAI'S DAUGHTER*

"The cross-cultural suspense story is as active as the traffic pattern at Dupont Circle... Japanese pop culture references, style, intrigue and the quick pace of *THE BRIDE'S KIMONO* combine... to attract hip readers."
—*Daily Press* (Virginia) on *THE BRIDE'S KIMONO*

"Sujata Massey takes readers on a thoughtful tour of contemporary Japanese youth culture in this accomplished murder mystery... deftly sketching everyday life in parts of Tokyo rarely seen by tourists, Massey tells a series of overlapping stories about identity, the popular media and the hilarious frenzy of comic book culture."
—*Publishers Weekly* on *THE FLOATING GIRL*

"A totally captivating experience. A unique plot, exceptional protagonist, and some subtle cultural lessons are as beautifully arranged as a vase of cherry blossoms."
—*Booklist* on *THE FLOWER MASTER*

"A gifted storyteller who delivers strong characters, a tight plot and an inside view of Japan and its culture."
—*USA Today* on *ZEN ATTITUDE*

"Sly, sexy and deftly done. *THE SALARYMAN'S WIFE* is one to bring home."
—*People* Page Turner of the Week on *THE SALARYMAN'S WIFE*

THE KIZUNA COAST

THE KIZUNA COAST

SUJATA MASSEY

THE IKAT PRESS
Baltimore, MD

Trade Paperback ISBN: 978-0-983661-05-4
Hardcover ISBN: 978-0-983661-06-1

Dedicated to the People of Japan

Rei Shimura Books in Order

The Salaryman's Wife
Zen Attitude
The Flower Master
The Floating Girl
The Bride's Kimono
The Samurai's Daughter
The Pearl Diver
The Typhoon Lover
Girl In A Box
Shimura Trouble
The Convenience Boy And Other Stories Of Japan
The Kizuna Coast

Other Books By Sujata Massey

The Sleeping Dictionary
The Ayah's Tale

About This Book

In 2008, I thought that my Rei Shimura books were done. Six years later, though, I'm releasing a new book in the series. You're still here, willing to read? Thanks, and you deserve the backstory.

Shimura Trouble, the tenth Rei mystery, came out in 2008 under a series of challenging circumstances, including a request to considerably cut its length. After working through a severe edit, I wasn't sure I had the energy to keep writing Rei books—plus I was spending more time in India than in Japan and had a lot of ideas in that direction. Therefore, I constructed *Shimura Trouble's* ending to tie up loose ends and address readers' hopes for Rei's love life. As far as I was concerned, the girl could hold hands and drink mai tais in the Hawaiian sunset for a while.

Rei and I embarked on an amicable separation. During the time that she was renovating an early twentieth-century cottage in Hawaii, I was taking a paintbrush to a 1913 house in Minnesota, and working the rest of the time on *The Sleeping Dictionary*, my first historical novel set in late British Raj India. It felt fresh and challenging to create a cast of new characters and also to build their storyline around real historical events in India.

Then came a very terrible Friday. It was March 11, 2011, and while driving through snow, I heard the radio report about a massive earthquake on Japan's main island, Honshu. By the time I reached a TV, the tsunami had already struck.

Once again, I became immersed in Japan—but in a way I never had before. The bright lights, luxuries, fast trains, and sweet cartoon images were replaced by hardship, power outages, meltdown, and the loss of almost twenty thousand people. It was the biggest horror the country had faced since World War II.

Like many around the world, I was filled with a desire to do something. For a while there were no flights into Japan for would-be volunteers. All we could do was give money and prayers. I imagined how frustrated Rei Shimura would feel, trapped on her Hawaiian island. And I knew she'd find a way around the barriers and get into Japan and the tsunami-ravaged Tohoku coast.

The first draft of this novel, *The Kizuna Coast*, took about six months to write: a speed record for me. But then I put it aside for a few years to deal with editing and launching *The Sleeping Dictionary* as well as moving from Minneapolis back to Baltimore. Therefore, I didn't return to seriously working on the book until 2014.

Because of the real framework of the 2011 earthquake, tsunami, and nuclear disaster, this book could probably classify as a modern historical novel within the Rei mystery series. Yes, there's a crime to solve, a love story, and the typical cast of characters... but it's different.

Kampai!
Sujata

Cast of Characters

Rei Shimura—Raised in California and trained in Japan, a world-class young woman who deals in antiques and personal intrigue

Michael Hendricks—Rei's new husband, a former spy who now works for an American think tank on Pacific Rim issues

Yoshitsune Shimura—Rei's great-great-uncle Yosh, whose son Edwin and daughter-in-law Margaret are Rei's relatives living in Hawaii

Yasushi Ishida—Tokyo antiques dealer who is Rei's most important mentor

Hachiko—Mr. Ishida's beagle-Akita mix dog

Richard Randall—Rei's beloved friend and former roommate who still lives in Tokyo with his boyfriend, Enrique

Norie Shimura—Rei's aunt who lives in Yokohama, married to Hiroshi Shimura. Their children are Dr. Tom (Tsutomu) Shimura, an emergency-room doctor in Tokyo, and Chika Shimura, an executive trainee in Osaka

Mr. Okada—small businessman who owns a *senbei* cracker-roasting shop and is a neighbor to Mr. Ishida

Dr. Kubo—veterinarian at Animal House clinic in Tokyo

Mr. Yano—volunteer director of Helping Hands organization

Mayumi Kimura—Mr. Ishida's eighteen-year-old assistant at the antiques shop and a lacquer artist. Her parents, Mr. and Mrs. Kimura, are lacquer artists.

Mrs. Endo—senior-citizen volunteer

Akira Rikyo—Mayumi's high-school sweetheart. His father, Mr. Rikyo, is a carpenter, and his mother, Mrs. Rikyo, is a textile artist. His sister is Hanako, and his nieces are Noriko and Sachiko

Mayor Kazuo Hamasaki—mayor of Sugihama

Mr. Morioka—owner of Takara Auction House in Sugihama

Michiko Tanaka—a nurse who is a co-worker of Tom Shimura and volunteers with Helping Hands

Nobuko—a professional cook volunteering with Helping Hands

Sgt. Lee Simonson—medical corpsman in the US Army

Private McDonald—a driver for the US Army

Dr. Nishi—a Japanese physician who is also a colonel in the Japan Maritime Self-Defense Force (JMSDF)

Miki Haneda—a seven-year-old Sugihama girl with mother named Sadako

Constable Ota—Sugihama police officer

Lieutenant-Colonel Uchida—a JMSDF officer

Petty Officer Oshima—a dog handler in the JMSDF

Glock—female artist and a roommate of Mayumi, along with another young woman artist, Eri

Yoshiko—beautician who works with Richard Randall at Blond Apparition

Mr. Koji—construction site boss

Queen Cake—bar manager in Tokyo

Masa—a teenaged boy from Sugihama

Mr. Fujita—a lawyer

Sgt. Kodama—Tohoku Prefecture police sergeant

Japanese Name Suffixes

Suffixes commonly follow surnames—or even first names—to show respect or kinship. The suffix "san" is the most commonly used one; it means Mr., Mrs., or Miss. "Kun" is the equivalent of "guy" and is typically used by young men and boys toward younger males, but now is sometimes used by young women for good friends of both genders. "Chan" means little one, and is used for children of both genders and young women; and sometimes when addressing parents or grandparents.

CHAPTER 1

_____

If you've been through an earthquake, you remember.

You recall where you were and exactly what you were doing; what you had for breakfast and the plan for the day's activities. What's harder is explaining the panic that rolled through you when the ground wouldn't stop shaking. The moment you learned that everything you trusted to be safe and solid, was not.

I've weathered a variety of earthquakes, large and small, in California and Japan. But the earthquake that still figures in my dreams is the big one: the Great Eastern Kanto Earthquake of 2011. Even though I wasn't even there when the earth buckled.

I was perched midway in the Pacific, playing mah-jongg, a thousand-year-old Asian game of tiles that moves fast and furious. My Hawaiian friends play with a set dating from the 1920s, so the tiles are probably ivory or bone. This gives me the creeps, although the set's owner, Pak Chang, claims that such old tiles carried great _feng shui_.

But that disagreement is just the start. Pak, my great-uncle

Yosh, and their cohort, my neighbor Lilia DeCruz, continually fuss about the right rules to follow: American, Japanese, or British. As a result, almost everything goes—including controversial "dirty" hands using tile pairs from more than one suit.

The night of the disaster, I was involved in a different kind of dirty mah-jongg—because Michael Hendricks, my brand-new husband, was at the table. This kind of mah-jongg meant a bare toe tracing its way up my calf, or a whispered code about something happening later on. Michael could make me blush with just three or four words uttered at an extremely low decibel level. I'd become flustered to the point that my attention disintegrated to Michael's level, and then both of us would lose.

Michael and I had failed so many times that it was becoming legend in the community. But what happened after those losses was the best part of mah-jongg night.

"I don't care what the governor says about feeling sorry for people, it's not right for people to live on the beach. Looks like a tent city," Uncle Yosh grumbled. He was talking about the stretch of beach that had become an encampment of homes for locals who couldn't afford Oahu housing.

"Then where you gonna put them? Nobody's got acres of land lying around for your great-niece to build them houses. Unless she knows something we don't." Lilia looked significantly at me.

Underneath the table, I flicked Michael's stealthy hand off my thigh so I could concentrate when answering.

"I wish there were a secret land parcel I could tell you about." Because of my work, I was considered a possessor of important information. About six months earlier, I'd put my antiques work on hold to help with the restoration of Ewa Landing, sixty small cottages that had been built in the early twentieth century for sugar-plantation workers. Abandoned when the plantation closed in the 1970s, these cottages were where Lilia, Pak, and Michael and I lived.

Michael winked at me. His blue eyes stood out against his sailor's tan, which had deepened since moving to Hawaii.

Great-Uncle Yosh shot the two of us a disapproving glare. "Not many men got the nerve to sleep in a house their wife paid for."

Michael laughed as if my uncle had made some kind of fabulous joke. But I was slightly embarrassed. Not because it was wrong that I'd been the one offered the cottage—but because white guys on this majority-Asian island were ribbed just a little bit harder than anyone else.

"It's modern times, Uncle Yosh," I chided him in a mild voice, just as Carly, Aunty Lilia's daughter, hurried up with a kid attached to each hand.

"Hey! When can we go out in the canoe again?" demanded Kai, the older boy.

"Nobody wants to canoe now! You folks hear what's happening?" Carly's voice was loud and urgent.

"Hold on, Carly," Aunty Lilia began.

"Go look at CNN!" Carly shouted. "An earthquake just happened in Japan, and the big wave's gonna roll over them, what you call it, cyclone or soonamee—"

"Tsunami," I corrected, feeling a chill steal over me, despite the fact it was eighty-two degrees.

Michael was already scrambling to get his cell phone out of the pocket of his cargo shorts. He shook his head as he looked at the screen. "Hank's called three times. Damn it, I never felt any vibration."

I'd made Michael silence his phone because I was tired of frequent, nonessential interruptions from his boss. Hank was a former navy captain working through the sorrow of not making admiral by acting like one in his new civilian job. As Michael sprinted off, phone at his ear, I felt guilty. Michael worked for a group that dealt with threats to the Asia-Pacific region. He was supposed to know about crises before they aired on CNN.

"I'm sorry to break up the game like this. But if Michael's on duty, I want to make sure he's got what he needs for a long night," I explained as I gathered up our tiles to turn in.

"Don't be silly," Lilia chided. "It's terrible about Japan. So many here came from there. Nobody got time to play mah-jongg after hearing such news."

"You woulda lost anyway, Rei," Uncle Yosh said, looking at the tiles I turned in. "Girl, I can't believe all your bad luck."

For *feng shui* reasons, I'd painted the door to our cottage a perfect Chinese crimson. The positive, powerful color was supposed to shield us from misfortune. Michael had been so hasty that he'd left this door ajar; I closed it behind me and took a few deep breaths before moving on.

I really hoped that Carly's reaction was overkill. Japan had planned carefully for earthquakes and tsunamis; state-of-the-art construction and evacuation routes would ensure optimum safety. But I had relatives and friends in Japan, where I'd lived about four years. This made the disaster a personal one.

Trying to calm myself, I slipped out of my sandals and walked barefoot through the dining room. The small room was furnished with just a few pieces: a persimmon-wood Japanese *tansu* chest, and a low paulownia tea table flanked by two indigo cushions. This was where I planned to serve our supper of grilled tuna, asparagus, and Japanese rice flavored with *kombu*.

In the back of the house, near the kitchen and bathroom, was the original bedroom that we'd converted into our study. The small room held an old mission-style desk from Michael's former apartment, his desktop computer, and a rattan daybed I'd covered with vintage Japanese quilts. This served our few guests and was a favorite lounging place near our only television.

Michael was in the study on his phone call, keeping his eyes on the wall-mounted flat screen. CNN showed an aerial view of the Pacific Ocean. Although the sound was muted, a scrolling newsfeed confirmed Carly's report.

Major Earthquake Hits Northeast Japan to be followed by tsunami. Thousands feared injured. Richter scale 9.0. And then, the message repeated.

The Richter scale reading was probably off, because I'd never heard of such a powerful earthquake. I raised the volume to low, so I'd get more details without disturbing Michael's call.

An American newscaster was reporting that the earth's plates had shifted under the Pacific about two hundred miles from the city of Sendai. The newscaster was chattering about the coast's many seawalls and sirens going off everywhere and people evacuating in an orderly fashion.

As he spoke, the picture shifted from the ocean to traffic-clogged roads and collapsed buildings of a town identified as Sugihama. Its name was familiar; I'd probably been through the area antiquing. With anxiety, I watched people hurry up steep outdoor tsunami evacuation stairs, past gawkers stopped along their route with cameras and phones pointed toward the ocean. I wanted to yell at them that this was not a YouTube moment, and they were slowing escape for others. But who would hear?

Michael finished his call and came to sit with me on the daybed. "It's Friday afternoon," he said in a low voice. "Plenty of fishermen are out on the water."

And everyone else was at work or in school, or out shopping or inside their homes. Sure, they'd hear the sirens, but not everybody had a car they could speed away in, or legs strong enough to run.

Michael's eyes were fixed on a foamy white line growing across the dark-blue ocean. "Hank says it's a couple of minutes away from hitting land."

"It's long, but doesn't look that high." After speaking I realized the overhead camera couldn't reveal the wave's height. I had no way to judge, until the event itself.

"I don't think there are any seawalls taller than fifteen feet," Michael said, as if he were thinking along the same lines. "Let's hope that's high enough for this little town. Oh, no, hold on. There it goes!"

The line finally turned into a real wave that rushed smoothly over a seawall. The powerful, monstrous surge was lifting up all kinds of things—houses, street lamps, buses—before sucking them under. More water kept pushing from behind, and soon the entire small-town landscape was no longer there.

All of it, gone.

I grabbed Michael and buried my face in his chest. I felt his heart beating rapidly against my wet cheek.

"It's the worst thing I've ever seen." Michael breathed deeply. "I'm really sorry, but I can't stick around. Hank's informed me that a complementary tsunami wave is headed for Hawaii."

"What the hell is that?"

"The rebound of the energy generated by the wave that hit Tohoku. Sirens will go off all over Honolulu and coastal towns in a couple of hours, and if people in this development want to avoid a massive traffic jam they should gather their valuable papers now and evacuate."

I stared at him, feeling this news was too much to process. "Will you tell them?"

"I've got to get to the Tsunami Warning Center, and I suppose I'll get my orders from Hank over there. You can spread the news at Ewa Landing."

My own cell phone rang, and I snatched it up. "Hello?"

"Rei-chan, did you hear?" All the way from San Francisco, my father's voice crackled with worry.

"Yes, Dad. Michael's here, too. I'm putting your call on speakerphone so we can all hear each other."

"Hi, Toshiro." Michael's voice was warm. "You must be worried for your brother's family."

"Indeed I am. I called his house and had no answer, even though it's a time that Norie should be home," my father said. "And I never heard of an earthquake measuring 9.0, have you? We've been told to stay away from the beaches because there will be a reciprocal wave coming from the earthquake's epicenter."

"I hear you. In fact, I'm just getting ready to help my office deal with our own potential tsunami." As he spoke, Michael was putting all kinds of communications gear into his briefcase.

"Please stay overnight at Honokai Hale. That is truly high

ground." My father was speaking of the cliffside home belonging to Uncle Yosh, his son Edwin, and daughter-in-law Margaret.

"Don't worry, Dad. I'll drive over with Uncle Yosh. He came to our neighborhood this evening to play mah-jongg, so it'll be very easy to get going."

"Good. I won't have to worry about any of you, then."

Two heavy knocks thudded on the front door.

"That may be him now. Michael, can you get the door?" I asked, but my husband had already vacated the room, leaving nothing but flip-flop sandals behind.

CHAPTER 2

Even with Uncle Yosh walking alongside me, my door-to-door encouragement of neighborhood evacuation attracted no interest. People wanted to huddle in their homes, watching the tragedy replay across each network. Lilia had been watching her TV nonstop and informed us the wave had been twenty-three-feet tall. Shaking her head, she told me, "We got nothing that we can't handle, compared to that."

Michael called my cell from his office to say he wasn't sure if he'd be released from work that night and hoped Uncle Yosh could leave a key near the front door.

"No need for locking; nobody messes with Shimuras," my uncle answered tersely.

"I'll try to take that as an invitation," Michael said, when I repeated my uncle's *bon mot*. "But don't wait up."

Uncle Yosh and I got in his vintage Toyota sedan around six, and quickly realized that outside of Ewa Landing, others were evacuating. Driving west on Farrington Highway, the Celica was quickly absorbed in a long line of taillights that reminded me of the candle-lit paper boats that floated on water during O-bon ancestor-remembrance ceremonies.

We rode mostly in silence; my brain was fogging as badly as the windshield of the twenty-five-year-old car. I knew the horror was just beginning. In the hours that lay ahead, thousands of people would remain trapped underneath buildings and debris or marooned in buildings surrounded by water. And then there were those who were without anything to cling to, who were swimming, floating, and drowning.

Yosh and I were received warmly by our relatives, who offered drinks and a *yakisoba* dinner. I found it impossible to relax, even after everyone had gone to their rooms and the living room was darkened for me to sleep on the fold-out sofa. Aunt Margaret must have heard me rustling, because she came in the wee hours with a container of Tylenol PM. The pharmaceuticals eventually did the trick, but over and over, I dreamed the wave had come to us. I was on a staircase, desperately trying to scramble higher, but an obstacle blocked me from safety. A dog barked somewhere, over and over, until the nightmare finally ended.

It was full-on morning; I awoke to sun streaming straight into my eyes and the smell of grease in the air. I was still sprawled on the folded-out sofa bed in the Shimuras' cluttered living room. My head was cloudy from the sleeping pills, and a line of pain ran across my midback, courtesy of the sofa bed's bar. Michael was on the other side; he'd slipped into bed when I was knocked out.

From the kitchen, I could hear my aunt and uncle talking about the local impact.

"Just a tiny one-foot wave hit Waikiki," Uncle Edwin scoffed. "All those warnings for evacuation made no sense. The lady at Safeway was saying our wave was too small even for a toddler to surf."

"Better safe than sorry. Remember the 1960 tsunami in Hilo?" Aunt Margaret's high voice reproached from the kitchen. "People knew it was coming, but some stayed to watch like fools and got themselves killed." She looked through to the living room and waved at me. "Rei, you and Michael gotta get up! Come watch over the veggie bacon Edwin got for you. Everyone else is having Portuguese sausage."

Rubbing my eyes, I went into the kitchen. The artificial bacon was sizzling on the stove; using a spatula, I flipped it, although it held no appeal for me. Looking toward the crowded kitchen table, I saw the little television Aunt Margaret always kept going. The TV was broadcasting a repeat of one of the morning news shows, and a newscaster was speaking about the results of the earthquake and tsunami. Then came the horrifying pictures of destruction and people searching for loved ones. I wanted to turn away but couldn't.

"Rei, did you speak with your Japanese auntie yet?" Margaret asked. "I bet you're worried. We all are."

"I couldn't get through to her last night. One time, I did get a recording from the phone company saying circuits were full." I stopped talking to listen to the television, where an American reporter in Japan was talking about schoolchildren who'd vanished on a kindergarten bus that was presumed taken by the wave.

"Rei, your bacon's burning!"

Michael rushed in wearing nothing but shorts and grabbed up

the spatula I'd forgotten. With soft eyes he looked at me, then put the burnt bacon on his own plate.

Still in a fog, I dropped Michael at Pearl Harbor a few hours later and returned to Ewa Landing. After doing some work check-ins, I left my office for a late lunch and settled down at the kitchen table with my phone. The first six times I called my Shimura relatives in Yokohama, there was neither a dial tone nor even a busy signal. Just a static-filled silence that was mystifying and only served to make me feel like the whole country had gone under. But on my seventh try, the crackling gave way to the usual double-beep of a Japanese phone ringing. My heart began pounding. If someone picked up, what would I learn? Maybe something I didn't want to hear.

Three more rings. Just as I was expecting the answering machine to pick up, my aunt Norie answered "Hai" as if it was an ordinary morning.

I was almost too frazzled to remember the proper telephone greeting of moshi-moshi. I blurted, "Obasan! I've been so worried."

"Rei-chan, it's very thoughtful of you to call. Don't worry. We are not near the devastation. But what a bump it was; the ceiling tiles fell down right on the flowers I was arranging during my class at the ikebana school."

"It sounds as if you were in Tokyo yesterday afternoon. Where were Uncle Hiroshi and my cousins?"

"Chika-chan was traveling for work in Osaka, where she didn't even feel the earth tremble because it's so far away." My aunt gave a half laugh at this. "Tom was at his hospital in Tokyo. He took care of almost a hundred people, stayed overnight, and is continuing work there today. Your uncle was on the train from

Tokyo to Yokohama. That train slipped partly off the track but fortunately did not turn over."

"Thank God!" I had not thought about the impact the jolting would have on the thousands of trains crisscrossing Japan.

"The situation in Tohoku is much more serious. So many people are missing from small towns along the coast. It's a blessing that you aren't in Japan," Aunt Norie continued. "Because of your work travels, you might have even been in that region where the wave hit so hard."

As an antiques buyer, I had traveled up and down Japan, looking for special things. The Sendai region was famous for furniture carpentry. I'd traveled to a spring auction there each year with my dear antiques-dealing friend, Mr. Ishida.

Mr. Ishida was the closest person I had to a grandfather, since both of my own were deceased. We exchanged a phone call every two weeks or so. Now I remembered with awful certainty that he had talked about going to Tohoku sometime during the spring.

"Have you heard anything about conditions in Sendai City?" I asked my aunt.

"Some people were killed by the earthquake, which was quite strong. Actually, Rei-chan, I must end our call soon. The government wants us to keep the phone lines as free as possible."

"Sure. I'm just glad to know you're all right. Give everyone my love." I hung up and went into my cell phone's web browser, typing in the auction name. Only Japanese language pages came up. As fragmented as my Japanese reading ability was, I could still make out that an auction of *tansu* chests had been planned for March 10, the day before the tsunami. This meant Mr. Ishida could have made it back to Tokyo that very evening. However, I needed to call him to confirm.

As I punched in the number, I pictured the interior of his charming shop, full of tall, polished wooden furniture, and dazzling Imari porcelain. It was a haven for wonderful historical objects, and the best part was that Mr. Ishida lived upstairs.

His answering machine wasn't turned on—something that happened with him a lot. Mr. Ishida had mentioned hiring a part-time apprentice, the same job I'd done occasionally during my years in Tokyo. I'd said a brief hello to her once when I'd called for him, but it had been so brief I'd never learned the young woman's name.

It was ten thirty; maybe the apprentice wasn't in yet. The most regular inhabitant of the shop at this hour was Hachiko, Ishida-san's recently acquired dog. She was a mixed breed of Akita and beagle. I'd asked Mr. Ishida to text me a picture, but his phone wasn't sophisticated enough, he said. He stayed loyal to his early-model Nokia, a semi-antique in its own right.

The phone rang on. Perhaps the lines were jammed and the call wasn't even really going through. Another possibility was that Mr. Ishida had closed the shop because nobody was in the mood to buy antiques in the midst of a disaster.

I didn't want to think about the third possibility: that he couldn't answer because he'd gone to Sendai on the tenth and never returned.

CHAPTER 3

As often as I continued calling Ishida Antiques, nobody picked up.

And since that same shop phone rang in Mr. Ishida's upstairs apartment, it seemed clear he was not in Tokyo.

On Saturday, when there was still no response, I phoned Aunt Norie and asked if she could go to the shop and check on him. But she told me that transportation was still halted, and there were rolling power blackouts throughout Tokyo. My aunt, however, pledged to keep calling, in case she had better luck than I did.

"Doesn't Mr. Ishida have his own family?" my old Tokyo friend Richard Randall inquired when I phoned to ask him if he wouldn't mind going to the Yanaka neighborhood to check on Mr. Ishida.

"He never had children. Other people in the neighborhood might know his whereabouts, but I think the people he was closest to are all in the senior citizens' *tai chi* group that meets in Ueno Park at sunrise." As I spoke, I doodled the *kanji* for "big energy," the meaning of *tai chi*.

"The subway isn't running today. There's no way, no how I'm getting to Yanaka or Ueno," Richard grumbled. "And we're not supposed to use taxis for anything other than an emergency. Why don't you telephone the police?"

"I already called his local precinct. The officer said a patrolman could check on whether he's in the store, but that I should expect not to have an answer for several days because they're busy with public-safety concerns. We can't wait that long, Richard. There might be a puppy inside who needs to be fed."

"Don't use *we* with me," Richard snapped. "And I can't be a pet sitter! I'm busy enough with my own demon cat."

"I'm not asking you to take care of a dog. I don't even know if the dog's there. But it's another reason to check on the store. If the only thing that's out of order is his telephone, that would be really good news. And I'll get off your back."

"Okay, okay. I'll bike over this afternoon. Ishida Antiques is on the main drag in Yanaka, right?"

"Yes. It's near a shop that sells roasted *senbei* crackers." I could smell them in my imagination, and that sent a rush of homesickness through me. "I'll forward an Internet link with a photograph of Mr. Ishida." I'd only found one picture online, but unfortunately Mr. Ishida was half-blocked by a teenage girl with blue hair.

Richard sighed theatrically. "You're lucky the salon's closed, so I have the time to undertake your errands."

"Which salon?"

"Blond Apparition. Did you forget that I started a cosmetology apprenticeship last year?"

"Yes, you did tell me. How soon before they turn you loose on actual paying customers?"

"I'm usually seeing four or five clients a day, thank you very much." Richard sniffed. "But right now the salon's closed. Our owner says she doesn't know *when* anyone will feel chill enough to come in for a blowout. You can't believe what the city's become like. People are saying it's the worst crisis since World War II."

Michael and I decided to spend that evening in our backyard watching the sunset. Sitting together on plastic garden chairs I longed to replace with teak ones, I told him that Richard had made it back from Yanaka and found Mr. Ishida's store locked up with the lights off. Per my instructions, he had rung the exterior doorbell to Mr. Ishida's private apartment located above the shop and had no response. A neighbor had said to him that he believed the shop had been closed since Thursday evening—and what was really strange, the neighbor thought, was that Mr. Ishida hadn't mentioned the closing to him—nor had he left a sign about the reopening date on the shop door, as was his normal custom if he traveled.

"Nothing is normal in Japan anymore," Michael said, twisting the top off his India pale ale. "Did you hear the latest about the nuclear power plant in Fukushima?"

"Well, I know the cooling system was knocked out by the wave, so the towers are getting hotter. One of them is melting down, right?"

"Tower four's on meltdown and one or two of the other six towers are on fire. The Japanese press has reported that plant workers put out a fire themselves... but our sources are saying otherwise." Michael paused. "It's really bad, Rei. This plant is just two hundred miles from Tokyo. If the radiation keeps spreading, the entire Tokyo-Yokohama area will have to evacuate."

"But that's more than thirteen million people. There's nowhere to go." I recalled some of the hokey disaster movies I'd seen with panicky mass evacuations. But this story would feature my friends and relatives and wouldn't have a Hollywood ending.

"There's the rest of Japan and nearby countries. Believe me, thousands of people are trying to get to Korea and Singapore. It's like some of the Jews living in Germany and France who had a gut understanding of the coming Holocaust six years before the camps."

It was so like Michael to assume the worst. After all, he was a former spy. Instead of telling him the analogy was inappropriate, I asked, "Do you think your boss might send you to Japan to figure out what the truth is? Such a big meltdown threatens Pac Rim security, doesn't it?"

"It threatens world security in many ways. But working at a think tank is more about reacting rather than acting." Michael took the last sip of beer. "It could take months for them to get a plan together."

"I wish I could get to Japan and do something." I finished the ginger lemonade I'd been drinking and put it down, noticing that it cut a clean circle on the table's dusty green plastic. "I feel so helpless."

"Better to raise money or do something helpful from here than walk into radiation," Michael said.

"That's hypocritical. You'd go if you were called—I know you would."

"Hey! Is that the landline ringing?" Michael inclined an ear toward the cottage.

He was buying space from me—trying to avoid being put on the spot. I shot him a glance that communicated my thought, but hurried into the kitchen where a cordless phone was attached to the wall. I picked up the receiver and saw that its screen was lit up by a jumble of unfamiliar numbers.

CHAPTER 4

———

"Hello?" I said, receiver clamped to my left ear as I returned outside. "Hello?"

Like a heavy wind, static swirled around a faint voice. "Excuse me, Shimura-san. This is Ishida!"

"Ishida-san!" I cried as joy, relief, and love surged through me. "Thank you for thinking to call me. I've been so worried. Where are you? I had no answer at your shop."

"I was near Sugihama when the earthquake came. I suffered a slight injury and am staying in a shelter in a place called Yamagawa." He added something else, but I couldn't understand. We were speaking Japanese, our usual language together.

"Ishida-san, I'm very concerned that you were injured but so glad you didn't drown. What is your slight injury? Are you stable enough to be transported to Tokyo?" I gave a thumbs-up to Michael.

"A closed-head injury. I wish the doctor would let me leave this shelter, but they are worried to let me travel alone. And I don't want to go yet."

"A head injury—you should see a good doctor in Tokyo. My cousin will help us find the right one. You must leave."

"I need you to help me here. I'm sorry, but—"

"You need me to help," I repeated. "Of course! What can I do?"

"My apprentice said..." Mr. Ishida's voice was disjointed.

"Said what?" I asked. The staticky sound overtook my ear, and then a loud beep signaled the call had ended.

"What's the problem?" I shook the phone as if that would somehow bring back Mr. Ishida. "Michael, Ishida-san survived. He has a head injury and is in a shelter in a town called something like Yamagawa."

"I'm so happy for him. For you, too." Michael came up and hugged me. "Did I overhear you offering to help him with something?"

"He said he needs my help. He can't travel back to Tokyo without supervision, and he said something about an apprentice. It might be the newly hired young lady who handles the shop when he's gone. I'll try the shop number again."

But nobody answered at Ishida Antiques, and when I redialed the long, unknown number, my call didn't go through. All I heard was static. Studying the number, I said, "It's not his cell or store number. The question is whose?"

"Let me see." After scrutinizing my phone, Michael said, "The area code and prefix make it likely the phone is a military one—perhaps connected to Misawa, the big US air base in Aomori Prefecture, or a Japanese base. If Mr. Ishida said he's still in a shelter, this could be a military-issue cell phone being handed around for the survivors' use. You could send a message to the shelter he mentioned. I believe the Red Cross can forward anything you give them."

"Great idea. I'd like the shelter staff to tell him that I'm coming as quickly as I can."

"But that's not efficient." Michael gave me an odd glance as we walked back to our chairs facing the ocean. "He could be placed immediately at a good hospital. I'm sure we can arrange for one of his friends or relatives to meet him—"

"But that's not what he wants," I protested. "He specifically asked me to help him. I've got to respect that."

Michael sipped his beer and took a long look at me. He shook his head and said, "Is that because he's your *sempai?*"

I shook my head. "No. I wouldn't call him that, although of course he is my *sensei:* teacher of the most important things I learned about Japanese furniture and art. But really, I want to go because of what he means to me. And he has no children or other relatives that I could find."

"You mean—he's completely alone? That's got to be rough."

"Well, he's got this new assistant—a young woman who picked up the phone a few times when I've rung the store in the last year. We never really chatted, and I don't know her name. But maybe something's up with her. He wouldn't have asked me to come get him if he could have asked her."

"She wasn't answering the phone at the store when you rang," Michael said, and I nodded.

"I wish I could just say to him, 'I'm so happy you're alive. I'll see you in Tokyo on my next trip.' But something inside me is saying I have to help him. He has this wordless way of communicating with me. We are that close." The tears I'd tried to hold back started. I cried silently, and Michael put his arm around me.

"I'm so sorry," he said softly.

I gulped hard. "This morning, before I knew whether he was alive, I researched flight possibilities between Hawaii and Japan. It turns out Narita and Haneda Airports aren't even open for arrivals."

"Narita might open in a few days, but just to outgoing flights. I wish I could pull strings to squeeze you in on a charter flight with the Red Cross, but the Red Cross groups involved are coming from other Asian countries, not Hawaii."

There had to be a way. "I'm going to ask Mr. Pierce tomorrow if he could spare me for two weeks."

Michael stared out at a cresting wave. "If you were to go, you wouldn't be able to guarantee a two-week turnaround. Ewa Landing is eighty percent built, and the goal is to be finished in what, six weeks?"

"That's where you could help me," I said. "We're at the stage that's just checking up on the contractors, pushing them along. They usually work till seven—you could follow up on things for me when you come back from work."

"You've thought of everything." Michael turned away from the crashing wave to regard me with a pained expression.

"Well, not *everything*. I can't figure out how to get a plane seat. But I've got to go. Mr. Ishida didn't live through World War II and seventy lonely years afterward to get stuck in a tsunami zone without anyone to help."

Michael stared out at the endless Pacific and didn't say anything. His MO was to get quiet when he was stressed.

"Do you think it's irrational for me to go?" I blurted, unable to bear the stillness.

"I think it's risky. But I understand that you love him, and love trumps risk." Michael shot a sidelong glance at me. "I was actually thinking about what you'd need in a tsunami zone. The water purification tablets from my last disaster training are still good. And I have an excellent sleeping bag and a lightweight pad to go under—"

I traded my chair for his lap and, after kissing Michael deeply, I said, "Thank you for this. But I still have the problem of no flight to Japan. We probably can't pull this off."

"I don't know about that. Another option is flying to Korea, and then get yourself to Japan—"

"Of course," I exclaimed. Michael had done covert work in South Korea for many years; the country was set as deeply in his heart as Japan was in mine. "Once I reach Korea, it's not too far to western Japan by plane or ferry. I can probably figure it out when I'm there."

"Given the panic at airports, the ferry is your best shot. I'll put together the itinerary for you, including this supergreat restaurant for black noodles near the ferry building." Michael sighed. "These secrets I'm sharing. Where's your laptop? Let me get the ticket for you with my mileage points. I've been hoarding them for a reason."

"Actually, that can wait. There's a marital concern that's much more important."

"What?" Michael looked quizzical, until I kissed him again and began unbuttoning his shirt.

When I'd married Michael, Richard had warned me that the relationship would subdue. The sexy spark would burn out along with spontaneity and real passion. But I liked the long-term sexual availability that came with wedlock. Who cared if Michael fell asleep right after dinner on a Friday? He would have lots of time on Saturday morning.

To my surprise, marriage had brought a new kind of sexual freedom. How liberating to trail my left hand with its proper-looking gold band and diamond solitaire along a body that had been promised to me for richer and for poorer, in sickness and in health.

How long until we have this again? I wondered as we ran holding hands into the cottage and slid down on the low platform bed. Part of the charm of our life was learning each other's ways, for we hadn't been that intimate before marrying. In fact, we were following romantic patterns of much older generations. Not that we were old-fashioned; not at all, I thought as our legs twined together. Over and over, the fan rushed cool air over the bed, billowing the white cotton sheet above us like a canopy, making the erotic experimentations underneath feel all the more secret. And making love now was important. I wanted Michael to know I wouldn't toss him aside for my old life in Japan.

When we were through, I lay spent in my husband's arms. I wondered how I could possibly leave him. But then I thought of the eventual reunion. How sweet it would feel to have each other again. We'd have years of this life together.

Michael wasn't going anywhere, and I was certain I'd be back soon.

CHAPTER 5

The noodles weren't exactly black, but the broth was: black from soy, spices, and long-simmered beef. I knew upfront that Michael's favorite Korean dish wasn't vegetarian, but I was too tired from traveling to search for alternatives. And I could use some extra iron for what lay ahead.

It was just two days since I'd taken Mr. Ishida's call. Michael was more anxious than ever because the nuclear reactors were still spewing, and even the Japanese government had agreed to a greater evacuation zone. Yamagawa, the Tohoku town where I believed Mr. Ishida was staying, was just ninety miles from Fukushima. It hadn't been evacuated, but I knew that could happen. If a new radiation boundary was drawn in the next day or two, I might not be able to meet him there, making my whole trip unnecessary.

On the brighter side, my Korean Airlines flight to Incheon International Airport was on time and quite smooth. Once I'd cleared customs, I saw Mr. Sook, a scarred, wizened fellow who was one of Michael's former sources. Mr. Sook drove me to the terminal building in a shiny black Hyundai Equus sedan, insisting I accept an envelope of Korean *won* because the noodle shop didn't accept credit cards.

It was hard to figure out exactly how cheap my noodles were, but I had no complaints as I slurped away. I drank glass after glass of water, rehydrating after air travel and preparing for the bumpy ferry ride.

When I went across the street a half hour later, the line of ferry passengers waiting to be ticketed was crowded with relief workers, luggage, and boxed supplies. I was rolling a small suitcase-on-wheels containing city clothes and toiletries, plus a duffel bag and backpack with gear for Tohoku. Michael had gathered a strange assortment of wilderness supplies that made me feel like a modern-day Daniel Boone. He'd held tightly to me in the airport, his eyes shining with unshed tears. "I'll be back soon," I'd whispered, and he had swallowed hard instead of answering.

As I handed over my ticket and boarded the ferry, my thoughts turned from the guy I was leaving to the one I needed to find. I'd first met Mr. Ishida six years ago. I was twenty-four and had arrived in Tokyo with a master's degree and the delusion that a person who couldn't fluently read Japanese would still be hired by a Japanese museum.

Once this plan fell apart, my next scheme was to cover my living expenses by working as an English teacher while slowly creating an identity as an antiques buyer. So, in order to check out the goods of some of Japan's most successful dealers, I went to the Heiwajima Antiques Fair at Tokyo's Ryutsu Center.

Heiwajima was a big sale that anyone could attend; there was no invitation-only list, as the most prestigious auction houses insisted on. The sale involved about three hundred dealers selling treasures and schlock at all prices, and bargaining was definitely allowed.

I'd really come to buy collectible antique *yukata* robes; but my attention was drawn to a stall selling wooden *tansu* chests. I passed by the most ornate, highly lacquered pieces to focus on one that was probably affordable: a dull brown chest with the flat, unfinished look common to country pieces. But the wood's grain was dramatic, and drew me in for a closer look.

"Are you interested in that piece?" A soft voice came from behind me, and I jumped to see the seller, an elderly man a few inches shorter than me. His silver hair was thin, but instead of having it closely cropped like most men would, it was uncombed and slightly wavy, surrounding his head with a silvery halo. He wore an ordinary collared shirt under a gray business suit.

"I'm not buying today, but it's quite lovely. I'm curious about the wood. Is it—could it be—persimmon?"

"You have a good eye," he said, as if he hadn't noticed me puzzling out the *kanji* sign atop the chest. "May I ask your name, please?"

"I'm Shimura Rei," I answered in proper backward fashion, bowing and bringing out my name card so he could know the proper Japanese spelling of my name.

After inspecting the card and tucking it into his bag, he handed me his own card. I could not read his first name, but his surname, Ishida, was decipherable, as was his address in Yanaka.

"Ah, I see from your card that you work with antiques. I just received that piece and haven't restored it. If it was in your stock, how would you care for that *tansu?*" Mr. Ishida cocked his head to one side and looked smilingly at me.

"I'd think about bringing out the grain," I said, choosing not to inform him that I didn't have a shop or warehouse to keep "stock." "It's not a traditional look for a country piece, but the wood seems fine. Just some scratches and stains that could be removed."

"Using what?"

"Linseed oil. After that, some beeswax. But not too much."

"How did you learn this?"

"I found an old volume on woodworking in the Jiyugaoka books district." I was tempted to say I'd read it but decided to be truthful. "My father translated a lot of it for me."

"Your father is Japanese. Of course, I see it in your face. And your mother?"

"She's American. I was raised in California, but now my home is here." I spoke these words, knowing I was labeling myself. But the elderly antiques dealer looked surprisingly pleased.

"California is a special part of your country," he said in precise English. "There is so much appreciation of Asian culture. And they bake very delicious round bread."

"That's sourdough," I said, grinning back at him. "I'm from San Francisco, just like that bread. Pacific Heights, not far from Japantown." I'd noticed an American couple had come into the sales space and were handling an Imari tea set. "Excuse me for taking your time. You have some customers."

"Perhaps customers; perhaps lookers." Switching back to Japanese, he glanced over his shoulder and gave the couple a friendly smile. "I will be in my shop in Yanaka on Monday. If it is convenient for you, please come. It will be my pleasure to offer you tea and some conversation."

What had I done to earn such a nice invitation? I wondered, looking at the courtly old antiques dealer. But that Monday, I arrived for the first time at his prewar stucco building, carrying a still-warm, square sourdough loaf I'd made in my Japanese bread machine.

Ishida Antiques was precisely ordered and spectacularly surprising at the same time. Imari platters rested in state atop glowing wooden *tansu* chests. *Obis* were furled into decorative blossomy shapes on antique dining tables, and lovely folios of woodblock prints were open for browsing. Although I could recognize pieces of decorative art that were greater than a hundred years old, the place did not feel like a museum. It felt like home, and Mr. Ishida explained that it had always been a business downstairs, and a private home upstairs, since his late father built it in 1925.

Mr. Ishida was pleased with the bread and went straight to the small kitchen in the back of the shop to fetch butter and a seasonal cherry-blossom jelly. He bade me to sit down with him on *zabuton* cushions set around a low paulownia wood table made a century earlier in Sendai. The scent of well-polished wood mixed with fragrant *mikan* oranges.

Mr. Ishida poured a mossy-tasting green tea from a cast-iron kettle I suspected was at least as old as him. As we ate and drank, he coaxed out the story of my emigration to Japan. He did not say, as others had, that it was irrational to keep trying for something better than teaching English. Instead, he told me I'd have to be quite smart about Japanese antiques; and that if I wanted to help him by staffing the shop when I had time, he would be very pleased. He couldn't pay more than a clerk's wages, but he would teach me all that he knew.

So I began visiting at least once a week and helping out; and traveling with him to antiques auctions and flea markets all over the country. And as four years passed, what Mr. Ishida gave me was far more than secret furniture-refinishing recipes. He trained me to recognize every possible sign of a genuine or faked antique and to look at my whole life in those terms.

More than once, he said: "Please remember, Shimura-san, not to pretend acceptance when your heart tells you otherwise. It is a flaw within many people and has led to more pain that can be measured." And: "One fool's heart knows the correct answer better than the heads of many people."

Often I sensed he was cautioning me not to fall into the trap of a good Japanese girl. Why had Ishida-san chosen me? I hadn't said anything particularly clever when we'd met. All I could conclude was that he'd liked my honesty, and San Francisco.

And now he was asking for my help. I felt haunted by the knowledge that if I'd still been in Japan, I would have certainly accompanied him to the March auctions. And if I'd been there, I would probably be in the shelter with him.

Unless I'd been among the thousands of unlucky people who'd died.

CHAPTER 6

Osaka was Japan's other capital: the biggest city in western Japan, a business hub that was a major stop on the bullet train's route to Kyoto, Nagano, and other western points. Today, I'd come by taxi from the city's dock to the Shin-Osaka railway station, where I awaited a Hikari Express to Tokyo.

As Aunt Norie had said, Osaka was so far from Tohoku that its residents hadn't felt any tremors when the earthquake hit. Japan Inc. was still flourishing in this part of the country. But Shin-Osaka's commuters seemed preternaturally quiet. Many heads were turned to look at the station's wall-mounted television sets tuned to coverage of the continuing Fukushima nuclear meltdown.

I heard from the ticket seller that national trains were fewer and mostly running late. Rolling electric blackouts meant that I'd wait about two hours, instead of the typical five to ten minutes, to catch a bullet train to Tokyo. This train would have added stops, changing the classic two-and-a-half hour journey to four.

From the time I'd left Honolulu, I'd been traveling, waiting, and traveling again for almost twenty-four hours. But I was lucky to have some downtime in Osaka, with its electricity, heat, and plentiful food and drink. I located a power outlet and plugged in my Japanese cell phone. I rang Michael first and found him in the middle of his workday with only two minutes to talk. He told me he was glad I'd made it to Japan; I imagined he wasn't saying more because Hank was with him.

Then I called Aunt Norie in Yokohama, who asked what the food situation was at the station and advised me to bring as much as I could carry.

"I'll get some bento box meals and pack dry ice around them. How many meals do you need?"

"Oh, we're all right at the house. I am thinking of you. When you reach Tokyo, you might not be able to get a train to Yokohama for some hours. You need to carry food for yourself."

The prospect of sitting around in Tokyo Station for a while, or possibly overnight, was unappealing. "My old friend Richard has an apartment in Roppongi. I probably could stay with him tonight."

"The little American boy?" Aunt Norie sounded anxious.

"Canadian," I answered while tapping out a text message to Richard. "And he's not so little. He's twenty-eight years old and has a partner."

"You really should not stay overnight with *any* type of single man." Aunt Norie sucked air through her teeth. "You are married now."

"He's my best friend. Remember, I lived with Richard for almost four years."

"Living together!" Norie sounded like she was choking.

I was relieved to see Richard's quick return text: *Hell yes. Stay as long as you like.* I told my aunt, "Okay, I'm set for staying overnight in Tokyo. I'll come to see you as soon as I can—*mo sugu.*"

Sugu, the Japanese word for *soon*, made a refrain in my head. *Sugu-sugu-sugu* became the sound, over and over, of the high-speed train rushing along its special track. When my train finally arrived, I had an assigned seat in the Green Car, where the seats were individual and soft. I closed my eyes, and from my head down through the rest of my body went the clickety rhythm: *sugu-sugu-sugu.*

Four hours was the perfect amount of time for a nap. Soon enough, I would be in Tokyo; and from there I'd have maybe one day before my next journey into the epicenter of trouble.

In Tokyo Station, only half the people who ordinarily would have been rushing around were there. It seemed like Sunday morning rather than Thursday night, except that nobody had the happy, today's-a-day-off expression. People's eyes were downcast and their mouths were set in tense lines. A quick can of hot coffee or a chilled energy drink might have helped, but the station's numerous vending machines were flashing empty signs.

My tired spirits revived at the sight of Richard and Enrique waiting just inside the Central Yaesu exit. Richard was rocking a flaming-red North Face jacket, while Enrique wore a rainbow knit beret angled over his long, wavy hair. Even if they hadn't been foreigners, they would have stood out.

I dropped my luggage to hug each of the boys. Richard took my wheeled suitcase and Enrique grabbed my duffel bag for the walk to Roppongi. I adjusted my backpack so it sat squarely between my shoulders and tried to keep up with their quick strides.

Richard fingered the sleeve of my boiled wool jacket, the warmest thing I could find at the Saks outlet in Waipahu. "I love that green; it's like a Granny Smith apple. Who made it?"

"The designer label was unfortunately cut out—but thank you. Actually, I feel like a hunchbacked granny." The backpack was heavy enough to pitch my body slightly forward.

"Look over there," Richard said. "The city ordered a blackout of Tokyo Tower to save power for more essential icons."

"That's sad. It's actually really kind of you to come all this way to bring me to Roppongi. I still know where you live."

"You'd never find your way on foot. Most of the buses are shut down, not to mention the subway—"

Richard stopped talking as the sidewalk beneath us started vibrating. I was so disoriented by the rolling that I fell forward and only saved myself by grabbing onto the back of Enrique's Lucky jeans.

All around I heard small shrieks as parents clutched children and those who were alone steadied themselves.

"Just another aftershock," Richard crowed, as I awkwardly let go of Enrique with a mumbled apology. "I've lost count of how many we've had today."

"At least five, wasn't it?" Enrique turned to me. "Don't be embarrassed for holding on. Are you okay, *querida*? Soon you'll become used to it."

I had hoped, almost a week after the quake, that the tremors would have stopped altogether. I shook my head and said, "As long as it's not another big one."

"We could easily have a really big quake," Richard said.

"Because of the way the fault line cracked, Tokyo's at greater risk. Actually, Rei, I can't believe Michael even let you travel here."

"Michael's not my keeper," I answered, having caught a tiny bit of contempt in Richard's tone.

"But Michael was once your boss!" Richard teased. "Which is actually hot. It reminds me of a great little movie called *Secretary*."

"Michael's body is soo hot," Enrique drawled. "In your Christmas card, I saw those washing board abs. *Ay, caramba*."

Richard sniffed. "Yes, he's physically appealing, but in that All-American Superman way—"

Now I regretted the photo of Michael and me canoeing on our holiday greeting card. "Stop it. You sound like you're talking about a blow-up doll. And you know that I was never Michael's secretary."

"No offense meant." Richard's laugh was light and silvery. "Tonight, let's just have fun. We'll help Tokyo launch its economic recovery."

As we approached the Roppongi Crossing intersection, I noticed that the popular Café Almond restaurant had its sign unlit and windows dark. "If Café Almond's closed, there's no hope much else is open in Roppongi. And I'm pretty tired; I'd just as soon get to your apartment and sleep."

"You will, in due time," Richard answered. "We should check the nightclub buildings around the corner before turning in."

But the nightclub towers were dark, too. Everywhere, shop, restaurant, and bar doors had closed signs hanging on them, if the missing lights didn't give enough of a message.

"We've got to find somewhere. It's effing Thursday night. We always go out on Thursdays." Richard's voice sounded strained.

"I'll call Salsa Salsa to see if it's open." Enrique pulled his cell phone out of his jeans jacket pocket and looked at me. "Do you remember that it's near Azabu Crossing? A bit more walking for us, if we go."

I didn't answer. From the animated conversation Enrique began with someone on the other end of the phone, it seemed clear he'd struck gold and found an open establishment.

"Let's go!" Richard said when Enrique had rung off.

After all they'd done for me, the least I could do was pay for a few drinks.

There was no electricity at Salsa Salsa, but candles glowed in the windows and random people were performing on the club's small stage. The usual glasses of water on the tables were missing; however, there was booze being poured at the bar crowded with eager customers. I stirred a room-temperature mojito while the men slammed down cosmopolitans. A Latin-Japanese girl came by with a platter of six empanadas. She said, "Complimentary!"

Richard reached for one and then made a face. "These aren't even heated."

Enrique said to him, "Don't take it, *querido*. There is no working refrigerator, remember?"

"But I'm hungry." Richard sulked. "I haven't had anything since our last crusts of bread this morning. The rice cooker won't work without electricity, and the instant *ramen* packages are finished."

Now I was glad for my heavy backpack and its contents from Shin-Osaka station. I handed each of them a bento box, explaining the regional specialties within: the breaded fried vegetable cutlets called *kushi-katsu*, the savory octopus dumplings, pickled vegetables, and *hako-zushi*, a kind of box-pressed sushi. "Michael suggested I bring packages of dry ice. You're welcome to drop some in your cosmo, too."

"Rei's *hermano* has beauty and brains," Enrique commented, opening his bento box with enthusiasm. At the tables around us, people looked on, their stern gazes alerting me that bringing outside food into a place desperately trying to unload its spoiling inventory was impolite.

"No, please," said a young male waiter, hurrying over. "We cannot permit the serving of food from other places."

Then Enrique popped an octopus dumpling in the waiter's mouth. With a furtive look to the side, the waiter chewed it fast and departed without saying anything else.

"This may be the best meal we've ever eaten together," Richard opined as he finished his box five minutes later. "Thanks for sharing. But why aren't you eating anything?"

"My time clock's crazy. Right now it's midnight." I yawned as I heard someone tuning an acoustic guitar. "I'm amazed that there's even a show here tonight. What's the saying about fiddling while Rome burns?"

"Tonight is amateur night, live and unplugged," Enrique said. "I may join them. It's not so frightening for me to sing when there's no microphone."

"Singing the oldies is Enrique's new hobby," Richard explained to me as his partner skipped up to the front of the room.

As Enrique crooned an old INXS ballad, "Don't Change," he stayed on key and looked deeply at both the girls and guys in the audience, which elicted plenty of giggling and cheers.

I turned to Richard to see if he was admiring his partner's talents, but his expression was critical and squarely on me.

He reached out to push back some hair that had fallen across my face. "Please let me cut that. It looks like a spent dandelion."

Self-consciously, I touched my shoulder-length layers. "I was trying out wearing it long. I thought it looked okay."

"Your hair was so gamine before, with zero maintenance. And if you're going into an earthquake zone, you're not going to have access to a curling iron. You really need something short, cute, and practical."

"Are you kidding? Michael would go into mourning if all my hair vanished." He liked it sweeping over his body as I bent over him.

Richard sniffed."Straight men usually have a long-hair complex. Tell Michael you don't want to play Asian Barbie for him."

"You and your game playing," I said, rolling my eyes. "Give my husband a break. Your bento dinner would have been spoiled if it wasn't for his dry ice."

"I suppose boring also can mean smart," Richard said as the whole bar began singing "We Are The World." "When you leave for Hawaii, maybe I'll join you and Mr. Handsome Hendricks for a few quiet days. Then I'd travel on to Winnipeg."

"That would be nice—but rather unexpected," I said. "Is everything okay with Enrique?"

"Better than ever." Richard paused. "But what if the radiation can't be contained? It could keep on rising until we all turn into Godzillas. Enrique's been through worse stuff when he lived in Peru, but this is the closest I've ever come to death."

I wanted to shake Richard for his drama. "Hey! When the quake came last week, you didn't die or even lose your apartment. Tokyo desperately needs foreign hairstylists. And how could you ever leave Enrique behind? It would be nearly impossible for him to get an immigration visa to the US or Canada. You aren't married."

"I know." Richard sighed. "I guess we're stuck here."

"I wish you two could live together wherever you want." It was on the tip of my tongue to add, *and get married like Michael and me,* but that would be pressing a tender point.

"I know. Well, sweetie, I hope you get Mr. Ishida out of the tsunami zone fast and solve whatever other problems he might have. In an e-mail, you were saying something about a dog?"

"That's right. I don't know where his dog, Hachiko, is right now. It could be that he took her along to sniff out termites." As Richard gaped, I explained, "Some beagles are trained to detect whether furniture is infested."

"You could go by his shop and look in the windows," Richard suggested. "I guess you have no way of getting inside."

I didn't answer. Back when we worked in the same office, Michael taught me the art of picking locks and unscrambling combinations to safes. I'd spent more than a month learning the skills. And since getting married, we'd developed a private lock-picking game. This one dealt with undoing the other person's zippers and buttons and clasps using anything except for one's fingers.

I blushed at the memory of the last afternoon we'd played. In fact, the particulars and outcome of that lock-picking game might have convinced Richard that Michael wasn't such a bore.

But this married lady wouldn't talk.

CHAPTER 7

Usually I awoke too early when I flew into Japan. This time, I could barely open my eyes. What did it was a heavy weight on my chest—Richard's cat Mutsu. We locked eyes, and she leapt off lightly, as she'd done her job.

It was already eight o'clock, and Richard was ambling around the apartment. I guessed that Enrique had already left for his morning capoeira workout.

"One good sign of life is people are walking to the subway," Richard said when I stretched and yawned a good morning. "I've lit the flame for the water heater—you can shower if it's not too long."

"That's great. I've got something for our breakfast." I dug into my luggage and pulled out a loaf of round, sweet Hawaiian bread.

"Oh, that's going to be perfect with my Georgia brand instant coffee." Richard showed me the water kettle he was heating atop his Tokyo City Gas heater. "Were you warm enough last night?"

"Yes, I was quite cozy in my sleeping bag plus your extra blanket. Hey, is there a car rental place around here?" I asked.

"A few blocks away, but even if you could rent a car to drive a few hundred miles out of here, how would you refill it? Most of the filling stations are closed. And you would need a lot of yen. I bet you forgot how expensive gas is here, even in the best of times."

He had a point. "What I need before anything else is more Japanese money. I have less than a thousand yen to my name, which in today's exchange is like twelve dollars, right? I only made it to Tokyo because I could charge my bullet train ticket."

After taking a very short shower, I put on makeup and one of the few "city" outfits I'd brought: gray flannel pants and a cream-white angora turtleneck I found on sale years ago at Mitsutan. This went underneath the spring-green jacket. Around my neck, Richard tied my vintage green-and-gold Hanae Mori scarf into a complex, elegant knot.

"You aren't the hippest girl on the planet, but you do look properly Tokyo," Richard said, fussing with my hair as he walked around me.

"Richard, I'm only going to the ATM." Kissing my friend goodbye, I headed out and soon discovered that every teller machine in the vicinity was out of service. I finally found an open Citibank, where there were long lines of people in need of money. When I came to the teller's window, I was asked for my passport before the teller ran my ATM card through a handheld machine. Minutes later, the young woman gave me an envelope fat with yen notes. I'd asked for the equivelent of $1,000 because I was doubtful about bank access when I reached Tohoku.

But there was no point in going to Tohoku until I checked out what had happened at Mr. Ishida's shop in Yanaka.

The subway was in operation with more trains than the day before. I caught the Chiyoda Line to Sendagi Station, the closest stop to the district of Yanaka. Mr. Ishida's neighborhood was a tucked-away, urban hamlet that had the superb fortune of escaping both American bombs and the Japanese building boom that came in the postwar period. The area was still a patchwork of small streets with tiny gardens, tall trees, and charming wooden buildings: the kind straight out of woodblock prints or children's picture books about olden times.

Yanaka had been my home for a few years, too, so I was distressed to find several small, familiar buildings had collapsed. But plenty of people were sweeping in front of their houses as usual, or had opened their shops for business. As I drew near Mr. Ishida's place, I saw the next-door *senbei* shop had its metal grille raised.

As impatient as I was to get into Ishida Antiques, I decided it was worth stopping to say hello to Mr. Okada, since he and Mr. Ishida had shops so close to each other.

In Okada Senbei, the wooden shelves that always displayed twenty varieties of crackers were bare, as if a horde of shoppers had bought up every morsel. But Mr. Okada was toasting new crackers with tongs held over a charcoal-filled brazier that had been his grandfather's. He looked up at me.

"*Irasshaimase!*" he said, the standard welcome greeting to customers.

"It's been a long time, Okada-san." I bowed, hoping he'd recognize me. "I'm Ishida-san's former assistant, Shimura Rei."

"I remember you, Shimura-san. You prefer seaweed-sesame crackers with a dark soy glaze." Mr. Okada was in his sixties now. He had a friendly, round face with plenty of smile lines, which now creased deeply. "I'm happy to see you again. But didn't you move to Hawaii?"

"Yes, I'm married now, and we own a little house by the beach. But I've come to help Mr. Ishida."

"He's away somewhere." Mr. Okada's tone was urgent, and his smile lines vanished. "Actually, I've been quite worried. I checked the morning after the earthquake to say hello, but except for his dog, Hachiko, nobody was in the shop."

I had so much to share with Mr. Okada, but I wanted to know the essential details first. "Did Ishida-san call you to ask for help with the dog? Or to say anything else?"

"No, I haven't had any telephone calls from him. But I'm his neighbor, so of course it was my duty to help the little dog. Unfortunately, city regulations don't permit animals on premises of a food seller. Because Ishida-san's apprentice didn't come around to get Hachiko, I brought her to stay at the neighborhood veterinarian."

It had been a long recitation, and the cracker Okada-san was roasting started smoking around the edges. Shaking his head, he dropped the burnt circle in a wastebasket.

"Mr. Ishida and I spoke only once on the phone, and that was March twelfth. He said he was in a shelter for injured people in a place called Yamagawa. My husband tried to get the Red Cross to send a message to a shelter in Yamagawa, but they couldn't locate a place."

"Yamagawa is one of those little towns hit hard by the tsunami," Mr. Okada said. "I heard its name mentioned on the news."

"Ishida-san was at an auction. I don't know whether he was actually caught up in the water, but he mentioned that he suffered a head injury and couldn't return to Tokyo without help."

"That would be a good job for his apprentice. But I haven't seen her since March tenth."

"Maybe she'll be at the shop today," I said, though I doubted it. "I heard her voice on the phone several times over the last few months, but we've never met. What's her name?"

"Mayumi-chan was what he called her; her full name is Kimura Mayumi. Ishida-san said the Kimuras are a well-known lacquer family originally from the Aizu section of Fukushima. They relocated to a small town in Tohoku Prefecture when Mayumi was very young."

Kimura meant tree village: a fitting place to come from if one was involved in the lacquer arts. The name carried a more peaceful association than my family name, which meant warriors' village. The two last names, Shimura and Kimura, sounded very similar. Maybe Ishida-san used Mayumi's first name to avoid tripping over old memories—or because he considered her a granddaughter.

I stifled this strange, swift flicker of jealousy and thanked Mr. Okada for helping Hachiko. I told him I planned to go into Ishida Antiques to look for more clues to Mr. Ishida and Mayumi's whereabouts and then stop at the veterinarian to see how Hachiko had fared.

"Won't you take some freshly roasted crackers as a small welcome back?" Okada-san offered. "I also can lend the key I have to Ishida-san's front door. It's quite simple to get into the place,

I'm afraid. I think he should have an alarm system, but he doesn't like wires."

Mr. Ishida believed that a guard dog was a greater deterrent than any alarm. He had once told me that Hachiko could sense if certain people were trouble. The dog once stalked a customer who turned out to be a shoplifter. Mr. Ishida had said, "When Hachiko put her paws and nose on the fellow, he quickly took a jade figure right out of his pocket and handed it to me!"

Mr. Okada placed three packages of seaweed-sesame crackers in a crisp navy shopping bag with a striped-ribbon handle. I thanked him for the kind gift and wrote my Japanese cell number on my business card and handed it to him. "Just in case I don't see Mayumi-chan at the shop, and you do happen to see her after I've gone to Tohoku."

"I will keep your card right by my *reji*," Mr. Okada said, gesturing toward the old-fashioned cash register. "And when you find Ishida-san, do call in case there's anything I can do here to make his return."

The fact that I didn't have to pick Mr. Ishida's lock was almost disappointing. Michael's little black case containing fifteen picks and four tension wrenches designed for narrow Japanese locks would remain inside my jacket pocket.

I walked around the building's stucco exterior, relieved to see no parts of it had crumbled. Fitting Mr. Okada's spare key into the old brass lockplate, the knob turned, and I stepped into the shop.

It didn't smell quite right. I was used to the scent of wax and green tea, but today I smelled some kind of spoiled food. A few more steps until I spotted two moldy oranges lying on the floor. They'd fallen, along with a square porcelain dish, from an ornately carved miniature Buddhist altar.

Unfolding a tissue from a promotional packet somebody had thrust at me by Sendagi Station, I gathered up the oranges and broken pottery and deposited them in a small trash basket near Mr. Ishida's fifty-year-old desk. Now, as I looked around, I saw more evidence of the earthquake. Several pieces of porcelain had fallen off display tables and lay broken on the shop's worn pine floor. Several drawers were hanging open on a step *tansu*, and some folders of shop receipts and records were scattered across the floor.

How surprising that Mayumi had not cleaned up. Uneasily, I looked on the desk for a note or other evidence of her last time in the shop. But there was nothing, and the store telephone had no blinking lights promising messages, because the power was off.

Next I moved on to scrutinize the aged plaster walls near the desk. Beside a museum calendar featuring old woodblock prints was a taped-up paper that looked like a printed reproduction of an Internet web page. This was the same picture I'd found online of Mr. Ishida and a teenage girl with hair dyed as brilliantly blue as an anime character's. Close by this weird picture was another shot of the blue-haired teenager posing with Hachiko. The girl was sticking up a couple of fingers to make rabbit ears over Hachiko's head: a classic move employed by young Japanese posing in photographs. Belatedly, I realized that the young, punk-looking girl could be Mayumi Kimura.

I felt shocked that Mr. Ishida had hired someone who looked like this to help sell his high-end antiques. I conceded that she was pretty, with sleepy-looking eyes and a full, pouty mouth. But she was about as far from me as he could get. And Mayumi's juvenile appearance was perhaps the reason he called her "Little Mayumi" and not "Miss Kimura."

I returned my attention to the Tokyo National Museum calendar. There, written on March 10, was the town name Sendai. On the eleventh was another Japanese word I could guess at, because it was in *kanji* characters that had multiple readings.

The Internet browser was down, so I couldn't use the *kanji* decoding website. I took out my cell phone and snapped a close-up picture to show my relatives at dinner. Aunt Norie and I had already confirmed via texts that I would arrive by seven.

As I put the phone in my pocket, my gaze fell on a familiar red lacquer box sitting on the desk's blotter. This cashbox was typically locked and kept in the bottom desk drawer. Touching the edge of the lid, it flipped up.

No money inside: not even a hundred-yen coin. This didn't make sense, because Mr. Ishida always kept a variety of bills and coins for making change. Perhaps he had deposited everything before his auction trip, although Mayumi would have needed cash on hand to make change if she'd stayed back to keep the shop open for business.

Perhaps a burglary had occurred. But then, more than money should have been missing. I'd not been inside the shop for over a year, so I didn't know the stock; although I recognized some very expensive pieces that apparently still hadn't found the right buyer. But then I remembered the shop's inventory list.

Mr. Ishida listed all his goods by hand inside ordinary lined notebooks. Dozens of these notebooks, going back for decades, filled a shelf above his desk. Inside the notebooks, each item in his inventory was described along with its date of acquisition, original price paid, and if applicable, the buyer, date of purchase, and sales price. He wrote the items' names in both Japanese and English because he wanted to be able to quickly present a precise description for foreign clients who might telephone or contact him by mail.

I opened the most recent notebook marked 2010 and recognized Mr. Ishida's handwriting on most of the pages. Over the last six months' dates, though, a new, tinier script had recorded most of the inventory information. Mayumi's entries were like a handful of sand in my eyes. She'd written in Japanese, not English.

But I would always know where the most valuable things were kept.

In a clear, locked glass case, I saw the shop's exceptional collection of *inro* and *netsuke*, the ancient snuff containers and coordinating fasteners that wealthy gentlemen of past centuries wore on silken cords attached to their *obi* belts. And in a tall rosewood chest, all the long boxes that should have held calligraphy scrolls were still full. Finally, I went to the heavy old safe in the kitchen. The combination was still the same: 060721, the date Mr. Ishida's father founded the shop. Inside the safe, I was relieved to open up some small silk pouches and find some small pieces of jade and elaborate gold-and-pearl jewelry. But there was also a three-foot-square black lacquer box that was empty. It was impossible to guess what might have been stored inside.

Clearly, some goods had been removed from the safe. I wondered if it had happened before or after Mr. Okada came in to get Hachiko.

I thought again about how I'd entered the shop. The door had been locked. Would a thief have bothered to lock the shop again after getting in? That could only have happened if the thief had found the store's spare key.

I went back to the desk's top drawer. The spare key rested inside an old cigar box, just as it had in my day. I also saw the sheet of important phone numbers. These were for Mr. Okada, Dr. Nakajima, Mr. Ishida's personal physician; the Japan Post Bank, Federal Express, and me. At the very bottom were two new numbers: one for Animal House Veterinarian and the other for Mayumi.

Perhaps there wasn't a burglary. I could be sending myself on a private trip to new, paranoid heights. Just because there was an empty lacquer box in the safe didn't mean anything was missing from it. Maybe Mr. Ishida just kept the box there. I could call Mayumi to ask her about it, now that I had her number. I pressed this number into my phone and waited, tight with anticipation.

Four rings, and then a high-pitched, cheerful woman's voice came on. *Mayumi here. Leave it at the beep! Arigato gozaimashita!*

As I struggled to think of what I should say, the phone vibrated, and Michael's number flashed on the screen. I hung up on Mayumi's voice mail to answer.

"Great timing!" I let out a gusty breath. "You've caught me inside Mr. Ishida's shop."

"That's right, you took the lock-picking set. How hard was it to get inside?"

"Too easy. I was offered a spare key from Mr. Okada, who owns the *senbei* shop next door. But now that I'm inside, I'm a bit worried something might have happened here."

"Like what?"

"Well, the earthquake threw some objects on the ground, but that doesn't explain why the cashbox is sitting empty on top of the business desk, and there's another lacquer box inside his safe that's empty."

"Think there was a break-in?"

I heard a sipping sound, and imagined that Michael was drinking his customary glass of ice water, having arrived from canoeing home.

"Very possibly. I suppose the police could figure it out—"

Michael interrupted, "Tell me more. What exactly do you see?"

"Okay," I said, looking around again. "A number of things are lying on the shop floor, mostly pottery, but I saw folders, too. Right away I noticed that a plate of fruit had fallen from Mr. Ishida's Buddhist altar. The oranges had rotted on the floor, and the plate was completely smashed. "

"Sounds like an earthquake. Can you tell if anything's missing? Sorry. You've not been in the shop for over a year, right?"

"There's an inventory list, but Mayumi's chosen to list the acquisitions only in Japanese. I really need the English to be able to understand what's what. It also seems that plenty of valuable pieces are still around. If a burglar came in and left behind the *inro* and *netsuke* collection, he was pretty clueless." I paused, not sure I wanted to give voice to my darkest thought. "Unless someone threw everything around to look like a burglary."

"Who's Mayumi?"

"She's the hip apprentice Mr. Ishida hired last year. I telephoned a number Mr. Ishida had for her in his desk, but there wasn't an answer."

"What's hip about her?"

"Well, she has blue hair. It's utterly ludicrous for someone working in a shop like Mr. Ishida's, you know?"

"Excuse me, sweetheart, but you had a navel ring the first six months we were together." There was laughter in Michael's voice. "I didn't ask you to get rid of it, either."

Hastily, I said, "I'm not going to judge her taste. But it's kind of teenagery to color one's hair like that. And if she's anywhere near Tokyo and hasn't come by, it seems irresponsible."

"Call her again," Michael advised. "Public transportation is still erratic, so perhaps she hasn't been able to get into the neighborhood. And you've no idea what her character is."

"It's irrational, but I have a weird feeling about her. I found out that Mr. Ishida's dog, Hachiko, was left alone in the shop during the earthquake. Fortunately, Mr. Okada went in the morning after with his spare key, found her, and brought her to a kennel. But you'd think Mayumi would have come to save the dog."

"At least you know Mr. Ishida's okay; he's got to be the person to untangle what happened." In the long pause, I could practically hear Michael thinking. "If I were you, I wouldn't call the police yet. It would be upsetting all around if you sicced them on an innocent person, whether it's Mayumi or this Okada guy, who seems to have just as much access. And don't forget that *you* could be detained. The fact you came in when the store was locked automatically makes you suspicious, should it turn out any valuables really are gone."

"You've convinced me. I won't call the police. But I'm really worried what Mr. Ishida will deal with when he returns."

"There's not much you can do until you see him. And he's probably more worried about his dog than anything else."

"Okay, the veterinarian is my next stop."

"Good idea. What kind of dog is a Hachiko?"

"Hachiko's her name, silly. She's really cute in the picture I saw that's posted near Mr. Ishida's desk. She has an Akita's thick fur and curling tail, but also a beagle's facial structure with the long nose."

Michael whistled. "What a mix. Akitas are loyal working dogs, and beagles have great temperaments and noses. My hunch is, once you see her, you'll want to be with her 24/7."

"The last thing I need is a dog." I shuddered. "Not with this possible burglary, an apprentice who's gone AWOL, and no ride yet to the tsunami zone."

My husband sighed. "Sometimes the little things are all we can pull off. But that doesn't mean they don't matter."

CHAPTER 8

After we'd said goodbye, I realized I hadn't asked Michael about his work or the renovation progress at Ewa Landing. I made calls to the general contractor and the plumber, but they didn't answer. I'd have to hope for the best. I also rang the *senbei* shop to ask Mr. Okada if he'd noticed the same disarray on March 12 that I'd just seen.

"Some things had fallen, but I didn't look closely because Hachiko was so excited to get outside," he explained. "I had similar problems in my shop, but crumbled crackers are not as much of a loss as broken porcelain. Are you calling because you'd like some help cleaning it up?"

"No, I can take care of that easily myself." I would do what I could, but leave all the broken goods in boxes for Mr. Ishida, as he'd surely be filing insurance claims.

Mr. Okada's directions led me to Animal House, a modern veterinary office near the train station. Animal House had a bright exterior sign featuring cheerful cartoon dogs, cats, and fish. The electricity was working here, although the overhead lights in the waiting room appeared to have been purposely dimmed. Mr. Sato, the front desk receptionist, had colored his hair straw-blond and styled it into a rooster-style crest reminiscent of Tintin. When I said that I'd come to see Hachiko, he clapped his hands in excitement.

"Yes, she is here! Since you're not her owner, I won't ask you to fill out paperwork—but Dr. Kubo certainly wants to speak with you. Please come this way," he urged, jumping up to lead me down a hallway decorated with pictures of people and their pets. "Our Good Owners Wall is for people who rescue animals in need of shelter. The picture in the far left lower end is Hachiko-chan and Ishida-san. We took this shot last spring, when she was a tiny puppy."

Mr. Ishida had raved about Hachiko, but he'd never mentioned that she'd been a rescue. How small the dog had been: a caramel-and-cream ball of fluff. This photo of the beautiful puppy in the lap of a smiling octogenarian owner seemed to radiate the hopeful emotions of a new attachment. In a way, it reminded me of my own wedding pictures.

We continued to a small examination room decorated with animal anatomy charts, and Mr. Sato showed me the plastic chair where I should sit until Dr. Kubo arrived. A few minutes later, a middle-aged woman wearing surgical scrubs decorated with prancing poodles joined me.

"I'm Dr. Kubo," she said, bowing. "I hear you've come for Hachiko?"

I gave my name and explained that I'd traveled from Hawaii to help Mr. Ishida come home from a shelter in Tohoku.

"Oh!" the doctor exclaimed. "I'd heard from Okada-san that

Ishida-san was away on business, but he did not know the location was Tohoku. Is he all right?"

"Ishida-san and I only spoke once briefly by phone, and he said something about a head injury. He will be allowed to travel home once he's got a companion helping him."

"You must be very close to Ishida-san to have traveled to help him. Do you also know Hachiko well?" She'd picked up a clipboard and begun writing notes.

"No. Ishida-san got Hachiko after I moved to Hawaii. But he spoke of her very fondly, so I have a positive picture."

"Of course," Dr. Kubo said, writing away. "She is his best friend. Now look who's here!"

Mr. Sato arrived with a frisky, midsize dog in tow. He dropped the leash and Hachiko trotted toward Dr. Kubo who cooed and produced a biscuit from the pocket of her scrub shirt. Chewing happily away, Hachiko looked at me, and then came forward to say hello.

I was cautious with dogs I didn't know, but Hachiko seemed gentle and friendly. Within seconds I was off the chair I'd been sitting on and on the floor with the dog half on my lap.

"We're making friends," I said.

"If she were a cat, she would be purring," Dr. Kubo agreed. "I'm glad the two of you are becoming close. Don't worry about the bill—Mr. Ishida will take care of things when he returns. I will give you printed instructions on her daily diet."

"I don't know why I'd need diet instructions," I said, wondering if I'd misunderstood something.

"Because you are taking her, *neh?*"

"Um—I'm sorry, but I can't take Hachiko right now."

"Heh?" Dr. Kubo stopped writing. "If you're not here to take her, why did you come today?"

"She's been here for five or six days, right? I wanted to visit, so I could tell Ishida-san how she's doing." The doctor's assumption made me feel awkward.

As if she'd sensed my stress, Hachiko gave a little shake that jingled her collar, stood up, and left my lap.

"It is unhealthy for a dog to stay in a place where she can't really exercise." Dr. Kubo watched the dog strolling the small room, as if she were seeking escape. "Our office doesn't have a dogs' playroom. Our kennels are intended for invalids needing a few nights' care."

I went to pat Hachiko, whose rounded tail wagged in circles that shook her entire bottom. I felt like she was forgiving me. "Like I was saying earlier, I'm leaving Tokyo as quickly as I can to bring home Mr. Ishida. But until he's here, there's no place Hachiko could stay and get personal attention."

"You speak Japanese so well yet have no friends or family?" Dr. Kubo sounded skeptical.

I thought about the Shimuras' house in Yokohama. They didn't have any pets. Maybe they'd welcome Hachiko, if I asked. I didn't think Richard was a good option because of Mutsu, but I'd ask him as well.

"I will check around, but it's not likely the people I know would take her," I said.

"You might consider bringing Hachiko with you to Tohoku. Ishida-san always said she was a good traveler."

The vet was acting as if I knew how to handle dogs. I imagined Michael laughing about it. At the door, Hachiko nuzzled my hand, as if saying, *of course you'll take me.*

I gave Hachiko one last neck scratch and turned back to the doctor. "I will try my very best to get Hachiko out soon. But it seems to me that she needs a place where she'll be allowed to stay indoors for her safety."

"I'm sure you'll make arrangements." The doctor's smile was serene. "You are a very good person to do this!"

I caught a Tokaido Line train to the Yokohama suburbs; they were running one an hour, instead of one every ten minutes, so the car I stood in was jammed. I breathed a sigh of relief thirty-five minutes later when the doors parted and I was released into the cool Yokohama air. It was a fifteen-minute walk to my aunt's house in a hilly suburban neighborhood near the station. The streets around her home seemed unusually full of parked cars, probably because of the government restrictions on nonessential gas usage.

When Aunt Norie opened the door, I found the power was off and the house lit only by candles. This created a lovely atmosphere. I embraced my aunt, who was in her late fifties but, because of her glossy black pageboy, unlined face, and trim figure, looked about fifteen years younger.

"I must apologize for supper," my aunt said. "I only had three hours to use my stove."

"But it smells so good." Indeed, I rarely spent more than an hour making an evening meal. Tonight, my aunt had prepared miso soup flavored with dried mushrooms and shelf-stable tofu. She'd also set out saucers of tiny dried fish, pickled radishes and carrots from her garden, and a green salad with mayonnaise-*yuzu* dressing. The main course was *oyako-donburi*: rice topped with a soy-mirin-onion flavored omelette. *Oyako-don* meant mother-and-child, so there should have been diced chicken cooked with the omelette, but not tonight, either for lack of chicken or her mindfulness about my vegetarian habits. The eggs were extremely local, because she now had two hens in a backyard coop that Uncle Hiroshi had built for her with a Tokyu Hands kit.

Uncle Hiroshi, a banking consultant, was at the table, his usually grave expression lightening as my aunt praised his carpentry skills. Shaking his head at all the flattery was my thirty-five-year-old cousin, Tom.

"This is really a great meal," I complimented my aunt. "I thought you were suffering from food shortages."

"Fortunately, my kitchen cupboard and garden provide. It must be different in Tokyo. I doubt Richard-san has a vegetable garden or hens."

"You're right. He lives in a small apartment high over a noisy street, and his giant cat, Mutsu, would make short work of any hens." Talking about animals reminded me of Hachiko. "Actually, I met a special animal today."

Everyone listened as I spoke about Hachiko and what the doctor had said about wanting her to leave the veterinary kennel as soon as possible.

"I'm sorry, but we can't help." Aunt Norie's voice had an anxious pitch. "We have chickens freely moving throughout the garden, and your uncle is highly allergic to dogs and cats."

"Oh. I didn't know."

"That's why Chika and I never got a pet." Tom gave me a wistful look.

"Do you know the legend of Hachiko, Japan's most famous dog?" Uncle Hiroshi asked. "Back in the 1920s, a male Akita would walk his master, a college professor, to Shibuya Station every morning. He'd return for evening pickup at exactly the right time.

Of course, he could not understand when the professor passed away. He loyally waited at the station for many years, until he finally died of cancer."

"I know that story well," I said. "So many times I've met up with friends by his statue at the station."

"Ah, but that is the *second* Hachiko statue," Uncle Hiroshi corrected. "The first was erected after his death in 1929, but during wartime, the statue was melted down for munitions. Only in the postwar years was the dog's honor restored with a new bronze statue."

His expression "melted down" reminded me of the current state of Fukushima, but nobody else seemed to have noticed.

"I'm very sorry we cannot take the dog," my uncle continued. "I like the happy nature of dogs, but they make me itch and sneeze terribly. It would be ideal if Mr. Ishida's apprentice could be found and she could make arrangements."

"I don't know if I'll find her." Even though I'd left a phone message for Mayumi, I wasn't sure I could trust someone who'd left Hachiko alone so long in the first place.

"You said earlier that you had photographed some word written on Mr. Ishida's calendar?" Aunt Norie asked.

"Thanks for reminding me," I said, getting my phone out of my pocket. My uncle, aunt, and cousin leaned in to look at the image that I zoomed so it was readable.

"Sugihama." Aunt Norie said. "Cedar tree shore. It sounds like a town name, but where is it?"

"In Tohoku," Tom said.

"When the tsunami hit, Sugihama was on CNN! But was Ishida-san actually there? He phoned me from somewhere called Yamagawa."

"Maybe he was carried some distance by a wave," Tom suggested. "That was the plight of many people."

"Or it could be that his shelter is in Sugihama, not Yamagawa, but he was confused," I remembered. "He does have a head injury."

As I thought about the various possibilities, the Shimuras' electricity returned with a cheerful snap. The pendant lamp above the table glowed warmly, and Uncle Hiroshi hurried off to rummage around his study. He returned with a deeply creased 1990 Japan Tourist Board map of the Tohoku coast.

"Sugihama is small—just a tiny dot—a few miles north of a place where an eight-meter wave hit. And it's below Yamagawa, where the wave was seven meters," my uncle said, examining the map he'd spread out on the table.

"Twenty-four feet tall," I translated and shuddered.

"How can you get to any of these towns?" Uncle Hiroshi shook his head. "It will take many more days or weeks before the train lines are restored."

"I don't know yet," I admitted. "I was told it's pretty unlikely I could rent a car."

"Some nongovernmental organizations are finding ways to go," Tom said. "One of our nurses is going to Sugihama on a chartered bus with the Helping Hands organization this Friday evening."

"You mean, tomorrow?" As Tom nodded, I exclaimed, "That's perfect! Can you put me in touch with this nurse?"

"Certainly. I have her number in my phone."

After Tom spoke, I saw he was blushing. Uncle Hiroshi didn't seem to notice, but Aunt Norie, who'd been hoping for a daughter-in-law, pounced. "You have taken this girl's number? Who is she?"

"Nurse Tanaka." Tom sounded irritable. "And it's very normal for staff to have each other's phone numbers, for professional reasons."

"Nurse Tanaka who?" Aunt Norie would not be brushed off. "How old is this nurse?"

I had a distant memory of a pretty nurse who had chatted with Tom about things other than medication during my stay at St. Luke's for a smashed knee. I asked, "Is Tanaka-san the one who worked on the trauma ward?"

"Yes. She's still there." Turning to Aunt Norie, Tom added, "Tanaka Michiko is two years younger than I am. And to answer any other questions you probably have, she has not married yet and seems to be a responsible, respectable person."

"Oh, Tsutomu." Aunt Norie beamed. "You must certainly call this nurse on Rei-chan's behalf. And if you can't reach her tonight, give me the number, please."

I could not reach Michiko Tanaka by phone, but that evening, I found an English-language website for Helping Hands. After a few exchanged e-mails with its director, Hiroshi Yano, I learned he was seeking volunteers who could commit to a minimum of three days of assistance in Sugihama. I expressed my willingness to help, but added that I hoped to also visit Yamagawa. Mr. Yano wrote back that this would be fine, and that he would reserve a seat for me on the free Friday evening bus. *Thank you so much!* I typed back before remembering that I still had a dog to worry about.

I pondered taking Hachiko from the vet to stay in the shop

alone. Perhaps Mr. Okada knew a neighborhood youngster who could feed and walk Hachiko twice daily.

But was that responsible? I considered the missing money, the empty box in the safe, all the scattered objects. I'd felt an odd atmosphere in the shop that had never been there before. If someone had already entered and stolen without hindrance, there was no reason to think he or she wouldn't return to properly finish the job.

No, I decided. Even though Hachiko was technically a guard dog, I didn't want her there.

CHAPTER 9

"This is your last day of comfort. Please enjoy it, because soon you will enter another life. Just twenty of you are here today, but ten more will be with us tonight on the bus."

In a packed Shinjuku conference room, Mr. Yano chose to start volunteer orientation on a gloomy note.

"I wish I could describe the conditions of the lodging where we will stay, but we are the first group going into Tohoku, so I cannot." Mr. Yano was a trim fellow about my age, who had a wispy beard that needed trimming—an atypical look for the Japanese. "Expect that sleeping, eating, and toileting to be very rough. There will also be no personal bathing, clothes washing, or wearing of contact lenses, because there is no place to wash hands with water."

No hand washing in clean-freak Japan? This was unthinkable, but all around me, serious-looking volunteers—mostly people in their twenties through forties—were nodding as if it was no problem.

"Do not come if you think you might get cold or tired or overpowered by bad smells. It's better to change your mind now than later, *neh*? Once you arrive, there will not be return bus transportation until Sunday."

People were raising their hands left, right, and center, full of questions about the length of the bus ride, danger of exposure to radiation on the trip, and so on. There was one question in the back of my mind that had been bugging me since the night before. Could Hachiko come? I was beginning to think it was the best option.

Soberly, we filed out a few hours later. I hadn't dared raise the question. Instead I read through Helping Hands' suggested packing list and decided to focus on obtaining a few items Michael hadn't thought of when he'd packed my duffel bag. A down jacket and a battery-powered phone charger were the only outstanding issues.

I rode the subway a few stops to Roppongi and went to Richard and Enrique's place. I entered through the unlocked apartment door and found Richard huddled on the futon with a blanket wrapped around him. He was drinking wine and reading a Hawaiian travel magazine that I'd brought. Glancing at me, he said, "Your island looks better to me all the time."

"Then come visit," I said. "Although we get cyclones a lot, and sometimes earthquakes and tsunamis, too."

"Yeah." He sighed. "Let me get you a glass of wine. What's the latest?"

"I'm definitely cleared for the trip to Tohoku," I said, accepting a small tumbler of Chilean red. "But I've got a couple of last things I need to bring along. Do you have battery-powered phone charger?"

"Sorry, I'm an all-electric boy. Anyway, I hear you can't find one of those chargers to save your life in this city. Everyone else wants one, too."

"Okay. Then would you lend me your down jacket? I can't stand the idea of buying a winter coat I really won't wear again at Tokyo prices."

Richard's face paled. "My North Face coat?"

"I'll be careful. Apparently the weather's really cold there—too cold for my jacket—"

Richard sighed gustily but stalked over to the closet and handed me the red jacket swathed in the shelter of a garment bag. Obviously, this was a highly prized item.

I gushed out my thanks and swore to bring it back in good condition.

"Okay," he muttered. "But what are you doing about the dog? Not that I'm offering to take her. She'd eat Mutsu within minutes."

"Well—I hope to take Hachiko with me to Sugihama."

"Is Helping Hands cool with that?"

"Actually, I've been afraid to ask, in case they say no."

"You're leaving tonight." Richard said. "If they don't let her on, you won't get to go at all. Right?"

"Sometimes you're just too logical," I grumbled. "Yes, I know. But I can't figure out the right move."

"Make the dog seem like an asset, not a liability. You could tell them Hachiko's a search-and-rescue dog or something."

"But that's not really true—"

"She's going to help you search for Mr. Ishida, right?" Richard paused. "I suggest you say something, rather than nothing."

Feeling Richard's eyes on me, I took a swig from my glass,

picked up my phone, and rang Yano-san's cell number. I was less hopeful than my friend about how the conversation might go. If Mr. Yano didn't think people should bring contact lenses, surely he'd take the same attitude toward pets.

Mr. Yano didn't pick up; his voice mail recording was on. I was about to start my plea but suddenly realized leaving a message could give the volunteer organizer plenty of time to concoct a strong rejection. So I hung up.

"I only got his voice mail," I told Richard.

Richard took a long sip of wine. "Getting back to the search-and-rescue idea. I think it could work. You could play some training games this afternoon, so at least the dog has the appearance of skill. You'll need yummy treats, of course—"

"I can't train a dog," I interrupted. "I've never had one."

"You said she has a beagle nose. Beagles are used all the time for searching suitcases in airports. People seeing those dogs expect them to be skilled."

It was true that appearances were important. I considered how I'd judged Mayumi because of her hair. "To make Hachiko look like a search-and-rescue dog to Yano-san, she needs to wear a red coat."

Richard had already picked up his cell phone. "I'm calling Isetan to see if they're open for business today."

Richard and I hadn't shopped together in a long time. Normally, we made pilgrimages to both the men's and women's departments, but today we headed to the famed department store's pet fashion boutique, which occupied almost half a floor. On a winter-clothing sale rack, I found a quilted red coat from Rich Dog World that looked big enough for Hachiko. The children's floor yielded two small Tory Burch T-shirts with appliquéd white crosses that would be easy to remove. One hundred dollars poorer, we returned to Richard's apartment, where I sewed the crosses onto the dog coat and Richard put Mutsu in the Meowtize cloak he'd impetuously bought for an upcoming party.

The fat cat did not look any better in black sequins, but I kept my opinion to myself and finished the last bits of packing. My duffel was quite heavy now. I decided to drop it off at Mr. Ishida's store before going to the vet's to retrieve Hachiko. With a kiss to Richard, I was off with my luggage by four o'clock.

As expected, I received a friendly reception at Animal House when I made it clear I was taking Hachiko away with me. Too quickly, her leash was in one of my hands and a red shopping bag with sedatives, lemon-scented poop bags, and dog biscuits was in the other. Dr. Kubo had also written a list of daily care instructions, which would have been helpful, except they were printed in tiny eight-point kanji.

Hachiko trotted out of Animal House alongside me. It seemed like her jaw stretched into a smile at the sight of the familiar Tokyo traffic. When we turned onto Mr. Ishida's block, she surprised me by breaking into a run. She yanked me the rest of the way and barked joyfully while I opened the shop door. Once inside, she hurried everywhere looking for Mr. Ishida.

"I'm sorry, Hachiko," I said. "But we'll find him soon, I promise."

Hachiko ran up the staircase in the back that led to Mr. Ishida's private quarters. I followed her up and found this door was locked and required a different key than the shop's entry. But I still had my lock-picking tools, so I was quickly inside. I'd needed to go into the apartment anyway to find clean, warm clothes to bring

Mr. Ishida, who might have been wearing the same garments for a week.

In the flat, all was neat, with the twin bed made and clothes all hanging in closets. Books and newspapers were everywhere, but in orderly piles. A few drawers had been rocked open by the earthquake. I wouldn't know if anything was missing, so I didn't undertake any kind of search but gathered two pairs of trousers, two sweaters and shirts, an extra coat, gloves, and four sets of underwear and socks. Everything went into a leather suitcase that was large enough to hold Hachiko's dog supplies as well.

I still had an hour to spare before leaving for the volunteer bus. Remembering what I'd said to Mr. Okada about cleaning up, I found the broom and dustpan and swept up all the china bits and put them in the empty lacquer box and returned everything to the safe. When that business was done, I called Michael. It was dinnertime in Tokyo, which meant it was late evening in Honolulu.

After I explained my plan to take Hachiko, Michael did all but cheer. "What awesome news. Is she on the manifest, or are you sneaking her along in your bag?"

"I wish I could, but she's too big."

"Well, I can't wait to meet her."

"I can't possibly bring her to Hawaii. You know the quarantine laws, and Mr. Ishida's going to get her soon, I hope—"

"Which is fine. But I'm coming to Japan! My proposal for communication action during the continuing nuclear crisis got accepted. Two of the guys and I are flying out of Hickam Field as soon as space is available."

The brief pleasure I'd felt at hearing he was coming was

immediately supplanted by worry. "But what is this proposal exactly? What could you do?"

"We'll fold ourselves into Operation Tomodachi, the US military effort to help relieve Japan. My role will be working with people in an attempt to improve communication."

"It sounds very noble, but that kind of talking has been going on for a week without success," I said. "And you represent a think tank. How can someone like you influence the Japanese government and TEPCO?"

"I'd like to think I can communicate with Japanese bureaucrats a touch better than the people sitting abroad yelling at them about the extent of the radiation spill." Michael sounded aggrieved.

"Are you going to do this from Tokyo?" When he didn't answer, I added, "Knowing you, it will be much closer to the danger zone. You shouldn't do it."

"So you're worried about my health." He snorted as if this were an irrelevant issue.

"Of course I'm worried! Think about what going to Fukushima might mean for the rest of your life. My life, too, since we're married."

"I hear you, but when I worry, it's about the hundred people still crawling around that TEPCO plant trying to put out fires. They're the ones who're going to die, and if a solution isn't found, thousands and possibly millions will also die. Really, I'll be fine. If I go to Tohoku, I'll probably be based on a ship near the plant."

"Probably." I sighed, letting out all the fear and frustration in my breath. "How soon do they think there's going to be a flight with space?"

"Maybe tomorrow."

"So I'll be in Tohoku. You might not be able to reach me when you land."

"I'll call this number."

"Well, cell service is still pretty erratic, and I may have trouble keeping my phone charged while I'm out there. I tried to find a battery-operated charger, but the stores are sold out."

"How can you go without a charger?" Without waiting for an answer, he huffed, "You can't leave the city until you have the necessary charger. I've got one packed."

"What do you mean, I can't leave? The volunteer bus leaves in a few hours. But don't worry, okay? I'll be back in Tokyo soon."

"Don't worry," Michael repeated sarcastically. "I can't be concerned about you, after all you said about my plans?"

"It's tough being apart. I wish I could make everything okay—"

"I'm not going to talk to you," Michael snapped. "You need to conserve power." And with that, he disappeared.

Great. I'd alienated him, just as I'd alienated every other man in my past. Now I was starting to think that maybe the problem wasn't the guys—but the way I communicated with them. Michael and I been married for less than a year. Fights like this—about travel and work and safety—were extremely painful for both of us. Maybe too painful for the marriage to hold.

I shook myself. I needed to take my mind off of Michael and back to getting Hachiko on the volunteer bus.

Dogs supposedly weren't allowed in the subway system, but since it was after rush-hour, fewer guards were on duty. It was the first–and only–opportunity to test out whether Hachiko, in her new red coat, could pass as a working professional.

Inside Sendagi Station, nobody stopped us. When I attempted to buy a ticket, the ticket-window man insisted that emergency workers and their pets could travel at no cost.

"Search and rescue!" a mother explained to her her young son and daughter as Hachiko and I stood next to them waiting for the subway to Shinagawa, the volunteer bus's departure point.

"Yes," I told the children. "We are going to Tohoku."

"*Gambatte kudasai!*"

"*Gambatte, neh?*"

Dozens of friendly requests for Hachiko to work hard at her duty followed us all the way onto the Yamanote line and out to Shinagawa Station. Feeling pumped up, I practically danced the remaining blocks to the designated parking garage, one of those sixty-dollars-an-hour places that always made me roll my eyes. This evening, not many cars were parked. Instead, the garage was dominated by a long tour bus with a sign over its front windshield that spelled out "Helping Hands" in English. Fifteen people were already loading up the baggage compartment with their own heavy backpacks and duffels. Those who were waiting in line to get near the compartment caught sight of Hachiko and began asking me if they were permitted to pet her.

"Sure. She's not on duty yet," I said, striving to behave the way a professional dog-handler might.

"Hello there, Shimura-san." Miss Michiko Tanaka looked just as I remembered: pretty and petite, with a placid face that turned incredulous at the sight of Hachiko. "Oh! Your cousin did not mention a dog was with you."

"If it's too much trouble, I suppose I could find another way to Tohoku—"

"But we are the first civilian volunteers arriving. There is no other group going that could take you." Tanaka-san bent to look closely at Hachiko, who was sitting with her head drooping like a disgraced schoolgirl. "I'm sure she could be very useful. I'm partnering with Yano-san on organizing this trip, so I'll put in a word for her. But where shall she go during the ride? Surely she cannot fit into the luggage compartment."

"She could sit on my lap," I suggested confidently.

We both looked at Hachiko, who, lengthwise, was about the size of a human five-year-old.

"I suppose." She still looked worried. "But I don't know who else would willingly sit with you and that dog…"

"I will sit with them," a male voice volunteered from somewhere in the crowd.

"I'd certainly like to hold the dog," an older lady cried out.

"What is cutie's name? She's so sweet," gushed two girls wearing Waseda University sweatshirts.

The Hachiko hubbub finally brought around Yano-san. Now wearing a tattered army jacket and jeans tucked into knee-high rubber boots, he looked even more laid-back than during the orientation. Surely he would turn out to be a dog lover.

"Yano-san, please excuse me." Swiftly I began my white lie, because he had an expression even more dubious than Miss Tanaka's. "Did you receive the phone message I left about this service dog?"

Yano-san ran his hand through his unkempt hair. "Sorry, I've been so busy. I heard many messages on my phone but may have missed or accidentally deleted a few. I didn't get any message about dogs."

"Dogs like this help find people. Please allow her to come," the grandmotherly woman said in a softly authoritarian tone.

"Which breed is she?" Yano-san looked dubious.

"Hachiko is an Akita-beagle mix. She belongs to the gentleman called Ishida-san whom I mentioned I'm looking for—"

"Helping Hands means *human* hands," Mr. Yano said. "There is another volunteer group rescuing abandoned animals in Tohoku, not Tokyo."

A man in his twenties with a cockscomb haircut like Mr. Sato's hurried up. "Excuse me?" he said, making a quick bow to Mr. Yano.

Good, I thought, a distraction. As the director turned to hear the young man's request, I gently brought Hachiko out of the garage for one last toileting opportunity. After returning, I encouraged anyone who hadn't yet petted the dog to meet her. If Hachiko became part of the group, it would be harder for the Helping Hands leader to reject her. But after what he'd said, I knew I was in danger of blowing my chance to rescue Mr. Ishida.

Shortly after I'd come back to the group, Mr. Yano's voice came over a microphone reminding everyone to take seats on the bus, as he hoped to leave town within ten minutes.

I took a deep breath and went up to him, Hachiko at my side. "What do you think? May I load my luggage and join you?"

After a tense pause, Mr. Yano spoke. "Yes. But please keep him on your lap at all times, and if there is any incident on the way up, we will have to leave the two of you at the gas station. It's a bit unexpected, you see...."

I wanted to fist pump the air but resisted. I hid my smile, bowed deeply, and said, "Thank you very much. What a great kindness to Hachiko and her owner."

"This dog will have to work, too," Yano-san said.

"Of course, of course."

As I kept bowing, Hachiko nuzzled my leg as if to say *thank you*. But my gratitude was being supplanted by nervousness. Hachiko's working-dog costume wasn't a reflection of who she really was. Just as Richard's red puffer jacket was hardly enough to shield me from the chilly uncertainty ahead.

CHAPTER 10

By the time I was cleared to bring Hachiko aboard, most people had already found seats. Hachiko and I wound up next to Mrs. Endo, the lady in her seventies who'd lobbied for her. Endo-san encouraged me to let Hachiko spread out over the two of us so she didn't get cramped during the ride. As I thanked her, Mrs. Endo produced a terry-cloth neck pillow and a cotton sleep mask.

"I shall sleep most of this journey, to conserve energy. Please excuse me." Mrs. Endo rested with a hand on Hachiko's back, and within minutes appeared to be in a more comfortable world.

A young man seated several rows ahead of me, across the aisle, turned and winked at me as Mrs. Endo began snoring. He was the one with the stand-up hair and black leather jacket who'd arrived last minute and looked even less equipped to volunteer in a disaster zone than me.

By the time the bus had proceeded up the Shuto Expressway to the Northeast, Mrs. Endo was murmuring in her sleep. After all that had happened, and my continued battle with jet lag, I tried to drift off, comforted by the heavy warmth of Hachiko's body on my lap. Sometime later, I awoke to an incessant vibration against my stomach.

Immediately I guessed that my buzzing cell phone held an incoming call from Michael. Instead, Tom's picture flashed up on the screen.

"Hi, Tom," I said, trying to keep my voice low because so many passengers around me were sleeping. "How are you?"

"Actually, that's why I'm calling. Did you manage to get Hachiko approved for travel?"

"Yes. Right now she's resting on my lap." I pressed the light on my watch. "We've been driving about four hours. Halfway there."

"I have a small update for you. I e-mailed someone at a hospital in Sendai who said that in Yamagawa there is a shelter for injured and geriatric patients. Perhaps this is the place from where Ishida-san called."

"Great. Is there an address?"

"I heard they're based in a recreation center. That shouldn't be hard to find once you're there. I hope you can get your friend out quickly and back to the city."

"Thanks," I said, just as the bus started shaking like a blender on puree cycle. The phone fell in my lap, and I looked frantically out the window to see what was going on, but all I could see was black sky and red taillights. It felt rougher than the earthquakes I remembered in California and Japan. Was it just because I was on a bus on the freeway rather than at home? I thought of Michael and how he'd already lost his first wife when she was traveling thousands of miles away. There would be too many parallels if I vanished.

Other volunteers were awakening and gasping and murmuring.

The driver had stopped the bus, and I could tell from looking at the brake lights of cars around us that they were also blindly riding out the awful, buckling experience. The bus jerked up and down, awakening all the sleepers. There wasn't a sound, but I felt the stiffness of our group fear. Even Hachiko sat up, whimpering and shaking.

"It must be an aftershock," Mrs. Endo said, her hand bumping into mine as we both stroked Hachiko.

"Rei-chan? Are you still there?" Tom's voice reminded me.

"Yes, yes! Sorry about that." I wouldn't tell him about the aftershock, as it would only feed into his concerns. "Tom, thanks for calling, but I'd better hang up. People around me are trying to rest."

I was too anxious to let myself fall asleep again after signing off, even though the movement underneath the bus had subsided and traffic had started up again. After an hour's worth of driving, the bus pulled off to a Jomo station for refueling. Despite the fact it was two a.m., more than a hundred cars were lined up waiting to enter the station. I worried about how long our fill-up might take before realizing that all those private cars were waiting for one pump, while buses and other official vehicles had sole access to the other.

The bus rolled to a stop behind two others, and I disembarked along with everyone else who queued for the toilets while I took Hachiko aside for her potty break. After Mrs. Endo was through with the restroom, she offered to stay with Hachiko so I could take my own turn. I barely had time to get into the putrid facility before Mr. Yano was calling into his microphone, "Helping Hands, now departing!"

Mrs. Endo was already seated with Hachiko when I jumped on,

making apologies for my tardiness. I glanced at my cell phone and found Michael had sent a text. As usual, it was short on emotion. *Where are u and what's going on? Dog okay?*

We're both on the bus doing well. I love you, I tapped back along with a string of heart emoticons. The fact that Michael had messaged me meant he'd cooled off. It was better going into Tohoku with neutral language from him than nothing.

I waited for an answering text, but it didn't come. Since the battery was already down to 70 percent, I clicked off the phone and pulled out my water bottle. My slight hunger reminded me of the *senbei* in my jacket. As I tore open a cellophane wrapper, the young man with cockscomb hair looked at me. He'd exchanged seats with someone and was now closer. I imagined that he could probably smell the aroma of the savory crackers.

Remembering the unwitting favor he'd done for Hachiko, I offered the second cracker page to him. "Please, go ahead. I've got more in my bag."

"*Ie, ore daijobu desu.*" As the young man politely declined with "No, I'm okay," I caught his Tohoku dialect, which before now I'd only heard when traveling to auctions or watching TV dramas.

"But our journey is several more hours, and who know what we'll have to eat when we arrive? Please take it."

"*Itadakimasu.*" Taking the package, he bobbed his head and murmured the phrase that meant, "I gratefully receive this food," which every proper Japanese person said before eating.

"Are you volunteering till Sunday or longer?" I asked after we'd each finished chewing. I found it amazing how delicious a freshly made cracker could taste.

"I will not return to Tokyo." Seeing my surprise, he added, "I've been in Tokyo for almost a year, but my family lives in Sugihama. They need me now and perhaps for a long time."

I'd guessed right that he was a northeast boy. "Are they okay? Your family, I mean."

"My parents' house is in the hills just outside of town, so the property came through fine. Some windows broke from the quake, but that was all. But my sister and her two daughters were in a low-rise apartment building near the harbor. They didn't make it."

"I'm so sorry!" Now I wished I hadn't been so nosy. My neighbor's composure was gone, and he wiped a hand across his eyes.

"If I hadn't moved away, I could have saved them," he muttered. "Little children are hard to move quickly by yourself. My nieces were age one and three."

A tear rolled down his cheek, and I felt a familiar, awful prickling in my own. Perhaps sensing my discomfort, Hachiko stirred. She sniffed in the direction of the man, stiffened, and made a low growl.

"Hachiko!" I was upset that she might make a grieving man feel worse. "I'm sorry, but I think she might be tired or hungry."

"What's her name?"

"Hachiko. You know, like the famous dog statue in Shibuya. She's actually a very sweet dog."

"If she's hungry, I can give this to her." He showed me that he had a cracker fragment left.

"She's got plenty of her own treats." I reached in my coat pocket and took out one of the sweet-potato biscuits from the vet's office. "Here, Hachiko. Yes, sweetie, just one snack until it's breakfast time." I yawned. "I suppose four a.m. would be harder if I wasn't still operating on Hawaiian time."

"I should introduce myself—after your kindness of sharing food," the young man said. "My name is Rikyo Akira."

"I'm Shimura Rei." As Hachiko munched away, I explained that I'd traveled from Honolulu to find Hachiko's owner, who'd had a head injury and might be in a shelter in Yamagawa.

Akira looked at me intently. "What is your friend's name?"

"Oh, you wouldn't know him. He's an elderly gentleman from Tokyo who had the bad luck to be here attending an auction when the earthquake hit."

"There's an antique auction house right in Sugihama that opened a year or two ago. Maybe that's where he went. What is your friend's name?" he repeated.

"Ishida Yasushi," I said, surprised by Akira's concern. "I heard there's an injury shelter at a recreation center."

"If you're going to Yamagawa, try finding the Morito Recreation Center. That's a nice, large facility for sports. It's too many miles from the water for the wave to have hit."

"Thanks," I said, surprised. "You know a lot about the area."

He shrugged. "When I played on my middle school's basketball team, we had games there. Yamagawa and Sugihama are only two miles apart."

"So you like basketball?" I continued, glad to have found a less loaded topic than the death of his sister and nieces.

"I'm tall for someone in Japan, so I did pretty well. But I stopped playing in high school."

"Japanese high school is so demanding." I felt sympathetic.

"It's a bit different than that. My father and mother wanted more help with our family business—since I was getting older."

"Was their business inside Sugihama?"

"No. My father's a carpenter, and his workshop is near the house. I was working construction in Tokyo, but now that I'm home, I'll help him repair people's homes and shops. It's too much for one person."

Now I noticed how his leather jacket stretched over broad, strong shoulders; Akira was as buff as any construction worker I'd seen in Western Oahu. Smiling, I said, "It sounds like you're probably the most essential person heading to Sugihama. No wonder Yano-san took you at the last minute."

I expected Akira to chat a bit more, but he only gave a slight nod and closed his eyes, just as Mrs. Endo had. I got the message. I was being too American and talking all over the place, while all the Japanese people understood this journey meant hours of precious rest before the onslaught of hard work.

Even Hachiko had the good sense to sleep. I let the rise and fall of the dog's body guide my own breath. This relaxation practice must have worked, because the next time I opened my eyes, the bus had stopped moving.

"Look at that!" One of the college girls sounded horrified.

"Unbelievable..." Her friend's voice trailed off.

The sky was light enough to reveal we were driving through the midst of what had recently been civilization. But mud covered the entire landscape. Dropped into filth were a variety of cars, uprooted trees, parts of houses, and many small silver scraps that I realized were fish.

The bus slowly zigzagged through, tires protesting against the mud. Mr. Yano sat behind the driver, leaning in and offering words of encouragement.

"So many fish." Mrs. Endo had finally wakened, and her eyes

widened as she gazed out the window. "The wave must have thrown them all on land."

And not taken them back. How many millions of fish and other sea creatures had been flung ashore to die? Crows circled and dived, enjoying their feast.

I watched a pair of Japan Maritime Self-Defense Force sailors wearing sinister-looking respirators force open the door of a Toyota hatchback, unleashing a miniflood of dirty water and fish. The men were carefully pulling out something using a plastic tarp. Judging from the bit of pink coat that showed itself from under the mud, I guessed the decomposed body was female. The next corpse to emerge was much smaller, with a dangling Mickey Mouse backpack. I thought this was the worst thing I'd ever seen—until the appearance of an even tinier body, with feet that suddenly flashed a thin ribbon of lights.

Toddler sneakers. My mind went to Akira's dead sister and nieces. I turned my head and saw Akira was looking in the same direction. Noticing my consternation, he muttered, "Not them. They were already found."

One sailor walked around with a notebook, stopping at the license plate to write it down. Another tied a ribbon to the car's side mirror and used a marker to write "3" on the driver's door.

I shut my eyes, wishing I'd never looked.

CHAPTER 11

I didn't dare look at any more cars with soldiers nearby as the bus slogged onward. The mud lessened as we moved upland, and a road finally emerged from the dirt. We traveled on it another mile, until the driver stopped at a cluster of stucco buildings. Mud and seawater had painted them a horrid, greenish-brown shade from ground level up to about three feet. Mr. Yano turned around to announce this was the volunteer headquarters and tsunami survivors' shelter. Then he thanked the driver for his service.

Everyone politely applauded the driver, but there was no hurry to get off the bus. When the narrow door opened, a sickening, fishy odor flowed in, and people slapped on the gauze facial masks typically worn when having a cold or hay fever. I hadn't thought to pack such a mask, and it was no surprise that Akira also was maskless. But as I stood in the bus's center aisle, trying hard not to inhale, Mrs. Endo dug into her purse and handed a new, plastic-wrapped mask to each of us.

"I always carry extras, *neh?*"

Once I'd thanked her and slipped the softness over my nose and mouth, I debated whether there was any lessening of the evil smell. It didn't seem like much.

Mr. Yano's voice was muffled as he spoke through his own gauze mask into the microphone, introducing the town's mayor, a fellow who'd come out of the dingy compound to greet us.

Mayor Kazuo Hamasaki was dressed for work in a hard hat, reflective vest, and rubber boots, with a respirator hanging around his neck. He welcomed us, explaining that the volunteers' sleeping dormitory would be up on the second floor of the school district headquarters building. The staircase was still too damaged to use, so we would all use a fire ladder set up on the western side of the building.

"Can your dog climb a ladder?" a woman whispered to me, looking worriedly at Hachiko.

"I may have to camp out below with her." But I didn't want to. The stench made my throat close and head spin.

"Where are all the townspeople?" Yano-san inquired. It was strange that the mayor was the only one we'd seen.

"Many are outside searching for lost relatives or trying to clean mud from their homes." Mayor Hamasaki's serious expression grew even more sober. "If the homes are not habitable, they are staying inside the shelter here, which is normally used as Sugihama High School."

"Have they eaten much today?" Mr. Yano asked.

"They've had cereal bars and water. So far, all provisions have been provided by the Japanese and American military forces."

"As promised, we have brought fresh food and will cook hot meals." Yano-san's cheer sounded forced. "We have portable stoves and plenty of propane fuel."

Nurse Tanaka came forward now and gave a little half bow. She said something in a low voice to the mayor, and I caught the words *potto*: the polite way to say "portable toilet."

"I'm sorry," Mayor Hamasaki answered. "The government hopes to bring some of those soon for everyone."

Where would we relieve ourselves? Some volunteers exchanged worried glances, but there was no complaining.

I was diverted by Hachiko, who was tugging hard on the leash, interested in something a few feet away. Following her movement, I saw an eviscerated, stinking fish being picked at by a crow.

Why did Hachiko like *this* fish? I wondered, shortening my hold on Hachiko's leash. There were so many dead fish. Then I realized: she was interested in the crow.

Hachiko saw life in the midst of all this death. She saw the opportunity to hunt.

And that was what I needed to concern myself about, too.

Akira insisted on bringing my backpack and duffel up the ladder to the second floor of the building. Returning to Hachiko and me a few minutes later, he said, "It's not bad up there; at least all the windows are closed. I'm going to my family now. Good luck with everything."

"Thanks. If you're doing carpentry around town, I might see you again." Following him out, I gave Hachiko a bowl of kibble and a very short walk.

As we returned to the volunteer shelter, I saw Nurse Tanaka waving energetically. She called, "Yano-san, the mayor and I were talking about you."

I felt my stomach drop. Maybe they'd decided there was no way Hachiko could stay with the volunteer crew. That she needed to be confined to a holding area for random animals.

"Oh, Hachiko," I whispered, reaching down to stroke her. How quickly she'd captivated me.

"The mayor suggested I tend to some injured tsunami survivors in Yamagawa this afternoon," Nurse Tanaka said. "Didn't you say your missing friend might be there?"

"Yes. Can you check?" But I desperately wanted to go with her.

"Please plan on accompanying me after lunch."

Had she read my mind? "Thank you!"

"Before we leave, I believe you've been put on kitchen duty, making the hot lunch. We hope to have a meal prepared for two hundred people in less than three hours, so this will mean working quickly."

Unlike our volunteer headquarters, the high school that had become the survivors' shelter was in an area just elevated enough not to have flooded. Therefore, the first floor gymnasium had become a sleeping zone, and the school kitchen, although devoid of electricity, was still a big, decent workspace. I tied Hachiko's leash to the railing of the kitchen door, suggesting to her that she settle down in an empty cardboard box that had held potatoes. Fortunately, she liked its smell.

The school's kitchen was a medium-sized room with a dead refrigerator and no working lights. It was so cold, though, that a refrigerator was hardly needed. Nobuko-san, a round-faced woman in her early thirties, was designated as the head cook, based on her real profession in Yokohama. She asked me to pull groceries from the seven boxes of food supplies brought up on the bus. The potatoes were already being peeled by Yuki and

Reiko, the dog-loving students I'd met on the bus, so I got to work chopping yams and then chopping onions. The rest of the stew's flavor would come from miso and the dried seagreen called *kombu*. By the time Yuki and Reiko had properly recounted the various problems with their parents, boyfriends, and professors, twenty pounds of vegetables were simmering in five giant tureens that bubbled energetically atop propane camp stoves. A teakettle also was on. Miss Nobuko explained we could offer green tea and serve it with packaged crackers while the stew was cooking.

"They need warmth—and tea will fill their bellies a bit as they wait for lunch," she told us.

I was dispatched to spread the news of a coming meal among the families staying at the school. It was a short walk uphill to the school. Inside, the families had staked out spaces inches from each other, defined only by dark green military blankets and borders made from pieces of cardboard boxes. People looked exhausted and somehow very small, like they'd shrunken to fit their miserable little pens.

But my offer of tea was welcome and quickly repeated from one boxed space to another. As if following the directions of an unseen teacher, the tsunami survivors fit themselves into a line and proceeded quietly behind me to the auditorium, where Yuki and Reiko served hot tea that was replaced an hour later by stew. I carefully served one cup of stew per person into cardboard bowls. Everyone gave profuse thanks.

About half the stew we'd cooked was left after the first round, but before I could offer anyone seconds, Nobuko-san told me to take away the partially filled tureens. Seeing my dismay she explained, "We will each have one bowl for our own lunch, and the remainder will be brought to feed people at the injured persons' shelter."

I'd been so busy with cooking and serving that I'd almost forgotten the afternoon plan. But instead of feeling eager, I was strangely anxious. I might find Mr. Ishida seriously or irreversibly injured. Our reunion could be the start of a long period of caretaking. There was also a strong chance he wasn't still at this shelter, but at a hospital or somewhere else.

After finishing every drop of the savory stew, I threw away the paper bowl and went behind the kitchen to see how Hachiko was doing. She'd fallen asleep in the box, shivering despite her coat.

As I petted her, a couple of dark green jeeps pulled up with two American soldiers in each. Encouraging Hachiko to come along with me, I went to greet two uniformed Americans in the first jeep. Pulling down my face mask, I said, "Hi. Are you our ride to Yamagawa?"

The soldier in the driver's seat took off his respirator to answer me. "You bet," he said, revealing a face so young it still was dusted with acne. "We heard a couple of folks were going over to work with us this afternoon."

His companion climbed out of the jeep's other side and put out his hand for me to shake. "I'm Sergeant Simonson. Private McDonald's my driver. Are you American? We didn't know any civilian nurses were here."

"Actually, Nurse Tanaka is Japanese and comes from a hospital in Tokyo. I'll have to find her," I said. "I'm just coming along to help with serving a hot lunch." I gave him my name and said I'd flown over from Hawaii.

"Hawaii!" Sgt. Simonson looked pleased. "I was posted at Schofield Barracks last year. What kinda mutt you got there?"

"Hachiko's part beagle and part Akita—and no, I'm not a dog pro, but would you let me bring Hachiko along for the ride? I'm trying to reunite her with her owner."

"I don't see why she can't come along. Is her owner also an American?"

"No, he's an elderly gentleman from Tokyo." As Sgt. Simonson and Private McDonald came back and forth to the shelter with me, helping bring boxes of medical supplies and food, I explained about Mr. Ishida's call for help. As we worked, Miss Tanaka hurried out to join us, dressed in a white uniform complete with an old fashioned nurse's cap and carrying a doctor's bag.

"So glad you can take us," she said. "Sergeant Simonson, I understand you are a medical corpsman who has already been to the injured shelter? I would like to hear about the general challenges of this population."

Hachiko sat politely, but with her nose quivering, between Nurse Tanaka and me in the back of McDonald and Simonson's jeep, while the second jeep, packed to the roof with supplies and food, followed. We reached Morito Recreation Center after a half hour's drive, although the distance was only five miles. My heart rate quickened at the sight of the single-story brick building. This could be the end of the road for me; the place Hachiko and I would find Mr. Ishida. I swallowed hard, thinking: *Let him still be there—and well enough to return to Tokyo.*

At the door, we were met by some Japanese nurses and medical corpsmen. They moved deferentially behind Dr. Nishi, a fit-looking military doctor who appeared in a flurry of quick footsteps. He bowed to us and had a pleasant expression until he saw Hachiko.

"Stop!" he said in Japanese. "That dog is not allowed inside. We must maintain a clean environment for the patients' safety."

"Oh. I'm sorry." I apologized. "This dog, Hachiko, is the companion of a missing person who may be in the shelter. That's why I brought her—"

"Perhaps, but dogs are not allowed indoors. They are very attracted to blood and wounds. One lick could bring serious infection."

"I'll keep her outside." I looked around, trying to figure out where to tie her leash. "Maybe I can find her owner by myself and then reunite them outdoors—"

"Only if the patient is stable. Are you both nurses?"

At this point, I was glad that Nurse Tanaka spoke up, explaining her abilities as well as that of the medical corpsmen, who clearly hadn't understood the Japanese doctor's comments to me, but were looking uncomfortable. Miss Tanaka added at the end that I'd brought green tea and a hot lunch for the patients whose orders permitted a normal diet.

"But we have no stoves," Dr. Nishi said, frowning at me. "It is thoughtful of you to try to help, but I don't believe you'll be able to serve anything hot."

"These soldiers have generously brought portable stoves and propane," I pointed out. "If it would be all right to set that up, we could feed everyone."

"What is it that you're cooking?"

"A miso vegetable stew." I recited the ingredients, and as I did, I saw the military doctor rub his lips together. Maybe his disagreeability had to do with sheer hunger. I added, "Depending on the number of patients, I believe we will have leftovers for the staff."

"Yes, Doctor, how many patients are here?" Nurse Tanaka asked. "I don't know that information."

"Our census was fifty-two this morning."

I began, "The gentleman I'm looking for is Ishida. Yasushi Ishida—"

But Dr. Nishi was already motioning for Nurse Tanaka to follow him. My question either had gone unheard or wasn't important enough.

"Please come along. I'll translate," Nurse Tanaka said to Sgt. Simonson and the other army medic who'd traveled in the jeep behind us.

Private McDonald and the other jeep's driver, Private Finley, made it clear they'd help with the food service. They set up the portable stoves on some picnic tables near the shelter, while I tied Hachiko's leash to a bicycle rack. The dog stood motionless but kept her nose aimed in the direction of the recreation building, and jerked on her leash each time someone opened the door to go inside.

"She's still cold. I'm worried about her."

"Yeah, maybe she shouldn't have come to this area," Private McDonald said. "It's ten degrees colder than Tokyo."

"If she were on a walk, she'd be warmer," I said, wishing I'd thought to bring her box and blanket along. But I hadn't, so I busied myself getting the teapot on the stove. As it came almost to a boil, I turned it off and began pouring hot water into white foam cups with green tea bags inside. Not many Japanese preferred tea-bag tea over loose, but the pleased reaction of the tsunami survivors earlier had assured me these cups would be appreciated.

I arranged two dozen hot cups of tea on two trays, and set up twenty-four more cups to steep, giving Private McDonald directions to remove the tea bags after exactly four minutes. He looked at me as if I was crazy but set his watch.

Inside, the sharp aroma of kerosene heaters somewhat mitigated more unpleasant human odors. I supposed that I would smell that way if Mr. Ishida were not here and I'd have to linger in the area searching. How would I do it?

I forced my thoughts away from Mr. Ishida and to the people right in front of me. Hospital gurneys were crowded into the room, with barely a foot's width between them. These gurneys were topped by frail, mostly middle-aged to elderly people under green military blankets.

As I approached the first row of gurneys, a walnut-faced lady sat straight up and greeted me. She'd seen the tray of tea. The patient lying on the gurney behind her followed suit.

Ocha, ocha... a murmur went through the area, and patients began pulling their hands out from under the blankets. And as I moved along, each face I looked at was grateful. But where was Mr. Ishida? Not here.

Within minutes I'd finished distributing the tea and promised others that I would be back with more. As I left the building to hurry back to the tea on the picnic tables, I passed by Hachiko, who whined and sprang on me. Had she been frightened I'd abandoned her? She was a shop dog, and I'd brought her to a wild, cold, smelly place.

I put down the empty trays to pet her, noticing that she'd moved around the bicycle rack so much that she'd twisted her leash between several rungs.

"She's acting like she's really your dog," Private McDonald said. "Those other tea cups are brewed just the way you wanted—I took out the tea bags already."

"Thanks. The patients are really happy about the tea." I unclipped and straightened out Hachiko's leash, then reclipped it to the bike rack. "Sweetie, I'll be back soon. I promise."

Hachiko sniffed, as if insulted, but settled down with her head resting on her paws.

"More tea," I called as I walked back into the shelter. Was this what it felt like to be a waitress on the Shinkansen train? I was doling out the second tray of tea when a murmur went through the room followed by laughter. I turned to see Hachiko bolting straight into the heart of the room, a chewed remnant of leash flying from her collar.

Hachiko moved gracefully around people and chairs and underneath gurneys. Within moments she had vanished. I didn't dare call after her because I didn't know if she'd respond, and also because Dr. Nishi, who was just ten feet away listening to someone's heart, might overhear. Hastily putting the last cups of tea into the hands of two confused-seeming patients, I tucked the empty tray under my arm and began serious pursuit.

Glancing around the room, looking wildly for Hachiko, I noticed Sgt. Simonson giving me a "what-the-hell" look. I shook my head, threw my hands up in the air, and hurried on.

"Are you finished with the tea, Shimura-san?" Miss Tanaka looked up from nearby, where she was taking a patient's temperature. Obviously she had not seen Hachiko passing underneath the gurneys.

"Yes, just looking for someone." I paused, trying to look normal.

"By the way, there is a list in the doctors' office of all the injured persons. You could check it when you're done serving, okay?"

I could not see Hachiko at all; but in the farthest corner of the room, some laughter came from a small group of patients who were sitting together on a few folded blankets. I made my way on the outer edge of the sea of gurneys toward them. As I'd feared, Hachiko was in their midst and was standing with her paws on one someone's shoulders.

"I'm so sorry. It was an accident that she came in," I said, grabbing up the end of Hachiko's trailing leash. "Stop licking! *Dame desu!*"

Hachiko seemed to understand *"dame,"* the quick command that meant "bad," "no," and "don't" rolled into one. She dropped her feet to the floor, allowing the bandaged man she'd accosted to wipe his face with a hand. Smiling, he looked up at me with warm brown eyes surrounded by a lifetime of creases. The silvery nimbus of his hair was flattened, and a large square bandage was taped to one side of his head. The man's shirt was grimy, but a blue-and-gray silk scarf was tied at his neck with flair.

I knew only one Japanese man who tied scarves like that.

Hachiko had found Ishida-san.

CHAPTER 12

So quickly, it was over. All the stress of the last week faded at the glorious sight of Ishida-san embracing his best friend.

"So good of you to come, Shimura-san," Mr. Ishida said, catching sight of me. "I didn't know you'd bring Hachiko."

"I'm very happy she found you." This was an understatement, but there were too many people around for me to confess how deeply affected I was to know he was well enough to be at a mahjongg board. "Actually, Hachiko's not supposed to be inside for hygiene reasons."

"I was so worried about Hachiko," Mr. Ishida said as if he hadn't heard me. "How did you know she was trapped alone in the shop?"

"Fortunately, Okada-san remembered Hachiko and brought her to your vet. She's been with me since yesterday evening."

I would have to explain that I didn't know where the dog would be allowed to spend the night, except that Sgt. Simonson had joined us. "So this is where she went. The doctor's going to be pissed."

"It was amazing: Hachiko found her owner," I explained. "I'll go outside with her now, as I have to bring in food, anyway. Ishida-san, can you stay with her outdoors while I serve the meals? Are you recovered enough?"

"You take her straightaway while I try to get permission from the nurses. They don't like us wandering around."

I only had a foot of leash left to tug Hachiko with, and she would not leave Mr. Ishida, so he wound up walking to the shelter doorway so I could get her to move. There wasn't anything left with which to tie her to the bike rack, so he sat on the step, petting Hachiko, whose tail was making so many circles that it looked like a golden blur. As I explained to Ishida-san about the food-service work I needed to do here and then later in Sugihama, he nodded, but then said, "Please don't go back to Sugihama without speaking to me again—I have something very important to tell you."

Maybe this important thing was why he'd asked me to come to Tohoku in the first place, I thought as I joined Private McDonald in ladling stew into disposable bowls.

"The sergeant told me your reunion's already happened. Kind of amazing it worked out so fast." Private McDonald grinned at me.

"Yes. Now the only challenge is getting Mr. Ishida out of here and finding a place for Hachiko to sleep. Ideally they should be together. But it's a couple of days until the volunteer bus will return to Tokyo."

It took about an hour to serve all of the patients the stew. Then, steeling myself for a potentially difficult encounter, I located Dr.

Nishi in a closet-like office with just a table and one chair. He had a laptop computer on it and pages of papers scattered all around.

"I'm very sorry to interrupt, Dr. Nishi. I brought your lunch and wondered if I could speak to you a moment?" I put the bowl down to the side of his laptop.

He looked at the bowl, then his watch. "Actually, I'm still doing morning rounds and it's already late afternoon."

"I just found Ishida Yasushi, my mentor who was missing from Tokyo. I've come to ask if you'll allow him to transfer to the main shelter in Sugihama until I take him and his dog back to Tokyo on Sunday."

The doctor slowly sniffed the stew, as if he was savoring it. "I've examined a patient called Ishida, but he's not from Tokyo. Are you sure you have the right person?"

"Of course. I know him, and he knows me." I handed the doctor a plastic spoon and paper napkin. "Ishida-san owns a shop in Tokyo's Yanaka neighborhood. He grew up there and has worked in it for decades."

"*Itadakimasu.*" The doctor murmured the words one always said before eating and took a sip of stew with his spoon. "Very tasty."

"Glad you like it," I said.

"When he didn't give an address, I suspected dementia. He kept wanting to go outside this building, and he was speaking about a blue woman—"

"Oh, that's his apprentice." I paused, thinking it would be helpful to learn from this doctor the story of Mr. Ishida's rescue in case my friend left out or forgot any information. "Could you tell me how Ishida-san wound up here—several miles from where he'd been?"

The stew was working wonders. Dr. Nishi had a few more sips, then spoke. "According to the police, Ishida-san was rescued in Sugihama from one Takara Auction House—a three-story business on high ground. He had fallen during the quake's impact, he said, and had a laceration on the right side of his head that required some stitches. He was likely concussed."

"Concussed. Is it serious?" I exclaimed.

Nurse Tanaka-san stepped into the small space. "Oh, there you are," she said cheerfully. "We are ready to return to the other shelter."

"Okay." Turning back to the doctor, I asked, "What about the head injury?"

"It makes me reluctant to let him go about on his own. He's under medical watch."

"Does this mean he can't come with me today?" I stared at the doctor, feeling as if everything that had been going right was suddenly heading in the other direction.

"He has not proved himself to be sound of mind or even to know his name. You've come in and claim he's from Tokyo—but if he doesn't support that idea—what am I to do?"

"I think you should call his doctor in Tokyo." I looked at his stew bowl. It was empty. Maybe he was still hungry, because he'd seemed to revert to his earlier officiousness. "Dr. Nakajima's office is in the Yanaka District of Tokyo. I can look it up for you—"

"Thank you. Maybe I'll be able to reach him, but telephone access has been difficult."

Trying to hide my irritation, I said, "I hope to speak with you tomorrow."

"I don't understand why any doctor wouldn't want to move someone out of this shelter," I muttered to Nurse Tanaka after Dr. Nishi had given us leave. "There aren't enough staff to care for everyone, it's cold, and the risk of infection from someone else has got to be high!"

"Protocol, I think. I'm sure it will work out tomorrow, Shimura-san. May I offer my congratulations on finding your friend? You must be very happy," Miss Tanaka said in a soothing voice as we walked back into the main clinic room.

"It's thanks to you that Hachiko and I were able to visit. Who knows how long it would have taken otherwise?" I shook my head. "Did you hear the doctor believes Ishida-san has dementia and didn't remember that he was from Tokyo? I think the doctor's the one with issues of confusion."

Nurse Tanaka put a gentle hand on my arm. "When you speak to Ishida-san, perhaps it's best not to mention this supposed diagnosis. It could make him nervous."

"Of course I won't say anything. But I do want to talk to him. He said there's something he wants me to know before leaving."

"I do wish there was enough time for him to chat with you and enjoy his dog." Nurse Tanaka took her comforting hand away from me to look at her watch. "But I'm expected back at the other building to continue health checks with the families staying in the Sugihama shelter."

"I could go back to Sugihama on my own."

"But we have this transportation right now! I don't see how you can." The nurse looked at me warily.

"On the way over, I noticed there's really only one working road dug out. It's impossible to get lost—and I've got good boots." The black suede Merrell boots were a gift from Michael for last winter's brief trip to visit his parents in New Hampshire. They wouldn't look new for much longer, but that was okay.

Nurse Tanaka permitted Ishida-san to come outside with me for a few minutes to say goodbye to Hachiko. However, my elderly friend hadn't a coat with him and was directed by her to wrap a blanket around his shoulders for warmth. I explained to both of them that now I knew where he was, I'd bring the coat and the other clothes I'd brought from his home as quickly as I could.

"I would like to vacate this asylum," he told me. "The challenge will be finding a lodging to accept both Hachiko and me. Can you find out if any hotels are open in this area?"

"Before I do that, why do you even want to stick around here? It's a disaster zone without toilets and—"

"We have portable toilets behind the building. You should take advantage, if there are none in Sugihama."

"I'll check it out later," I said, as the two of us started walking with Hachiko between us. The dog now had a military-issue rope attached to her collar, courtesy of Private McDonald. "I'm glad you stayed a bit longer to talk. I must tell you about Mayumi-chan."

"Your new apprentice. I believe you mentioned her during the phone call you made to Hawaii that was unfortunately cut off too soon—"

"Yes, yes. I cannot leave this area without Mayumi. She didn't even want me to come to this auction—and look what happened."

I ran over the words he'd just spoken. They didn't make sense. "Do you mean that your apprentice Mayumi was here with you during the earthquake and tsunami?"

"Actually, it was a surprise that Mayumi-chan joined me in Sugihama," Mr. Ishida said. "She had said she heard the antiques house had a bad reputation; but it was quite a new place, so I told her I would visit and decide what I thought.

"Then, the day before leaving, she told me an important client was coming to Tokyo on the eleventh and wanted to see me in the shop. I could not ignore this, so I telephoned Fujiwara-sama. He had no plans to visit Tokyo. Mayumi-chan had been confused."

"Very confused," I said.

"So I left. I'd been traveling for two days already when she rang me on my cell phone to say she would rush to Sugihama to bring something I'd forgotten."

"Goodness! What item did you forget?"

"My *inkan*. It was my first time dealing with the Takara Auction House, so she reminded me I needed it. Always it's in my bag, but I'd forgotten it this time."

Mr. Ishida was talking about a special hand-carved stick with a calligrapher's *kanji* interpretation of his name. Although many Japanese last names were identical, supposedly each person's *inkan* was unique and therefore valuable proof of agreement when stamping official documents. It was conceivable an auctioneer would prefer an *inkan* to be used for a bill of sale. But Mr. Ishida also had a driver's license and plenty of business cards. I thought he could have closed a deal without having his personal stamp.

I put my skepticism on hold as Mr. Ishida continued.

"Mayumi-chan caught the bullet train to Sendai and then a bus to Sugihama. She met me midway through the auction. About thirty minutes later, the quake struck." He shuddered. "I don't remember everything, I'm afraid. There was such a terrible shaking with items falling all over. Everyone who could move was trying to get outside."

"Yes," I said, "I heard that's what people did in Tokyo, too. It's an instinctive reaction. Nobody wants to be buried in a collapsed building."

"I hit the ground hard and remember putting my hand to my head and touching blood. Mayumi pulled me back up to my feet. She was crying and wanted me to come outside with her and make an escape. However, I was quite weak, and we hadn't my van to drive away in—I'd gone by train. Mr. Morioka, the auction owner, said that he was moving his valuables as quickly as he could to the top floor, and if I needed, I could stay up with him."

"So you decided to take advantage of this shelter?" I asked, remembering Dr. Nishi's summary of what the police had reported. "But how incredibly lucky you were. So many people who stayed on upper floors of homes drowned anyway."

"I didn't immediately go upstairs. Mayumi-chan ran outside, trying to find space for us in a vehicle driven by any of the other auction-goers. She took my satchel because she thought showing people my identification might lead to our being assisted."

I nodded. Mr. Ishida was a senior member of the Tokyo antiques community. His name had opened important doors for me. Probably Mayumi thought it could open at least a car door.

"She didn't come back." His voice broke. "I waited, but in a few minutes, I spotted the wave from the window sweeping through the lower part of the town. I guessed that there might have been room for just one person in a car offered to her—and she'd had to go so fast that she could not tell me. In any case, Morioka-san allowed me to stay upstairs along with a few other people who didn't drive cars to the auction. I remember Morioka-san saying that the building was tall enough and so strong it wouldn't be swept away."

"He sounds quite confident for someone who is a newcomer to

Tohoku," I said, remembering what Akira Rikyo had said about Mr. Morioka.

"And he was correct! The wave flooded the ground level, where the auction had been held, but did not come up to the second and third floors. It was frightening nonetheless to be up there for so many hours—to see the destruction from the window." He shuddered slightly. "The next morning, we were rescued by boat. But when I came to this shelter, I couldn't find anyone who had heard about Mayumi-chan."

If she hadn't been found, it meant that she'd gotten out of Tohoku altogether—or that she hadn't survived.

"While I was upstairs, I thought I heard her voice calling, but I knew it must have been impossible." He shook his head. "I should have told her to stay with me instead of letting her look for transportation. I did not protect her."

"She sounds like she had a mind of her own," I consoled. "Everyone reacts differently in emergencies. But what we can guess is that she didn't return to Tokyo, because there was no sign she went back to the shop."

"I know that she would not have left Tohoku without finding me. The thing is," Mr. Ishida said, lowering his voice, "Mayumi is a girl who's had some hard times. She looks at me like a grandfather."

So he felt the same way about her that I felt about him. "It must be hard—"

"And her family probably has no idea what's happened. They would be so worried. Shimura-san, I beg you. Help me find Mayumi."

CHAPTER 13

M y job was supposed to be over. But now that Mr. Ishida had made his plea, a new ordeal was beginning.

I sent Michael a text message laying out the new problem. There was no response. Perhaps he was busy at work, or actually traveling to Japan, or was somewhere without wireless access. Or he was asleep. By the time I'd walked from Yamagawa to Sugihama, it was five—which translated to ten p.m. in Hawaii.

While trudging, I had plenty of time to think about the irony. Mr. Ishida was besieging me with the same feverish request to search for someone that I'd presented to Michael just a week earlier. I knew Michael hadn't believed a rush trip to Japan was really necessary.

Now I wondered how I could possibly suggest I didn't have time to help. There were about two days left before the volunteer bus returned to Tokyo. To learn where Mayumi went was probably just a matter of checking records of rescues and deaths. The end result of the search, however, might be bad news.

My first opportunity for research came during the evening dinner hour. I'd arrived just in time to assist with the shelter dinner: another miso-based stew, though this time it featured kale, turnips, and tomatoes. When Mayor Hamasaki appeared in front of me, I held onto my ladle for an extra moment before serving him and asked about the day's progress.

"I was overwhelmed to see another road cleared," the mayor said. "Sometimes I think, why were we so lucky to get your group helping us? There are quite a few towns with similar destruction, but not a committed volunteer group."

"Sugihama deserves the help—and I wish I were doing more. So far I've fed people. I haven't done any outdoor cleanup. That's the hard part."

"Didn't you travel on the medical detail to Yamagawa?" The mayor studied me with kind eyes.

"Yes." I realized this was a good opening for my query. "When I was in Yamagawa, I heard from someone about a young woman who disappeared in Sugihama during the tsunami. I would be grateful for any advice on the best way to find out if she survived."

The mayor put down his bowl. "Sorry, I'm confused. I heard from Yano-san that you are searching for an elderly gentleman?"

"Yes. I was thrilled to find my mentor, Ishida-san, in good health at the injured persons' shelter." I paused, remembering how incredible that moment had been. "But Ishida-san is quite anxious. He told me his apprentice was with him at the Takara Auction House. He lost sight of her between the earthquake and the tsunami."

"Oh, that's very tough. Did he tell you her name?" Mayor Hamasaki's voice was soothing, and I imagined he'd said this kind of thing hundreds of times over the last week.

"Kimura Mayumi. She is not a Sugihama native, but a nineteen-year-old from a town about an hour away, Kinugasa. She moved to Tokyo about a year ago." I explained about Mayumi helping Ishida-san after his fall and then rushing outside to find passage for both of them to escape the tsunami. I added that when she didn't return, Mr. Ishida had gone up to the building's third floor with Mr. Morioka.

"It was his only option," I explained. "He cut his head during the fall and was disoriented. He talked about sirens and hearing Mayumi calling. I understand that deciding to stay in the tsunami zone went against evacuation orders, but fortunately he and Morioka-san survived."

"That auction house is quite tall—and it's at the top of a street, which gave it higher elevation. I've been making rounds of all homes and businesses, so I spoke to Morioka-san when he was cleaning up a few days ago. There was flooding on the first floor only. But he was very upset about whether his insurance would pay to replace the floor." The mayor shook his head. "Floors can be replaced. They are not as important as people."

I nodded, thinking that with a few words, the mayor had effectively communicated his disapproval of Mr. Morioka. "I'd like to talk to Morioka-san about the events, just in case Mayumi came back. I gather from what you said, he didn't shift to a shelter, despite the problems on the first floor?"

"No. He's done some preliminary cleanup and felt strongly about staying on his second and third floor. Everybody who has a chance to stay home does that."

"Can you tell me the way to his shop?"

Using a pen from his coat pocket and a paper napkin from the stack near the tureen, the mayor drew a map. "It's about three kilometers from here, but no car can go all the way because of obstructions. So many people tried to drive through that road to escape, but unfortunately the tsunami caught them. Cars were tossed about, blocking the road."

"Is it possible for Mayumi Kimura's name to be added to all the search lists? I've heard that her hair is colored bright blue. Is it possible to note that down as well?"

"Blue hair?" he repeated, his eyebrows rising. "Certainly I shall alert the police, military, and hospitals."

"And how about *all* the Tohoku shelters? Just in case she wound up in another town like Mr. Ishida did."

"I'll do my best, but please know that if someone hasn't been reported found by this date... the news is probably not going to be good."

"I agree with you. And I'm sorry I've kept you so long. You must be very hungry," I said, belatedly remembering to spoon stew into his paper bowl. I looked to see how many people might have been waiting behind him, but saw nobody else.

Of all the displaced people in Sugihama, the last one to take a meal was its mayor.

It was eight o'clock when I finished with my labors and was able to return to the volunteers' dormitory to carry down some refreshments for Hachiko's evening meal. I found the personal hygiene situation had also improved. Two enclosed toilet stalls stood about thirty feet from the shelter. Someone had placed a framed picture of a cartoon little girl on one stall's door; the other stall was decorated with a collectible baseball playing card showing the smiling face of a Yomiuri Giants baseball player.

I carried a bowl of food to Hachiko, who did not get up from where she was lying near the high school's cafeteria door. She looked despondent, although I might have been projecting my own worries on her. After eating, and drinking the bowl I filled with water from my bottle, she nuzzled my hand.

"You're very welcome, Hachiko. And you'll stay with Ishida-san once I get him out," I whispered to the dog as I walked her away from the building to relieve herself. "It's really better for the two of you to go straight home than stay in the shelter here—don't you think?"

Hachiko thumped her tail, and I thought she was agreeing with me until I realized that a little girl who looked around seven years old had slipped out the kitchen door and was following us.

"Please may I pet your dog?" she asked. She was wearing a school uniform with a coat, which was grimy enough to look like she hadn't been able to change in the eight days since the tsunami struck.

I had seen enough of Hachiko to know she was good with most people, so I smiled my assent. The girl's small fingers went straight underneath Hachiko's chin, ruffling the soft fur. I wasn't sure how Hachiko would react to the child's bold greeting, but her lips curled charmingly. Could a dog actually smile?

"We have an Akita at home, only he doesn't have patches like this one. Is yours a boy or girl?"

"She's a two-year-old girl named Hachiko. Her owner is staying in the injured persons' shelter in Yamagawa, so I'm taking care of her for a bit. But tell me about your dog, please."

"My dog is a big boy, about seven years old. He's called Butter, because he's the color of butter." When she spoke the name, she grinned, revealing an adorable gap between some upper teeth. So her grown-up teeth were coming in.

"What a cute name. Is he like yellow butter or white butter?"

"White. Have you seen him?" Her eyes widened hopefully.

"Not yet. Sorry."

"Well, my father probably has him. He was looking for Butter when my mother took my sisters and me away in our neighbor's minivan. Butter was scared by the earthquake, so he ran away."

"I've heard a lot of animals got scared," I sympathized.

"We waited for Otoochan to come back with Butter, but the sirens were loud and the neighbors said we must drive away right then. No more waiting! I didn't want to, but my mother was yelling and crying."

I nodded, bending my head toward Hachiko so the girl wouldn't know that my eyes had started to water. From what she'd said, it sounded like both her father and dog could have died.

"Otoochan and Butter are coming later. There are too many trees and cars thrown about in the street. That is why they haven't arrived."

Hachiko was leaning into the girl's palm, looking up at her with melting eyes. As the little girl giggled, Hachiko rolled onto her back, offering up her stomach.

"I wish Hachiko would sleep with me until Butter comes."

"I'd really like that too, but Hachiko's place is supposed to be here outside. Look, I've made a big box for her with her blanket."

"People inside our area have dogs," she whined. "Why can't I?"

"That's nice they've been allowed." I gestured toward the darkening sky. "It was very nice of you to visit. May I walk you back to the other side of the building, so you can see your mother? She must be worried."

"Only if Hachiko comes. I want them to see her."

Cautiously, I said, "As far as they'll let me bring her—"

"Come, come! What's your name, anyway?" The girl gave a polite half bow. "I'm called Miki. Age seven years and two months. My sister Chieko's three, and Baby Miho is one. My mother's twenty-nine."

When we came into the shelter and met her mother, I was shocked. Japanese women typically look younger than their age: a combination of genes, near constant humidity, and zealous precautions against the sun. But Sadako Haneda was so worn-looking she appeared a good bit older than me—and I was slightly her senior.

The overwhelmed, fatigued woman was so busy giving a bottle to a baby wrapped in a pink blanket that she barely looked up at us. At her side, a three-year-old daughter who looked like a miniature version of Miki turned the pages of a grubby picture book.

The Hanedas had been assigned a small space on the high school's auditorium floor that was bordered by unfolded cardboard boxes. There were families in similar confinement on either side of them. The only thing softening these dismal pens were coats and dark-green military blankets.

"Okaachan, we have friends, and they're not from Sugihama!" Miki beseeched her mother to look up, and she made a tired smile and head bob in my direction before anxiously returning her attention to the whimpering baby.

I introduced myself as one of the Helping Hands volunteers, and Hachiko as a dog who was awaiting reunion with her owner.

"Hachiko and Miki-chan enjoy each other so much. If there's ever a time you don't know where Miki-chan has gone, it's probably behind the cafeteria door. That's where Hachiko's been tied up."

"Hachiko doesn't like the tying," Miki said. "Look, she's trying to eat her leash!"

"Shimura-san, thanks for bringing Miki back. I was a bit worried I didn't see her, but I didn't want to move her sisters and start a search. I also thought, where could she possibly go? There are no streets anymore—just mud." Sadako's voice was soft and sad.

"I'm so sorry about the conditions here. If Miki-chan can visit Hachiko when she's bored, it might be a good thing."

"Yes. She will enjoy playing with your dog because she really misses our Butter."

"Okaachan, Hachiko-san is so cold sleeping outside. Can't I please give her this for the night?" Miki bent over a pile of clothes and pulled out a large black down parka. I grimaced, imagining how quickly it would be covered with fawn-and-white dog hair.

"But that's Otoochan's," Chieko, the middle sister, protested.

Sadako Haneda reached out a hand to stroke Hachiko, who cocked her head and looked soulfully at the woman. "Yes, she can lie on the coat. If the dog would like it, she is welcome to sleep here with us."

"Okaachan!" Miki squealed, her face pinkening. "Truly?"

I was momentarily speechless, because the offer was so unexpected. "But... isn't... that's too great an imposition," I stammered. "Your space here is limited, and you have the girls."

"There's a family two rows over with a St. Bernard," Sadako said. "The thing is, Miki usually sleeps with Butter, because her little sister and the baby still sleep with my husband and me.

Having a dog to cuddle keeps Miki from being lonely. And it will be much warmer for all of us."

"That would be absolutely wonderful. I'll bring her food and bowls to you, so she can eat right away tomorrow morning. And I thank you from my heart." I thought to myself, *three small children without their home and a missing husband. Yet she had the generosity to take Hachiko in.*

Hachiko clearly understood the outdoor alternative, because she didn't whimper when I left her. I walked the short, chilly stretch to the volunteer shelter, feeling glad that yet another thing had gone surprisingly right.

Upstairs I found almost everyone had unrolled their sleeping bags and tucked in. Here and there, white lights glowed: volunteers were using their cell phones to read or send messages. My sleeping bag was wide enough that I could change into the double-layered, cotton long-underwear set inside of it. Only a three-foot-high wall of supply boxes separated our side of the room from the men's—not that any of them were looking.

Reiko and Yuki, the college girl friends, had set up their sleeping bags on one side of mine. Nurse Tanaka was on my other side. I thought she was asleep until I heard a choking sound.

"Tanaka-san, are you okay?" I put a light hand on the part of her sleeping bag where I guessed her shoulder was.

"Yes." She rolled toward me, and I saw that her cheeks were wet. "It's just that I talked to so many people who lost family members today."

"It's unbelievable," I whispered, thinking I'd probably done the same when talking to the Hanedas.

"If all the preparations the government made couldn't save them, what is to stop this from happening again?" Tanaka-san wept softly. "Why should we give anyone hope this place is safe to live in again? Cleaning up and rebuilding is futile."

"Every effort is meaningful." Mrs. Endo's calm voice came from a bit farther down the row of sleeping bags. "We have had the honor of giving them their first hot meals and cleaning homes and streets. Nurse Tanaka, you touched people with your hands who are in pain but will now recover. The local people will decide for themselves whether to stay here or move. It's like the prime minister says: right now, we all should practice kizuna."

Mrs. Endo was using a unique word that meant something like "bonds of loving kindness." This was different from the general western concept of love because of the aspect of giving to others. I thought kizuna was a beautiful word and had noticed the press and government officials using it repeatedly when praising acts of help to those hurt by the disaster.

Nestling down into the warmth of the down sleeping bag, I turned on my cell phone for the first time all day. Michael had left me three text messages. I was eager to read them and text back that I'd found Mr. Ishida. But as I attempted to read the first message, a tiny whirling circle appeared on the screen. I knew what it meant. As the phone's face went black, I swore under my breath.

Oddly enough, Reiko—who'd snored through the conversation between Mrs. Endo, Nurse Tanaka and me—stirred. Poking her head out of a Hello Kitty sleeping bag, she whispered, "Dead telephone?"

"Yes. And I don't have the right kind of charger—"

"You can use mine." She sat up and reached around to grope in her backpack. After a moment she handed me a small but heavy black plastic box.

"I'm all charged up. Please. You use it now."

"Thank you so much. I hope this doesn't use up all your battery power."

"No worry about that," she said with a light laugh. "We are only here one more day and then go home."

She would go, but I had a feeling I wouldn't be with her.

CHAPTER 14

Sunday morning I awoke to electronic bells playing a wake-up song from an outdoor speaker. I wasn't surprised; many Japanese towns played a ritual daily minute of canned music. Sometimes the music was played in the morning; other places rang chimes around dinnertime. Some foreigners thought it was a touch of Big Brother to have this loud, corporate-designed music take the place of birdsong. It always seemed to me that it was a way of reassuring everyone that community systems were operating as normal.

Sugihama's town song was a lightweight approximation of the Beatles' "Eleanor Rigby." The Beatles were perennially popular in Japan. This remake was all keyboards and synthesizers, but mentally, I put in the missing lyrics.

I'd seen plenty of lonely people in the shelters. The rest of them were scattered throughout the towns, freezing in their damaged homes. It was clear where they'd come from. The question was, where would they go?

Teeth chattering in the early morning cold, I pulled yesterday's clothes over my long underwear and went down the staircase to sit outside by myself in the winter sun, eating two granola bars as slowly as I could manage.

At least my cell phone was fully rejuvenated. I spent some time checking text messages. A contractor had sent an irritable message about the nonstandard window sizes in three of the Ewa Landing cottages. And Michael had sent ten messages with varying levels of concern about not hearing from me. I began a response with *Found Mr. Ishida!* and would have included a lot more if Nurse Tanaka hadn't touched me on the shoulder and said it was time to join in calisthenics. I threw on a few heart emoticons, pressed "send," and then turned off the phone again.

The volunteers' morning exercise assembly was being held outdoors on the other side of the building. I went around to a cleared area where the masked volunteers had arranged themselves in six shivering lines. I fell in with Tanaka-san as Mr. Yano clapped his hands.

"Ichi ni san! Ichi ni san!" He bellowed the one-two-three count into a megaphone and began high-stepping until everyone had joined him. After two minutes, I was exhausted, but then came squats, kicks, and punches. In Japan, group exercise for students and employees was common, aimed to build unity and daily energy. But the tsunami volunteers had already spent many hours lifting rubble and slept in an uncomfortable, cold room. People moved slowly. I felt myself stumble over something and scrambled to keep my balance.

"Good morning, Rei-san!"

Miki had slipped into the calisthenics assembly and brought

Hachiko with her for good measure. Behind me, I could hear her whispering to Hachiko to follow along.

"Hey there," I whispered, turning around to ruffle the fur on Hachiko's thick neck. "Let's give Hachiko breakfast right after this. I'll see my friend Ishida-san today and tell him how you're helping. He will want to meet you before they return to Tokyo."

"But she's with me now. Why would she go away?" Miki's voice wavered.

"Remember when I told you that she belongs to my friend? Yesterday, Hachiko found him at a shelter in Yamagawa When the doctor thinks it's all right, they'll go home to Tokyo. Just like your family's going to stay together."

Her mouth quivered. "Everyone but Otoochan and Butter."

I couldn't begin to address that point. "Soon you'll leave this shelter. Your family will stay for a while in a trailer that you can decorate just like an apartment. That will be cozier than staying in a gymnasium."

"But I want to go home to *our* apartment. It's so nice. And right outdoors we have a playground and a community garden. I can show you next week. The *suisen* will start blooming then, Okaachan says."

She was speaking of white narcissus, the first flowers that showed their faces in the spring. I nodded, but in my heart, I didn't believe the flowers would come. In the nearby town of Rikuzentakata, just one pine tree from a giant forest had survived the wave. The land was changed forever, just like Miki's family's life.

"You'd like to deliver lunch at the injured persons' shelter again? I can guess why," Mr. Yano said with a slight laugh when I raised my hand to ask permission to travel again to Yamagawa during the group assignment time.

He probably believed I was thinking of myself and not the group. And I had accomplished my objective of finding a lost friend—why wouldn't I do something more helpful to others? Awkwardly I explained, "I'd like to go back there, if it's not too much of an inconvenience. A lot of the people are bedridden and enjoyed seeing a friendly face. They were also so happy to have their first hot meal."

"Well, you can volunteer here this morning and bring lunch to them—but not the dog. I heard from Dr. Nishi about that."

Blushing, I said, "Of course, I'll do whatever's needed here before I go. Hauling garbage, shoveling mud—"

"I shall try to match the work with your skills."

I was assigned to give out antiseptic wipes and fresh socks. Foot hygiene. The simplicity of my job reminded me of how minimal my abilities were. Still, I was becoming tougher. And I didn't feel like gagging when I put on the gauze mask to load up the military jeeps that had returned to take Nurse Tanaka, Mrs. Endo, and me to the injured persons' shelter for lunchtime service.

Upon arrival at the Morito Recreation Center, I checked in with Dr. Nishi, who wanted to know the lunch menu. I told him.

Shaking his head, he said, "Don't make the *ramen* too hot. It will be easy for the patients to suffer burns."

I knew that by the time the soup was spooned into bowls and carried on a tray indoors, it would lose ten Fahrenheit degrees—at least. And noodle soup like *ramen* was only good when it was blistering hot. But I kept that opinion to myself.

"About the patient, Ishida Yasushi." The doctor cleared his throat. "This morning, I made contact with his personal physician you mentioned. Dr. Fujita is comfortable with Ishida-san returning to Tokyo, but agrees it would be better for him to travel with a companion."

I hadn't realized how stiffly I'd been standing until I felt relief wash through my muscles. "Thank you, Doctor. He will be so pleased about that."

"Actually, I'm not sure what his reaction will be." Dr. Nishi pressed his lips together. "I will sign the discharge paperwork and have it ready for you to take when you depart with him later today. It's a good thing you came. Otherwise, I wouldn't have known how to consult with his doctor in Tokyo."

"Thanks. But Ishida-san could have told you—"

"He never even said he was from Tokyo. Very strange, don't you think?"

Leaving the little office, I thought about Mr. Ishida's resistance to disclosing his address. I guessed that he'd kept it quiet because he didn't want to be sent out of Tohoku without finding Mayumi. But how frustrating for him to have been kept inside all this time with nothing to do but throw mah-jongg tiles.

"Ah, you come again with lunch," Mr. Ishida said when I made it to his little playing group about a half hour later.

"It's miso-*ramen* today," I said. "I do hope it's hot enough."

"I heard that I can leave today," Mr. Ishida said, smiling widely. "But the question is, where will I stay?"

"I'll get things sorted out with Helping Hands. But I think we should go to Sugihama together today. Hachiko's waiting for you there," I added as an extra persuasion.

"By herself?"

"Actually, she's enjoying some time with a little girl called Miki. She and her family were able to keep her inside the shelter with them last night."

"Hachiko likes children." Mr. Ishida sounded approving. "I only hope she doesn't lead them on a hunt for me. Her nose is all too powerful."

"Yes. She put on quite a show yesterday when she found you."

Mr. Ishida glanced at his watch, a round-faced Seiko model with a simple leather strap that dated from the 1950s. "About how long are you staying here today?"

"At least another hour. Let me finish serving the whole room, and then I'll come back so we can talk about the situation."

Easier said than done. It took longer than usual to serve today, because a number of the shelter's residents remembered Hachiko's dramatic run and wanted to chat about it. By the time I'd thrown away the empty paper bowls, more than two hours had passed, and I didn't see Mr. Ishida in the mah-jongg group anymore. As I glanced around, debating where to look for him, I saw someone waving hard at me from the door.

Mr. Ishida had already changed into his clothes from home: a brown tweed coat, corduroy trousers, and a black beret. He gestured again, looking impatient.

"I've decided to start my search at the Takara Auction House. If you would come along, I'd be obliged."

I hesitated. "It won't be long until I'm packed up to return in the jeep. We can get everything to the volunteer headquarters. After that, it should be easy to get directions to the auction house."

"It's already three o'clock. Once it's dark there won't be time. And my goodness, I'm ready to walk."

"But..." I trailed off as Mr. Ishida walked out the door. I stepped out after him and saw Mrs. Endo looking questioningly at me from the picnic table where she was taking empty tureens off the camp stoves.

Hurriedly, I went over to her. "That's my friend. He's been discharged but is insisting on walking to Sugihama. I'd better go after him."

"He certainly is a fit gentleman. But give him a mask." Mrs. Endo reached into her pocket and pulled out one of her plastic-wrapped gauze face masks. I grabbed the petite mask in my hand and my small leather messenger bag in the other and took off with some murmured thanks.

I scurried after Mr. Ishida, who was now carefully picking his way through tsunami wreckage some distance from the shelter. Breathlessly, I said, "Here's a mask for you. Yesteday I found that the walk between Yamagawa and Sugihama takes almost an hour. It's hard walking, with mud and obstacles and plenty of ups and downs. And I didn't see an auction house yesterday. Really, the jeep will take us—"

"I believe I'll recognize the area," Mr. Ishida said calmly, opening up the mask and slipping the elastic over his head.

"Well, let me ask him." I pointed toward a JMSDF sailor wearing a rugged camouflage suit.

I'd barely uttered my question about directions before the sailor, whose nametag read Uchida, immediately offered to take us in his jeep. This wasn't entirely surprising, because I found that when asking a Japanese person for directions, he or she usually felt duty-bound to bring me all the way. I gave the news to Mr. Ishida, who agreed to go once he was satisfied that the young seaman knew Sugihama's waterfront shopping district.

"So kind of you," Mr. Ishida said with a warm smile as Petty Officer Uchida reminded us both to fasten our seatbelts.

"One of our duties is inspecting and repairing streets in the shopping area there as well as in Yamagawa," Petty Officer Uchida told us as the jeep rolled along. "The place you are going was in a low area. It was hit hard, but there were some tall buildings that survived."

"I spent the tsunami on the third floor of the antiques store there," Mr. Ishida said.

The petty officer shook his head. "You were lucky to have survived. There were many deaths around there. Five boys thought they could climb up high on a school's playground equipment to survive the wave. The jungle gym was eight feet tall, but the wave was nine. Four of them died."

"Do you know about the dead from this area?" I asked. I gave him Mayumi's name, and Mr. Ishida described her appearance, including the clothes she'd worn and the blue hair.

"I'm not sure," Petty Officer Uchida answered. "I haven't seen anyone fitting that description, but we have long lists of names. If you give me the exact *kanji* characters for her name, I can give it to the help center, and they will send a text if there's any confirmation of death."

"That would be kind," I said. "Tell me—is there a registry of survivors?"

"Yes. If people enter a shelter, of course their names are recorded. But if they stay in their homes, or go off to stay in another place, that would not automatically be known to us. We only know to look for somebody if we have a request."

"I asked at the injured persons' shelter for a search to be made for her," Ishida-san said. "They put her name on a missing list. But I didn't hear anything again. It's been six days."

"Maybe Mr. Morioka will know something. It could be that she returned days after the tsunami to look for you," I said as we turned onto a road plastered in black mud and packed with wreckage: cars, broken buildings, beams, shop signs, and the contents of ruined stores. A couple of pigs crouched in the shadow of a ruined bakery devouring a muddy loaf of bread.

A long pole with a basketball hoop lay across most of the road. This must have been ripped from the ill-fated playground the soldier had mentioned. And then there were all kinds of other debris.

"I can't believe something made of porcelain is still in one piece," I said, pointing at a big, round blue-and-white brazier. It was the kind of thing that people used today as a table base, umbrella stand, or planter.

"Yes, glazed stoneware can be surprisingly strong. It probably floated all the way here from the auction house. How about that Buddha?" Ishida-san pointed toward a four-foot-tall, bronze Buddha statue sitting upright on a heap of rubble.

"It almost looks like someone's made an altar," I said.

"Yes indeed," the driver said. "People are doing this out of respect and hope. Several more Buddhas are watching over the streets of this town."

"Ah, there is the auction house," Mr. Ishida called out. "We are exactly where we need to be."

I followed his gaze to a stained stucco building with blown-out windows on the first floor. But the third-story windows were unbroken, and I caught a glimmer of warm light glowing from one of the windows. Only one stone lion-dog was left near the doorway; its mate must have been torn away by the wave.

After thanking the JMSDF men profusely, Mr. Ishida and I gingerly climbed out of the jeep and headed for the shop's front door, which had a "CLOSED" sign. However, the knob turned easily.

"*Ojama shimasu,*" Mr. Ishida politely called out the stock phrase that meant "sorry for bothering you." But I didn't see anyone in the dark, dank, muddy interior. Dozens of chairs the auction goers must have sat upon were turned over or on top of each other, with smashed pieces of china and wood thrown over them. And of course, there was the ever-present fishy odor, although some smokiness in the shop's air lessened it. Evaluating the color change on the wall from brown to beige, I thought that the wave had reached about eight feet and then subsided. Peering through the gloom, I saw a wooden staircase that was only discolored on the lower half.

"Perhaps Morioka-san is upstairs in his living quarters. Shall we go a bit farther?" I suggested.

"But of course," Mr. Ishida said.

I went up first, and when I reached the last filthy step, I carefully stepped out of my boots, holding onto a wiggly railing for support. I waited on the next step until Mr. Ishida had done the same with his sturdy Clarks lace-up shoes. Then the two of us continued in socks up to the second floor.

Our voices must have been overheard, because a middle-aged man with scant hair and a sweaty face appeared at the top of the second floor. Behind him, I saw an office that was being warmed by a wood fire burning inside a wide hibachi. A stone lantern glowed on a wide desk and a blue-and-white hibachi sat on the floor, a burning scrap of wood inside. Now I realized from where the smoky smell had emanated. But it was cozy and warm, and I felt myself instinctively leaning toward this second-floor sanctuary.

"Sorry, but I'm still closed for business." The man shifted uneasily, blocking the enticing view I'd just seen.

"Morioka-san, excuse the interruption. I am Ishida, who stayed with you." Mr. Ishida spoke quickly, which meant he was embarrassed. "I've come to say hello after being in the injured persons' shelter all this time."

Mr. Morioka's hand went to his mouth. "Of course, Ishida-san! I was so caught by surprise that I didn't realize—is this your relative?" He nodded, looking at me.

"I'm Shimura." I didn't bother using my first name; the two men were operating in a traditional universe where first names didn't matter, because they would never be spoken aloud. Probably Mr. Morioka hadn't recognized my mentor because he looked a lot less dapper than usual after living for a week on a basketball court. I knew that I didn't look attractive. My hair had lost its shape and was days from a chance at being washed and styled. "I'm a former coworker who's here to help him get home."

"Ah so desu ka," he said, the lines on his forehead smoothing out. "What a tough time we had that day and night. But when the rescuers took you, Ishida-san, I thought they would take you back to Tokyo more quickly than this."

"It was a much more complicated situation," Mr. Ishida said with a sigh. "We must find Kimura-san, the young lady who was with me during the auction. You remember her, of course."

Mr. Morioka paused, his gaze going from me to Mr. Ishida.

"Sorry, I don't actually remember her. It was quite a busy, urgent time."

I cut to the chase. "So you're telling us that no young woman with blue hair ever came back to find out what happened to Ishida-san?"

He looked at me quizzically. "I haven't seen any female looking like that! Tokyo, of course, but not here."

Mr. Ishida said, "The thing is, she did come from Tokyo, though she's really from a small town in Tohoku called Kinugasa—"

Mr. Morioka interrupted him with a gentle hand gesture. "This is all rather confusing. Won't you two come inside and tell me about this?"

CHAPTER 15

I offered to help Mr. Morioka make tea, but he was too courteous to permit it. I watched him move awkwardly between the hammered iron teapot he'd set on a grate over the hibachi and his tea canister. We'd obviously caught him by surprise. I got as close to the hibachi as I could and slipped off Richard's down jacket, enjoying the warmth.

Mr. Ishida and I both murmured *itadakimasu* and complimented Morioka-san on his green tea, although its dull flavor revealed it had been brewed at too high a temperature. A century ago, Japanese people cooked and brewed tea perfectly over wood-burning fires; but now fuzzy-logic rice cookers and electric kettles had taken away such skills.

Mr. Ishida began recounting the story of how Mayumi had arrived during the sale. After greeting Mr. Ishida, Mayumi had offered to go straight to the checkout table with his *inkan* and some cash to pay for the items he'd already purchased.

"She thought we would be leaving right away, but I said that

I wanted to stay a while longer," Mr. Ishida remembered. "She argued with me a little about it. I wonder if she'd had a premonition. Just think—if we had gone out and caught a taxi to the station, we would have been away from the coast when the tsunami came an hour later."

"Why did you want to stick around, if you weren't buying any more particular items?" I asked.

"Well, I'd arrived right as the sale was starting, so I hadn't a chance to make a full examination of the wares. All the catalogs had been taken, and I was curious what was coming up."

I nodded, because I would have felt the same way, having traveled so far to a new auction house in Tohoku.

"Morioka-san had set the reserve prices on most items very low," Mr. Ishida said, looking at our host with a smile. "I was curious about the impact of this on the bidders: whether they would rise to pay much higher prices—or not bid against each other and wind up with real bargains. Fascinating group psychology comes in play in auctions, doesn't it?"

Mr. Morioka seemed to flinch at Mr. Ishida's description of his setting the low reserve prices, but did not protest.

I asked, "Ishida-san, what did you successfully bid on?"

"A very fine *negoro-nuri* lacquer kettle that appears to have been crafted in the Edo period. I was almost certain it was made in Wakayama."

I caught my breath. "What an exciting antique!"

"Yes. The red lacquer overlaying the base black lacquer had aged in such a way that there was a delightful, red-black patina. Today, painters try to copy that finish, but there's nothing like the real thing. I could have easily sold that piece to several of my best customers."

"Yes, it was one of the best pieces in the sale," Mr. Morioka said. "Did you manage to take the kettle with you? I would feel badly if it was paid for and lost."

"Once Mayumi-chan paid and brought it to me, wrapped properly in tissue and its box, I placed it in my satchel. Mayumi went out with my satchel after the earthquake, along with everyone else."

"Ran off, eh?" Mr. Morioka snorted. "I suffered the same. The assistants I hired to help me that day all just left when the quake hit. The young these days are not so loyal. One of the furniture-moving fellows returned to see me yesterday, and I said he certainly didn't have a job with me anymore."

"Mayumi-chan was trying to find space in a car that was evacuating," Mr. Ishida explained. "No taxis were answering her calls, and we needed a ride because we had come here by train and then bus. Unfortunately, I could not accompany her outside because I was too shaken to move quickly."

"Yes, you had fallen and cut your head," Mr. Morioka said. "It was quite a struggle to get you upstairs, remember?"

Mr. Ishida bowed his head toward the auctioneer. "I thank you for your help. You did save my life."

"No, of course I would help. I remember the condition you were in. Very confused and anxious."

"Do you own a car, Morioka-san?" I asked.

"I have a Honda Stream van, which is excellent for transporting large pieces. It was swept away with some other cars that were in the lot behind my building. I've spoken to the insurance already, but they say it will take time to make a claim."

"Did you ever consider driving to higher ground?"

"If I hadn't had so many valuable items on the first floor, I would have gone. But I needed to move everything that I could upstairs. Of course, the heavy pieces of wood furniture that I couldn't move up the stairs are ruined. If just one man had stayed to help me carry, it would have been different."

Complaints again. I thought it irrational that he believed his workers should ignore a tsunami warning to help him protect items that were probably covered by insurance. And I wondered what Mayumi's choices had been as she stood outside, desperately looking for an exit from town. She might have caught a ride with someone too panicked to wait for her to bring Mr. Ishida—just as Miki's neighbors couldn't wait. Or perhaps there had only been one seat in a car, and she'd taken it.

To either safety or her death.

I decided to follow this line of thought. "Morioka-san, have you heard anything from the customers who left? Have they called to say they reached safety?"

"No. I would not expect them to call me. Phone service has been so limited that people are only calling relatives and close friends."

I nodded. "Okay, then. But would these customers have parked in the same lot where your Honda Stream was?"

"Yes, if they could have found room. There are only six places."

"Excuse me, but do you know who parked there that day?" Mr. Ishida chimed in.

"Well, I keep a parking sign-in list by the register. All the customers write down their car model and license number and mobile number. That way I know not to report them for illegal parking."

"I can't read Japanese fluently, but Mr. Ishida could review that list—if you still have it," I said.

"I doubt that I brought it up with me when I was moving things to safety. I was more concerned with cash and the valuables. I'll check, though."

Mr. Morioka got to his feet and made his way through the clutter to a desk in the back, where he began sorting through papers. He had a frown on his face while doing so.

"I can understand that the list could be helpful—but we don't want to impose," Mr. Ishida murmured to me.

"If we have any phone numbers, we can follow up ourselves to find out whether someone did take her or saw her run off. It's not so much trouble, in a case of life and death," I whispered back.

"That is—if the people who drove cars away are still alive themselves."

Mr. Morioka turned around in the chair he'd taken in front of his desk. "Excuse me, but I've gone through all the papers I brought up with me. The parking list isn't here."

"Morioka-san, would it be all right if I looked for it downstairs?" Without stopping, I added, "Even if I don't find the parking list, I might be able to locate some of the valuables you are worried about. Volunteers are coming around to help with cleaning all the businesses, but this would give you a little head start on the process."

He sucked in his breath. "I'm not letting unknown people in here to do any so-called cleaning. I could lose many things."

"Shimura-san has a master's degree in the Japanese decorative arts," Mr. Ishida said soothingly to Mr. Morioka. "Not only can she find things, she can advise on restoration. I will help her look, if you like. It's good for me to move after sitting in the shelter so long."

"Mud is slippery," Mr. Morioka warned. "You could fall again and be hurt."

"Please, Morioka-san." I tried to sound humble, but I was growing irritated. "If we don't find a parking list, we might find an auction attendance list. A person on that list might have seen whether Mayumi went in someone's car or took the evacuation stairs up into the hills."

"All right, all right. I will go down with you to help guide you to the right places," Mr. Morioka said, looking resigned. "Wait just a moment while I get my work boots."

Five minutes later, we had donned coats and footwear and were back on the ground floor, searching. Late afternoon sun streamed in, illuminating the gloomy, filthy room. I started my search in the desk area, using the edge of an antique abacus to scrape mud off stacks of swollen, waterlogged papers. As I'd expected, the papers were all in Japanese, but I wasn't too worried, because a parking sign-in sheet would feature license-plate numbers. But I couldn't find any paper list containing license plates, although I did come across a giant wad of damp, brown 10,000-yen notes.

"Here's some money!" I called out to Mr. Morioka.

"Thank you," he said, taking the muddy wad of bills in his hands. "Thank you very much."

"I've found what look like Edo-period *ema*—horse pictures that people hang at temples," Mr. Ishida said from across the room. "These can be cleaned gently. No detergent cleaners because the paint is vegetable and could deteriorate."

"Yes, yes. Thank you for finding them." Mr. Morioka's mood seemed to be improving.

I didn't feel as pleased. From what I could see, all the dirty papers on top of the desk were too ruined to be of any use. Papers that had been inside of desk drawers were in better shape but had no license numbers or anything to do with parking.

Mr. Ishida was stooped over, gently pulling things from the sludge, looking very much like a rice farmer tending young shoots.

"This is curious," Mr. Ishida said, lifting something soft from the mud. "It feels—"

I looked at him shaking mud off the item and then examining it.

"I've found my satchel!" he exclaimed, unzipping the top. "I don't want to touch it any further with dirty hands, but I see my wallet and mobile phone are inside. Even the package with the lacquer kettle is inside. Oh, this is good news."

"Yes, very wonderful. I will get some hand sanitizer and towels," Mr. Morioka said. "Just a minute. They are upstairs."

"I'm so pleased for you," I said to Ishida-san, as Mr. Morioka hurried off.

"But why was it inside? I thought that she had it. Maybe I didn't remember right and had it with me." Mr. Ishida sounded confused, and I recalled Dr. Nishi's snap diagnosis of dementia.

Mr. Morioka clattered back down the stairs with a squeeze tube of Kirei Kirei hand sanitizer. In Japan, the words for "clean" and "beautiful" were the same. Handing Mr. Ishida the sanitizer, he said, "It's so strange. If your satchel was downstairs all this time..."

Mr. Morioka didn't need to finish his statement. His spooked expression mirrored my own feeling. Suddenly, it seemed possible that if the satchel had been left on the flooded first floor, Mayumi's body might be, too.

In short order, the small cleanup we'd begun expanded to include a couple of JMSDF sailors I hailed from the street. They brought portable halogen lights that lit up the darker corners of the shop. Still, several inches of mud coated the ground so one had to tread very carefully not to smash porcelain and all the other delicate antiquities that had floated in the wave.

"This building was already marked as containing no deceased victims," said a soldier who was slowly pulling a rake through the mud. "If a body was here, it would smell strongly. But one can smell fish, mildew, and earth. Not much more."

I sincerely hoped that he was right and we wouldn't find Mayumi.

Bringing mud-logged chairs outside to allow the military searchers more space, I tried to imagine the scenario. Mayumi would have rushed with Mr. Ishida's satchel in tow. Then she would have returned to the shop, put down Mr. Ishida's satchel somewhere, perhaps because she was distracted and looking for him, because she wanted him to ride somewhere with her. Had he gone upstairs at this point? Perhaps she couldn't find him. In any case, she'd gone out again without the bag or her boss.

"I think all possibilities are exhausted," the skeptical soldier told us at the end of an hour's hard work.

"I am grateful for your help, and also not to have immediate bad news," Mr. Ishida said. "I cannot thank you enough for your kindness."

"I thank you as well." Mr. Morioka was the only one who seemed cheerful. "You went to a lot of trouble searching for the missing person. Also, moving the big pieces that fell over saved me quite a bit of work. I thought I would prefer to do everything alone. Now I realize how valuable others' help is."

I looked at him and sighed inwardly. What a marked change from the selfish way Morioka-san had spoken earlier. Perhaps he'd finally felt the light, unexpected touch of *kizuna*.

It was about five o'clock when we said goodbye to Mr. Morioka and began our walk toward the Sugihama volunteer headquarters two miles from the shopping district. Mr. Ishida wanted to talk more about Mayumi.

"She's really quite a gifted artist. When we find her, I'm looking forward to your seeing some of her work."

"I'd like to see it. I heard from Okada-san her family makes lacquer?"

"Yes, and it's still her art form, which is exciting. Her family makes traditional objects like boxes, tea bowls, and plates, but she has taken to decorating wooden buttons with beautiful lacquer designs. She would like to sell them directly to clothing designers and shoemakers. But her parents didn't like that idea so much."

"Why not?"

He paused. "Before I explain that—I'll tell you how I met her," he said.

"Yes. I was wondering how you came to hire her." I tried to keep the suspicion out of my voice.

"I was at the Roppongi shrine sale one Sunday morning last spring. I always arrive very early, and this time I noticed a young lady with some very fine Aizu lacquerware spread on a quilt before her. Of course, this young lady was Mayumi."

"Oh, so she was selling for another dealer?"

"Not quite. First, I asked the prices. I was startled that she knew the pieces' age and provenance quite well—yet was asking far too little money."

"Do you mean it was too much of a bargain?"

"Exactly. To sell at those prices would have been a big mistake. I convinced her to put everything back in the little cloth bags they came in and bring them to my shop for a formal appraisal."

"You were extremely kind to suggest that to her."

"When we were talking inside the shop, the truth emerged," Mr. Ishida said. "She confessed the lacquer came from her family who lived in Tohoku. She'd had an argument with her parents and taken their heirlooms away when she moved to Tokyo."

"What was the argument about?"

"They wanted her to stay at home and continue learning the lacquer craft as an apprentice, making the style of lacquerware that was profitable for them. Instead, she wanted to study at Geidai, the arts university, where she could take a modern-art approach to lacquer.

"Mayumi had secretly applied to the school and been admitted, but her parents refused to let her attend. She rationalized taking the lacquer by believing she would eventually inherit it, and she needed the goods now. If she sold everything, she thought she'd have enough for one school year. That was quite naïve. There were twenty pieces, so actually, she could have paid for much more than an arts education."

I was unable to let go. "But the parents hadn't given her any of it, right? The police could pursue her for theft."

"She thinks her parents didn't take police action because they didn't want her to be convicted of a crime. However, her parents sent a message to her mobile phone saying that her name had been stricken from the family register. And that made her feel depressed."

So maybe Mayumi's conscience had returned—albeit, a little too late. I said, "I don't believe in disowning family members, but I very much understand the parents' anger. She'd taken their history: something they'd passed on for many generations that was even more emotionally important because they are still working in lacquer. And she would do a thing like sell it off?"

"But the collection's still safe," Mr. Ishida reminded me. "I said that if she needed money for school, I'd give her a part-time job, although it could take a few years to reach her goal of school tuition. I also convinced her to let me keep her family lacquer in the shop's safe for the time being, while she thought a bit more about the situation."

"Um, I checked the safe when I was in your store, but all I saw inside was some papers."

"There should have been many cloth pouches holding lacquer, all stored within a cedar box."

"An empty cedar box," I said. "That I saw."

"Oh, that is terrible news. " He gazed off into the distance for a moment. "Someone must have broken in! Okada-san always told me to put in an alarm, but I thought Hachiko was enough."

"When's the last time you checked the safe?" I asked.

"About a month ago, when I put something else in temporarily. A month or six weeks ago?"

"So we don't know when the lacquer was taken—and whether Hachiko was there or not. She's a friendly dog to most people. And unfortunately, your combination is easy to guess."

"I don't think so. It's a combination of numbers only of personal significance to me."

"The combination is the date your father founded the business. That information is embossed on a plaque mounted on the building's exterior."

Mr. Ishida was silent for a moment, then shook his head. "I

didn't think about that. But it's true, with the information outside, anyone might know. Maybe someone guessed who frequents the area and figured out that I was away. Someone like the boy with rooster hair!"

"Let me tell you what I noticed," I said, not wanting him to vanish on a tangent. "If a burglar came, he—*or she*—passed up many obviously valuable things such as the jade you keep in that glass case. So it wasn't a smart burglar, right? Or else the burglar was someone who was only after that lacquer."

"Are you suggesting Mayumi? She would never do something like that without telling me—"

"We don't know that. She was with you for less than a year."

"The only reason I could think of her taking out the lacquer was because she wanted to return it to her parents. Yes, doesn't that make sense? If she was joining me in Tohoku, she might have taken it out because she wanted to return it to them."

"Did you ever contact Mayumi's parents to let them know you had the lacquer?" I felt like I was losing my breath under the mask. I was growing tired from the trash-strewn, uphill climb and the reshuffling of ideas.

"No. I did call them from the injured persons' shelter on March thirteenth, hoping that Mayumi had somehow made it to their home. But they said not, and I believe they're looking all over for her, too."

"And during this conversation, the fact that you'd been holding the lacquer safely for them, was never mentioned?" I was suddenly very worried for Mr. Ishida, because he could be accused of being an accomplice to theft.

"I saw no reason to say anything about the lacquer. Their daughter had disappeared, which was enough of a shock. I told them that I really did try to convince Mayumi-chan that she didn't need to bring my *inkan*," Mr. Ishida continued in a miserable tone. "Mayumi told me it was such a short day trip, that it was no problem. She said she'd phone my friend Okada-san, who owns the *senbei* shop, if she had any delay returning. Therefore I had no worries about Hachiko's care."

"Okay. I still think we should talk to her parents, just in case they've located her and neglected to call you. Did you happen to know the name of their lacquer business?"

"No, but her father's name is Shosuke Kimura. He's quite well known, and their town is called Kinugasa. There are a number of Kinugasa towns in Japan, and this one is a magnet for lacquer artists."

I reached into my messenger bag, fingers searching for the familiar cool steel of the cell phone. I touched my wallet, lots of receipts, a granola bar, and a MAC lipstick. Feeling frantic, I dug into my coat pockets, and then all the pockets of my jeans. It was pointless. My cell phone was nowhere to be found.

CHAPTER 16

"I can't find it." I told myself that there was no reason for panic. This wasn't the first time I'd lost a cell phone; it wasn't like losing a person. It was a hassle, but I'd live through it.

"Your phone is missing? Perhaps you left it at Morioka-san's auction house." Mr. Ishida grimaced in sympathy.

"It might have slipped and fallen when I grabbed up my bag and ran after you leaving the shelter," I said, mentally retracing my actions. "Or during the jeep ride. I wouldn't have heard it fall if it landed in mud. Oh, and even if I do recover it, the moisture will probably have destroyed it."

"What a shame," Mr. Ishida said. "We should tell Mr. Morioka, in case he finds it."

"Really, the worst thing is that I won't know when Michael arrives. His employer is sending him to Tokyo to work with different people on the meltdown problem."

"That sounds like valuable work. And don't worry—I can help

with those phone communications. My phone is surely still in my bag."

As Mr. Ishida bent his head to examine his phone, I heard the groaning sound of a large vehicle approaching. Pulling up alongside was a long white truck painted with a *tanuki*, a Japanese wild animal similar to a raccoon, on the side. The *tanuki* was believed to be a crafty creature, and this version wore a pair of overalls and held a saw. The *hiragana* type on the side of the truck said *Tanuki Carpentry*.

"Shimura-san! Are you going to the volunteer headquarters? I can take you," a strong young male voice called out.

Leaning out the driver's window was Akira Rikyo, the friendly young man I'd met on the bus ride.

"Thanks a lot. As long as there's room for two." As I spoke, I felt a sudden squeeze of my right arm. I glanced at Mr. Ishida, concerned that he might be losing balance. He was fine but was regarding Akira with a shocked expression.

"Ishida-san, this is my friend Rikyo Akira, who came back from Tokyo to help his parents. Rikyo-san, how are you and your parents managing?"

"Thanks for asking—as well as can be expected." His voice was as rough as the long beams of wood in the truck's open back. It seemed his Tohoku accent had strengthened in the time since we'd spoken on the bus. "We had the cremation ceremony and funeral for my sister and nieces yesterday. Now it's back to work."

Mr. Ishida bowed his head slightly and said, "I'm very sorry for your loss. It's kind of you to stop, but we won't trouble you for a ride. The volunteer headquarters is close."

"Oh, is that so?" Akira paused, sounding uncertain. "Well, see you later."

I'd expected Akira to protest. Instead, he put the truck in gear and accelerated away from us a bit too quickly, so that mud spun out from the backs of the tires as he left.

Shaking my head, I said, "I wish you hadn't turned him down. It's still got to be a half mile or so to the shelter."

"It's a bad idea for us to ride with him," Mr. Ishida said in a tight voice. "Anything might happen."

As if on cue, an aftershock roiled the ground beneath us. I grabbed Mr. Ishida's torso to keep him from falling. We held each other, the ground buckling, and I prayed no fault line would swallow us up. I wanted to scream, but I held back, gasping instead.

The terrifying tremor was about a minute. When it finally subsided, I waited for my heartbeat to slow. "What did you mean when you said anything might happen? Did you have a premonition a tremor was coming and not want to be in the truck?"

"I didn't want to get in the truck because I don't trust that fellow."

"But I've talked to him for *hours*," I protested. "And I worry we hurt his feelings, maybe acting like we were too good to ride in the truck. By offering us that ride, he was only trying to show *kizuna*—"

"I recognize him from Tokyo," Mr. Ishida said tersely. "I mentioned to you a suspicious young man with hair like a rooster? He's the one."

"Akira's hair does stand up a bit, but he doesn't do anything with folk craft or antiques. There must be someone else for whom you're mistaking him."

"I recognized the name, too. Rikyo Akira is Mayumi's old boyfriend from high school."

"But that's amazing. If there's such a connection—and he's local—maybe he can help us look for Mayumi. After we call her parents to double-check whether she's been found, of course."

"Didn't you hear what I said?" Mr. Ishida's voice was uncharacteristically sharp. "Mayumi disliked him! She was always trying to avoid him."

I paused, letting this sink in. Suddenly, I remembered Hachiko growling at Akira on the bus. Maybe she'd been trying to tell me something, and I'd been too jet-lagged to notice.

Carefully, I asked, "Are you saying Akira is a stalker?"

Mr. Ishida put his head to one side, as if considering the idea. "I can't make that judgment. But Mayumi asked Rikyo to please leave the shop each time he stopped in. And it wasn't that she was merely irritated by the attention. It seemed like something more."

"Something like?" I asked, because he'd fallen into silence.

"Something like fear."

CHAPTER 17

After what Mr. Ishida said about Akira, I began questioning myself a bit more.

Akira had jumped on the volunteer bus at the last minute with no luggage. Had he been underprepared because he'd noticed me going into Ishida Antiques and decided he'd better follow me? Did he know something about the opened safe? Or, if he really was stalking Mayumi, did he trigger her abrupt decision a week earlier to travel to Tohoku?

I'd liked Akira. It was unsettling to think I had gotten someone so wrong. But I couldn't beat myself up about it, because there were more pressing issues at hand. Mr. Ishida and I had just arrived muddy, cold, and tired at the Sugihama survivors' shelter. And he wanted to see Hachiko.

Remembering that Miki had pledged to watch over the dog, I led Mr. Ishida into the gymnasium full of families. His aged eyes widened with distress at the sight of the cardboard-bordered dwellings. I pointed out the Hanedas' space, and led him toward the family.

At the sound of Mr. Ishida's voice, Hachiko jumped up and banged her front paws on the cardboard boundary, causing it to collapse. The family next door looked startled, and as Mr. Ishida grabbed hold of Hachiko's collar, I apologized to them.

"Who's this?" Miki, who'd fallen asleep next to the dog, came awake, looking worriedly at Mr. Ishida.

"Miki-chan, here is Hachiko's owner, Ishida-san," I began.

"Oh, Hachiko, your father's here." Miki's expression relaxed into a smile. "Your daddy's come back. Just like ours will."

"Oh, Miki," Sadako Haneda said, sounding anxious. She was rocking the fretful baby while her other daughter, Chieko, played with an electronic game.

"Thank you for being so nice to Hachiko. I'd like to take her outside for a short walk. You will be able to play with her after supper again, if you like," Mr. Ishida said.

Miki assented with a quick nod. "Go on with them, Hachiko. It's time to be with your daddy. He missed you very much."

"I'm surprised how that turned out," Mr. Ishida said as he took Hachiko's rope leash and walked with me from the high school shelter toward the volunteers' building. "Although the mother had tears in her eyes. I gather that the husband is still lost?"

"Yes, since right before the wave. It's really awful," I said. "Don't you think the way Miki was urging Hachiko to return with you seemed like she was acting out her own dream of a reunion?"

"Maybe it is. They are in the same situation as I am, not knowing if there's reason to keep worrying, or to start mourning." He sighed. "I heard some talk about supper and actually am a bit hungry. When will it be?"

"Usually around six thirty. I can almost guarantee you it's going to be a soup or stew with a miso base." With a sinking feeling, I remembered that breakfast wasn't covered for the volunteers. I only had one granola bar left in my stash.... What would he eat?

"I have no complaints about miso at any time of day," Mr. Ishida said. "In the meantime, I'll take care of feeding and walking Hachiko."

"I forgot to mention the dog food and water bowl are still with the Hanedas."

"Good. That will give Miki a chance to help, if she likes."

I decided to use his absence as a time to inquire about sleeping arrangements for Mr. Ishida. I wasn't sure if there was even room in the displaced residents' shelter, or if he'd qualify, coming from out of town.

Mr. Yano and Miss Tanaka were doing paperwork a quiet corner of the dormitory space and greeted me as I approached them.

"I'm glad to see you again, Shimura-san. Unfortunately I'm leaving tonight," Miss Tanaka said softly. "My workplace insists. At least I can tell your cousin how well you've been doing here."

"That would be great. Excuse me, but I have a bit of a favor to ask you, Yano-san." I described Mr. Ishida's release and desire to stay a bit longer in Sugihama while he searched for Mayumi.

"Of course there's room for him to be sheltered," Mr. Yano said. "The mayor keeps the list of everyone going into the big residents' shelter, but there is also space with the volunteers."

"For us to stay near each other would be ideal. But are you sure the volunteers wouldn't be inconvenienced?"

"Three-quarters of the volunteers are packing up to return to Tokyo this evening on the same bus as Tanaka-san," Mr. Yano answered. "It won't be until the day after tomorrow that more volunteers will arrive. There is certainly room for him."

"That's very kind of you—"

"Not kind. Just practical." Mr. Yano told me where to find an extra bedroll, sleeping bag, and woolen socks donated by the military. Miss Tanaka mentioned that toiletries would be available from the Red Cross for him, as well as breakfast snack bars and water. All I needed to do was fill out a form with some details about Mr. Ishida for organizational records.

I was rushing through the paperwork—Mr. Yano assured me writing in *hiragana* and English would be fine—when Mr. Ishida arrived with Hachiko at his side.

"Nurse Tanaka, it is very nice to see you again."

"You, too, Ishida-san. Are you feeling well?"

"Quite well. With the help of Shimura-san, I feel much stronger and enjoyed a long walk today." Turning to bow to Mr. Yano, Mr. Ishida introduced himself and thanked him for allowing me time away from volunteer duties to help with his release from the injured persons' shelter. After that, he asked if he'd heard anything about the whereabouts of Mayumi Kimura.

"Shimura-san gave the information to Mayor Hamasaki and me, and it turns out because her parents knew she was missing, her name was already on many search lists," Mr. Yano said. "But so far, there is no news of her being taken in for shelter, or confirmed dead or injured. I'm quite sorry."

"I suppose that because I'm out of the shelter, I should go look wherever the bodies are kept. In case she's there, but was not identified. Because she is not a citizen of this town, nobody would know her."

He'd forgotten about Akira Rikyo.

"The bodies have been brought to various school gymnasiums to await identification," Nurse Tanaka said. "The police can take you to these places, but unfortunately, a number of the unidentified have already been cremated. Therefore, you will not necessarily have the right answer."

"Perhaps Hachiko could help search around the town for Mayumi," Yano-san said. "Wouldn't you rather do that, now that you've got the dog again? It will be a nice time together, since Hachiko cannot sleep upstairs—"

"But the volunteer with animal allergy is going back on tonight's bus with me," Nurse Tanaka said. "Perhaps Hachiko could indeed sleep upstairs. It's so cold—she will keep Ishida-san warm. And the new staircase is working well."

Mr. Yano paused, and then said, "All right, then. As long as Ishida-san thinks that it's a good idea."

"Both of us would like it very much." Mr. Ishida bowed again and again. "I am not deserving of such kindness, but I am so grateful for it."

The next morning, Mr. Ishida told me he'd slept well. He joined me for the morning exercise drill, following all movements until the jogging and jumping sequence. With a shrug, he shifted into a *tai chi* routine. How gracefully he moved, one movement flowing into another. With his hands, he pushed, and I had the sudden image of a beautiful wave that rose and subsided within the stretch of his narrow arms.

"I see a good idea for exercise modification," Mr. Yano called out from his position in front of the assembled group. "Maybe Ishida-san can lead *tai chi* routines for the evening program."

"Yes, please," people called out. I didn't know how anyone could still have energy for the evening program, which I'd missed each night because I needed to sleep.

After exercises were finished, I said goodbye to Mr. Ishida, who decided to go with military transport to the places where the dead were awaiting identification. Trying to take my mind off the grisly scenes he might encounter, I went into the kitchen and helped Nobuko-san chop onions. These tears hurt—but I'd trade them any day for emotional ones.

By ten o'clock, the stew of dried black mushrooms and wakame sea greens was simmering in a thick stock of miso and water. I looked up at a sound and saw Miki come in.

"Rei-san, I'm sad. Very sad."

"Oh, no." I felt my spirits crash. Probably her father's body had been found.

"Hachiko is not in her box outside the kitchen," Miki said, tears running down her face. "She's not upstairs where the volunteers sleep. Now she's lost, just like Butter—"

I crouched down so we were eye-to-eye. "Sorry. I forgot to tell you that she stayed in the dormitory last night with Ishida-san, and then the two of them went out today. I promise you they'll be back."

"Where did they go?"

"Oh, just driving. Looking around." I didn't want her to know about the morgues.

"But why is her bed with my daddy's coat gone from outside?" Miki's voice didn't sound reassured. "That's her afternoon nap place."

"If she's with Ishida-san, he'll make sure she naps—just like you make sure of your younger sisters. And I must give back your father's coat to your mother—I brought it upstairs to the volunteers' sleeping area yesterday because Hachiko really likes it."

"Okay." Miki wiped her tears away with two chubby fists. "I know she likes to snuggle in it, but I should brush off the dog hair today so it's clean for when Otoochan comes."

Biting my lip, I turned back to stir the pot. I couldn't bear facing her when my thoughts about the likelihood of her father's arrival were so different. It might only be a few more days until Miki would hear bad news about her father not coming back. Until then, she should have some good times. I promised her that later in the afternoon, I'd ask her to take Hachiko and me on a walk to wherever she wanted.

The count for people wanting lunch was 20 percent lower than the day we'd arrived. Yano-san explained that many of the residents had dispersed to their relatives' or friends' homes in undamaged cities and towns. Also, people whose homes were remotely habitable preferred to stay in them and continue cleaning up. Many of the worst obstacles in the streets had been removed, and traffic was beginning to flow.

After lunch, I decided to hang the used dishcloths outdoors. It was cold, but any wind would help dry them. As I draped the cloths over a bicycle rack, the sound of tires crunching over rubble made me turn. The Tanuki Carpentry truck stopped at the front of the building. Akira emerged from the side of the truck closest to me, while a tall man in his fifties with similar features stepped out of the driver's side.

I pinned up the last cloth quickly and went back into the

kitchen, my heart thudding. So Akira and his father had come. They'd caught me off guard, and I needed to think before speaking to them. But what would I say? The opportunity to find out came quickly when Akira appeared in the kitchen doorway a few minutes later.

"Sorry to disturb you." His voice had a rasp to it, as if he'd caught a cold. "My father came to get some instructions from the mayor. How are things with you and the volunteers?"

"I'm fine." I tried to smile at him normally, but it was tough. "As you saw yesterday, I've found my old friend, who survived the tsunami without serious injury."

"When we met on the bus, I didn't understand that your friend was actually someone I knew. There are so many people named Ishida, *neh?*"

"*Actually,*" I said, repeating his word with emphasis, "you did know whom I was talking about. Especially after you recognized Hachiko."

"It took me a little bit of time." Now he sounded apologetic. "Since the dog was without the person who usually walked her, I didn't make the connection."

"That person is Mayumi Kimura, right?"

"Yes." His voice cracked as it rose higher. "Have you heard where Mayumi-san has gone?"

"Before we get into that, I have a question." I was striving to keep a neutral tone, despite the agitation I felt. "Why did you take the volunteer bus to Sugihama on the same night as me?"

"It was the only way to reach this area. I heard about Helping Hands on the television news. When I e-mailed Yano-san, I wrote that I come from Sugihama and wanted to return to my family for the funeral and so on. Yano-san was kind enough to give me the last seat. Now, please tell me where Mayumi is."

"When we were chatting on the bus, I remember you saying you didn't know what had happened to your girlfriend. You weren't even sure that she was alive. Why wouldn't you know what had happened to her, a full eight days after the earthquake?"

A pink flush spread across his cheeks. "The last time we saw each other was March tenth, when she was walking Hachiko near the shop around five o'clock—the dog's dinnertime," he added. "If Mr. Ishida was working with a customer then, she'd take Hachiko out for a little walk."

"Okay," I said. "So what happened next?"

"I went home. The next day, I was at work when the earthquake hit. Some of the guys working on the building fell, so after the ones who needed to get the hospital got in ambulances, the boss closed down the site for the day and we all went home. The construction project stayed closed down for the next couple of days, so I had time to check if Mayumi was okay. I didn't see her going in or out of her apartment, and when I went to the door to ask, her roommates wouldn't answer it. So I went to Yanaka a couple of times during the hours that Ishida Antiques is usually open. But it was locked up. Did Ishida-san close the shop because of the power shortages or interior damage or something like that?"

"No, he didn't. Let's sit down for a minute, Rikyo-san." I indicated the scrubbed steel table in the center of the room.

He looked relieved by the offer. "Great. I really appreciate it. And wouldn't you rather call me Akira? People our age are more casual."

"Okay, Akira-kun—call me Rei, if you like. Getting back to

Mayumi: you were on the right track when you thought she wasn't in Tokyo."

"Really?" He began to smile. "Did she go home to her parents' house?"

"Mr. Ishida made a call to them, and they said they didn't know where she was. I'm sure they're extremely worried, too. All Mr. Ishida and I know is that Mayumi left Tokyo early in the morning of March eleventh. She took a bullet train to Sendai, transferred to a bus, and arrived at the Takara Auction House around one thirty."

"You mean—the auction house here in Sugihama?" His eyes bugged out at me, as if all the implications hit him. "Was she here when..."

"Yes. When the tsunami came. Since Ishida-san was released from the injured persons' shelter, we've started a search."

"Oh, no. I can't believe it." For a moment, he sat with his head bowed. Then he looked up. "I must speak to Ishida-san. I've got a truck, so I can drive all over looking for her."

"Right now, Mr. Ishida's seeing if she's among the dead who've been laid out in various school gyms around Tohoku."

He stood up, tears filling his eyes. "I must join him."

I felt guilty for all of my suspicions, because his emotion seemed very real. "I'm sorry, Akira. I think Ishida-san might prefer to do that job by himself. And he's quite capable. He saw Mayumi that day. He knows what she was wearing."

Akira's mouth settled into a tight line, revealing a similarity between his face and that of the older man who'd come out of the truck. "Yesterday he would not accept the ride I offered."

"That's because you've done some things that made him anxious about Mayumi's safety."

"Like what?" Akira's voice was defensive.

"You were often hanging around the shop area, watching for her. The times you went in, she asked you to leave."

"She didn't know what she was doing," Akira said roughly. "I love her—and I kept going back because she needed to know that, and also about her family's change of heart."

"What about her family?" I was suddenly on high alert.

"A few months ago Mayumi's mother telephoned my parents to ask them to tell me something. It was that if Mayumi returned the lacquer, they would forgive her and she could return home. This was really good news, because I know Mayumi felt rotten about what she did. But I couldn't reach Mayumi by phone or text—she blocked my calls. So I came to the store each week or so, just to see if I could break through, but she wouldn't even let me near."

"So what happened next? Did *you* return the lacquer to the Kimuras?" I asked, thinking about the empty safe.

"But how? I couldn't visit her apartment—the roommates would never let me in. And I don't know if she kept the lacquer there, anyway. I know she was thinking about selling it."

He sounded as if he didn't know the lacquer had been in the safe; although that could be a ploy. "All right, let's return to Mayumi's situation on the day of the tsunami. Since Sugihama is your hometown, do you think she might have phoned your family or anyone else she met through you for help evacuating?"

"No. Mayumi and my mother don't get along. She must have been alone when she vanished." Akira's voice broke, and when he continued, he was sobbing. "If only I'd been here. I wasn't able to help my sister and nieces. Not Mayumi, when she needed me most."

Akira stumbled to his feet, and his chair tipped and fell,

startling Miki. She shrank against the wall as he rushed past her into the hallway.

"Who's that?" Miki asked. "Why is he crying?"

"He can't find someone he loves." I felt my throat close up, a precursor to a sob.

"Too bad," Miki said. "I wanted to tell you that Ishida-san's back. It's time to walk Hachiko."

The carpentry truck was gone by the time Miki, her sister Chieko, and I had caught up with Mr. Ishida and Hachiko. I longed to discuss the details of Akira's conversation with Mr. Ishida, but felt tongue-tied because of the two little girls running alongside us, pointing out what they recognized of their devastated town. Chieko kept trying to pick up stray toys that were scattered across the landscape, while Miki held fast to Hachiko's leash, preventing her from eating anything.

"I hope the smell doesn't bother them too much," Ishida-san said, observing that only Chieko had kept the gauze face mask in place.

"It must have smelled pretty bad where you went."

"They're using many chemicals there—it was all right. And I was relieved not to find Mayumi."

"Were you able to find out about any unknown people who might have been cremated?"

"Yes, I did talk to some people who'd released bodies of victims to be burned. Nobody remembered a victim with blue hair."

"I should tell you that Akira stopped by the shelter."

"For what reason?" Mr. Ishida stopped walking.

"He thought we might know where Mayumi was. Apparently, he had no idea she'd come to Sugihama." I explained how I'd asked a number of pointed questions to find out what he might know about her disappearance or the missing lacquer. "He sounded very clueless about everything—for instance, he was genuinely shocked that she'd been in Sugihama during the quake."

"He *appeared* shocked."

"Maybe. It's hard to know what's true. He told me he'd been following her only because he loved her so much, and he wanted her to return the lacquer to her parents."

"It was more than that." Mr. Ishida shook his head. "I know it."

About thirty feet ahead of us, Miki was turning off from the main road toward the ravaged waterfront. The little sister followed dutifully. I thought ahead quickly. The sea wall was gone—this was a dangerous place.

"Just a minute, please. You are moving too quickly. Wait for us!" I yelled.

"It's pretty by the water," Miki called back. "Butter used to like playing here."

But the waterfront wasn't pretty anymore. It was a junkyard of buildings and cars and toppled trees. Hachiko buried her nose near some overturned vending machines, halting the girls' progress and giving Mr. Ishida and me time to catch up to them.

"Hachiko, that's enough," Miki said, trying to tug the dog's head upward. I saw that the group of vending machines had fallen into each other, creating a collapsed metal-and-plastic sort of teepee. Hachiko had her nose in the gap between two of the machines and was whining. Judging from an unpleasant, sweet odor, I imagined that crushed cans of soup and sweet beverages were underneath.

"No, Hachiko. People's food and drink is not good for dogs," Miki scolded.

"Let me help," Mr. Ishida said and clapped his hands hard. "No!"

Hachiko looked at her owner and sniffed, as if she dismissing him. Then her tapered beagle snout returned to the crack between the machines.

"She rarely disobeys me." Mr. Ishida crouched beside her and peered into the dark. "Shimura-san, please look."

It was a command he'd given me numerous times when we scouted antiques. I squatted next to him and squinted in the darkness. I first thought he was pointing out a couple of small, thin sausages. But then I saw fingernails.

"Yes," Mr. Ishida said in a very low voice.

Ever since entering Sugihama, I knew I'd see some corpses. Now these fingers appeared to be the start of something awful that I didn't want to see. I couldn't believe Mr. Ishida was putting me through this.

Then I thought suddenly of the girls. They shouldn't have any idea what was going on. Obviously, the military or police needed to address the body under the vending machines—but I'd have to get the children away.

"Miki-chan, let's walk Hachiko a little closer to the water," I suggested. But Hachiko would not go. She pushed her nose in the opening, lowered her ears, and groaned. And then to my horror, she reached out her tongue and licked.

"Hachiko!" Cringing at the dog's crude brazenness, I grabbed hard at her leash and finally got her away.

"Don't eat from the street, Hachiko," Miki chided.

And now there was a new sound. A whimpering. And it wasn't Hachiko talking, because it came from the area where the fingers were.

"Did you hear that? Someone's underneath," Miki shouted.

Mr. Ishida reached into his satchel and took out a small flashlight he always carried for examination purposes. Now he shone it into the gap, unaware that Miki and Chieko were peering, too.

"Shimura-san—get some help," Mr. Ishida shouted. "The person trapped under these machines might still be alive."

I asked Miki and Chieko to walk with me to find some soldiers or police to help, but Miki insisted on remaining with Mr. Ishida, her eyes glued on the gap. And Chieko wouldn't go with me, either.

So I left them in Mr. Ishida's custody and sprinted off as best I could in the uneven, sticky terrain. My heart was pounding from the exercise and excitement. With thousands still missing on the coast, it probably wasn't Mayumi who was lying trapped underneath. But it was someone.

I found soldiers working on the main road, and they ran back with me to the vending machine wreckage. Within minutes, they'd radioed for an ambulance. I'd expected the six men to quickly begin the heavy lifting, but instead, they walked around the perimeter, viewing the toppled vending machines from all angles.

"As each machine is lifted, the other two might shift position and crush the injured person," the commanding officer told me. "We do not want to cause more injury or worse. It's also best to send the children away."

"I can't get them to leave." I kept a hand on each of the sisters, wishing they would not stare so hard at the operation. As two men counted down to three and heaved up one machine, the others held the remaining machines beneath steady. Mr. Ishida crouched down to help keep a soft-drink machine lifted six inches from the ground, while the one on top was brought up.

After the first two machines were pulled off, a pair of legs in muddy tan trousers were visible, although the body's trunk and head remained hidden. A soldier crouched down and tugged down a sock, touching bluish-white skin near the back of one ankle.

"There's a pulse!" he said.

Miki whispered, "Those are Otoochan's shoes."

I agreed with her that the brown loafers we could see were men's shoes—but it was highly doubtful they were her own father's shoes, as many men in Japan wore brown loafers. I didn't say it, though, just looked at Mr. Ishida.

"Miki-chan," he said softly, "please step back a bit."

"No," Miki said, her little voice rising to helium heights. "It's Otoochan. I know it!"

As the third vending machine was lifted, the fourth one underneath shifted, and I forgot about the girls and rushed forward to grab it along with two other soldiers. The pain in my shoulders and arms was almost unbearable, but in a half minute, this machine was hauled up and away.

The man lying on his side in the mud hardly looked human. His face was bruised and covered with cuts. A trickle of fluid ran close to his mouth, and a mountain of empty cans lay nearby. It was clear how he'd survived. For twelve days, this man had managed to feed himself canned coffee and soup and soft drinks.

"Otoochan!" Miki squealed. "Otoochan, can you see me?"

Tears pricked the edges of my eyes. Nobody could tell who this man was.

"Miki." He groaned her name, and briefly his eyes flickered open. They shone with tears. Then they closed again.

Could it be? Dimly, I heard the soldiers exclaiming to each other about the situation. Another man found alive! After almost two weeks.

Mr. Ishida put a hand on my shoulder and whispered, "He knows Miki's name."

"I told you it was Otoochan," Miki shouted, and then called out to her sister. As both little girls hovered over him, his eyes opened again.

"Chieko. Did..." The man's breath came in short gasps. He could not finish.

I pulled down my face mask because I felt like I was losing all breath. Tears were running down my face; I brushed at them, forgetting about the mud on my hands. I was a physical and emotional mess.

"Don't cry, Rei-san," Miki said. "He's going to be fine."

"Haneda-san, you have been strong for so long," Mr. Ishida said. "Your whole family is safe. Don't worry about anything. The terrible time is over."

In the midst of the laughing and crying and cheers, I reached down to pet Hachiko, who was sitting just like the model of a good dog. Hachiko thumped her tail on the ground, as if to say: *Yes. I told you so.*

CHAPTER 18

After the ambulance lurched off through the rubble to take Miki's father to a working hospital, we all hurried back to the shelter.

Sadako Haneda was fast asleep, lying under an army blanket with the baby snuggled nearby. "Oh, back already? What time is it?" she said, sounding fuzzy. "I was dreaming."

"We found Otoochan," Miki yelled.

Various people huddled on the other sides of cardboard enclosure reacted to the news and passed it on. An elderly woman whispered, "The girls' father—"

"Really found?" another person murmured to yet someone else. Mrs. Haneda shook her head. "Please, Miki."

"Hachiko found him," Miki shrieked. "She smelled the way to him. He doesn't look very handsome, but they'll fix him at the hospital."

"Haneda-san, it's absolutely true." Mr. Ishida spoke quietly.

"I'm delighted to tell you that your husband has been found alive."

"Truly?" She rubbed at her eyes, and I imagined she thought this encounter might still be part of her dream.

"His identification was in his pocket," I assured her. "But just as important, he was conscious and recognized his daughters by name. Miki never gave up hoping, and he didn't, either."

Miki was so excited that she couldn't stay still; she spun in circles around her mother. "He's going to a big hospital in Sendai, Okaachan, and someone will bring you there right away—"

"Yes, you must go to him once the medical people call with his location. Ishida-san and I will watch the children," I pledged.

Mrs. Haneda's eyes shone with tears of joy. "But where did you find him? How could you find him when the soldiers didn't?"

"Hachiko knew that someone was underneath some broken vending machines near the waterfront. She wouldn't budge until they were removed."

"That wonderful dog," Mrs. Haneda cried. Others in the room came over to smile and offer congratulations. Quite a few people cheered, while others wept.

"I'm very surprised she found him," Mr. Ishida said, patting Hachiko, who'd marched straight into the shelter and sat with nose lifted, as if she was inhaling all the praise. "Hachiko has no formal training for searching—except for termites!"

"She's been sleeping with Mr. Haneda's coat for a few days," I reminded him. "Perhaps that smell imprinted on her, so when she recognized it near the vending machines, she was thrilled."

"Hachiko will find Butter next," Miki said happily. "They'll be great friends."

"Oh, Miki," her mother answered softly. "We should mainly be grateful about Otoochan...."

"But we need Butter!" Miki burst out. "The family isn't right without him. He could be underneath some other vending machines. But he doesn't have fingers. He cannot open food and drink cans like Otoochan. We must find him."

As Miki began weeping, I put my hand on her small shoulder. It wasn't enough, but I had no words. Later that night, when I was able to borrow Mr. Ishida's phone to leave a text message for Michael, I condensed all the day's excitement in a few lines.

Great day. Hachiko found a father of 3 who'd been trapped for 12 days. We are still looking for Mr. Ishida's apprentice. No idea when I'm getting out. I love you.

Then I hit send.

Hachiko's future was a lot more certain. The story of her latest discovery spread throughout Sugihama. By the next morning, Mr. Yano asked Mr. Ishida whether he was willing to have Hachiko undergo a short training to do more work assisting the searchers. He agreed with the caveat that the two of us needed to accompany her.

"This is exactly what we need," he told me afterward. "Hachiko will visit places where Mayumi might be trapped. If she's anywhere in Sugihama, Hachiko will find her."

So shortly after breakfast, Ishida-san and I fell into step with a search group led by Petty Officer Oshima of the Japan Self-Defense Force. His second-in-charge was a frighteningly large male German shepherd called Ninja.

Upon the dogs' meeting, Hachiko had stepped forward to sniff hello with Ninja, but it didn't go the way I would have expected.

Ninja growled threateningly and regarded Hachiko with a dominant stare. Hachiko lowered her head and backed off.

Like dog, like owner? I wondered as the training continued. Mr. Oshima kept a straight back and serious expression similar to imperial army soldiers from old photographs. He immediately exchanged Hachiko's rope leash for a proper harness and leash, which he kept a firm grip on. Sternly, he nudged Hachiko toward various piles of rubble that had different smells. Paradoxically, the dog that loved to smell and taste everything suddenly showed no interest.

Petty Officer Oshima told us that in addition to observing how Hachiko reacted to scents, we all needed to be aware of subtle signs like raised ears or fear of certain areas.

"Dogs don't usually think death smells good. In that way they are like us," he muttered.

"Hachiko's prior professional experience was with sniffing for live termites," I said when Hachiko finally caught interest in some fallen beams of wood and started barking.

"Very good, Hachiko!" Mr. Ishida reached into his pocket for one of the sausage treats the petty officer had allotted at the start of the walk.

"You must not reward her for finding termites," the dog handler corrected. "Now she is rewarded for finding people."

"Some of the survivors at the shelter want her to smell their loved ones' clothing and go hunting for them. That seemed to have worked well yesterday. Can her skills be improved even more strongly in this direction?" I asked.

"Such searches are typically conducted over days or weeks," Petty Officer Oshima answered. "They're also limited to the dog following the scent of one person. It would confuse even a professional search dog to follow many different smells at the same time."

"But surely she would recognize the scent of someone she'd known in her daily life," Mr. Ishida suggested.

"Maybe. But the most important training for your dog in this vicinity is that of a cadaver dog—which means, finding dead bodies. And in such a short time, not much can be expected. Hachiko will spend her time serving as back up to Ninja. Knowing this, are you still interested in continuing this training?"

Hachiko wasn't my dog, so I kept quiet. Mr. Ishida bowed slightly to the handler and said, "If it's all right with you, I'd like her to try a bit longer."

We resumed the slow, sniffing journey, with Mr. Ishida holding Hachiko's leash this time, and Petty Officer Oshima leading the way with Ninja. While Ninja was docile with his master—and ignored Mr. Ishida and me after a few quick sniffs—he obviously felt differently about Hachiko. Ninja turned his head and barked whenever Hachiko tried to lead Mr. Ishida off in a different direction. And I'd thought mothers were the only ones with eyes in the back of their heads.

Still, Hachiko continued to forget Ninja was the boss, because she kept creeping up to sniff his hindquarters. Ninja's tail swished angrily the first time this happened, and the second time, the shepherd turned his head to reveal bared teeth.

"Hachiko lives just with me. She doesn't have much experience with other dogs," Mr. Ishida apologized.

The petty officer didn't answer him, because he was busy listening to his walkie-talkie emit beeps followed by a crackling sound. The words that I could make out sounded like someone was saying that a body had been found. It turned out I'd heard right.

"This is just the cadaver training that your dog needs." Petty Officer Oshima sounded cheerful. "We will allow Hachiko to lead us to the body and then give her a very good reward."

Because the area was a mile away, an army jeep pulled up to take us. Mr. Oshima and his aide took the front passenger seat, while both dogs jumped into the back with Mr. Ishida and me. I made sure Ninja was on the exterior right side, with me next, then Mr. Ishida, and finally Hachiko on the left exterior. The farther apart the two dogs were, the safer for everyone.

The day was a bit warmer so the jeep's plastic windows were unzipped, and Hachiko craned her head out, inhaling the foul air. We turned onto a narrow street that crossed the main street with Takara Auction House. Hachiko's ears pressed forward, reminding me of what the dog handler had said about animal reactions.

"Look at Hachiko's ears," I exclaimed.

"Actually, we're headed to a butcher shop," Petty Officer Oshima said. "Knowing this dog's interests, she's probably smelling meat."

I couldn't tell which building he thought was a butcher shop; there was only the shell of one building left. Underneath was a cluster of people—soldiers, and a person in a Red Cross jacket, and several civilian volunteers I recognized from the shelter.

"Stop here," Sgt. Oshima commanded his driver. To us he said, "Now it's time for Hachiko's lesson: discerning human remains from those of animals."

"Should we come all the way inside?" Secretly, I was hoping he'd forbid it.

"Only if you want to keep training the dog." The dog handler looked at me with contempt.

Earlier in the day, he had spoken about a dog's first reaction when someone was detected. He might cringe or rush forward, depending on his temperament. As we took the dogs out of the jeep, Ninja barked and strained toward the ruins of a shop. But Hachiko stayed put and whined softly.

"Let Hachiko lead you," Mr. Oshima told Mr. Ishida and me. "Let her sniff all the various things, but do not reward. You may give a half sausage for her reward, once she's come up to the body."

"Come now," Mr. Ishida said, pulling Hachiko along on the leash. I trailed the two of them, looking everywhere but ahead. I felt ashamed of myself for wishing that I'd stayed on kitchen duty. Not that I felt like eating anytime soon.

Holding my breath, I took the last few steps to join the group. Four soldiers were already inside the building, standing around something on the ground. Despite the respirator on my face, I sensed the air was particularly vile, in a sweet and musky way.

"Just a short time," the petty officer said, indicating the dogs should come forward to smell the thing that must have been a corpse.

Hachiko walked slowly forward. But instead of sniffing, she laid her head straight on the corpse's shoulder. I was horrified, but Mr. Ishida didn't pull her away. He stood rigidly, his attention following Hachiko's inspection of the corpse.

Trying to be brave, I looked as well. The body was not terribly long, and its legs were curled up against the stomach, the way a side sleeper might lie. But that was the only inkling of the body's former humanity. The flesh was black and swollen. I could not guess at age or gender, if it hadn't been for the light-blue skinny jeans and purple and pink sneakers. A towel had been placed over the corpse's face; I wondered if this was routinely done out of respect or because the decay was so horrific.

The corpse's top half was dressed in a short, flaring white coat that was unbuttoned. The coat buttons were feminine: lacquered rounds with a pink flower set on a blue background. The pink of the flowers matched the hand-knitted scarf tucked around her neck. At the end of the white coat's sleeves, the dead woman's hands were not really hands anymore. Just squirming maggots.

Mr. Ishida had said something about Mayumi designing lacquer buttons. But what else did I know about her?

Fighting revulsion, I bent to look at a few strands of turquoise-blue yarn slipping out from under the edge of the gray towel. Then I realized the strands weren't yarn. They were thin and silky: human hair.

I wanted to look back at Mr. Ishida to see if he was all right, but I couldn't even turn my head. I was overcome by everything. The sight of her, the overpowering smell, and the end of the search.

Petty Officer Oshima was saying something unintelligible. I was losing air inside the respirator. I tugged it up so my voice could be heard. But when I did that, the poisoned air swept into my nose and throat, making me gag.

"I think it's..."

That was all that I got out before my eyes filled with all the turquoise blueness, and I was gone.

CHAPTER 19

Eventually, I returned to my senses. I was lying across the back seat of the military jeep, only there were no dogs beside me. A Red Cross medic was waving something under my nose that smelled sharp and medicinal. I struggled to lift myself onto my elbows, and I saw Mr. Ishida looking down anxiously.

"You weren't feeling well," he said. "I'm so sorry. Death after more than a week's time is especially hard to encounter."

Taking a shallow breath of air—air that was wonderfully devoid of everything except fish—I asked, "Is it her?"

"Yes." His voice was low. "I recognized her coat."

"Lacquer buttons..." I couldn't say more without thinking about the body and wanting to throw up.

"Yes, those were hers. And she had knitted the scarf—during quiet times in the shop, she liked to knit." Mr. Ishida's voice was soothing.

"I'm sorry," I said, tears leaking out of my eyes.

"Nobody blames you for fainting. It was difficult in there.

Everyone has stepped away. They are waiting for the corpse-removal crew."

I'd meant that I was sorry he'd had such a terrible discovery of the young apprentice he'd cared about. But I couldn't put together those words. My head hurt, and every part of my body felt tight, as if rods inside were forcing me into a tense sitting position. I took another shallow breath and asked, "Did you tell them it was Mayumi?"

"Yes, but they would like the Kimuras to have a chance to see her before the identification is officially confirmed."

"And Akira needs to know," I said. This news would devastate him.

"Someone else will tell him. Don't you worry."

"Where's Hachiko?" I asked.

"She is right here," said Mr. Ishida, and I looked down the short length of his right leg to see the dog sitting on the ground. But her head was turned, as if she was still trying to see Mayumi.

"It was very hard to get Hachiko to leave." Mr. Ishida wiped a hand across his eyes. "And despite what I said to Oshima-san, I'm sorry that now she has learned to recognize the smell of human death."

"It's so foul. I still smell it."

"During my years fighting with the imperial army, it was almost impossible to erase this smell of death from around myself. I've been told we will be brought to a bathhouse where we can clean ourselves. This is a very good idea, if you're willing."

A bath sounded like good therapy. But it wasn't as easy as Mr. Ishida thought. "I hear the nearest open bathhouse is in another town. And our clean clothing is at the volunteer shelter."

"The driver will bring us to the shelter first, to fetch those things. He will be eager to sanitize the car after we have gone out. And then we'll ride back, clean and calm. Don't worry, Shimura-san. I'll take care of you."

It was about an hour to the town of Takamachi. You could tell there had been flooding in the town, but luckily, it was not as severe as what had happened in Sugihama. We were dropped off outside a traditional wooden-walled bathhouse that had a yellow lamp shining in welcome and a blue *noren* curtain fluttering in the doorway. The fee for a bath was still advertised as 350 yen. Unsurprisingly, there were long queues of people patiently waiting.

People who joined the line for the women's section stood a slight distance away from me. Perhaps Mr. Ishida's hyperbole about the smell of death was true. My embarrassment increased when the old lady who managed the women's section came up and whispered to me that I had special dispensation to go straight in.

"Take as long as you like in the showers," she said emphatically. "There is much soap. But if you don't mind, please do not enter the communal bath today. It's a little inconvenient for you, but we have to think of everyone else. I'm very sorry, but..."

She understood the smell of death.

Inside the ladies' changing room, I took off all my clothes and put them in a plastic bag inside a small square locker. Then, shielding my lower half with a miniscule towel, I staked out my territory in a far corner of the women's showers. Then I did the same as everyone else: fitted myself on a tiny stool near a tap and started dousing myself with buckets of water. The warm water felt purifying and soothing. Using the liquid soap that came out of a dispenser on the wall, I lathered myself from head to toe. As I scrubbed, I glanced jealously at some female bath patrons just a few feet away from me, soaking in the deep, steaming bath. They looked so comfortable; but as their words floated back to me, I lost all envy.

"We cannot find our daughter. According to the Red Cross, it's quite typical...."

"The insurance agents won't pay to build another house. They say..."

"Matsumoto-san's deceased husband was found yesterday. He was covered in so much mud they thought he was a log. But his watch alarm went off..."

Outside of my cell phone, I had lost nothing. I had no friends or loved ones who'd died in Tohoku. Mayumi wasn't someone I'd even spoken with—so logically, I couldn't mourn her with any more depth than I did all the people I'd heard about on the news. But I did because of all Mr. Ishida had told me.

It was especially poignant to find her curled into herself, as if sleeping in the butcher shop. In the old days, Japanese people who butchered meat were regarded as a kind of untouchable. I remembered the writhing maggots and wanted to vomit, but there was something else that disturbed me.

I glanced at the bath, where the sober conversations continued. And then I recalled the recent words one woman had said to her friend.

He was covered in so much mud he looked like a log.

Mayumi hadn't been muddy. In the short time I'd seen her, I'd mentally cataloged that her blue jeans were dark blue and her accessories were candy pink. I could make out the floral patterns of the handmade lacquer buttons on her winter white coat. No wave could have rushed over Mayumi and kept her clothing in such immaculate condition.

Something else caused her death.

This thought was so jarring that the plastic bathing pitcher slipped out of my hand and the precious warm water spilled over the floor. Hastily I collected the pitcher and refilled it, anxiety streaming as fast as the water. Mayumi had come to the ruined butcher shop *after* the tsunami. Somehow, she'd survived the wave, and then entered the butcher shop and died.

What did this mean? Perhaps someone had killed her elsewhere and transported her to the butcher shop after the tsunami. On the other hand, Mr. Ishida had revealed that she was emotionally troubled. I quickly dismissed the idea of suicide, reasoning anyone in such a state would not have run from the wave but straight into it. Perhaps Mayumi had been disoriented after the tsunami. If she needed a daily medication for a chronic condition and missed too many doses, she could have died.

Half an hour later, I met Mr. Ishida, whose thin white hair was still damp from his own cleansing experience. I shivered, because I wasn't wearing a coat. Richard's down jacket had such a terrible stink that I'd kept it in the plastic bag with my other dirty clothing.

"The shower was a relief," Mr. Ishida said, sighing slightly. "I did not go into the bath, just to be careful I didn't spread the odor."

"I was warned not to do that," I said. "Ishida-san, I was thinking about something when I was showering. Did you notice anything strange about Mayumi's body?"

"What isn't strange about the body after decomposition? Nature takes its course."

"I thought Mayumi's clothes were unusually clean." When he didn't react, I added, "How could her clothes stay clean if she had been covered in eight feet of water?"

"But surely she drowned." Mr. Ishida looked puzzled. "One could tell that water had gone up to the ceiling of that butcher shop. All that mud."

"Yes, the room had been filled with water, but I think she must have entered it later on. If her clothes weren't muddy on top, she wasn't touched by the wave." I continued, "This means something else caused her death. Did she have a preexisting health condition? Maybe something that required daily shots or medication?"

"Not that I know about. When working for me, she never took any sick days." Mr. Ishida sighed heavily. "You are right that the situation is strange. Perhaps she was confused and distraught and fell and hurt herself after the tsunami. But why would she have gone into that place?"

"For anyone to know the cause of death, she should be examined by a coroner." I said the word in English, because I didn't know the Japanese version. When Mr. Ishida looked blank, I added, "I'm talking about a doctor who performs medical examinations on the dead: someone who'd know if there was a trauma injury or a knife wound."

"That kind of doctor is called a *kenshi-kan*," Mr. Ishida said. "There must be such a doctor in this area."

I had never wanted to leave Tohoku more strongly. The smells and sights of death and rot had clotted themselves into a bolus of horror. Nothing should have kept me any longer. But I heard myself say, "The only way to account for Mayumi's death is to have a *kenshi-kan's* examination."

"You may be right. And if the death is not caused by accident or illness, there may be someone walking around who is responsible." Mr. Ishida looked soberly at me. "Akira might have been away, but his family was here. Didn't you say they disliked her?"

"He did say his mother had a problem, but who has time to commit murder when a tsunami's happening?" I shook my head. "Hey, I just thought of something. Was the family lacquer with her when they found her?"

Mr. Ishida was still for a long moment, then shook his head. "I was overcome by the body. I don't recall anyone finding possessions near her. She did bring her backpack to Sugihama. I saw her put her telephone inside."

"Okay." But did the fact her backpack was missing point to anything else?

"You know, if we hadn't been right there to identify her, she might have gone straight for cremation," Mr. Ishida said. "I would not have known anything."

"I'm so sorry, Ishida-san." I took his hand, which was cold as ice.

We made it back to shelter about an hour after supper had been served, but Nobuko-san had kept leftovers for us in the kitchen. Once again, it was miso stew—this time, with fewer vegetables. I had little hunger for it, as the death smell kept flickering through my nose.

"You look very clean," Nobuko-san commented. "I hope for a

ride to that bathhouse tomorrow along with the other volunteers during our free-time hours. Was the water hot?"

"Actually, I didn't go inside the soaking tub—just the shower, which was lukewarm. But the bath looked nice and steamy. Please tell me something honestly. I may look clean, but do I smell that way?"

Nobuko came closer and inhaled as if she was sniffing her stew for seasonings. "You're fine. Don't worry."

"Ishida-san and I came close to a dead body, and I've heard that the smell can follow. That's why I couldn't enter the ladies' bath, although I was allowed to shower."

"Oh, dear. You are not alone in this. Lots of our volunteers have come near the dead."

I caught a glimpse of Mr. Yano briskly passing by in the hallway. "Nobuko-san, please excuse me. I must speak with him." I put my paper bowl in the garbage bag and hurried after him.

"Yano-san, do you have a moment?"

He stopped. "Yes. By the way, Ishida-san mentioned that the two of you and Hachiko found his missing apprentice. I'm very sorry about the circumstances."

"Thank you," I said. "Did Ishida-san mention that we don't think she drowned?"

"He said something strange. I wasn't sure I understood."

"Here are the facts." I told the volunteer coordinator about Mayumi's clean clothes and the way her body had been found in a muddy butcher shop, where the water marks went all the way to the ceiling, showing that it had been flooded during the course of the storm.

"That does seem very odd," he said after a pause. "But we are only volunteers, not experts in disaster recovery. Miss Kimura could have died from another natural reason. Maybe she was struck by an object or she fell. By the way, the Kimura parents came to our volunteer center when you and Ishida-san were at the bathhouse in Takamachi. They'd already been alerted by the military about their daughter being found and were transported to Sugihama to identify her. They stopped to thank both of you for your search, and also Ishida-san for employing her during her months in Tokyo."

"Are they still nearby?"

"Oh, no, they went back home. However, they left their business card."

Thank God for Japanese name-card etiquette. I grasped the card quickly as Yano-san handed it to me. It was a plain white card, tastefully bordered in red, with the *kanji* for "Kimura" and "lacquer" on it with an address and telephone number.

"Please be careful not to upset them any more," Mr. Yano cautioned. "They were very sad when they left."

"I'll do my best."

CHAPTER 20

———

Mr. Ishida was similarly wary about phoning the Kimuras. Shaking his head, he said, "If they just learned the bad news, this concern we have about unnatural death could be overwhelming. I suggest we get some sleep and speak to them tomorrow."

Normally, I would have agreed with him. But things didn't operate reasonably in disaster zones. "If we aren't able to share our concerns, the Kimuras will surely go ahead with plans for immediate cremation. And then the chance to know the truth might be lost, which they would ultimately regret."

He looked behind him, as if anxious that anyone else might be listening. However, most volunteers were involved with the electronic devices they'd not been near all day long. "I'm surprised by the urgency you feel for someone you didn't know," he murmured.

Not only hadn't I known her, I'd built my own picture of her as a thoroughly dislikable young woman. I'd been appalled at the idea that Mayumi had left Hachiko, shocked she'd tried to sell family heirlooms, and dismayed that Mr. Ishida had trusted her enough to work in his shop. With all these strong instinctive feelings, I should have thought, *it's a sad story, but at least it's done.*

But lying in front of me was a ruined girl who'd curled up to die. Something about her physical position spoke to the hopelessness she'd felt. And this made me ashamed of my early judgment. "She would want us to know the truth. About everything: what she was going to do with the lacquer, and how her life ended."

"Perhaps you have a point in calling tonight, then," Mr. Ishida said. "I believe you have more strength than I for this type of communication."

The first call didn't go through; there was only some dead air that was typical of dropped phone calls since the disaster. But I kept trying, and eventually the phone did ring. But almost instantly, a pleasant woman's voice spoke. "This is Kimura Lacquer Goods. Sales hours are ten till six daily except for Mondays. Please leave a message if you would like to place a special order. Thank you very much."

They might be too distraught to check their shop line for messages, but I still went ahead and explained who I was, that I was sorry about Mayumi's passing, and that I had some information about her situation.

"Very well said," Mr. Ishida commented after I'd clicked off. "You were calm and did not make any assertions. That is the proper manner."

"I just hope I wasn't so vague they'll put off speaking to us until after the cremation."

"We cannot manage their decision," Mr. Ishida said gently. "I'll go to sleep now, but if you like, you can take the phone with you. In case they call back... and for any other reasons you might have."

Mr. Ishida's phone had come back to life after it had spent the day in a sealed plastic bag with plenty of dry rice to absorb moisture—a tip from Nobuko-san. I tapped in a brief message to Michael. *We found Mayumi, but she wasn't alive. Don't think she died from the wave. Don't know how the hell she died. I love and miss you.*

As I wrote, I imagined him putting his arms around me.

I saw from the phone's blank face the next morning that I had no e-mail, text, or phone message from Mayumi's parents. But I couldn't brood on that, because another problem was looming. I had no more granola bars. This meant no breakfast for me, or Mr. Ishida, who had come with nothing.

I supposed I could have run over to the residents' shelter and asked for a breakfast bar; that's what the military had left for them. But we'd expressly been told by Mr. Yano not to go after military food supplies, for reasons of accounting. I had gone out of the box so many times, I didn't think I should do so again.

But I had to tell Mr. Ishida, because I'd had food for him the day before. When I saw him standing outdoors, slowly warming up with his *tai chi* routine, I apologized for not remembering to look for food when we were in Takamachi.

"I don't eat much at my age," he said, obviously trying to make me feel better. "Did the Kimuras answer your call?"

Shaking my head, I said, "I don't know if they haven't heard my message yet or just don't want to talk."

I went through the morning exercises feeling faint. No hunger last night, but plenty this morning. Afterward, I went to the survivors' shelter to get busy with lunch preparations. I had just started organizing my cutting board, wondering if I could sneak a carrot piece, when little Miki Haneda ran up and hugged me.

"Good morning," I said.

Miki stepped back and opened her hands like a magician might when performing a show. In each palm was a plastic-wrapped rice ball. This particular o-nigiri—made of sesame-flecked rice wrapped in seaweed, with a pickled plum in the center—was ordinary in Japan. But I adored it.

"Where did you find these?" I didn't think any shops had reopened in town, so I was stunned by the timing of this gift.

"There was a 7-Eleven near the hospital in Sendai. We all went yesterday and got lots of good food."

I couldn't express how thrilled I was, and also touched that she'd thought of me when her father's situation was paramount. In a community flooded by chaos, here was one thing that had gone right.

"Thank you!" I hugged Miki, inhaling the smell of Sugihama mud overlaid with some sort of sugary pastry.

"Okaachan wants to say hello. She's around the corner with my sisters and Hachiko. Ishida-san is already there." Skipping, she led me out the back of the building, where Mr. Ishida was standing with the dog at his side. I let Miki present Mr. Ishida with the o-nigiri, which he politely refused twice before gratefully accepting. He ate as slowly as I did, savoring the taste of fresh, soft rice.

"You already had breakfast," Mr. Ishida scolded Hachiko, who was watching as if a grain of rice might drop into her mouth at any moment.

While we ate and chatted with Miki, Mrs. Haneda had crouched down drawing a chalk picture on the sidewalk with

Chieko. When she looked up, I felt as if I were seeing a different person. She looked a decade younger.

"Shimura-san, I'm sorry that I didn't yet thank you and Ishida-san for rescuing my husband," she said, her voice bubbling with warmth. "So I'll tell you now. He owes you his life, and we owe you all our future happiness."

"There's no need to thank us!" I demurred. "It was all Hachiko's work. The most important question is, how is your husband recovering?"

"He only had a broken shoulder—he is quite lucky in that regard. The problem is his skin was wet for too long. He has some bad bacterial infections but is taking an antibiotic. He will feel better soon. The doctor would ordinarily release him to heal at home, if only we still had one."

"Yes. I'm so sorry about that. Are you going to stay with relatives?"

"If we do, it's just temporarily. My husband works for the town of Sugihama, so he wants to return and rebuild. By the way, Ishida-san was just saying Hachiko located someone else yesterday. How are you?"

"I'm fine," I said, holding back other words.

"I think that person was dead," Miki said in her no-nonsense tone. "Did you know that? Her parents visited our shelter yesterday, looking for you. The lady cried, and the man yelled, telling her to stop. So mean!"

"I don't think the father was mean. Think how angry you felt the other day about Butter," her mother said gently. "There are strong feelings when loved ones pass away."

Miki shook her head. "Butter is not dead. Just lost."

"Maybe that's true. Do you remember how much Butter liked

swimming?" Paddling her arms, Mrs. Haneda said, "I think our Butter took a long swim on top of the wave, all the way to another part of Japan. But she will find a child there to make sure she gets fed."

I bowed my head, not wanting any of them to see my face. I prayed that if I ever had a child, I would not have to tell that kind of story.

"How far away is this part of Japan?" Miki put her hands on her mother's shoulders and gazed intently into her eyes. "Where, exactly?"

Mrs. Haneda's happy voice cracked. "I don't know, Miki-chan."

Miki pulled away from her mother and looked straight at me. "The father who came here yesterday was not very nice! He was rude to that handsome young man."

"Which young man?" I asked.

"The one with the leather jacket. He was crying in the kitchen before, remember?"

If Akira had crossed paths with Mayumi's father, he might have been told about the death on the spot. I needed to talk to him, to see how he was doing.

Glancing at Mr. Ishida, I said, "I'm going to skip calisthenics this morning. Will you apologize to Yano-san for me?"

"Why?"

"I need to visit the Rikyo family."

Mr. Ishida shook his head. "You mustn't go alone."

"When I'm alone, he's more willing to speak." I was in a difficult position, because my going against a respected person's wishes would make everyone present feel awkward. I threw in a second, face-saving argument. "Don't you think one of us should remain here today? If the Kimuras return to the volunteer headquarters, someone needs to speak with them."

"That is true. I will stay here," Mr. Ishida acquiesced. "You will take Hachiko, for extra protection."

I didn't want to mention that Hachiko didn't like Akira. Instead I smiled and said, "That's a grand idea. Hachiko will get her day's exercise going up the mountain and back."

"If I come with you and Hachiko, we can look for more missing people. I'm really good at it," Miki offered.

"Miki-chan, I'd appreciate your help here teaching more children how to play mah-jongg," Mr. Ishida said, coming to my rescue. "Shimura-san will bring Hachiko back within two hours."

"Probably within three hours," I said, thinking that the walk would take some time. Especially since I wasn't sure where I was headed.

The temperature had warmed to about fifty degrees when we set out. I was grateful for the sun, because I was still airing out Richard's parka and had switched back to my fashionable fleece jacket. Hachiko strolled beside me with her tail in the air and nose hovering just above ground level. The distance was approximately two miles. I figured that a forty-minute walk would give me time to compose my thoughts and also perhaps speak to any police I saw. I'd heard that station had been swept away; my best chance was finding someone working the streets.

When a policeman in blue emerged from a jeep, Hachiko barked happily and wagged her tail. *Good public relations*, I thought, waving at him. The man, who'd had his head down and been heading toward a building with a clipboard, stopped.

"Do you need help?" He wore the typical constable's cap of a community police officer. After all the military police gear I'd recently seen, the cap was reassuring. Hachiko's friendly nose on his leg brought a small smile to his face.

"I don't need help—but I have some information I would like to share." As the words came out, I wished I didn't sound so self-important. That was the problem when Japanese was one's second language. "I'm a volunteer with Helping Hands. This dog and I went with a team that found a deceased young woman in the butcher's shop. After I left the scene, I realized there were some details that meant she could not have been a typical drowning victim."

"A woman found in the butcher's shop? I believe I heard about that." The policeman began tapping into his phone. After a minute he said, "Do you know the woman's name?"

"Kimura Mayumi."

"Yes, there was an initial identification made of that deceased victim in late afternoon... It was confirmed by her parents at six p.m." He paused in his reading. "The military report says death by drowning."

"That's what I think is wrong. You see, there was no mud on her. She came to the area after the wave had subsided."

He looked quizzically at me. "How do you know when she came? What are you saying? And this report doesn't mention clothing. No, not at all."

"Well, if water had passed over her, wouldn't her clothing be muddy?" I was trying to seek agreement, but his immobile expression told me that I appeared insane. Striving to sound intelligent, I added: "As you know, the water that rushed over this town held a great deal of earth and debris. Her coat was white and her jeans were blue. Therefore, no water passed over her."

He looked from me to his crackling walkie-talkie. "Excuse me, but I must answer this."

"Of course, but I just want to know—were pictures taken at the scene?"

"None are attached to this report. Hello, hello!" The cop spoke into his walkie-talkie. A brief conversation about moving someone's car transpired. When the call finished, he patted Hachiko, who seemed to smile up at him. "What a nice dog. I'm sorry you are so upset about this death. Would you like to sit down? I can bring a social worker."

"No, thank you. We're out for a walk. I'm perfectly fine. By the way, how can I reach a coroner?" I knew my question was abrupt, but it was clear I would have to go elsewhere to raise the alarm.

"I'm afraid the coroner died. He was in Yamagawa when the wave struck." His expression had darkened, and I realized the coroner must have been someone he knew, perhaps even a friend.

"I'm so sorry," I said, unable to imagine all the losses of friends and colleagues this man must have gone through.

"The deaths are so widespread that right now our concern is trying to save any remaining lives." He spoke quickly, as if fearful of crying. "Unfortunately, there is little time to evaluate how each person died."

When I told the policeman that I understood, I meant it. I thanked him for his time and walked on, thinking, *that damned wave.*

Before I'd left for the walk, I'd consulted with Mayor Hamasaki. He said that a gas station was the landmark for the turnoff to the mountain road leading to the Rikyos' home. When a long tanker truck passed me along the way, it confirmed that I was headed the right direction.

When I reached the gas station, the tanker was parked and in the process of fueling the various gas pumps. A short line of cars waited, the owners standing outside their vehicles and watching the process with hopeful expressions. The station's shop's window sign glowed "open."

"*Irrasshaimase*," a young lady with a green kerchief over her hair called as I stepped inside.

"It's so nice that you're open." I smiled back at her, all the while quickly scanning the shelves that were half stocked with breads, cookies, noodle packs, and candy. I imagined a lot of local people had reached the shelves before me; but there was still enough that could be carried away for Mr. Ishida's and my next day's breakfast. Or several breakfasts.

"Last night we had our first delivery since the tsunami," the salesclerk confided, coming up to offer me one of the shopping baskets I'd bypassed in my excitement to inspect the edibles. "It's just great! I really hope there will be enough for all the shoppers who'll visit today. Good thing you came right now."

The shop's owner could have taken advantage and raised prices, but the shrimp chips and Pocky sticks and sweet bean cakes were selling at typical convenience store prices. I gathered up an assortment of crackers and cookies and *inari-zushi*, the sweet tofu-skin pockets that were stuffed with vinegary rice. I was buying enough to buy some of her time. "Excuse me, were you here the day of the tsunami?"

"Yes, I was. I haven't met you before. Are you a volunteer?"

"I came from Hawaii." I watched her smile grow wider. "Actually, I'm trying to trace the path of someone else who came from outside the area who vanished during the tsunami. She was a nineteen-year-old woman with shoulder-length blue hair. I know it sounds unusual."

"Blue hair? I would remember seeing that—but maybe not. Things were very busy the day of tsunami, as we were trying to close down everything except the gas pumps," the girl said. "Did she fill up with gas here?"

"No. I was thinking she might have passed through in someone's car, trying to evacuate. This young lady had been at Takara Auction House when the quake struck and was looking for a ride to safety."

"I've heard of that auction house." The clerk stopped smiling. "Nobody really knows the owner. He didn't participate in our town's summer festival last year—or the year before. He did tell one of the other girls working here that she talked with an accent. How weird." She sighed. "Anyway, I don't remember seeing a blue-haired girl the day of the tsunami."

"She knew the Rikyo family, just up the hill."

"Akira Rikyo?" Her face transformed to sunshine. "I know him—he's so nice, but he was away all last year. But he's back. Akira-kun and his father came in to say hello earlier today."

"I'm going to visit them at their house," I said. "I was so sorry to hear about the family they lost in the tsunami."

"Yes, the father keeps so busy with work, but the mother has not come down here once. I worry that she is too sad to leave her place. Will you please tell her the milk delivery will come later today? I'd really like to see her."

"Yes, I promise."

"If you need directions, I can give them. You see, Akira and I were in high school together. He didn't really know I existed because he had some out-of-town girlfriend, but…"

Eventually, she gave the directions.

CHAPTER 21

Twenty minutes later, I rang the Rikyos' doorbell, which was elegantly installed in a pillar beside the gate to their attractive, cedar-shingled home. There was no trace of physical destruction here, but I was concerned about Mrs. Rikyo's condition. She'd lost her only daughter and two granddaughters about a week and a half ago. It was a terrible time for a stranger to intrude.

I rang again, and nobody came. I glanced around, thinking. A Toyota Camry in the driveway made it seem that someone could be home. There was an intercom microphone close to the doorbell, but that hadn't been answered. Looking at the intercom again, I saw no light.

How stupid! If the electricity was out, so too was the doorbell. I opened the gate and went straight up to the sliding-door entrance and knocked.

"*Hai, hai!*"

I heard a female voice calling from within, and in short order, the door slid open, and I faced a woman about fifteen years older and just a bit shorter and rounder than I. Her complexion was unlined and youthful, but she was dressed in a conventional, middle-aged style: a scarlet wool sweater with a chicken embroidered in the center, and knife-pleated khaki pants accented by a crazy patchwork apron. She looked 100 percent motherly and appeared as cozy as Otafuku, the folk goddess of hearth and home. I'd been worried about meeting a thin wraith dressed in black, so this was a relief.

"Excuse me for bothering you." I made a quick, polite introduction, giving my name before asking if she was Mrs. Rikyo.

"Yes, but we've given our information on damage and loss already. Thank you for checking." She'd summed me up, just as I'd evaluated her. The door was sliding closed.

"I'm sorry not to have explained straightaway. I'm not here about damage. I came to see your son. We met on the volunteer bus?"

"Oh, the Helping Hands who were so kind to give him passage." She smiled at me with real warmth. "He's out on a job with his father but will return for lunch. Please come in—it probably won't be long." She glanced at Hachiko, who was standing nicely at my side. "The dog's okay, too. I like dogs, but my husband never wanted one."

"If I'm really not bothering you—"

Mrs. Rikyo waved me into the house's *genkan*, a stone-floored entryway where an assortment of boots and shoes were lined up in a burled walnut shoe case that looked handmade. The case was topped by five handmade *kimekomi* dolls clad in tiny, intricate kimonos, all with slightly different facial expressions and classical hairstyles.

"Will the dog mind staying in the *genkan?*" Mrs. Rikyo asked, looking at Hachiko.

"She won't mind at all. I will give her something to enjoy," I said, taking a rawhide bone out of my pocket. I signaled she should lie down, using the sweeping, palm-down motion I'd seen Mr. Ishida use. Hachiko lay down and began working on the rawhide. She was so pleased to be indoors with a treat that she didn't mind us moving on.

"You know, my son also wanted us to have a dog. But I was so busy with him and his sister, I never saw how." Mrs. Rikyo ushered me into the main room that was warmed by a glowing kerosene heater. The *zabuton* seat cushions around the maple *kotatsu* table were hand-embroidered cotton.

"What gorgeous cushions. I love the embroidery," I said.

"Really? I made them from old fabric and did the embroidery, too. I like all kinds of sewing. Best of all is making dolls."

"*Kimekomi* dolls like the ones in the *genkan?*" I asked. "They are absolutely stunning. What gentle expressions on their faces. So lifelike; and the costumes are charming."

"Those dolls are early practice ones, not good enough to sell." She deflected my praise, but from her skin's flush, I could tell she'd appreciated my noticing them. "Shimura-san, I beg you to overlook the disorder here. We've moved a lot of things around because of the tsunami. We have friends staying in my sewing room, which means the sewing materials had to come to the living room."

The living room was cluttered, not just with sewing materials. I saw stacks of carpentry magazines and a few suitcases that probably contained some of their friends' possessions. Only one spot was almost completely clear: the *kotatsu* table I'd noticed earlier. Two framed photographs sat in the center: one of a young teenager dressed in the fashions of about ten years earlier; the other of a toddler in a strawberry-patterned sunsuit.

Following my gaze, she said, "I am making dolls in honor of my late daughter, Hanako, and granddaughters Noriko and Sachiko. I made the clothes they wore in those photographs, and because I have some of the cloth left, the dolls will resemble them quite a bit. Well, as much as dolls can. They are not alive."

She bent her head, trying to hide her emotion.

"Akira said they died in the tsunami. I'm so sorry for your tragic loss."

"You're kind to care. It was quite terrible. You see, my daughter felt the quake and heard the sirens, but she could not get my granddaughters packed up quickly. When she began driving toward our house, she telephoned me because they were stuck in traffic. I kept talking to her, talking, talking... and there was a rushing sound. The wave caught them." She looked down for a long moment. "Soldiers found them the next day in their car. She was holding both of them."

"Oh." I bent my head and got out a tissue. She'd probably told the story enough times that she didn't cry anymore, but I couldn't stop myself from wiping my eyes.

"At least we don't have to live with worry and false hopes. And I know we're lucky to still have Akira. He's a good boy to have come back from Tokyo to help."

"Yes. Why did he go to Tokyo in the first place?" I asked, putting my tissue away.

"Well, he worked some construction jobs and the pay there is higher than what he could get working for my husband. And he followed a girl—such a silly thing. But now that's over."

"Is the girl you mentioned called Mayumi Kimura?"

"Yes. She perished in the tsunami. This is a real shame, and I must say, quite a sad surprise, because she doesn't live in our town. Her home is inland; it escaped the wave."

"It's incredible that you heard already." It made our conversation easier, but also made me wonder how she knew.

"Akira was at the volunteer center yesterday and recognized Mayumi's parents. They told him the news. When he came home, he told us. He cried so hard, he made us cry, too. I warned him years ago that the girl would only break his heart."

"I heard Mayumi was from Kinugasa. That's not quite the village next door. How did they happen to meet?"

"Well—even though I'm a rather unskilled needleworker—I have been requested often to bring my dolls and embroidered pieces to festivals and sales all over Tohoku. One time, I brought Akira to help me at a sale in Sendai. Mayumi was on the other side of the hall, selling lacquer at her family's table. The two made eyes at each other and exchanged telephone numbers. I wasn't happy because she was just fifteen—and he was seventeen. In those years, it's a big age difference."

To a parent, but not to a kid.

"She was too young: a mischief-maker and also disobedient to her parents, I later learned. Not like our daughter." Mrs. Rikyo shot a wistful glance at the photograph of the deceased Hanako. "Akira took the train after school to some area to meet her. But more often she came downtown. Sometimes he didn't even come home for supper, he was so busy with her. His grades dropped, and he became a completely different son. This went on for three years."

"That's a long time for a high-school relationship."

"I hoped very much that he would outgrow this interest, but after she finished school, she ran away to Tokyo and convinced Akira to follow her. This was very hard on my husband, who had always expected Akira to continue our carpentry business. He was working then as his apprentice. Just as Mayumi's family expected her to finish high school and then work with them at their shop selling lacquer. It's the way we do things here, isn't it?"

I made an apologetic expression. "Sorry, I'm confused. I thought Akira went to Tokyo to encourage Mayumi to return home to her parents?"

"He never said that to us. He just said he found a job and apartment and not to worry about him. But I am his mother. Of course I did worry. Wouldn't you?"

"What was your husband's feeling about their relationship?"

"Oh, he thought boys will be boys. We should not interfere, he said, because he always believed Akira would come back to work with us. I suppose he's been proven right. I only wish Akira had come when the whole family was still alive, instead of after losing three members."

The front door slid open with a grating sound. *"Tadaima!"*

I recognized Akira's confident voice announcing his arrival home. But anything else he might have said was quickly drowned out by sharp, wild barking.

"I'm so sorry. Hachiko's being awful." I got to my feet and rushed to the *genkan*, calling, "Hachiko, *dame desu!* No!"

Akira had escaped the home and was now peering through the sliding front door at Hachiko and me. I grabbed the leash and pulled Hachiko next to me, apologizing all the while.

"How did *she* get in here?" he asked as he reentered, keeping a careful distance from the two of us. "Did she bite my mother?"

"I brought her—and your mother's fine. I'm so sorry. I didn't think about you coming into the *genkan*. Your mother mentioned you'd be coming back for lunch."

"Better keep her close to your side on that leash," Mrs. Rikyo advised, seemingly unfazed by Hachiko's display of aggression toward her son. "I'm just putting the water to boil for *ramen*. We will have it with a packaged sauce—I hope you don't mind," she added to me.

"Please don't go to trouble on my account," I said. "Really, I could take the dog out. I did want to speak to Akira-san."

"Is that so? Why didn't you tell me about Mayumi?" Akira's voice was bitter. "You had my mobile number. I learned from *them*, and they even blamed me for it!"

"B-but that's why I came here this morning," I stammered. "When the discovery was made yesterday, I couldn't have called you, because I've lost my phone."

"Here," Mrs. Rikyo said, handing her son a large pair of shearling slippers. "And don't forget to put the boots outside."

"So, do you know where was she found?" Akira asked coldly after he'd come back from disposing his boots. "The Kimuras wouldn't answer any of my questions."

"Her body was found in a butcher shop around the corner from Takara Auction House."

Akira gaped at me. "But that can't be. In Tokyo, she became a vegetarian—she would never have gone inside a butcher shop. Are the police really sure it was Mayumi?"

"Mr. Ishida recognized her clothing. A white coat with special buttons she'd made. And I guess if her parents came later, they saw her, too."

"Ishida-san was there?" Akira paused, then said, "And you weren't?"

I'd blown it. God, this conversation was hard.

"Yes, I was there. Akira-san, I'm really sorry." I watched the young man as he bent his head and hid his face in his hands.

"You didn't cry like that for your sister," his mother sniped. Her voice surprised me; I'd been so focused on Akira I'd forgotten she was behind me.

"How would you know? You told me about them over the phone. You weren't with me after the line went dead." Akira shot back. "I miss Hanako. She was my only sister, and she was just great. And I will never forget Sachi-chan and Nori-chan. But at least the three of them were together when they died. Mayumi was alone."

Alone. This was my sense of it—although I had no idea about the truth. Why had he said the same word I'd thought about when I reflected on Mayumi's curled body?

"Akira-san, do you think Mayumi might have seen somebody she knew in Sugihama? I mean, other than Ishida-san at the auction house?"

"That's almost like what her parents asked." He looked at me with eyes that glistened with the remnants of tears. "They thought I'd lured her back. I had to explain that I was working in Tokyo when the quake and everything else happened."

But Mayumi's death occurred *after* the quake. I thought a moment and then asked, "If you want to put them at ease, could someone you know tell them where you were from the day of the quake through last Friday, when you rode the bus out here with me?"

"Of course. I was working construction on an apartment

building in Ebisu. There were about thirty of us and a supervisor who sent us home right after the quake. We talked about it already, remember?"

"You said you walked around looking for Mayumi on those days," I said.

"You looked for her?" Mrs. Rikyo interjected. "Akira, I thought everything between you two was over."

"I can't help caring about someone I've known for four years, okay? I just wanted to make sure she was safe. I also wanted her to do the right thing. The lacquer—" he shot a glance at his mother. "Yes, I told Shimura-san about that."

"Her parents telephoned about her taking their heirlooms. It's terrible enough, but I can't believe they tried to involve me in their family business," Mrs. Rikyo said.

"Ishida-san thinks she might have had the lacquer with her when she came this way." I paused, thinking about how much further to go. "It seems like Mayumi might not have drowned. She could have died for another reason."

"Not drowned?" His mother's eyebrows rose. "But the tsunami—"

"When she was found, her clothing wasn't muddy." Telling them this was a risk, but I figured that seeing their reactions was important. Mrs. Rikyo looked hard at me, and Akira gasped outright.

"That sounds improbable. Who told you?" Mrs. Rikyo demanded.

"It's just my idea, based on her clothing."

"As I said, Mayumi had no reason to be in a butcher shop—she had to be brought there." Akira said. "I always worried something bad could happen to her in Tokyo. But now it turns out that the village where I grew up was the real killing field."

"Sugihama is known for fields of rice—not for killing anything. Don't be dramatic, Akira," Mrs. Rikyo chided.

"Mayumi couldn't tell dangerous types from good types." Akira continued speaking in a rush. "Perhaps someone from her Tokyo life followed her here on the eleventh."

"Dangerous types?" I mulled over his phrase. "Whom did she socialize with?"

"Lots of people. She lived near Chiba Station, sharing an apartment with strangers—young people do that in Tokyo," he added to his mother, whose lips were pressed disapprovingly together. "I was lucky that one of my friends here had a cousin in the city. He said I could stay as long as I needed and the rent would be affordable, with all the construction jobs I could get."

Construction was considered a 3K job—*kitanai, kiken,* and *kitsui,* which roughly translated to dirty, dangerous, and demeaning. Because many foreign laborers had been deported in recent years, Akira, who was both a Japanese citizen and had carpentry training, would have been in high demand.

"The police could probably follow up on the people Mayumi knew by looking at her cell phone," Akira said. "If she didn't drown, that would mean her cell phone didn't get flooded, right?"

"I don't know if the searchers recovered a phone." When Akira looked skeptically at me, I added, "I fainted when I saw her. I woke up in a military jeep outside the butcher shop, heading to the bathhouse in Takamachi."

"Her cell phone is in a bright blue Totoro case," Akira said, mentioning the famous cartoon character. "She was still using it in Tokyo. And she always carried a backpack. It was black; she got in on sale at the Coach store."

"That was nice of the military to bring you to a bath," Mrs. Rikyo commented, as if she wanted to end all talk of Mayumi. "Our water service is still running in this house and we have been very grateful for it. In fact, if you need to use the facilities..."

"Thank you very much."

After I'd washed my hands and come out, Mrs. Rikyo ushered me toward the door, handing over Hachiko, who had been lying quietly at her side.

As I retraced my path, my thoughts circled. Akira's mother had been both critical and defensive of her son. This was standard operating procedure for many mothers. But was her attitude toward Mayumi fair? Was it any different than mine had been?

Akira's point about Mayumi's cell phone also gave me something to contemplate. Mayumi could still have had Akira's home phone number stored in her phone or memorized. Trapped in Sugihama without transportation, she might have called that number. If Akira's mother had been on the phone with her daughter, it was unlikely she'd end that call to take one from an unknown number. Or maybe, the phone call that Mrs. Rikyo had engaged in with her daughter hadn't been as long as she said. Somehow, during the process, she could have picked up Mayumi.

I'd thought Mrs. Rikyo was the picture of a cozy-looking homemaker and seamstress. She was even going to make me noodles for lunch. But I'd come away without a meal—and the knowledge that her dislike of Mayumi was needle-sharp.

CHAPTER 22

W hen I made it back to the survivors' shelter, it was past lunchtime. Mr. Ishida was seated on a two-foot-high stool at a child-sized table with a mah-jongg board in front of him and a handful of children clustered around. Judging from the distracted behavior of the children, I could see the lesson was going slowly. They were too accustomed to hand-held, blinking amusement.

Mr. Ishida looked at me reproachfully. "Back at last. I was becoming worried."

"Where is Hachiko?" Miki asked.

"She's just outside the kitchen door resting. Actually, she may need some more water, after our long walk. I don't suppose you have time...."

"Yes! I'll do it!" Miki said, and the other children got up, leaving a clattering mess of discarded mah-jongg tiles. This left Mr. Ishida and me alone for a few minutes. I bent to pick up some scattered tiles. I thought of asking Mr. Ishida if he thought these tiles were bone but decided against it. With plenty of unknown dead trapped into the Tohoku landscape around me, I didn't even want to say anything that made one think of skeletons.

I placed the missing tiles in front of Mr. Ishida, and he scooped them into a small cloth bag. As we repeated the movements, I summarized the conversation at the Rikyos' home. At the end of my recitation, he sharply pulled closed the bag's drawstring.

"So Akira's showing concern. We don't know if it's honest," Mr. Ishida said.

"Or if his mother's being completely truthful about the situation. It seemed clear that she disliked Mayumi."

"If she caused Mayumi's death, she wouldn't want you to know that, would she? She would have behaved more softly and appeared more compassionate," Mr. Ishida said. "I wonder if it was a good idea at all for you to give them the details of the death as you did."

"I'm not sure, either. I hoped to catch their reactions. It was interesting that Akira was all in favor of an investigation, and he raised a point about Mayumi's cell phone probably harboring information. I said I didn't know what happened to her phone. Was a phone ever found?"

"The soldiers checked her pockets for identification, I remember, and they were empty. I described her backpack. They looked around for it, but it wasn't nearby."

"Was it a Coach backpack?"

"I don't know about brands. It had a 1960s style pattern of Cs on the fabric, though."

"Sounds like Coach. Akira's young; he knows the brands. I wonder if more searching would bring it to us..."

"But we really don't know if Mayumi died of unnatural causes.

We must not get ahead of ourselves. It's like counting money in the cashbox before we've sold anything that day."

Mr. Ishida's words about the cashbox reminded me of his empty safe at the shop. What had happened to the Kimura family lacquer? It really could have been a factor in Mayumi's death. Now my thoughts turned away from the Rikyos. A thief could have killed her for it—or even her own parents.

"My hips are tight after sitting on that little stool," Mr. Ishida said, placing his hands on the low table to aid him while he stood. "I'll feel better after *tai chi*. I agreed to teach a beginner's workshop for the shelter residents this afternoon."

Exercise was a good way to cut stress. As I watched Mr. Ishida slowly shuffle out of the room, I considered following him, but I could see Mr. Yano heading my way with a clipboard and an intent expression. Guiltily, I realized he might have come to address the fact that I was continuing to go AWOL from volunteer duty.

"Excuse me for my absence this morning," I began.

"Actually, I wanted to say that I've a message from Petty Officer Oshima, who is working on searches with dogs. He said that because Hachiko did not come again this morning, it's probably better for her not to continue the search training. I hope that's all right with you."

"Ishida-san wanted her to take a walk with me this morning. I'm really sorry. I should make an apology—"

"It's no worry," Yano-san said. "Apparently Ninja doesn't perform as well with the distraction of another canine. And it would be best if the trained military dog is able to work at top level, *neh?*"

I nodded. At least Hachiko had enjoyed lots of hugs, strokes, and acclaim from volunteers and tsunami survivors the day before. It was too much to think she'd find Mayumi's backpack.

"We are running a bus back to the city midafternoon tomorrow. Some volunteers are going home and fresh ones are coming in. You and Ishida-san may want to take advantage of this—otherwise it will probably be four days till we run another transport."

"Thank you, but I'm not sure if we should take that bus," I said. "There are some issues regarding Mayumi's death that aren't resolved. I will talk to Ishida-san about it, though—"

"If anything's unresolved you would surely want to talk to Mayumi's parents. And the timing is good because they're back."

"In Sugihama?"

"Yes. They arrived here about twenty minutes ago. The father is in conference with Mayor Hamasaki. Why don't you see the mother, who stayed out of that meeting because she wanted to be sure to speak with you?"

Feeling anxious, I followed Mr. Yano to an unoccupied classroom that was crowded with boxes of military meals and blankets. Mrs. Kimura was seated on a child-sized chair and had her head bowed as if she was praying or thinking deeply. As we walked through the door, she looked up. Her hair was classic for a middle-aged Japanese woman—a smooth pageboy, black shot through with a little gray that revealed she wasn't afraid of passing years. She was quite attractive; the wide-set eyes, pert nose, and rosebud mouth strongly reminded me of Mayumi's photograph.

As I drew closer and she stood to bow, I caught the scent of death. Mrs. Kimura probably was wearing the same dark-gray pantsuit she'd had on when she viewed Mayumi's body the day before. The combination of the lady's proper appearance and horrible smell was hard to comprehend.

"You must be Shimura-san, who telephoned us. I'm the mother—Kimura Emiko," she said in a soft Tohoku accent. "I came to thank you and Ishida-san for identifying my daughter yesterday. The soldiers wouldn't have known who she was if you hadn't been there."

"It was Mr. Ishida who recognized her clothing. Can we walk outside for a moment? Maybe we will find him practicing *tai chi*. He wants to meet you."

Not only did she need to see him, the wind might blow the death smell away from her a little bit. The few moments we'd spent together were already triggering nausea and horrible memories in me.

"I would like to meet the gentleman who gave our daughter a job," Mrs. Kimura said, following me out the front door to the dismal landscape where wind whipped at a tarp-covered mound of rubble. "And I apologize for missing your telephone call yesterday evening. My husband and I were still going through formalities with the police."

"I wanted to give you some information."

"Really? I heard that you lost consciousness when you saw her. I'm very sorry it was so traumatic." The wind blew hair across her face, and she raised a hand to brush it away. Many small, light scars marred her fingers.

"Please don't worry about me. You must have suffered so much, first thinking that Mayumi was safe in Tokyo during the quake, and then realizing she'd actually come here."

"But I already knew that Mayumi was in Sugihama," Mrs. Kimura said.

"You knew? Ishida-san didn't mention it."

"She'd telephoned me for the first time in six months the day before the tsunami—on March tenth. She told me that she had to come for business travel on the eleventh and that she very much wanted me to meet her."

"Is that so?" I used noncommittal words; but inside, I was extremely startled.

"How I wish I'd heard from her earlier so we could have planned for a meeting. The situation was difficult—on the eleventh we had an important department store buyer coming to our shop and studio to decide which pieces to take," Mrs. Kimura explained. "My husband planned to spend all day showing our lacquer, and also the scenic areas of our town—which meant I needed to manage the shop. My husband was firm about keeping the day's plan in place and not changing things around for Mayumi, who had caused a lot of trouble in her last years home. Therefore, I telephoned Mayumi back and told her we'd be glad to see her at our home that evening, but we could not meet her in Sugihama." She wiped a hand across her eyes. "I made a terrible mistake."

"You couldn't have known what would happen." I consoled her.

"The quake rocked our town very, very hard. Immediately, I knew our daughter was in danger. The buyer who was with my husband had a car, so he departed immediately back toward Tokyo. We found the phone network wasn't working; I called and called but could not reach Mayumi's cell phone."

"What kind of phone did she have, by the way?"

"An iPhone she'd received about six months before leaving. We kept her on the family plan despite everything. You see, I thought if we could talk to each other, the trouble could someday be fixed."

"I'm so sorry," I said. "You mentioned Mayumi causing trouble. She told Ishida-san that she took some of your family's lacquer with her to Tokyo. Do you think her phone call to you was a sign that she wanted to return the lacquer and become part of the family again?"

"She didn't mention the lacquer in her call," Mrs. Kimura said. "I had a hope she hadn't sold it, but I did not want to push things in the conversation. Mayumi seemed upset when I said that I couldn't meet her in Sugihama. She told me she didn't really care, and that she was supporting herself quite well. I didn't know if this meant she'd sold the lacquer already or was receiving enough salary. I didn't want to ask about work—one hears girls do all kinds of things to make a living in the city. All I could think of saying was that I hoped she might somehow be able to visit in the future." Mrs. Kimura twisted her hands; again I noticed the thin, white scars. They made me nervous.

"Actually, I had some extra information," I said. "The thing is, I believe she survived the tsunami."

She gasped. "You don't think that body was Mayumi, then?"

"Sorry. I'm using the wrong words. What I meant to say is that she couldn't have died from drowning. Her coat was white, and we could make out the designs of the buttons on her coat. She would have been blackened with sea water and mud if the wave had touched her."

"Oh. I see." Mrs. Kimura put her face in her hands. "But that's—terrible. It doesn't make sense."

"I'm wondering if the police said anything about how many days ago they think she might have died—because of her body's state of decomposition? I'm sorry. I hate to use such language about your daughter."

"No, they didn't talk about the time or cause of death. They just asked us to sign saying it was her."

"If a forensic autopsy were performed, the truth could emerge about what killed Mayumi. But I have no sway with the police, who are terribly overworked and not prone to look into things closely. If you and your husband requested an autopsy, though, there might be a chance."

Looking back at me, Mrs. Kimura shook her head. "I don't think it's possible. Her body has already been transported to our town, where the funeral will be held followed by cremation. I want to invite you and Ishida-san to the service."

"Thank you. I understand about holding the funeral soon. But after hearing this, could you postpone the cremation, just in case—" I broke off, seeing that Mr. Ishida had come around the shelter wall accompanied by a man I hadn't seen before.

Mr. Kimura was tall for a Japanese person but not thin; he was broad-shouldered and had a thick torso, which looked even bigger because of the black down coat he wore. His eyes could barely be seen because he was squinting against the wind, or perhaps was filled with extreme tension or grief.

Mr. Kimura might have heard that I was American, because he put out his hand to me instead of bowing. As I let his firm, warm hand surround my smaller, colder one, I noticed his fingers bore some of the same markings as his wife's. Suddenly I recalled seeing such scars on someone else. It was in a close-up photograph in a museum of a lacquer artist who was one of Japan's Living National Treasures. The scars were leftovers from lacquer burns to the skin. The oil used for making sticky, shiny lacquer came from the same plant family as poison ivy and sumac. While milder than these infamous plants, it could also cause many skin problems and scarring.

I shook Mr. Kimura's hand and bowed. After introducing myself, I said, "I'm very sorry about your daughter. We really had hoped to find her alive."

"Well, at least there is no more worrying. And Ishida-sensei has reassured me that our daughter lived safely in Tokyo and enjoyed time exploring the art world and working in his shop. You will be interested in that," he added to his wife.

"I explained to your husband that Mayumi-chan was a pleasure to know and great help to me," Mr. Ishida said quietly to Mrs. Kimura. "She was a lovely, brave person. And a most talented artist."

Addressing his wife again, Mr. Kimura said, "Ishida-sensei believes our family lacquer collection might be lost somewhere in this town or else in Tokyo. Unfortunately, the collection is not in the shop safe, but he will search for it when he returns."

"That is kind of you, Ishida-san. The lacquer was very important to us before—but it seems such a superficial thing, now that she's gone." Mrs. Kimura sighed, a soft release of breath that seemed full of sorrow. "Shimura-san mentioned to me a possibility that Mayumi might not have drowned."

"What?" Mr. Kimura was speechless for a moment and then shook his head. "This woman hadn't met our daughter once," he said to his wife, as if I weren't there. "How could she know her? Of course she's dead. We saw her body with the hair, the coat you bought her, and the lacquer buttons she's been making for years—"

"I agree with you that the body was hers," I said, trying to keep my voice low and reasonable-sounding. "But her clothing was clean. I thought about it and realized that if she'd been caught up in a wave, she would have looked much worse. So we don't know why or when Mayumi died."

Mayumi's father was silent for a moment, looking at a ground. Then he looked up and said to Mr. Ishida, "It could have been the earthquake that killed her. Falling down killed several people across the country."

"She was with Ishida-san during the earthquake," I said, looking at Mr. Ishida for support. "She survived that without injury and went outside to look for transportation. She may have briefly returned to the auction house, because we recently found Mr. Ishida's satchel containing his purchases there. She'd carried that bag outside with her when she was looking for a ride."

"Your satchel? What about another bag that might have held our family lacquer?" Mr. Kimura's voice rose to an alarming, angry pitch.

"Mayumi had her backpack that day, which would have had plenty of room for your family treasures," Mr. Ishida said evenly. "The police have a description of the bag, so perhaps it will turn up. We could ask them together or look around some more today."

"We don't have any more time to waste in this town," Mr. Kimura said bluntly. "We need to return home to be ready for tomorrow's funeral and cremation. Relatives are arriving and need our attention."

"Are you sure you want to cremate so early?" I pleaded. "There's still a chance for Mayumi to undergo an examination to determine the cause of her death."

Mr. Kimura took a deep breath, and in my eyes, the six-foot

man appeared to grow in size. He took a few steps toward me with an expression that seemed no longer tense, but furious. Instinctively, I backed up. Then I lost balance; my heel slipped on something. I righted myself, kicking away another dead fish.

"Our daughter died of natural causes, just like more than fifteen thousand people in Japan! There's no reason for detection. This is not *Strawberry Night*."

I felt hot with embarrassment from his mentioning the popular NHK-TV drama from a few years back that starred a cute, young female detective. "I didn't mean to disturb you. I'm very sorry. I don't think it's any sort of detective game."

"Let's go," he said to his wife. "Some soldiers said they could drive us back to the place where we left our car."

"Yes." Her voice faltered. "I was just telling them about the funeral—"

"It's not their business."

I felt myself shuddering, just as Mrs. Kimura was. In a shaky voice she said, "Remember that yesterday we spoke about inviting them—"

"No matter what my wife may have said to you, our daughter's funeral is for family only. None of our family needs any more talk of crimes. Please leave us in our grief."

"I never said crime—" I began.

"We're sorry. Very sorry," Mr. Ishida said over my words.

Mr. Kimura put an arm through his wife's and hustled her out to the mud-covered road.

CHAPTER 23

I didn't need to ask Mr. Ishida whether it was something I said. He'd been right all along. I looked sideways at my mentor and said, "I put my foot in it again."

"I only hope he doesn't take things out on his wife," Mr. Ishida answered.

"Why would you think that?"

"Just a worry. Mayumi once said that his bad temper was another reason that she was glad to leave the house."

Belatedly, I felt a chill of the air on damp skin. I hadn't stopped sweating since Mr. Kimura's *Strawberry Night* insult. "What else did she say about her father?"

"Nothing more. She really wasn't a complainer." He sighed. "On the other hand, Mayumi's father might have spoken so harshly because he is overwhelmed. Yes, his town did not flood, but if the government extends the radiation danger zone into Tohoku, he may lose his home and studio."

I thought again about the bad news continuing to flow out of Fukushima. Michael wouldn't go there, I hoped.

"There's so much to lose right now," I said. "Look at the people we know from the shelter, quietly hoping their loved ones are alive. I feel like Mr. Kimura was incredibly focused on the lacquer collection, not her."

"For some people, though, ancestral treasures are loved in the same way as a family member might be. Such a collection was the root of everything his forebears were—and also formed his own pride and identity," Mr. Ishida said.

"So where do we go from here?" I asked.

"With our invitation to the funeral revoked, I see no reason to stay in Tohoku anymore. If we return home, I can check in with my doctor, get my shop in order, and possibly find the Kimura family lacquer."

We were on the edge of something that was as messed up as the landscape around us. It was hard to leave it alone, just as it was hard not to want to pick up Hachiko's waste, even though the landscape was full of filth. But we couldn't right the situation in Tohoku in another week—or two weeks.

"A bus to Tokyo leaves tomorrow," I told him. "But we should tell Mr. Morioka that we're leaving, just in case someone brings in the Kimura family's lacquer with the mistaken idea it was lost from his store."

"Yes, that's a good idea. And in the meantime I shall continue teaching my *tai chi* class, and you can provide whatever help is needed until the departure."

"I should do something outside. I've been a little too absent from Helping Hands."

"Do not forget that one of our absences led to saving Miki's father," Mr. Ishida reminded me. "And another time, we did identify Mayumi."

"Yes, we did do that. But it feels useless to have shared what we discovered when nothing will come of it."

My black mood held sway throughout lunch and all afternoon, when I joined some volunteers outside for trash separation. Hours later, my back ached from being bent, and I thought it was a good thing that we were leaving the next day. But when I woke up the next morning, my back didn't hurt anymore. I felt fairly rested—though far from relaxed.

Mr. Ishida and I breakfasted on pumpkin snack cakes that I'd bought at the gas station the day before. Soon he would be in his cozy home enjoying bread and jam. In Yokohama, I could enjoy my aunt's homemade miso soup and some pickled vegetables—or, if I stayed in Tokyo, a scone and caffè latte. Everything was possible, now that we were leaving behind the tragedies of Tohoku.

As I stepped out into the chilly morning, dressed in jeans and my fleece jacket, my thoughts turned to Richard's odiferous jacket packed inside two plastic bags. Would the smell of death ever leave it?

Mr. Ishida held Hachiko's leash loosely while she trotted beside us. Her curlicue tail was upraised, and I wondered if she knew that we were almost on our way home.

Sugihama still looked like the disaster zone that it was, but there was now a clear way in and out. Rubble had been heaped alongside the roads, so cars and trucks could pass where there was no access before. Just outside the infamous butcher shop, I saw the Rikyos' carpentry truck.

"I suppose they could be repairing the place," Mr. Ishida said. "It's their town. I'm sure they're working in many places."

Or Akira could be searching for any possibly incriminating evidence. How could we just walk by and never know?

"I'll go in to say goodbye to him," I said to Mr. Ishida. "It doesn't make sense that we would say goodbye to Mr. Morioka but not to Akira."

"That's not the only reason why you want to speak to him, is it?"

"No, it's not."

"Hachiko and I are coming along." Mr. Ishida's voice was firm, and this time, I didn't mind.

The smell was milder than before, but each step I took in the mud was heavy. Like the last time, the dank abattoir was lit by battery-operated lanterns. But this time Akira was the only one on the premises. His back was to the door, so he didn't seem to notice that we'd walked in, even though Hachiko was whining. His back was bent as he vigorously shoveled mud from the room's center toward the edge. Then I saw a thin cord running from his ears into his jacket.

I came around in front of Akira, and he hurriedly stood up and reached a hand into his pocket to click off his electronic device.

"Music makes the work go faster," he said.

"What were you listening to?"

"Taylor Swift. And it's good to take a break. Any news about Mayumi's death?"

Hachiko strained on the leash, but this time she didn't growl. Her curlicue tail was rolling. She whimpered softly.

"She may believe that Mayumi is still here," Mr. Ishida said, holding her leash. "After all, she remembers finding her."

"Oh. Good morning, Ishida-san," Akira said, bowing to him.

"Good morning."

"I can hardly believe that you landed this grim assignment," I said to Akira.

"I wasn't sure I wanted to take it, but my father said we had to. You see, the butcher hired us to replace the floor and redo the walls. But nothing can be done until all the mud's gone, and the other junk."

I tried not to show my indignation. Had the police been concerned about Mayumi's death, they would be the ones raking mud. But they weren't involved—and therefore, the young man who might know something important about the girl's death was in charge of the scene.

"I'm glad you stopped in," Akira said. "You said you fainted when you were in here before, so it must have been hard to come back in. If it's not too upsetting, would you show me where she was found?"

I paused, thinking Akira might know and just be trying to play naive. I looked at Mr. Ishida, who didn't speak, either.

"I'm not sure anymore," I fibbed.

"Okay. I suspect that she was here." Akira followed a trampled line of many footprints to a slight depression. "The mud is rather dry on the surface around this spot," Akira said pointing. "Her body would have kept the mud underneath her damp."

Mr. Ishida's face had a blank expression, the one he used when when he was examining items for sale and didn't want to tip his hand. But we both knew this was where Mayumi had lain.

"We don't know whether she walked in here or was carried in, so I've been looking at footprints. Your feet are large—I noticed that before," Akira said, nodding toward the Merrells I wore.

"It's true," I said. "But looking around here, I can't possibly tell my footprints from anyone else's. So many people came in when Mayumi was recovered."

"Her feet were small and delicate. She usually wore Air Jordans. She fit into one of the larger youth sizes, if I remember right. We bought matching shoes once." Akira's voice was wistful. "I looked for small female shoe prints but didn't notice any. However, look at those."

A single line of widely spaced, large footprints trailed from the back of the shop—a direction quite opposite from that of the searching group. And now I saw a small, gaping opening in the back wall to an alley. This low doorway—like the larger one in front—must have been blown out by the tsunami.

"These footsteps look like a path from the back door taken by a man who walked into the muddy shop after the water had gone down."

Mr. Ishida proceeded with Hachiko to examine the line of footprints and the back wall. I stayed in place to continue the conversation with Akira.

Akira continued, "When I'm carrying a load that's heavy, I move slower, with my feet farther apart. Just like that."

I glanced down at his boots. Timberland was a popular brand in Japan.

"See this?" He dug one foot into the mud between us. "The tread on my boots radiates out from the center. The other shoe or boot's tread is a zigzag."

"I'm not accusing you," I said. "And really, those footprints could have been someone in the search party—"

"Could have been," Akira said. "But everyone else was

together. We just looked at those footprints. Did you ever talk to Mayumi's parents?"

"Yes, we both did." I glanced over at Mr. Ishida, but he was still looking closely at the back door Akira had pointed out to us.

"What was their reaction to you saying she didn't drown?"

I hesitated again. "It's hard to say what they felt. Mayumi's mother seemed to understand, but her father was against the idea of asking the police to conduct an autopsy."

"That sounds like him!" Akira blurted.

"Really? What kind of man is Kimura-san?" Mr. Ishida asked. Without my noticing, he and Hachiko had quietly returned from the building's edge.

"Someone who thinks his decisions are always right. And the truth is that he's quite a sharp businessman. There are plenty of lacquer artists in his town, but he's the one who's managed to become famous. When I was in Tokyo, I recognized his lacquer in the windows of a gallery in the expensive Omotesando district. He even published a book about the family's lacquer history, with photographs of the heirloom pieces and stories about the shoguns and lords who used to commission *netsuke* and *inro* from the family."

"But what is he like as a person?" I pressed.

"I never saw much of him, because he was so angry about us being together. Since we weren't welcome in their house, we met in outside places—usually around here, because her school ended an hour before mine, so she used that extra time to take two trains to get here. Mayumi's mother said that as long as we met in public, it was all right." He shook his head. "They needn't have worried about us getting in trouble. Mayumi didn't really like being touched."

"You must have cared about her a great deal," I said, thinking some boys would have moved on to easier territory.

"I loved her. And I will forever regret scaring her away from Tokyo, since it is here that she died. My cursed town—my fault!" His lower lip trembled.

"She came back here for a work reason," Mr. Ishida corrected him. I looked at him, wondering if he was mellowing. But he walked to the main doorway and stood. He was silently reminding me that we needed to get to Takara Auction House, speak to Mr. Morioka about the family's lacquer collection, and return by early afternoon to get the bus.

"Akira-san, we'll leave for Tokyo tonight," I said. "I hope things get better for you."

"When you go to Tokyo, you could talk to my roommate. Will you do that, please?" His eyes seemed to beg, and I felt confused.

"To talk about what?"

"Ask my friend Abe Toshi about where I was during the tsunami and the days after. He will tell you the truth. And then you will stop looking that way and not telling me everything. I didn't kill her—and I didn't take any lacquer, either."

"No one is accusing you," I said, but he took out his cell phone and read off his friend's number to me, which I wrote down on a receipt I found in my own pocket. Feeling duty-bound to reciprocate, I gave him my own business card, scribbling down the home numbers for my aunt's house and Richard's apartment.

"If you have anything else to tell me, you can try me at these friends' numbers, because I've unfortunately lost my mobile phone."

"Okay. I don't suppose he'll ever stop being angry at me." Akira glanced toward the entryway, where Mr. Ishida was stooped slightly, trying to soothe Hachiko, who was whimpering and straining to return to the butcher shop.

"Ishida-san, perhaps you should let her make one last check of the area," I called out to him. "She might have picked up the scent of something important."

Mr. Ishida shrugged and let the leash slip from his hands. Freed of her owner's hold, Hachiko took a moment to sniff the air on all sides. Then she padded through the mud toward Akira and me. Akira held his ground, but his expression tensed. I had been foolhardy in my directions and now could only hope no attack was imminent.

Hachiko walked straight up to Akira, placing her nose to Akira's muddy leg, sniffing. Then, to my shock, the dog softly licked his hand.

Akira had put his other hand on Hachiko's back and stroked it awkwardly. He looked at me and said, "Unbelievable."

Hachiko nosed his leg again, made a snuffling sound, and then trotted back to Mr. Ishida's side.

"She doesn't mind me anymore," Akira said, sounding as puzzled as I felt.

CHAPTER 24

After saying goodbye, Mr. Ishida, Hachiko, and I walked around the corner and down the block to the Takara Auction House. We had a lot to think about.

"Rikyo clearly wants to be trusted," Mr. Ishida said. "But his point about his boots was nonsensical. How many pairs of boots could a construction worker have? Plenty."

"Actually, the prints could be from men's shoes, not just boots. But I agree."

"I don't want to keep telling people that Mayumi didn't drown," Mr. Ishida said. "The situation with Akira becoming involved is only bringing confusion. However, I do feel strongly that we should pursue the issue of the missing lacquer."

I wasn't sure if I could hold myself to Mr. Ishida's standard of not telling. And finding a handful of tiny *netsuke* and *inro* would be a lot harder than finding a dead body. "All right, but it could be anywhere in the country. With anyone, or stuck in mud—"

"That is not something we can accept. Her parents are

Kimuras—wood people. Those wooden treasures were carved by their ancestors, so they must be returned."

We'd reached Takara Auction House. The entrance now had a new black door fitted in place. I tried turning the knob, but it held fast. I knocked on the door, waited a minute. But there was no response.

"He may be out," I said to Mr. Ishida. "That's why the shop door is locked."

"Oh. Here's a bell. Surely this will bring him downstairs." My mentor pressed the doorbell, "Hello, hello," Mr. Ishida called, looking through the shiny new windows that had filled the open gaps we'd seen on our last visit. Mr. Morioka had been fortunate to have these repairs already done. But the new windows were also a frustration, because they kept us from being heard. I glanced around for anyone who might be able to tell us if Mr. Morioka had gone out, but I didn't see a soul.

"There's one thing I can try." I reached into the inside pocket of my fleece jacket and took out the lock-picking set.

"Oh." Mr. Ishida sucked in his breath. "What interesting tools. Are they for woodworking?"

"No. They can open doors." I selected the medium-sized pick, and with a couple of gentle twists, the door opened.

"Excuse us—we've rudely arrived." Mr. Ishida called out the standard greeting one made whenever entering another's home. The sales room was much better organized than before, which was a good sign, although the lights were still out. As we started toward the staircase, I heard the telltale ringing of a cell phone. It was a cascading shower of bells, which happened to be my ringtone.

Immediately I began hustling off in the direction of the sound.

It seemed to be coming from upstairs. I didn't take the time to kick off my shoes but headed up the wooden staircase and straight through the unlocked door leading to the second floor business office, Hachiko loping along behind me. Just as the bell melody cut off, I spotted the purple-encased mobile phone lying on the center of Mr. Morioka's desk.

How long ago had he found it? Obviously, he'd charged it, because the battery signal appeared to be at 100 percent. And Michael had just rung me.

I was just getting ready to push redial, when heavy, fast footsteps came down from the third floor. Hachiko's hackles rose, and she emitted a low, nasty growl.

Mr. Morioka rushed in, his face reddened. He was holding a section of broken wood. Either he'd been in the process of repairing something or had grabbed it up as a self-defense weapon.

"Sorry!" I began apologizing as the auction house owner paused, taking in the sight of Hachiko. His jaw unclenched, and he blinked his eyes.

"I'm—I'm sorry, too. I reacted very quickly. I thought you were thieves!" Morioka-san lowered the piece of wood. "My door was locked."

"Not quite all the way," I said quickly, because Mr. Ishida was coming up the staircase, and I didn't want him to volunteer anything about my interesting tool set. Technically, I had broken and entered.

"But why would you come into a closed shop?" Mr. Morioka asked. "I am not yet reopened for business. But will be soon."

"We sincerely apologize for alarming you," Mr. Ishida said. "But we really wanted to see you, and it didn't seem that the doorbell was working. We had to let you know about some recent developments."

"And then I heard my telephone," I added. "I thought it was lost forever. Thank you so much for finding it."

"Ah, it's yours? That's good news. I considered bringing it to the police, but then I thought they would tell me it is a lost cause. The streets are full of lost mobile phones. Because this one had foreign calls coming in, I assumed it belonged to one of the big city antique dealers who came."

"And you had the right charger for it. What a coincidence."

"Those iPhones are popular in Japan, too," he said. "Ishida-san, what is the news?"

"Unfortunately, it is confirmed that my former apprentice, Kimura Mayumi, passed away. Her family knows, and we are returning to Tokyo today."

Mr. Morioka's expression grew very serious. "I see. I'm very sorry for your loss. I know you will miss her very much. It's a hard time for everyone, but at least now her family and friends won't worry she's lost."

His words were well-intended, but I certainly didn't feel closure. I couldn't explain about Mayumi not drowning because of Mr. Ishida's recent request not to divulge details. Quietly, I said, "Thank you. And please tell me where and when you found my phone. I thought I'd never get it back."

"Let's see—it was yesterday, as I continued cleaning downstairs. It must have fallen when you were looking at some papers. It's quite fortunate you stopped by to retrieve it. Let me give you a cup of tea."

As Mr. Morioka went to the kitchen to fill his kettle with water, Mr. Ishida and I settled on *zabuton* cushions close to the kerosene heater. I sent a *got my phone back—more later* text to Michael. Mr. Ishida patted Hachiko, who now wanted to leave the room and return downstairs. All morning, the dog had been confusing me.

As tea preparations continued, I scrolled through my phone's text messages, e-mails, and phone calls. They were marked with the bright blue bullet that signaled unread. And there must have been one hundred of them.

Most of the communications were from Michael, either details of his travel itinerary or pleas for me to leave a message about my whereabouts. In an increasingly serious tone, Michael reported that Richard and various relatives were all concerned not to have gotten any calls, e-mails, or texts from me. Not to mention himself.

I felt awful.

"All caught up?" Mr. Morioka asked when he emerged from the kitchen carrying a lacquer tray that held the teapot, three Imari cups, and a matching small plate of Koala March cookies.

"Not quite," I said. "But I've got a long bus ride in a few hours. I'll try to respond to every message."

"Mayumi ate those cookies every day," Mr. Ishida said, sounding wistful as he accepted a small, bear-shaped cookie. "I suggested she choose fruit sometimes, or her teeth were in danger of rotting."

A picture of Mayumi's rotted face flashed into my mind. I shut my eyes tightly, willing it away; when I opened them, I saw both men looking worriedly at me.

"Sorry," I apologized. "I'm still feeling some stress. But it turns out that my husband has just arrived in Japan. Now we can see each other."

"I look forward to finally meeting him." Mr. Ishida turned back to Mr. Morioka. "You made the tea in your kitchen today—instead of on the kerosene heater. Does this mean your gas line works?"

"No gas yet. But the electricity is on in this section of town—and I have an electric stove."

"But the doorbell wasn't working, was it? And the lights weren't on downstairs," I pointed out.

"The doorbell is new; the circuit hasn't yet been connected. I will turn on the lights when the shop reopens, which may be tomorrow."

"Wait—I thought this was an auction house. You're also a shop?" I asked.

"Well, I know that people returning to their homes badly need furniture. Antiques are not the first choice for simple local people, but I have a number of chests and tables and even ceramic hibachis they can use for burning wood or coal. They won't be as fussy about small damages to furniture, given the dire situation. Now I can finally attract them as customers."

"Is that so?" Mr. Ishida's words were noncommittal, but I wondered if he was remembering post-war Japan, when black marketers had exploited the population by charging exorbitant fees for food, matches, blankets, and the like. "Speaking of buying and selling, there's something I want you to know about."

"Of course."

"When Mayumi died, there's a chance she was carrying something valuable that could still be found. That's why we came today—to let you know to look out for some special pieces of lacquerware that might come to you in upcoming weeks or months."

"Or that you might hear about someone else selling," I added.

"Of course. What kind of lacquer?" He leaned forward attentively.

"These are small lacquerware treasures from her family's personal collection."

"I don't know her family, I'm afraid."

Mr. Ishida said, "Her father is a well-known local lacquer artist: Shosuke Kimura."

Mr. Morioka scratched his cheek. "I may have heard of him somewhere, but I'm not aware of his style. What are the pieces like?"

"I'm talking about antique pieces crafted by family ancestors. They are mostly Edo period with some Meiji and Taisho. I recall an extremely fine black *netsuke* and *inro* set with a golden crane design. Also, a cat *netsuke* and mouse-shaped *inro* set; a red lacquer memento box ornamented with ducks, and another *netsuke* and *inro* set with a grasshopper in gold leaf on a silver lacquer setting..."

As Mr. Ishida recited details, Mr. Morioka took notes on a legal pad. I listened, thinking that the collection went far beyond Mr. Ishida's description of "very valuable." It sounded like museum quality.

I stared into my cup of green tea, thinking. Mr. Ishida had clued in Mayumi about the lacquer's tremendous value. If she sold to anyone in Tokyo, he would likely hear about it. However, if she sold the goods to someone whom Mr. Ishida didn't know—who was based in another part of Japan—she might get away with it. Was Sugihama too close to her home to pull it off, though?

Not if she was selling to someone who'd arrived in Sugihama for the auction and was returning to another place entirely. Again,

I wished for the list of auction attendees—the list Mr. Morioka said was lost.

"One last question. Are you sure these family pieces were lost in my shop?" Mr. Morioka's voice broke into my thoughts.

"Not at all," Mr. Ishida said. "The last place I saw them was in Tokyo—in fact, I was keeping them safe for her to return to her parents. But there's a chance she brought them here, initiating the return herself."

"I will look out for them. If someone brings any in wishing to sell, I will certainly telephone you straight away. In any case, the parents should have insurance covering the items' damage or loss. Are they making a claim?"

"I didn't ask if they had special insurance for the lacquer." Mr. Ishida paused, and I imagined he was thinking that the Kimuras probably hadn't bought a special policy. To them, the lacquer collection was personal, not a collection worth hundreds of thousands of dollars.

"You've been very kind to see us before leaving," Mr. Ishida said.

"Yes. And I realize that I came up here without stopping to take off my shoes—I'm really sorry," I added. "I'd be happy to sweep off the stairs or something, before we go."

"Of course not! Those stairs are still dirty. Don't worry at all," Mr. Morioka reassured me.

Only six of us, including Hachiko, boarded the early-afternoon bus for Tokyo. I was concerned about the future of the cleanup project, but Yano-san assured me a full load of city volunteers would be getting on board as we stepped off.

With few outbound passengers, there was plenty of room to spread out; even Hachiko got her own seat. But I felt bittersweet about leaving because of how the goodbye had gone with Miki.

"You shouldn't take Hachiko. My father needs to see her. And she'll miss me." Miki had resisted when I'd tried to give her a hug.

"Yes, she will miss you," I'd said, bringing Hachiko forward for some more petting. "But you and your family can always come to Tokyo someday to see her and Ishida-san. And maybe, when you're a young lady, you can fly to Hawaii and meet me."

"Miki-chan, they must go," Sadako Haneda had pleaded. "Please don't make them late."

In fact, our bus had left twenty minutes past schedule because of the number of shelter children who needed to say goodbye to Hachiko. But eventually, it pulled off.

The bus had a powerful heater; it was the coziest place I'd been since the Takamachi bathhouse. I unzipped my jacket, knowing that seven or eight hours of heat stretched ahead. Mr. Yano had explained that the ride might be slightly longer, because the nuclear danger zone had expanded to a greater area that included some stretches of freeway. Again, I thought of Michael; my texts to him were going unanswered. How I hoped he was all right; that I wouldn't lose him to the radiation. It was an unfathomable idea until I considered that so many people in Sugihama and Yamagawa had suddenly perished. Michael's first wife had died, too. He never wanted to talk about it, but it had been a man-made disaster that had shaken the world's conscience for a while. Then it was forgotten by almost everyone, except the loved ones left behind.

How warm the bus was. If I closed my eyes, I could pretend I was lying out on a sunny Hawaiian afternoon. But I kept my eyes open as I went through all the messages and e-mails on my telephone, and began returning them. I texted Richard and Aunt Norie about my forthcoming arrival; sent e-mails to my people in Hawaii about the construction project; and after phoning and getting no answer, texted a heartfelt note to Michael about how much I'd missed him. I also remembered to text Toshi, the friend Akira had asked me to contact. I wasn't sure what to say but eventually came up with something about meeting Akira in Tohoku and wanting to bring Toshi a message from him.

Moments later, Toshi's return text came. Blessedly, it was in a mix of simple *hiragana* and *katakana* characters. He asked if I could meet him at seven the next evening in Ueno. He'd mentioned a place, Summer Grass, that I hadn't heard of. A quick browser search gave me an address near Ueno. I answered that I'd see him there.

Across the aisle from me, Mr. Ishida was asleep, his white head resting against a sweater he'd folded against the window. I looked around and it seemed everyone—Hachiko included—had entered the land of nod.

My desire to let go of everything—all the tensions, unsolved questions, and sadness—overtook me. I made a pillow out of my backpack and let the bus's motion take me to the place where my fellow travelers had already gone.

I dreamed I was in Hawaii, snorkeling with Michael at Hanama Bay. As I slowly kicked my way across the warm water, I saw bright fish flicker beneath me. But they weren't ordinary fish, they were lacquered ones, as beautiful as the buttons that Mayumi had painted. I was slowly pursuing a fish that had swum out of view after Michael had pointed at it. Somehow I knew this was the most important one.

"Wake up, wake up! Welcome back to Tokyo. Don't forget anything you brought, please."

After hours of rest, Mr. Yano's voice was disorienting. We'd made it back to the Roppongi garage where the journey had started. I saw several dozen new volunteers dressed for work lined up near a mountain of duffel bags.

"But we are not leaving for several hours." Mr. Yano sounded surprised. "I don't know why these people have come early. And I was expecting twenty people; this looks like double the number."

"At least the line isn't as long as the one for Disneyland," I said.

I put Mr. Ishida's plastic bag containing his few possessions on my arm while he concentrated on leading Hachiko off. She took the steps down the bus carefully, and as she alighted on the clean cement, made a yawning sound as if she was relieved to be back in the familiar city.

"Rei-san, over here!"

Hearing a familiar masculine voice, I glanced at the thick line of waiting volunteers and was startled to see my cousin Tom standing close to the front with his hospital friend, Nurse Michiko Tanaka. Tanaka-san wore the same clothes she'd worn volunteering the week before, but completely clean. Tom was dressed in an emerald-colored down jacket, crisp blue jeans, and thigh-high wading boots. The ballcap on his head had the emblem of the San Francisco Giants. He didn't look like a doctor at all.

"You must be very tired from your long week of service, Shimura-san," Nurse Tanaka said. "And Ishida-san, it's very good to see you finally returning home. Yano-san sent me an e-mail with the information about your apprentice being found. I'm very sorry."

"Thank you," Mr. Ishida said, bowing his head.

"Are you two going on the trip together—or did Tanaka-san just come to say hello and goodbye?" I asked.

"The Sendai hospital contacted all the Tokyo hospitals asking for temporary physician assistance. I will be working at both the injured persons' shelter in Yamagawa and a community hospital in Sendai. Nurse Tanaka was also approved for temporary duty. Before, she had to take vacation—but this time, it is no problem."

"I appreciate your help arranging that situation," Miss Tanaka said, blushing. I suspected the two might be excited about the trip for more than altruistic reasons. I was glad. Tom had taken entirely too long to find a serious girlfriend.

"Tom-kun, if I'd known you were coming, I would have warned you to bring a lot of food for breakfasts—nobody cooks breakfast for volunteers," I explained. "And I hope that you have enough tissue for the *potu*—"

"I know!" Tom said hurriedly. "Michiko-san explained the hygiene situation, and my mother has packed enough breakfasts to feed a whole bus. Which reminds me, Mother expects you to sleep at our home in Yokohama tonight. Do you think you can manage the train journey? Everything's running on time, but it's close to rush hour."

"I'll be on my way," I promised. "Right after I drop off Ishida-san and Hachiko."

CHAPTER 25

After the ride in from Tohoku, the forty-five-minute journey to Yokohama was quick. It felt like a dream to disembark just after nine p.m. from the cocoon of the train out into a suburb where street and shop lights glowed and cars and buses waited patiently for late-arriving commuters. Shiny bikes, motorcycles, and scooters moved smoothly through unobstructed streets. People clad in light spring clothing walked home, many of them texting or chatting into cell phones. Tulips bloomed gaily in pots set outside shops and houses. On Aunt Norie's hilly street, the plum trees were in full, ballerina-like bloom.

I slid open the unlocked door and gently called out my arrival. Soft lights glowed from tables and ceilings, and the air was scented with sauteed ginger and onion. The big-screen TV in the dining room was showing a news story about panda bears. I exchanged my grimy boots for cheerful tartan slippers decorated with an embroidered ribbon that said "Happy Hearts."

Aunt Norie rushed out of the kitchen and threw her arms

around me. "It was too long until you texted me. How could you be that way?"

"I'm very sorry. Remember, in that text, I explained that I lost my phone for several days."

"At least Tom heard some things from that nice Tanaka-san," she said. "Tanaka-san told him that you found Ishida-san on the first day there. You could have come back straight away."

"It's a long story."

"And our Michael-san was here in this house for one night—but now is gone away. He knew just as little as we did. Your husband deserves more respect." My aunt talked nonstop while leading me into the little laundry alcove that was just off the first-floor bathroom. "I imagine everything in your duffel and backpack is filthy. But what's in that plastic bag you're carrying? Is it waste?"

"A down coat and some jeans and a sweater. I'm not even sure that cleaning will save them. The laundry service in Tohoku couldn't get rid of the odor."

"We will try my special detergent," Aunt Norie said, tipping the contents of a blue bottle into the washing machine.

"Attack," I translated the characters on the label. "That sounds extreme."

"Yes. Each pellet contains microbugs that eat dirt. If it doesn't clean it well the first time, I will try again. But I won't start the washing machine until you've showered and bathed."

"Bugs?" That had to be an exaggeration. I dropped the remaining soiled clothes into the high-end, fuzzy-logic Samsung washing machine. "And I really have tried to reach Michael. I don't know why I haven't heard anything back from him."

Aunt Norie handed me a towel to wrap around myself while

I took off my underwear. "You won't hear from Michael. Like a maniac, he went to Fukushima two days ago. I can't get through to him either. The telephone reception between here and there is terrible."

I froze in place. Michael's old texts had said nothing about Fukushima. Instead, he'd mentioned an airbase. Aunt Norie might be wrong. How I hoped she was.

"He texted that he was going to be in Misawa for a few days—"

"Yes, he was leaving with some military people to fly onto ships on the Fukushima Coast. What do you think of his travel plan?"

Picking up a bottle of Kanebo shampoo to take with me into the shower, I said, "I'm certainly concerned if Michael went to Fukushima. Even if the latest fix on those reactors is working, radiation takes a while to subside in the environment. Like months or even years—"

"I think so. But if all the international people work together, an answer will be found. Now, let's take care of you." Aunt Norie's voice was cheerful as she handled me a small bucket and ladle, necessary equipment for a Japanese shower.

"Be sure to wash your hair several times. And every single bit of skin. I don't want to hurt your feelings, but there's a strange smell. I hope Tsutomu doesn't return with this same odor. What is it?"

Death, I thought of saying, but knew it was too much.

I made sure to wash four times in the shower before lifting the lid off the square, steel-lined soaking tub. Inch by inch, I slowly lowered myself into the steamy water. It felt like being poached. I thought of the bubbling reactor, the radiation washing into the ocean, and perhaps into my husband, too. Even if Michael left Fukushima tomorrow, the radiation exposure could haunt him. What would be the long-term outcome? How ironic if this new job of his—the so-called think tank—would turn out to be more dangerous to his health than serving in the military and the CIA had ever been.

I stepped out of the bath a half hour later, unable to tolerate any more heat. I felt very clean, but I was tired. I only had the appetite to eat a bit of fluffy white rice and seaweed salad, just two of the many dishes that my aunt had prepared. I could not bear to taste the grilled mackerel after all the rotted fish I'd encountered in Tohoku.

Frowning, my aunt began putting away the leftovers and sent me to bed in Chika's empty bedroom. I lay gratefully down on a soft futon and turned out the light. Before I knew it, though, my phone was ringing.

"Shimura-san, are you awake?" It was Mr. Ishida.

"Yes, of course, Ishida-san." Stifling a yawn, I checked the time on the phone's screen. Seven thirty. I was finally on Japanese time.

"Sorry to have called this early, but I didn't want to miss you."

"Is it about the store?" I asked. "Did you find many things stolen?"

"Not exactly... but too much is in the wrong place. An earthquake couldn't have moved things from one side to another."

"Are you calling the police?"

"I haven't decided. But can you come by the shop this morning? Hopefully, you're not too busy."

"Michael's still out of town, so I have no plans." I warmed to the idea. "I'll just have a quick breakfast here and then meet you.

I could help you look through the shop. You've probably noticed I didn't touch a lot of the mess before going to Tohoku."

"I'm sure you left things so I could inspect for inconsistencies, which was a good idea," he said. "Already I've looked through everything, hoping to find Mayumi's family lacquer somewhere in the shop. But it really seems gone."

"I see."

"I've been thinking about the possibility of a professional burglar. If such a thing happened, it could perhaps be a factor in her death."

"Hmm. If the thief thought she knew his identity, maybe he followed and killed her?" The prospect seemed convoluted, but it couldn't be ignored.

"That's my first thought. But I don't want to forget about checking Mayumi's apartment to see if the lacquer is there."

"Do you know where she lives?"

"Yes. I dropped her there one evening by taxi. I know the building and watched her go into a second-floor door."

"Do you think her roommates are likely to be at home on a Thursday morning?" I was skeptical, knowing that most Japanese left for work early.

"Sure. They're neat."

I didn't get it. "She told you they were tidy?"

"Oh, no. N-E-E-T." Mr. Ishida enunciated four letters in English. "It is one of those modern slangs. Not engaged in employment, education, or training."

I chuckled. "And these NEETs can afford a Tokyo apartment?"

"Technically, it's Chiba City."

Chiba was known for its busy shipping port and Japan's busiest international airport, Narita. Real estate here was increasingly popular, as it was relatively cheap and an easy train ride into Tokyo. Because of Ishida Antiques's northeastern Tokyo location, the journey to Mayumi's neighborhood was about sixteen minutes.

The time was ten a.m. when we got off the Chiyoda Line. The commuters had departed, so it was easy to take a good look around. The neighborhood seemed tidy and safe, although the beige midrise building that Mr. Ishida had identified as Mayumi's seemed to sag in its position midway along the block. It wasn't a matter of construction. But the place hadn't been painted for a decade or so, and grime and mildew had focused on a few patches.

The building had outdoor stairways that went directly to each apartment's door. I heard Mr. Ishida's regular breathing as he followed me up. I was pretty tired, too, by the time we reached the sixth floor. Ringing the bell, I said between deep breaths, "Are you sure you want me to do the talking?"

"It's probably better. You are of the same generation."

The apartment door opened a few inches. The chain was still on, so I could only see a sliver of a young female face. A reddened eye bearing residue of both mascara and sleep blinked at us.

"Hello," I said, smiling and bobbing my head slightly. "We've come about Mayumi-san."

"She's not here. She's been away since the earthquake." The girl's husky voice had the sound of someone ready to end the conversation.

"Yes, we know she's been gone—"

The reddened eye widened. "Is she okay?"

I gave Mr. Ishida a look that said, *please take it from here.* He cleared his throat. "The fact is, we have some news about what happened to her. But it's serious. I'm sorry—is it possible for us to come inside and explain?"

"Who's that talking? Is a man with you?" The girl's voice was suspicious, and I realized that Mr. Ishida was not in clear view.

"Yes. I'm Mayumi-san's old employer," Mr. Ishida said, shifting into the space where the door opening was. "My name is Ishida Yasushi. You were speaking with the person who worked with me a bit before Mayumi did. She's called Shimura Rei."

"Okay, I've heard of you," the girl said, unchaining the door and stepping back so we could walk inside. "I hope she's still got her job."

Glancing around, I understood why she'd been reluctant to open the door. The roommate was still in a fuzzy blue robe tied over checked pajama pants. The small apartment was messy, with papers and clothes strewn everywhere. The walls were painted in chaotic-looking streaks of chartreuse, gold, and black. Posters of art shows and concerts were taped up here and there. I squinted, shocked to see an old ceramic urinal leaning against one wall. Another young woman was bent over it, doing something mysterious that I couldn't discern. The floor was covered with old *tatami* mats stained with paint and who knew what else. I wondered the last time the landlord had come around. Maybe he didn't care because he knew he'd get a large security deposit back when they left.

"We're artists." The girl who answered the door confirmed my suspicion.

"Oh. What's your name? Are you a painter?" I guessed, looking at the walls.

"I go by Glock. I specialize in graffiti. Eri-kun paints *benki*."

"Urinals?" I repeated in disbelief.

The other one, Eri, turned her head to address us. "I appropriate masculine vehicles for female purposes. What do you think of that?"

"How interesting," I said, thinking the comment had been aimed at Mr. Ishida, who was nodding as if the art wasn't strange at all. I walked closer and saw the urinal was being painted with cartoonish pink and purple princesses. It was nothing I'd ever collect.

"Can you just tell us what's going on with Mayumi? It's rude of her not to call and tell us, don't you think?" Glock put on a pair of smudged eyeglasses that were lying lenses down on a table and regarded us. They were Lennon-style glasses, not the most flattering.

"That's why we came," Mr. Ishida said. "We are wondering if Mayumi told you where she was going, the day of the earthquake."

"That morning, she said she was going to be out all day," Glock said. "I didn't think anything strange was going on, but when the earthquake hit that afternoon, I was worried and tried to reach her. I got no answer on her phone—and then she didn't get in that night."

"We'd hoped it was because the subway was closed, and that she stayed overnight at your shop. You have an apartment upstairs, right?" Eri said.

Mr. Ishida nodded. "The thing is, I was out of town. I just returned."

"Well, where did she go?" Glock cried. "Just tell us!"

"Don't worry," Eri chided. "If she was hurt, we would have heard."

"Actually, she did get hurt," I ventured. "Mayumi went to Tohoku, where Mr. Ishida was on business."

"But that's where the tsunami was!" Glock wailed.

"When Shimura-san joined me in Tohoku, we looked for her." Mr. Ishida's voice was soft. "But I'm sorry to say that she had died."

"Died." Glock sat down on a worn *tatami* mat and put her head in her hands.

Something about the clumsy way Glock moved made me think she might be drunk or high. And the other girl was strange, too. She had turned away from us and resumed painting the urinal.

"Her parents are holding a private funeral today, followed by cremation. You would have been invited, I'm sure, if they'd known about you. But they didn't know much about her Tokyo life," Mr. Ishida said.

"I can't believe it. I cared about her, and she was such a talented artist." Glock sniffed, as if she'd started to cry. "Did you know about her talent, Ishida-san? I know she just sold things in your shop."

"I understood she had tremendous artistic gifts," Mr. Ishida said. "Artists need enough for food and shelter in order to work. That is why I hired her."

"Did Mayumi seem frightened of anyone?" I asked. "Did anything strange happen in the weeks or days before she left?"

"Not really. Although she had a boyfriend from a year ago who followed her here and was always nagging her to return home to the countryside—as if she'd ever go." Glock rolled her red eyes upward.

"That sounds like someone we've met. What else do you know about him?" I asked, feeling uneasy.

"He was a carpenter and worked jobs around the city. He used to wait around on the street and often called and sent her texts. Before she blocked his calls, I saw some of these texts. He kept saying he loved her and thought if she stayed here terrible things would happen. And then he stopped coming around, although she sometimes saw him in the neighborhood where she worked."

This pretty much lined up with what Mr. Ishida had noticed. I asked, "Did Mayumi tell you what kind of terrible things he predicted would happen?"

"She never told me anything specific," Glock answered after a pause. "Mayumi was just annoyed. She wanted to cut herself off from everyone in her past."

"She didn't really cut herself off, did she?" Eri interjected. "It was her mother's birthday a few weeks ago, and she was anxious about whether to call or not. She did call her and was crying in the bathroom afterward."

"Did she tell you about their conversation?" Mr. Ishida asked.

"Yes. Apparently her father got on the line and shouted that she needed to bring something back to them. He's a mean bastard." Eri's voice was cold.

"How mean?" I asked.

Eri shrugged.

"Her father wanted her to work like a dog in his studio learning lacquer his way," Glock said fiercely. "He didn't appreciate that she wanted to make modern art with lacquer. And she was really talented."

"How long was she living here with you?"

"Nine months," Eri said. "So we'll have to find a new roommate. Get rid of all her stuff. That will be hard."

"Perhaps we can help," I said. "Will you show me where she kept her things?"

The second room was no tidier than the first. Glock and Eri slept on narrow futons that they'd unsurprisingly left out for the day. Mayumi's was rolled up and put in the sliding-door closet that ran along one wall. I opened one door and peered in to see plenty of boxes, suitcases, and a box fan. Mayumi's worktable was also in this room. It was a basic melamine model covered with newspaper and an array of jars, a cup of brushes, and endless tiny containers of various pigments. There were also a few pairs of work gloves and an artist's sketchbook of drawings, many of them filled in with colored pencils.

"It's hard to do lacquerwork in a bedroom. There can be strong smells," I said.

"True. We didn't want to inhale those odors while we were doing our work in the other room, so Mayumi worked in here and kept the windows open and used the fan. She only made art a few hours each week, because she was at your shop a lot." Glock looked reproachfully at Mr. Ishida.

On the table, thirty buttons were laid out, all with different raised designs that were all exquisitely tiny and detailed. And what images: faces, flowers, geometric shapes, and swimming fish. I'd dreamed about lacquered fish; here they were.

Mr. Ishida gently picked up a button. "Not finished, but already so beautiful."

"What do you think?" Glock asked me.

"I've never seen any buttons as beautiful. A high-end fashion designer would swoop on them. You could take a very simple, monotone garment and make it spectacular with these buttons."

"Yes, she was really ready to go into the big time. But her father wanted her to work for years doing little jobs—dropping rice husks to make patterns and other old-fashioned techniques. He said she needed five more years of practice before she would be allowed to paint the smallest flower on any lacquer piece that he'd sell."

"Lacquer apprenticeships can last ten years," Mr. Ishida said. "It seems tedious, but that is the way of most skilled artisans. But Mayumi did not want to be told what to do."

"How do *you* know what Mayumi wanted?" Glock shot back.

Glock probably didn't believe that Mr. Ishida could know because he was old and the opposite gender. I thought about telling her what a great friend he'd been to both Mayumi and me, but that would have embarrassed my mentor.

"I know a little of her feelings because we talked about it," Mr. Ishida said quietly. "But I didn't know she'd called her mother. I would have supported her traveling home anytime. Then she wouldn't have gone to Sugihama when she did."

I was still for a moment, feeling everyone's sorrow, but then recalled the visit's purpose. "Would you mind if we packed Mayumi's things to bring to her family?"

"I suppose that's okay. I couldn't do it myself." Glock shook her head, making a single crucifix earring shake.

Mayumi had kept all her clothes in three small plastic bins. I felt sad folding up her tiny wardrobe of jeans, T-shirts, and sweaters. Her socks and underwear were plain cotton and appeared worn from many washings. She possessed what seemed more like two weeks' worth of clothing than the wardrobe of someone who'd lived in the city for almost a year. Clearly, she hadn't gone shopping for any new or fashionable clothes since her arrival.

From the futon closet, Glock dragged out Mayumi's Samsonite

hard-shell suitcase. I packed it up with the clothing, toiletries, and the sketchbook and asked for a plastic bag to hold the lacquer buttons. Whether or not we found the antique lacquer, we still had Mayumi's own lacquer to give her parents.

"What about any other lacquerware? Maybe pieces she owned, but hadn't made?" Mr. Ishida asked Glock.

"I don't think so, but she's got some dishes in the kitchen area. You could look there."

Mr. Ishida headed into a small galley section of the room and began opening and closing cupboards. I followed him, noting dead insects and a pathetic assortment of plastic bowls and leftover take-out food containers. After that search was finished, he said to me, "Well, this must be it. I will bring the first bags we've assembled downstairs."

"Is there a place where she kept valuables she was worried about being stolen?" I asked, knowing this was the only chance to find anything in the apartment.

"What are you getting at?" snapped Eri, who was still painting away. "Are you really looking out for her—or are you here to take advantage?"

"I'm looking for some of her family's property—and if you don't believe me, you could certainly call them," I answered. "Here's my card, with my number. And I'll put their information on it, too."

"What property?" Glock asked as I scribbled.

"Did Mayumi ever talk to you about antique family lacquerware—or show you anything fine? Specifically, *inro* and *netsuke?*"

The girls exchanged glances and were silent.

"You did hear something—"

"Yeah, he took it from her." Eri looked accusingly at Mr. Ishida. Mr. Ishida's face flushed red. "I was keeping it safe!"

"Well, whatever the situation, it wasn't here," Glock said. "You saw what she had in her closet. Almost nothing."

Despite the harsh words delivered against Mr. Ishida, I felt grateful to both girls for having let us in to search, so I told them that. Eri sniffed and turned back to her painting, but Glock helped me move the heavy suitcase downstairs and out to the street, where Mr. Ishida was trying to hail a cab.

"I hope it's not too hard for you to make the April rent payment with Mayumi gone," I said as we reached the ground floor.

"Not really." Glock's voice was hard. "Eri could easily pay that whole portion because of her side job."

"What's the side job?" I asked.

"*Enjo-kousai.* I think it's disgusting."

The slang term she'd used meant "compensated dating," a contemporary custom in which older men gave money or gifts to younger women—especially teenaged girls—in exchange for their company. One could look at it as a very downscale, modern version of the geisha-patron relationship.

"But you two don't seem to—" I wanted to finish by saying they didn't appear to like men, but I realized that was unfair. They might have just been reacting to Mr. Ishida, since they'd believed he'd taken Mayumi's lacquer.

"Eri meets a lot of men in hotels and restaurants and clubs. She puts up with them because she needs the money." Glock shrugged. "If someone's really awful, she gets revenge by painting his likeness at the bottom of one of her urinals."

"Do the guys ever show up to the apartment?"

"Yes, if they have cars."

If Akira had been watching, and seen a number of men going to Mayumi's apartment door, he might have been upset. Especially if Mayumi ever went along.

"What about Mayumi? Did she have to do a little *enjo-kousai* as well to make the rent payment and save for art school?"

"No!" Glock's red eyes blazed behind the round Lennon glasses she wore. "I mean, she had to talk to them every now and then if they came by—I did, too—but she didn't date."

I considered going back into the apartment to ask Eri more about this, but she was a lot less friendly than Glock. I decided to play it cool. "Well, if you ever think of anything more—maybe one of Eri's friends who paid a little too much attention to Mayumi—would you let me know?"

"Okay. You gave Eri your name card, right?"

I reached into my purse, got out another card, and pressed it into her hand. Mr. Ishida had flagged down a white Mercedes taxi and was beckoning with one hand for me to join him. I said goodbye to Glock and made it down with the remaining luggage.

As I approached the taxi, its trunk lid floated upward. I readied myself to put the suitcase in, but the driver came around to take it from my work-chapped hands into his white-gloved ones.

"Thank you very much." I was still flustered by the niceties of a functioning city. As I settled onto the seat next to Mr. Ishida, I felt my mobile phone vibrate against my hip. I reached for it eagerly; this time I wouldn't miss Michael.

It wasn't a call, but a text from a blocked number. *Hiragana* characters, with the exception of the *kanji* character for "water." Putting it all together, I read:

Water washes the past away. Stop asking questions or you'll pay for it!

This was a rather infamous proverb. Politicians liked to use it in place of apologizing for atrocities. But with the tsunami, the mention of water seemed especially pointed. Not to mention the bold threat that came right after. What did it mean, that I'd pay for it?

CHAPTER 26

Abruptly I turned to look out the taxi's rear window. Immediately behind was a TEPCO utility truck. A Nissan Tilda moved slowly in the lane along the taxi's right side; its driver was a young mother shouting at her two young children strapped into booster seats. Another car was behind the Tilda, but I couldn't discern anything about its occupants.

"Did you forget something at the apartment?" Mr. Ishida asked, watching my movements.

My first thought was that Eri or Glock had sent the warning. But I didn't want to say anything until I'd figured out who sent it for sure. So I improvised. "I don't know this area. I'm curious to look around."

"Yes, whenever we ride the subway, it's convenient—but we miss seeing the world. You have probably never traveled by taxi to my shop. It's a very interesting journey." Softly, he let out his breath. "It's almost like old times, having you here. I feel a good five years younger."

"My aunt packed a nice lunch for us," I said, relieved to have steered the conversation back to safer ground. "I left it in the shop refrigerator, so we can eat it when we return. Then we could reopen the shop for business."

"A good plan," he agreed. "And you being there will also give me the chance to take Hachiko for her walk."

Hachiko was waiting for us, nose pressed to the shop's glass window, when we came back. She barked joyfully and let herself be petted by Mr. Ishida while I unpacked the lunch. Fortunately, it wasn't the type of food that would attract a dog. Aunt Norie had filled a bento box with containers full of delicious vegetarian items. There was steamed chard with soy and sesame seeds, vegetable-fried rice, and spicy fermented daikon root. She'd included *mikan* oranges and two packages of almond wafer cookies that we savored at the end, along with cups of Mr. Ishida's best green tea.

After we'd rinsed off the dishes, I turned on the lights in the front and hung the blue *noren* curtain outside, signifying Ishida Antiques was open for business. A few hours passed without anyone stopping in. I realized that a two-week closing might have convinced people the shop was permanently shut.

As I dusted and rearranged the shop's contents, I thought about whether Mr. Ishida should run an advertisement for a sale tied to cherry-blossom season to reinvigorate business. At the very least, he could put all his antique baskets on discount, because they'd look stunning with cherry blossoms inside.

Just before closing time, the door opened with a gentle ring of the old temple bells strung up by its top. Mr. Okada from the nearby *senbei* shop walked in with two bags of freshly roasted crackers—seaweed flavor for Mr. Ishida and the other—bonito fish flavor—for Hachiko.

"I would have brought your favorite flavor, Shimura-san, if I'd known you were coming back to Tokyo," Mr. Okada said apologetically. "Come to the store later for a complimentary bag. I want to thank you for your good work in bringing my friend home."

"If Shimura-san hadn't made her trip to Tohoku, I would still be sitting in the injured persons' shelter playing mah-jongg," Mr. Ishida said.

"You always said that Shimura-san's specialty is locating rare, old things," Mr. Okada joked.

"Yes, it is." Mr. Ishida's smile faded. "However, we took a while returning because we stayed to search for Mayumi-chan."

"Your Mayumi-chan who works here?" Mr. Okada asked. "I didn't know she was in Tohoku. You did find her, didn't you?"

"We did find her. Unfortunately, Mayumi perished."

"I would never expect—how terrible. I'm so sorry—she was such a nice girl." Mr. Okada bowed his head and was quiet for a moment. Then he looked up. "But I thought she would care for Hachiko and keep the shop open?"

"That's what I thought, too. Mayumi-chan asked if she could come up just for the day, and I'm very sorry that I agreed. It seems unjust that an old man like myself survived"—Mr. Ishida touched his own chest—"and a young person with so much promise lost her life."

"Be glad for good health in old age," Mr. Okada chided. "We all must. But I also wonder, if she went to meet you in that town, how was it that she drowned and you did not?"

"We were separated," Mr. Ishida said. "I stayed in the auction house and she was outside." Somberly, he explained we'd come upon her body during Hachiko's brief rescue training—and that the two of us did not believe she'd drowned. "The police are not interested, nor is her family. But we wonder if someone meant her harm. Okada-san, think carefully about whether you noticed anyone suspicious on our street. Your eyes are better than mine."

Mr. Okada sighed. "This street is always full of strangers: so many tourists coming to look for old-fashioned Tokyo. Because my shop is in the *Lonely Planet* guide, many of them are foreigners. A T-shirt with a marijuana design here, a tattoo there—all of it mixes in my mind."

"But did you ever see a specific person watching Mayumi-chan?" Mr. Ishida queried. "Perhaps a tall, strong, young Japanese man?"

Mr. Okada thought for a while and then nodded. "I've seen someone with a strange hairstyle who would often come around in the evening and buy a few *senbei*. Since he was becoming a regular, I asked whether he lived or worked nearby, and he said, no. He did not explain any more."

"What time in the evenings did he arrive?" Mr. Ishida pressed.

"Around seven. I was usually getting ready to close and sold him the last warm crackers I had."

"I typically sent Mayumi home between six thirty and seven," Mr. Ishida said. "To reach the train station for Chiba City—one usually walks along this street. That boy could have hung around in order to watch for Mayumi leaving."

"Once I saw them together when Mayumi-san walked Hachiko."

Mr. Ishida and I exchanged glances. I put my hand on Hachiko's back, wishing the dog could tell us what had been said on that walk. But she remained as inscrutably furry as ever.

Mr. Okada looked at the old Seiko grandfather clock, then made a regretful face. "I'd better leave. My wife likes my help pulling down the shop's door."

After Mr. Okada's departure, Mr. Ishida made phone calls to the six customers who'd left messages on his answering machine. I went through the whole store again, looking for the Kimura lacquerware, in case Mayumi had hidden it somewhere else on the premises. But no luck.

"I'd really hoped we would find the lacquerware in Mayumi's apartment." As he saw me out the door, Mr. Ishida sounded discouraged. "But chances are, it was lost in Tohoku."

Not necessarily, I thought. If someone was trying to derail our search in Tokyo, it probably meant the lacquer was nearby—or that person had it and didn't want to be discovered. I wondered about the things we'd taken from Mayumi's apartment.

"Do you mind if I take Mayumi's sketchbook with me for the evening?" I asked. "I'm interested to look at everything before we send it back to her parents."

"Of course. I've just unpacked it," Mr. Ishida said, walking back to his desk.

Taking the cardboard-bound sketchbook into my hands, I said, "Do you need help getting Mayumi's possessions upstairs? It might be wise to keep them away from public view."

"Yes, we certainly don't want anyone asking to buy those buttons. Let's take up the big suitcase together. I can manage the little bags by myself."

With two hours left until my appointment with Toshi, I decided to visit Richard to explain the delay in returning his down jacket. My aunt had texted that she was putting it through another cycle and hoping for the best. But when I called the men's apartment, Enrique was on the way out the door to teach his capoeira class and said Richard would work through early evening.

"Richie read me your text about coming back," Enrique said. "He was very pleased. You could say hi to him at Blond Apparition, if you have time."

Blond Apparition was located near Harajuku's most famous crepe stand. Looking at the giant, flat pancakes slowly turning golden on the round skillet reminded me that I needed to eat more to make up for my week of food deprivation. With anticipation, I ordered the crepe with strawberries with cream. It had been my favorite years ago.

The crepe-maker seemed flustered. "My apologies, but strawberries aren't available today."

"What? It's your best-selling crepe!"

"The thing is, we get our strawberries from Fukushima. And there's no produce coming out of there these days. So sorry. How about Nutella-banana?"

Thinking about whether I'd ever feel safe enough to eat Fukushima strawberries again, I accepted the substitution and wolfed it down. Then I wiped my mouth with one of my few remaining tissues and went into Richard's salon, a small building decorated on the outside with a Warholish rendition of Marilyn Monroe.

Inside the pink salon's main room were half a dozen Japanese women with foil-covered heads, reading magazines or tapping on their smartphones. A Japanese receptionist with a halo of lavender curls and a heavy gold necklace with a pendant reading 'Yoshiko-Girl' chirped out the usual *irasshaimase* greeting. Since Yoshiko was only a name for females, the pendant seemed a little overexplanatory.

"You're Richard-san's friend, *neh?*" she asked after I'd given my name. "I know all about you! His styling station is just around the corner."

"Thanks, Yoshiko Girl." I couldn't resist.

What a friendly workplace—just the spot for Richard. I turned a corner into the back of the shop, where Richard was teasing a woman's caramel-colored hair into a whipped tower straight out of the 1950s. When he glanced in the gilded mirror and saw me behind him, he lowered the comb.

"OMG, Rei Shimura!" he trilled. "Your hair looks like it went through its very own tsunami."

"Thanks," I said, over the caramel-whip chick's giggles. "I washed it yesterday evening, by the way. Twice."

"Well, it looks stripped of moisture and full of frizz. A year of sun damage in Hawaii really shows." He tut-tutted with his tongue and then said, "I did see your text about finding Ishida-san. Congratulations, babe."

"Thanks," I said, feeling somewhat put out by his evaluation of my hair. "I would have brought your coat with me today, but I'm washing it. You know, if it doesn't come out exactly like it was before, I'll definitely get you another one."

I expected Richard to jump on what I'd just said but he was studying me with a strange smile.

"What is it?" I asked apprehensively.

"You need more than a blow-out to fix that hair. Sexy gamine is your true look. I have an opening after I finish up with sweet Miya-chan. Then I'm busy again."

"You should try. He's very good," Miya said, beaming at me.

"Richard, I don't have time for a haircut, but I'd love to talk."

Miya's beehive was finished within five minutes. Despite her praise of Richard's skills, she looked taken aback as Richard put her tiny beaded Anya Hindmarch purse back into her hands and marched her out to the receptionist's counter. Miya probably expected a few more minutes with her exotic *gaijin* stylist.

When Richard returned, he held his arms out to me. I went into them, thinking that since Mr. Ishida had spilled the story to his good friend, I could do the same. "I don't know where to start. So much happened. And not much of it good."

Richard pulled a bottle of sherry out of the stylist's drawer and motioned for me to take the vacant customer chair. While he massaged my temples, I explained how the search for Mr. Ishida transformed itself into finding Mayumi.

I told Richard how devastated Akira had seemed, while his mother remained critical of Mayumi even after her death. And then I spoke of the potentially abusive relationship between Mayumi's mother and father, and about Mayumi's feminist roommates. This was the part of the story that most interested Richard.

"If one of Eri's *enjo-kousai* guys ever saw Mayumi at the apartment and wanted her, he could have been involved in her death. Forget Akira. You've got God knows how many men to investigate."

"If the police in Tohoku had shown any interest, they might communicate with their Tokyo counterparts. But that's not happening, and I have no resources to pursue a bunch of unknown men."

Richard sighed. "I bet you wish you stayed with Michael in Hawaii."

"Actually, Michael left a message on my phone that he did arrive in Japan. But he's not in town. He's doing something in the nuclear zone. Let's hope it doesn't involve a hose and a white suit."

"And you didn't tell me this *first*? Have another drink." Richard frowned. "Actually, you've barely taken a sip. Don't you like sherry anymore?"

"It's more fortified than I feel at the moment," I said. "I'm surprised they let you openly drink on the job here."

"We serve drinks because it relaxes the clients; and as you were saying, you've been through hell and back. You can hang here twenty more minutes and then shop along the street until eight. After that we'll go to Night Flower for a drink and somewhere else for dinner."

Out of all the gay bars in Tokyo, just a few admitted foreigners. Night Flower was the friendliest gay bar, open to men and women. In the old days, I'd had more than a bit of fun inside with Richard, Enrique, and their posse. Regretfully, I said, "That sounds very diverting, but I have an appointment tonight. Akira wants me to meet his roommate, who also worked with him on the construction site."

"A real Japanese construction worker, with the split-toe boots and the baggy jodhpurs? Bring him, too!"

"Toshi will be off duty, so he's going to be dressed normally. He texted that he'd be wearing a Yomiuri Giants baseball jacket. I guess he's a fan."

Richard snorted. "Why can't you meet us after you're done?"

"I've got to get back to my aunt's in Yokohama. She's expecting me." I felt the phone vibrate in the pocket of my new jacket and reached in hopefully. Maybe it was Michael. But another text message had appeared. I read:

Stick to shopping if you know what's best for you.

I bit my lip and shoved the phone back into my pocket.

"What was it?" Richard pounced. "Let me see."

"I've been getting some strange texts today. This was another one."

Richard reached his hand into my pocket and pulled out the phone. Instead of looking appalled, he giggled. "Does Mitsutan's marketing department have your phone number?"

"It's not a department store come-on. I think the message is from the same anonymous bastard who sent me another creepy message earlier today." I went into the conversation's history and showed the first message ordering me to stop my search.

After reading it, Richard gaped. "I take back what I said about marketing. I think you should skip traveling to meet the unknown construction worker. Just hang here with us."

I shook my head. "My meeting with Toshi is a half hour from now. I'm sure he's on his way already. How can I cancel?"

"I wish I could go with you, but I've got a customer coming."

"Yes, you said that a few minutes ago, Mr. Popularity."

"Don't worry. I'll send you a text after I'm done and maybe even a picture of the construction worker."

Summer Grass, the bar Toshi had suggested, was tucked in one of the many small streets near Ueno Station. As I drew near, I heard Johnny Cash droning from speakers mounted over a faux-aged wooden door. It was five after six when I arrived; I was just a touch late. I surveyed the room for a young man in a Yomiuri Giants baseball jacket. Several men wearing jackets sat alone at tables against the wall, but it was hard to see exactly what these jackets looked like in the bar's dim lighting.

Since there weren't any likely prospects sitting at the tables, I went to the bar and ordered an Asahi Super Dry beer. It was 6:20 p.m. Like every other solo person in the place, I took out my cell phone for messages. Nothing from Toshi, but Akira had sent a text message.

Did you find the lacquer? If not yet, I have an idea! Call me, Akira.

Since nothing else was going on, I texted him back but got no response. I thought of phoning, but it was too big a risk to have our conversation overheard. And was Akira part of the game? What if he'd followed me back to Tokyo—perhaps a day later, by train or bus—and was interested in getting the missing lacquer for himself?

Putting the phone away, I turned my mind away from this jittery vision and back to the missing construction worker. John Denver's "Country Roads" was playing, and I thought of all the broken roads in Tohoku, and the broken families I'd met. My beer glass was half-empty; I was not a half-full type of person. Now I was consumed with the thought Akira had set me up.

While I'd been pondering my silent cell phone—and the increasingly confused state of matters—a chunky man in his midthirties had casually settled himself onto the barstool next to me. He wore a bomber jacket, black jeans, and shiny Gucci loafers. He smiled as though he knew me.

Quickly, I put my phone away and said good evening.

He winked at me. "Hey, do you have a sister?"

What kind of line was this? I shook my head. "Sorry, I don't know who you're looking for."

"Are you American?"

My accent was not that obvious, so he probably had been given background on me but was hesitant to say my name. This oddity was Abe Toshi? Uncertainly, I said, "I'm so glad you found me."

"But of course. I've been looking for you all my life." He grinned, exposing a gold tooth.

"Are you Abe-san?" He looked a little bit heavier than I would have expected for a Japanese construction worker—older, too.

"Sure. You're Rei-chan, *neh?*"

"Yes. I'm surprised you aren't wearing the jacket—"

"You don't like this jacket?" He pretended mock-offense.

I laughed politely. "No, no..."

But why hadn't he worn the baseball jacket? Scrambling through my memory, I asked, "So, Abe-san, what's your opinion on Okazaki Kaoru?"

"A good place to drink. By the way, this place isn't my favorite. How about we take off somewhere quieter for dinner? My car's in the alley."

Alarm number two. If this man didn't know who the Yomiuri Giants's head coach was, he could not be a fan.

"Come on, let's go," he repeated.

"Um, I don't go off with men I've just met."

He looked pointedly at the rings on my left hand. "If a young married will play with one guy, why not another?"

This was most un-Japanese behavior. I said, "I think there's been a mistake. I'm waiting for someone else."

In the time we'd been talking, the real Toshi could have walked right by, thinking that I wasn't the woman who wanted to speak with him, but some other guy's girlfriend, or just a tourist looking for a one-night stand. Anxiously, I looked around one more time. No baseball jackets that I could see. I either was hanging with a really bumbling pick-up artist—or a very dangerous stalker.

"Think you're too good for me?"

I wanted to snap at the stranger to leave me alone, but I didn't want to let him know I was scared. By law, Summer Grass had to have an exit other than the door straight into the bar. But I couldn't let him think I was going to split. Not if he had a car.

"Do you believe in birth control?" I asked, lowering my voice.

"I—" he blushed slightly. "It's a thing for ladies to worry about, isn't it?"

"Mmm," I said, realizing just how creepy he was. "The thing is, my procedure is a little bit complicated. Would you excuse me?"

His skin flushed, but he no longer looked embarrassed. Just ridiculously pleased. "Take your time, *onee-chan*. I'll have another drink."

I slid off the stool and swaggered into the tiny back hall. When making my close survey of the bar's population, I'd noticed that near the restroom doors was a narrow doorway that went to a kitchen—if you could call a place where chicken wings were microwaved by that name. Two workers looked at me in surprise as I whispered a *sumimasen* and fled through the open door to the alley past a windowless black van with mud on the license plates. Why didn't this surprise me?

I wove a different path this time to the train station, knowing I probably didn't need to run, but walking as fast as I could. I had no idea who the man had been. If he'd actually been Akira's reference, I certainly wouldn't have paid much heed to what he said. But I thought it was extremely unlikely. The faster I walked, the more suspicious the man's approach seemed.

The phone buzzed in my pocket signaling a text. As I waited at an intersection for the light to change, I took out the phone. The sight of another anonymous message in *hiragana* made my stomach drop. But I felt too vulnerable to read it out in the street.

Slipping into a convenience shop, I sheltered myself from view behind a tall cardboard display of body shampoos and read:

You aren't following my directions, bitch. Ueno has many trains. But wherever you go tonight, I'll be following you.

CHAPTER 27

I began walking through the shop, seeing but not seeing the items on the shelves. And then I looked at the people. A few tired-looking older shoppers; some giggly, uniformed middle-school girls; and a male clerk covertly eying the girls. Excepting the clerk, nobody appeared creepy. I went to the back of the store, where nobody else was hanging, and phoned Richard.

"Texter knows I'm heading to Ueno," I whispered in Pig Latin. "There's a message just like the others about it."

"Oh." Richard paused. Pig Latin was harder for him to understand than Japanese. "I suppose you better come to the police station the safest way you can think of. You know, the station with the really big strong guys."

This was code for Night Flower, I imagined. Richard was acting the way Michael had in the past when my phone had been tapped. Oh, God—maybe it was. Who else had access to my phone? The female volunteer who'd let me recharge it when we were in the volunteer dorm. Mr. Morioka: since the phone had been lost in his shop. And a very long time ago, Akira had carried the backpack with my phone in it upstairs to the volunteer dormitory.

After saying a muted goodbye, I turned off my phone entirely. How would I get to Richard? It seemed unwise to travel through Ueno Station again.

Feigning interest in a rack of gardening magazines, I kept an eye on the window until I noticed a cab slowing farther up the sidewalk. I sprinted out and slid in before a young couple heading toward it could reach it. The driver looked disapprovingly at me as I settled myself in.

"To Shinjuku, please. And put your foot on it."

The man understood old movie lines, but there were limits to how fast a seventy-year-old man wearing white gloves would drive through Tokyo's busy, nightlife-ridden streets. We pulled up to Night Flower thirty minutes later with the meter reading just over 8,000 yen. At least I didn't have to worry about tipping, and it didn't appear we'd been followed by another vehicle.

After passing muster with a black, leather-clad bouncer who checked my name off the guest list, I slipped inside the dark, techno-thumping lounge that smelled of various e-cigarette vapors. Richard and Yoshiko were huddled at a cozy table in the back that had a good view of the dance floor. But neither seemed interested in the gyrations of the thirty or so men dancing to Shakira. Richard was chatting on his mobile phone, and Yoshiko was filing her nails into pointy spears.

Richard saw me and waved. As I arrived, he said, "Laters, honey," in a faux British accent and clicked off his phone.

"Was that Enrique?" I sat down.

"Yep. Something came up—he can't join us. Were you followed?"

"I'm not sure. I turned off my phone, in case there's something about my phone that's leading my stalker along. But I don't really want to sit out here in public; he could walk right in."

"Not tonight. Did you notice you were on a guest list? It's a special night for the Shakira Lovers Club. Nobody who isn't a member of that Facebook group can walk in, unless someone put them on the list."

"Richard, I'm starting to feel like my life's paralleling Mayumi's. Mr. Ishida said she acted as if she was being stalked by her old boyfriend, Akira. Now I'm being stalked, though I can't be sure who's doing it."

"Now you've got more reasons than ever not to go to Yokohama tonight. I'm just saying."

"I know. The path from the train station to my aunt's house has plenty of isolated stretches. I almost got hurt walking around there a few years ago."

"Don't tempt fate again," Richard crooned, causing Yoshiko to look up from her nails and nod in agreement.

"Aunt Norie won't like it at all." I sighed. "I don't want to use my phone again tonight. May I borrow yours to call her and make an excuse?"

"That's already done." Richard's voice was smug. "When I got your recent SOS, I called her. No, I didn't say you were being followed. I made up some bullshit about a reunion with Michael tonight—that satisfied her."

"You have my aunt's phone number?"

"In my history."

"Okay," I said. "I'm sorry to be so distracted. It's just so frustrating to have this going on. Anyone could be waiting outside the bar for me."

"If so, that's his or her mistake. This bar keeps surveillance on people outside."

"Seriously?"

"You bet. Most patrons here are closeted—so window shoppers are not welcome. There's a security camera running, and if someone does lurk, the bouncer takes his picture—with a really prominent flash. They tend to run away then." Richard sighed. "Hark, the bar-boy is finally coming over. You want a glass of water?"

"I heard it's full of radiation. Coffee would be better." I couldn't relax vigilance, even for a half hour. "So I guess I'll be staying with you and Enrique tonight?"

"Are you nuts? I don't want your phone ghost knowing where I live. You need to stay somewhere else that's a little more secure."

"Hmm. For me to go to Mr. Ishida is perhaps what the stalker wants. But hotels aren't secure at all."

"What about a gay bathhouse?" Yoshiko said. "There's a members-only one nearby. It's even harder to get into than Night Flower."

"That might work." Richard turned to her, looking surprised. "Enrique and I have a membership to that very bathhouse you mention. We could probably squeeze Rei in."

"What—a gay bathhouse membership? I thought you and Enrique were monogamous."

"Oh, come on. There's no reason not to enjoy the best bath in town with a couple's discount." He peered critically at me. "You go into baths with other women—why can't we go into baths with men?"

Having bathed just a few days earlier in such a place, I couldn't argue about that point. "I had a shower and a bath last night, and again this morning. My skin's as dry as my hair's become. Really, I'd much rather have a room with a bed."

"Boys Bath is a full-service establishment. There are group and private bedrooms as well as the disco, karaoke room, and movie lounge."

"We could consider it. If I can really get in—"

"You will, after your haircut."

"How can you give me a haircut now?"

Richard patted his waist, which was still adorned by his cowhide stylist's pouch with a couple of pairs of shear handles poking up.

Only short acts could be committed with those scissors—I knew from the gleam in his eyes. "Please don't give me a man's haircut."

"Spare me the gender bias, okay? I'll give you the Audrey, which is a far cry from a buzz cut. It was the best cut you ever had."

"Audrey Hepburn died too young. I don't know the karma's right to replicate that hairstyle on me, given the circumstances—"

"I cut an Audrey for a client six months ago. She's still alive." Richard paused. "Yoshiko, there's a photo collage of patrons near the bar. Be a honey and see if they'll let you borrow it for a while."

Yoshiko jumped up obediently. When she came back, she was holding a large framed picture filled with oddly cut photos of mostly male customers. The women had more of a variety of styles, including a short, cropped cut on the woman Richard said was his client.

"It's too big a change," I said, eyes sliding from the pretty twentysomething's picture across to a shot of another female with short hair, and a friendly face made even rounder by her double-circle, wire-rimmed glasses.

"Glock," I exclaimed. "The one with Lennon specs is Mayumi's roommate—whom I just saw today. If she's a regular here, she's probably a lesbian. And she was very close to Mayumi. What if a shift in sexuality was the reason Mayumi dropped Akira?"

Richard yawned. "Sexuality doesn't shift. What happens is that it becomes expressed."

"Look at this." I reached into the backpack and pulled out Mayumi's design notebook. Both Yoshiko and Richard leaned in as I slowly leafed through. Pictures of flowers, cats, and traditional art motifs all shown in circles. Following these was the picture of the women's faces pressed together. Another button design looked like a set of female lips. And then, without a doubt, a breast with a small, rosy nipple.

"The art's not proof of anything—but to think of this all being done in traditional Japanese lacquer is pretty wild," Richard said. "There are some blank pages at the end. I wonder how much farther she would have gone with her female-centric buttons."

"Glock was very close to Mayumi. And she seemed positive that Mayumi had no involvement with any men," I mused aloud. "I wonder about the situation with Eri. She seemed kind of anti-male, but she's got that *enjo-kousai* racket going on—"

"Who cares? Let's get going on your hair."

Richard jumped up to capture a temporarily vacant barstool. Carrying it toward the restroom, he inclined his head toward me. I followed him, thinking that getting a free haircut in a mixed-gender restroom was just another adventure to add to my life story.

In the tiny restroom, which was decorated with multiple vending machines and safe-sex-instruction signs, Richard positioned me on the barstool so I faced away from the mirror over the sink. I felt water flicking all over my head and then steel on my neck.

I kept smiling at the men and women coming in and out the door, acting as if I was supposed to be there, getting the haircut. Most restroom users wanted to know whether Richard was going to turn me into a wavy blond like Shakira. When he shook his head, they lost interest.

"We can get you some clothes from the lost and found," Richard said. "People get hot here, take their clothes off, and forget to put them back on. Yoshiko's out looking."

"A lot of Japanese men are the same size as me," I said. So much hair was falling. I couldn't see it, but I could feel my head becoming lighter. Freer. I hoped against hope that when I saw Michael again, he'd still like the way I looked.

Richard continued cutting, singing the Shakira song that was playing through the doorway, "Waka Waka, This Time for Africa." Richard entreated me to join in, but my cooling cup of coffee wasn't enough to put the same music in me.

Yoshiko hustled in after fifteen minutes with her arms full of clothes. She also apologized for not learning anything useful about Mayumi and Glock.

"So the staff is protecting the girls' privacy," Richard said. "It should make me feel safe, but at the moment it's irritating."

I suggested, "Maybe if I explained Mayumi is dead, it would be different—"

"Why would they believe you? Parents hire undercover detectives to find out what their unmarried adult children are doing. The staff here won't let you stay on the premises if they think you're asking too much. You haven't been here in years, and you aren't even a bona fide Shakira Club member."

"It's a bit hard because you are a double outsider here—not gay and not Japanese," Yoshiko said. "But don't feel bad—you look wonderful as a boy. I'll draw a moustache on you with my eyebrow pencil."

"Please, don't. It's not Halloween."

"Hold the whiskers for a sec. Audrey Hepburn has returned from her untimely demise and is ready for action," Richard swiveled the stool so I was facing the mirror.

I opened the eyes I'd squeezed shut to view the side-swept bangs and a sleek brown-black cap of hair that was about two inches long. The hair was gone. I didn't look like the thirty-year-old married woman who played mah-jongg with her senior citizen friends. I looked younger and more edgy.

Richard walked around the stool, scrutinizing. "I may have left you too feminine around the front—but that'll be good later on. Yoshiko, see if there's a hat we can put over my masterpiece. And let me use the eyebrow pencil to create some five o'clock shadow."

A tweed newsboy cap soon arrived to top off the hair, thanks to a loan from Yoshiko's friend on the dance floor. The cap coordinated nicely with a chamois shirt, denim jacket, and oversized jeans she'd brought out of the bar's lost and found, along with a pair of typical male, brown loafers. Richard suggested that I put my wedding and engagement rings in my backpack, which Yoshiko would carry out when we all left.

When I stepped out of the restroom in the borrowed clothes, all the men and two women waiting in the long line gave me the once-over. So I really did look like a pretty boy, or perhaps a transgendered one.

Richard, Yoshiko, and I went the club's back door, armed with sharp-tipped umbrellas liberated from the lost and found. I was tense, because we had to pass through two alleys to reach the fabled bathhouse. I remembered the black van parked behind Summer Grass.

But no cars or vans passed us in the narrow old lane. Richard whispered the plan to me: he would walk me in and introduce me as his special guest. I'd have to come up with the 3,000 yen for the price of a bath and a couple of drinks, because it was important that I appeared to be interested in recreation. A bit later I could act tired and pay the 6,000-yen fee for a private room.

"Sixty dollars is a pittance for a night's stay," I said after Yoshiko had said goodbye and split for the subway and the two of us continued. "But could the staff think you're cheating on Enrique? Things could be awkward the next time he's here."

"I suppose wagging tongues would be a pain to deal with," Richard admitted. "Okay, I won't ask for the room key right away. You could get fake-drunk, and when I book a room for you later on, they would think I was behaving like a humanitarian friend. The main point is get you through the door and convince people you're a gay man who doesn't speak Japanese."

There was no welcoming *noren* curtain outside Boys Bath's heavy steel door, nor were any prospective customers lined up for admission. The only clue that this place was a private-admission, men's-only bath club was the doorman, who wore a long, blue-and-white *yukata* robe tied over jeans. Richard greeted the doorman by name and was answered in the friendliest of manners: a kiss. Richard put his arm around my shoulders, introducing me as Raymond Shimura, a "Rocku Staa Banana," who had dreamed of visiting a very special bath.

Once inside, the charade continued. In quick, whispery Japanese, Richard told the concierge that Raymond Shimura was a Japanese-Korean boy-band performer from Canada. Apparently, I'd finished a sold-out gig in Yokohama and had come to the city for some rest and relaxation. The concierge whispered a question to Richard about how fluent Raymond's Japanese was. Richard whispered back that Raymond looked Asian but regrettably only spoke English. This is what made Raymond a banana. Yellow on the outside, white on the inside, and rumored to be delish.

"Take him right to our Wild Cats Lounge," the concierge instructed. "And you know, his VIP guest admission ticket includes two free drinks."

The recommended lounge was small, but appeared even smaller, because of its black walls, low lighting, and plush stuffed tigers, cheetahs, and panthers posed around the place. The seat cushions on the bar stools were zebra-print velour, and the gleaming bar appeared to be a facsimile of ebony. A sexy Japanese bartender sporting dyed red hair and the classic black-leather-vest-with-nothing-underneath-it motioned for us to take two prime seats.

"One cosmopolitan with an extra twist, please," Richard said to him in Japanese. When my friend turned to me, he spoke English. "What'll it be, Raymond?"

"Just a beer, please," I answered. "Whatever's on tap."

"Ah, he is American," the bartender commented.

"Raymond is from Toronto, Canada. We went to school

together. He is a boy-band performer who just gave a concert." Richard trotted out the lies he'd dreamed up.

"But of course," the bartender exclaimed. "I think I saw him on television this morning."

"It must have been someone else, because Raymond's contract doesn't allow filming," Richard ad-libbed. "You see, he has a pending deal with a soft-drink company. Only they can promote his image."

"I want to know more about your band," the bartender tried in stilted English. "Are you the lead singer? Is everyone else also bananas?"

"I'm going bananas," I started saying, while Richard pinched me.

"Raymond not only sings but plays bass guitar."

The bartender laughed. "A true *talento*. Two ways is better than one, *neh*? I recommend our very special beer cocktail."

The big crepe I'd eaten in Harajuku had been absorbed long ago, so the beer cocktail—a mix of white ale, bourbon, lemon juice, and bitters—hit me hard. I was beginning to feel less fearful of the texter, and also starting to think maybe the Mayumi search was not really worth the work. I would talk to Mr. Ishida about it the next day. But tonight, I'd maybe have another nightcap. Get a room, sink into a bed. Everything would be all right.

"Raymond, I'll be here tomorrow morning to pick you up for your news interview. Don't have too much fun tonight," Richard said, kissing me lightly on the lips.

I hadn't realized how much time had passed, but it was midnight. I'd been intrigued by the bartender's flirtation with me, and the shy, smiling admiration from the Wildcat's other customers. Now, without Richard's help, I wasn't sure I could continue carrying off the rock-star charade. Someone might bring me a guitar or flute or drag me into the karaoke lounge. When I really couldn't sing.

"Here, Raymond. Gift from a friend." The bartender slid a glass toward me and gazed eagerly for a reaction. I took a sniff of the drink that had odors of Coke, Curacao, and something else. Did Rohypnol have an odor? I knew I shouldn't try it.

"*Oishii*," I said, although it did not look delicious at all.

"Raymond-chan said *oishii*. His Japanese is very good. He knows Japanese!"

And so it went. Because Richard's protection was gone, the other customers dared to come closer. "Oh, Raymond-san, have you tried a Japanese bath before? I will show you everything."

"Americans wash in the morning," I rumbled back. "How early does this bath open?"

"Aren't you Canadian? You may learn Japanese ways—"

"If he's *toransukei*," one man said to the other in soft Japanese, "he could be shy."

The concierge who'd handled my admission stepped into the room and signaled to the bartender. As they stood ten feet away, chatting and looking repeatedly at me, I felt nervous. Something had come up, and Richard wasn't around to help me.

"Raymond-san, will you please come with me?" the concierge said in English. "Let's go upstairs."

"I will come, too," suggested one admirer, a middle-aged gentleman in a salaryman's typical gray suit.

"No, no." The concierge crossed his arms in a protective X before me.

"Thank you. I'm ready to roll." I practically fell off my bar stool, I was so eager to go. Richard had surely come through with the room arrangement. I tried to walk unsteadily, so I looked quite drunk.

"Sorry to interrupt conversations with new friends," the concierge said in English. "Raymond-san, we have a special customer already waiting."

Shaking my head, I said, "No customers, okay? I must sleep alone to give a good concert tomorrow."

"The customer is called Burukkusu-san. He is older, handsome, looks like a *butcho*," he said, using the word for senior corporate executive. "Maybe a music producer?"

"No, I do not know him. Please tell him I'm sorry, but I cannot go to him. May I buy a key for my own room instead?"

"Of course, of course, you can have your own room, too. But I must take you to Boroku-san. He *paid* for you."

"For me!" I was both outraged and frightened. Perhaps someone who'd been in the bar earlier decided to go for broke with a private invitation. But the concierge seemed nonplussed.

"I said to him: Raymond-san is a rock star, not rent boy. Still, he gave a small financial gift to us just for a favor of bringing you for an autograph and whatever might come. He would like to give you a bigger gift, if you want it."

What a conundrum. All I wanted was to lie down in peace. But I also had to appear like a curious, up-and-coming rock musician. Such people did sign autographs. And have random sex.

Glumly, I followed the concierge into an elevator decorated with pictures of the bathhouse's various luxuries—a screening room for erotic films, the bar, a restaurant, and numerous baths including one that contained a low-level electric current. Seeing me looking at it he said, "That bath is our most stimulating one.

Because of the electric crisis, though, TEPCO has asked us to refrain from running it, at least for this time being."

"Yes," I said as the doors parted with a cheerful ring and he waved me ahead of him into the hallway.

"I am bringing you because Burukkusu-san is very private. He does not want his room number spoken aloud. His tour guide was most specific."

"Tour guide?"

"Tonight is a big night for our having international visitors: a good thing after the tsunami. Our government is afraid no more tourists will come. It made us afraid, too."

The mention of the tsunami put me on edge. Could my stalker have booked himself into a room? How private and members-only was this club? I remembered the famous Groucho Marx line about never wanting to join a club that would have one as a member. If Boys Bath had allowed me as a guest, it might also admit another dubious individual.

The manager stopped at door thirteen and knocked smartly. "Burukkusu-san, hotel management has come," he called out in English.

But there was no answer.

As I deliberated whether to start walking away, the manager fished a key out of his pocket and gave me a wink. "Master key opens everything. There, you go ahead."

"Can we go in together? You might need to translate for me, because all I can give is an autograph."

"I met him. No translation will be necessary. And he wants to see *you*," the concierge whispered, putting his hands on my shoulders and propelling me inside. He closed the door and, too quickly, his footsteps faded off.

I could have run out myself, but I paused. I checked out twin beds that hadn't been slept in, and between them a low table with an iPod dock and a small basket with the typical sexual accoutrements of any Japanese love hotel, plus a big box of tissues. There was also a notepad emblazoned with BOYS BATH and a cute image of two little bears scrubbing each other. Tearing off a page, I carefully wrote "To Burukkusu-san, Keep on Rockin! Raymond Shimura" in English script. My job was done. The concierge would get his tip, and I'd get my private room.

The bathroom door was cracked open. I heard a slight sloshing sound of water and smelled the aroma of eucalyptus bath salts. The man called Burukkusu-san was apparently in the bathtub. I had a new thought. If he were in a bath, I'd have the physical advantage. I'd get a good look at him to satisfy my worries and be gone before he could get out. If he tried anything outrageous, I would snap a full-frontal photograph that could be shared with the police.

This meant turning on my phone again. I did that and then got into camera mode. Then, counting silently to three, I gently pushed open the bathroom door.

As I'd anticipated, the bath was full and a naked man was inside. He was far too long for it, with his legs folded up like pretzels. But what I could see of him was darkly tanned and pretty hunky.

I knew that body. And that face. Familiar blue eyes met mine, but instead of holding happy recognition, they looked panicked.

"Get the hell out," my husband shouted.

CHAPTER 28

"I mean it, guy!" He was starting to rise out of the tub. "How'd you get in here?"

I held out my arms. "Michael, it's me! Your wife!"

Michael stopped yelling. His eyes ran over my masculine outfit, the phone in my hand, and then back to my face. Clearing his throat, he said, "That's a hell of a cover."

"Speak for yourself. I was scared to death coming up here. Why are they calling you Burukkusu-san? Hendricks-san would have been enough."

"B-R-O-O-K-S. I thought you'd recognize my old code name." He shook his head, still looking me up and down. "Enrique promised that Richard would bring you sometime tonight. I just didn't think you'd look this way."

I was growing more confused. "Did you not specifically request Raymond Shimura, a boy-band member?"

Michael shook his head and started to laugh. Together we both said: "Richard."

"And look what he did to me half an hour ago." I pulled off the newsboy cap to reveal my new haircut.

Michael stopped laughing. "You cut your hair."

"I worried you wouldn't like it. Well, at least hair grows back."

"It's not bad." Michael paused, studying me. "It would look prettier after you, ah, remove the faux beard. That washes off, right? I could help you."

"Just a sex. I mean, sec!"

Double-locking the door and putting a chain on it, I went to the bedside table with the dock and looked at the songs loaded onto my phone. What was the right music for the place, moment, and man? The late, great LCD Soundsystem doing "I Can Change."

When I went back to the bathroom, I was singing along tunelessly, and the lost-and-found guys' clothes were slowly coming off to reveal the same old me.

I got into the tub. Between long kisses, Michael explained that he and his colleagues had been transported by helicopter from Misawa Air Base and dropped onto a navy cruiser stationed in the waters.

"Just like old times, huh?" I said.

"Not quite. Looking at those steaming reactors was worse than anything I've ever seen in a disaster movie."

"Um, how close were you?" My old anxiety for him returned.

Michael dropped his head, looking uncomfortable. "We were about twenty kilometers away. But you do know the big blaze is out, right?"

"I didn't know. That's great news. But did you guys really have to get that close?"

"Nobody made us do anything. But you know, being operational was the best way to find out what's really going on."

"So, I'm sitting in the water with you here... could it be radioactive?" As my question formed, I realized how stupid it sounded.

"If the Tokyo drinking water's got radiation, I'm sure the bath water does too. Don't blame me for that," Michael said.

"I won't."

"After things stabilized, I got clearance to take off and visit you. I was in Sugihama yesterday, but you'd already headed out."

"You never texted me you were planning that. I would have stayed!"

"I wanted to surprise you. At least I caught up with Tom. He filled me in on what he knew about you finding Ishida-san's apprentice, and I shared some of the things you told me about Mayumi's death. Hope that was okay."

"Of course. Those were my old concerns. You haven't heard about my phantom texter." I described the menacing text messages that had been flowing since my arrival in Tokyo and the disturbing man I'd met at Summer Grass.

Michael's voice was tight. "My first question is: who have you recently met that has your phone number?"

"Akira knows it and so does this guy called Toshi. Also: Mayumi's parents, and the antiques dealer Mr. Morioka, because I briefly misplaced the phone at his store and he found it. Oh, and I told Glock today as well."

"Did you bring the phone to this hotel?"

"Of course. It's in my backpack in the other room—" Before I could finish my sentence Michael had stood up and was shedding water as he stepped out on the tiled floor. Grabbing a tiny hand towel, he strode into the bedroom. "What's your password?"

"After the SIM card went in, I skipped putting the password

back on. I had a lot on my mind. I didn't think..." I stood up from the bath and reached for the remaining small towel to dry myself. Then I put on the crisp *yukata* robe hanging on the door.

Michael was sitting naked on the edge of one of the small beds, my phone in his hand. "Okay, I've gone into the phone's settings and can see that someone's activated your GPS. I've also discovered that every outgoing e-mail and text message, as well as your voice mails, is being forwarded to a Japanese address. It's in *kanji*. Can you read this?"

I scrutinized the inscrutable array of characters and numbers. "I could ask my aunt what this means. It would be fabulous if it turned out to be someone's name—but I'm guessing no stalker would be that stupidly transparent."

"You never know. The tracking that was put on was very straightforward. But Rei—" He shook his head. "You must not have spent any time examining your phone when you got it back, because this is all stuff you could have figured out."

"No," I admitted. "But I wasn't expecting to be tailed."

"It's easy enough to undo," Michael said. "We'll stop all the e-mail and GPS forwarding. I'd like to add a different GPS tracker just between your phone and mine, so I'll know where you are, if you run into trouble."

"Will that address the issue of the harassing texts? My number's still the same."

"I want a full record of those texts. They can be used to prove guilt if the police ever respond to this situation."

There weren't many things sexier than a gorgeous, irritated man wearing no clothes. I put my arms around Michael and said, "I want to forget about all of it for a while. Let's have some fun, and then I've got to leave you for the private room I told the concierge I wanted."

"No," Michael said. "I'll go to the mat to keep you with me for the whole night."

"Prove it." I smiled encouragingly as he pressed me back on the blanket.

No bones about it. A straight married couple making love in a gay men's hotel room was downright subversive. If the concierge happened to pop in again with his master key, how would he react to me lying exposed while Michael slowly stroked my breasts? As we moved together, relearning each other's bodies, I fantasized that I might actually be a sexy young man called Ray who'd checked into a Japanese bathhouse because he was curious and succumbed to the desires of a powerful, older producer. Other people did this kind of thing all the time. I didn't know what Michael was thinking as we made hard, fast love that night, but I felt different: outside of my body and reckless. He was above me, behind me, beside me.

Everywhere I wanted him.

"Hey, the group bath might be empty at this hour." I sighed as Michael emerged from the bathroom's minuscule shower the next morning.

"Unh-unh. The baths manager advised me bathing hours are nine to midnight." Michael was drying himself with the face cloth-sized towel he'd used the night before.

"You spoke with the baths manager yesterday?"

"Yes. I went in for a dip with Enrique because my back hurt from the helicopter ride."

"Hold on. You soaked in a bath with a bunch of gay men?" I could imagine the ripples of excitement this muscular *gaijin* would have created.

"Actually, soaking in a jetted tub with other guys is hardly a big deal. I've done it other places in Japan and Korea as well. Here, it was rather mind-opening."

Now I was angry. "Come on. It's like you getting naked with a lot of horny sorority sisters."

Michael made a time-out sign with his hands. "Enough, Rei. The mind-opening thing I'm trying to tell you about is I now understand what it's like to be a minority."

"What do you mean, Michael? You're waspier than almost anyone I know."

"It's about sex. Whenever you and I check into a hotel, people look at us and assume we're okay to sleep together. You might be Japanesish, I might be Connecticutish, but it's no matter to anyone. We've got our wedding rings."

"I don't see a ring on your finger today," I said archly.

"Hey, what about you, Mrs. Hendricks?"

"It was Richard's idea that I take it off," I admitted. "It's in my backpack in the locker downstairs along with my regular clothes. By the way, do you have any extra clean underwear I can borrow?"

Michael shook his head. "Forget the underwear. There's a larger picture to worry about. How can we get you out of here looking like you did when you came on to me last night? Your moustache and beard went down the bathtub's drain."

I pulled away from his caress and looked into the mirror across from the foot of the bed. Adjusting the tweed cap over my new short hair, I thought I looked like one of the Hardy Boys. "I'm passing as transgender—here, it's known as *toransukei* or *nyu hafu*. Richard and Yoshiko say it's still hard to be gay in Japan. You can't be out unless you work in entertainment, fashion and beauty, or the arts. And Tokyo's much more gay-friendly than other small towns."

"Sexual identity may have been Mayumi's struggle, and why she really left Sugihama," Michael said. "That's if she actually was playing for the girls' team. Going to a gay bar a few times is no proof. You're the living testimony."

"Now I'm wondering about Eri, the third roommate," I said. "She paints urinals—as you know, those vessels are colloquially called *benjo*. And *benjo* is also the slang term for a straight girl who hangs around with lesbians."

"Maybe that adds a double meaning to her art," Michael said.

"I want to see those women again," I said.

"There's a risk to that," Michael said.

"I know."

CHAPTER 29

Michael had prepaid his room the previous evening, so there was no need for conversation with anyone at the front desk when we left Boys Bath. He escorted me straight out, an arm protectively shielding me from view, although my reputation must have spread, because a number of staff pulled out phones and took pictures. I ignored autograph requests and kept my face pressed to his bicep.

After making our break, we high-fived each other and ran all the way to the west entrance of Shinjuku Station, where Michael planned to take the subway to a meeting in Kasumigaseki.

"I'm so glad you're just seeing people in Tokyo today," I said. "No more ships, no more radiation, no more fires. Right?"

"That's the working plan," Michael said. "After my morning and afternoon meetings, I'm focused on you."

We kissed a long goodbye, causing a mother to cover her child's eyes and glare angrily. Smiling, I tilted my cap at her and walked back around Shinjuku to Night Flower.

It was early. No doorman or guest list at this hour—but the door was unlocked.

"Oh, do you have a delivery for us?" A chubby man wearing a well-stretched Lady Gaga concert T-shirt looked up at me from behind the bar. I hadn't seen him the night before. Coffee was brewing in a little Sanyo coffee maker placed on the counter, reminding me I'd missed breakfast.

"Sorry. I'm a friend of Richard and Enrique's," I began, using the same casual Japanese he had with me. "My name is Rei."

"And they call me Queen. Queen Cake," he said with a grin. "But the scene here doesn't start until much later, *onee-chan*. I can give you coffee now, but that's about it."

"That is very kind of you," I said, taking the cup he poured. "I had coffee here yesterday evening, too. I was wondering about a girl who's come here before? She's called Mayumi and has blue hair."

"Oh, I've seen that girl a few times. She's not available, *onee-chan*. She goes with another girl called Glock."

"I know. And I met Glock the other day to give her some very bad news. I might as well tell you, too."

"I like to know news. Even if it's hard." Queen Cake put his thick forearms on the counter and leaned sympathetically close.

"Mayumi died."

His lightly lined eyes blinked rapidly. "Oh, how awful! She is young—eighteen or so?"

"Nineteen, and yes, it was a terrible tragedy. I'm not employed by the police, but as a friend to this community, I'm trying to figure out some things about her unfortunate death."

"A crime of hatred, maybe." Queen Cake pressed his lightly glossed lips together in a hard line. "I wonder if I can help. Our bouncer photographs outsiders who watch this place. We keep the phone here all the time."

"I'd be interested to look at the pictures."

He opened the cash register and from a drawer, pulled out a mobile phone in a rainbow-striped case. "You can look through."

There were hundreds of pictures. Most were of men with ages in the twenties through the seventies. I guessed that plenty of them might have longed to go inside the bar, but not felt the courage. Other snapshots captured middle-aged women, almost all with worried expressions—but neither Mrs. Rikyo nor Mrs. Kimura were among them. I focused on the men until I found a snapshot of someone I recognized.

Akira Rikyo had a baseball cap covering his rooster hairstyle. Still, the black leather jacket and anxious, pressed lips gave him away. He'd looked similarly stressed much of the time I'd seen him in Sugihama.

"You took a picture of this young man on March first, according to the data line on the photo," I said to Queen Cake. "Do you remember him from other times?"

He shrugged. "It's hard to know. All I can say is keep looking...."

I spent the next fifteen minutes going through the rest of his photo archive, but Akira didn't reappear. Maybe seeing Mayumi arrive here one evening was all he needed to know.

I thanked Queen Cake for his help and left, promising to let him know if it proved Mayumi had met with foul play. I also left my business card, in case anyone at the bar remembered something.

Walking along Shinjuku-dori, I quickly scanned my phone for messages and e-mails. Michael had sent a message asking whether the phantom texter had been in touch. I answered quickly no, that

I was fine. There was also a phone message from Akira asking me to call him. I did so, and he picked up on the second ring. "At last, Rei-san. Didn't you get my message to call yesterday?"

"Yes, but I didn't know what it was about—sorry, I ran out of time."

"I called to apologize that my friend Toshi couldn't meet you. He's sorry for the inconvenience."

"No problem. But I'm surprised he didn't contact me directly."

"The fact is, he's a bit nervous now. He received an anonymous text message he wasn't sure he understood, so he forwarded it to me. Rei-san, the message to him was a warning to stay away from a dangerous woman called Rei. Who do you think sent that?"

"I don't know," I said, feeling tightness in my stomach. If my anonymous harasser had contacted Toshi Abe, this meant he knew about Akira, too.

"Toshi doesn't want to speak to you now," Akira said. "But you could still verify my whereabouts that day by calling my boss, Mr. Koji."

"Why would he give information to a stranger over the phone?"

"Shimura-san, you have good ideas. I'm sure you can think of something."

Flattery didn't work on me. Clearing my throat, I said, "I'm glad that you called, because there's something else I need to ask you about."

"Sure."

"On March first, you were photographed hanging around a Shinjuku gay bar called Night Flower. Why?"

"I never went in there!"

"That may be true, but you remained *outside* the door long

enough for the bouncer to think it was worth recording your image. Why was that?"

"Because of Mayumi. She was walking through Shinjuku with one of her roommates and went in. My plan was to wait nearby to make sure she left safely."

"Isn't that a little overprotective?"

"I wanted to know if there was a new boyfriend. She'd been with some older guy recently. He looked like a bad sort. But when I saw the kind of guys going into Night Flower, I realized I didn't have anything to worry about. I left an hour later, after she and her roommates left together. Just a girls' gathering, you know."

I decided to ask him straight out. "Did you ever think Mayumi might be bisexual or lesbian?"

He gave a choked laugh. "Not really. But it's true, we never did it."

As I deliberated over whether to say anything more, his quick words cut into my chance.

"I must return to work. But let me know when you've spoken to Koji-san. I don't like you thinking bad things about me, Rei-san. It's not correct."

After ringing off with Akira, my phone buzzed again. This time, I saw it was Michael on the line.

"Hey. Are you already through with your meeting?" I looked at my watch and saw it was past twelve.

"Did you ever have breakfast?" Michael asked.

"No. But it's a bit late—"

"Let's do lunch. I'm on the west side. Remember that little place in Roppongi where they cold-cure the salmon with salt and lemon?"

"Ew. I still can't stand the idea of fish."

"You pick the place then. I have a gap until my next meeting."

"There's a *ramen* shop I like in Shibuya. It's called Usagi. Or is it Usago?" "Never heard of it. Do they have a website?"

"I'll just look..." As I took the phone away from my ear to open the browser, I saw a luminous line of *hiragana* text marked Sender Unknown.

Damn it. No texts for a half day had lulled me into a sense of complacency. But now I could feel someone breathing on my newly shorn nape.

"Can you give me those spellings again?" Michael asked.

"Sorry, I just got a text." I put the phone back close to my ear. "It says Sender Unknown, but for the first time, there's a scary emoticon attached to the text."

"What kind of emoticon?"

"A gun."

Michael exhaled sharply. "Sounds like an escalation. I'll come to you right now."

"Yes, but... hold on. Let me read the message—there's a bit of *kanji* in it, for a change. I might have to use my online decoder."

But the text turned out to be rather straightforward—and once I figured out the sender, I relaxed. "I think it's okay. It's a message from one of the girls I met yesterday. It just says, 'We need to talk to you. Come back, because Eri knows something.' What could that be?"

"But Eri or Glock may have been texting you all along," Michael pointed out. "And if there are two of them against you—in an apartment with a closed door—I don't like it. Even if they're women."

"The gun is probably Glock's sig line—get it? But what does Eri know? Is it about the lacquer, or, like Richard suggested, a spooky man who came through the place and hankered after Mayumi?"

"Could you just ask the gun and urinal artists to lunch? This sounds like a good conversation to be held in public."

"They're not going to spill anything with *you* at the table."

"I won't be at your table, but nearby. Hey, I'll bring my own lunch date. I'm really hungry, Rei. I'll get there before you."

"Okay, but where? I hardly know where to suggest—"

"Let's try CocoLo, which isn't far from where you are in Shinjuku. Double Cs and the L in caps. If the gals refuse, call me back with where they'd rather meet."

"They may not want to go out at all—"

"What did you say they were, NEET? Unemployed people are usually up for a free meal. Especially if you throw in a bottle of wine."

An hour later, I was seated in a charming café with walls lined with cheerful, cartoonlike images of circus animals. Glock and Eri were across from me; Glock in paint-stained overalls and glasses and Eri in a simple, stylish black dress. She did clean up nicely, I thought. And Michael had been right about the wine. Eri was quick to suggest the most expensive rosé on the tab.

The host had put us at a central table that had one unique characteristic. Right behind was the only table with the only foreigners in the place.

My husband had scored not one lunch date, but two. He was with Richard and Enrique, who both looked rather hung over. Judging from sporadic bursts of laughter, it seemed the trio was recounting antics from the past evening. I only hoped that Michael wouldn't kiss and tell.

"Please choose whatever you want. I'm just so glad you were able to join me," I said. "Oh, the wine's already half-gone. That's no fun. Should I order another?"

I was very glad when my shiitake and tomato omelet arrived; the wine only made me feel hungrier.

"How did you know about this place?" Glock said after we'd all eaten a bit. She'd ordered a chicken cutlet with salad and potatoes, and Eri a salmon salad that I couldn't quite look at.

"I used to live in the city," I said.

"It's gay-friendly," Glock said. "By the way, you look different today from yesterday. Now you are cute."

"You were with your boss, Ishida-san, yesterday," Eri said. "Maybe that's why you dressed down."

"Ishida-san is not my current boss," I corrected her.

"Then why did you two come yesterday?" Eri asked.

"He's my friend—and he really loved Mayumi like a granddaughter. As he mentioned to you, he thinks she may have had something with her—some little pieces of lacquerware. Now that she's passed away, he believes she would have wanted it returned to her parents." I paused. "How are you both doing today? I'm so sorry I had to give you terrible news. You knew her very well."

Glock swallowed down the remainder of her third glass of wine. "I will never forget her."

"So, you wanted to tell me something?" I asked.

"We might know about what you're looking for," Eri answered in a voice considerably more controlled than Glock's.

"The lacquer collection?"

"Yes. We didn't tell the whole story because he was there," Glock interjected. "We can't have police coming around."

"Thank you for trusting me," I said, although my inner radar had snapped on. How bad was their confession going to be?

"It started like this," Eri said. "I was going to go out on a date with a guy I know. Glock said she told you about what I do for extra cash."

"Yes." I smiled, trying not to look judgmental.

"It's no big deal to me," Eri said. "Well, Asao-*kun*—he's kind of a weirdo, but I've seen him for a while—had a business associate with him one night. He asked me to find another girl to come to dinner. Mayumi was keen to do it. You see, Asao and his friend—a guy called Daigo—sometimes sell things. And Mayumi had been trying to figure out what to do with her lacquer."

"Was she thinking of selling it?"

"Yes," Glock said. "I didn't want to say so in front of Ishida-san, because he had already put it in a safe for her and had mentioned to her several times he would pay for insured postage if she wanted to mail it to her parents. But she didn't want to give it up. You see, she couldn't save everything she earned at that shop job... it all was used up on housing, food, and so on. She still needed money to pay for art school, which costs hundreds of thousands of yen."

"School is expensive," I agreed. "But getting back to the night with the gentlemen Eri knows..."

"I did Mayumi's makeup for her and lent her a long black pageboy wig, because I didn't think the blue hair would suit Daigo—Asao warned me that he was quite a bit older, almost a grandpa age. So with that hair, and in a mini skirt and heels, she looked quite different. Prettier," Eri added.

"In your opinion," Glock huffed. From the grumpy expression on her face, I could see she hadn't liked the idea of Mayumi having a date with a man.

Eri continued, "We went to Tony Roma's to eat. Asao and Daigo asked Mayumi about herself, and she said that she worked part time in antiques. Daigo bragged that he made way more money than any dealer in town and didn't have to pay a wholesale price, rent for a storefront, or any of the usual stuff. Mayumi asked him more about it, and he said he worked closely with a dealer out of town. Mayumi got even more interested because she realized—"

Glock interrupted, "If she could sell the lacquer to someone outside Tokyo, Mr. Ishida wouldn't know! And she might make 24 million yen! She could go to school and buy an apartment with an art studio. I would go there, too."

Two-hundred-forty-thousand dollars was an out-of-this-world estimate for twenty pieces of lacquer. "Did Mr. Ishida quote that figure?"

"No," Glock answered. "He said it was worth more. But she figured that since both Daigo and the retailer would get a cut, she'd take away about that amount."

"Wow. This is really something. Do you know if Daigo went into Ishida Antiques and removed the lacquer from the safe?"

"No. Mayumi took it herself, a month before the earthquake, because she knew the combination. She met Daigo at another restaurant and gave him everything. Ooh, he paid her nicely for it—with more to come, after the lacquer sold."

"I'm confused," I said with a sinking feeling. "Did the lacquer already sell?"

"That's what we're not sure about," Glock said. "Daigo gave her a receipt, just like it was a regular business. He said she'd get all the cash after everything sold."

"How much do you trust Daigo?"

"I don't know him well at all. But my boyfriend would break his legs if he didn't come through." Eri moved a finger quickly from the outside edge of her eye to her lips.

She'd made the symbol that meant *yakuza*.

"Daigo didn't tell Mayumi where the stuff was going to be sold," Glock said. "But about two weeks after she'd given it to him, a catalog about an upcoming antiques auction came by mail to Ishida Antiques. There weren't any pictures, but she saw a listing with information about her stuff going up for sale at an auction house somewhere. We didn't know it was Tohoku, so that's why we were so surprised yesterday."

"Did you ever hear the auction house name, though? Was it Takara?"

"She never showed me the catalog—she threw it in the trash at a train station, so Mr. Ishida wouldn't see it," Glock said. "But she was worried because if it was in a catalog, her parents might hear about the sale. She also knew Ishida-san was planning a spring buying trip that would include auctions."

"Ishida-san told me Mayumi tried to talk him out of the whole trip to Tohoku," I remembered. "But I don't know how anyone could keep him from an annual business trip he really enjoys."

"A few days before the trip, she lied and said an important client had phoned and wanted to see him on March eleventh. But that didn't change his mind. She was desperate, so she removed his *inkan* from his satchel, reasoning that he'd have to come back to Tokyo because he couldn't purchase goods without having it."

"But that wasn't really true, because he's well known," I said.

"I don't know. But she took a trip to deliver it to him. She thought if she was there, she might be able to distract him during the time at the auction the items were going to be sold."

"And we know she also contacted her parents and tried to get them to meet her there." I paused. "It's so strange. Why would she expose herself like this to both of them?"

"She didn't tell me she contacted her parents." Glock looked surprised.

"She might have wanted one of them to vouch it was their property to the auction-house owner," I mused. "But her parents would of course ask how the items reached the auction in the first place."

"Ishida-san was there. He would have told them everything had been in the safe, waiting to go back to them," Glock said. "It could have all turned out okay."

This was a very childlike way of looking at the situation. I shook my head. "Well, excepting for the fact Daigo's business deal would have been shot. And he would not have liked that at all."

"Mmm-hmm," Glock said. "That's why we think she might not have died in a tsunami—but for a different reason."

CHAPTER 30

By the time I paid for lunch and said goodbye to Glock and Eri, it was one thirty. The three of us had turned possible situations around in our heads so many times that we were thoroughly confused. But the upshot was Mayumi had created a situation far more dangerous than I'd realized. Now there were leads on where the lacquer might be—but the chance of regaining it would be next to impossible if gangster intermediaries were involved.

I had seen Michael, Enrique, and Richard leave the restaurant, still in high spirits, a while back. A text from Michael revealed he'd gone to his second meeting. *Tell all at 5,* he'd texted, suggesting as a meeting point the Hachiko statue outside Shibuya Station. He also mentioned that he had custody of my bag that Richard had kept safe for me the previous evening.

I still had some spare afternoon hours. I could stop in to see Mr. Ishida. If I told him what I'd learned at lunch, many of the beliefs he held about the helplessness of his apprentice would be shattered. Still, there was a chance that the receipt for the lacquer was among the papers we'd taken. I didn't know what we could do with such a receipt, if the go-between was a gangster. But Mr. Ishida had been in the business for a long time and might have an idea.

Mr. Ishida was reviewing his accounts when I stepped over his threshold. Hachiko trotted to the door to greet me with many circular tail wags. I baby talked to her, allowing her to come close enough to my face to smell the mushroom-sun-dried tomato-goat-cheese pizza I'd had for lunch. No meat or fish but she still seemed approving.

"Ah, good timing. Five minutes later, and Hachiko would have taken me on our evening walk. Say—you look a bit different today. What is it?"

I took off the newsboy cap, expecting him to comment on my short hair. But instead he said, "Aha! It's a new hat, but just like the ones from the 1950s. I quite like it. By the way, are you finished looking through Mayumi's sketchbook?"

"I think so. You can look at it, too, although some of the art within is a little—unorthodox."

"Ah, that's what makes it art. So, what have you been doing?"

"I visited a few places between yesterday evening and this morning. There are some things that I've learned. It would be better if I could tell the whole story."

Mr. Ishida listened carefully as I showed him the record of subtly threatening texts I'd been receiving since going to Glock and Eri's apartment. I explained that Michael had figured out my e-mails had been sent on to another address, and that my voice mails and texts also had gone to the same anonymous individual.

"We removed all the tracking and forwarding from the phone, and that seems to have stopped the text messages," I continued.

"But then Glock contacted me about information she and Eri had about Mayumi that they were afraid to share yesterday."

Mr. Ishida's expression seemed to close as I narrated how Mayumi had accompanied Eri on an *enjo-kousai* evening and decided to put the lacquer in the hands of a gangster who told her he could fence it outside of Tokyo. He shook his head when I said that she'd figured out his safe's combination and passed the lacquer onto Daigo, taking a receipt and trusting the sale would go through. And then she saw her family's lacquerware listed in a catalog for an auction on March 11.

"When she couldn't draw you away from your planned business trip during that time, she decided she had to go. The girls don't know the name of which auction house it was, but I'm guessing Takara. Perhaps she went out there to explain to Mr. Morioka about the goods coming from gangsters or belonging to her parents."

He was silent for several minutes. "When I reached the auction house, of course I picked up a catalog. The Kimura lacquer was not listed."

"Maybe she reached out to Morioka-san ahead of time. If so, he should have told us."

"He surely would have told us after we described the lacquer to him. No—it could be a different auction house. Or perhaps the roommates' story is wrong."

"Maybe. But they seemed quite honest."

"Why would they tell you this, anyway?" Mr. Ishida sounded impatient.

"Because they think Mayumi might have been killed. And if gangsters are involved, it's a threat to them if the police know. It's all a big mess—"

"What did they say about Akira? He could have killed Mayumi."

"They didn't talk about Akira. But I have confirmed with him that he followed Mayumi and Glock to a gay bar, although he didn't really understand those implications." I stopped, realizing this probably was the first time Mr. Ishida had heard anything about Mayumi's private life.

"That she preferred women?" Mr. Ishida said into the silence. "I'm not shocked, Shimura-san. This kind of thing has quietly gone on for all of recorded history. Look at some of those old *shoujo manga* prints that fetch high prices. There are even a few in this shop."

"Back to Akira," I said quickly. "I made a quick call this afternoon to the construction company where he worked, and the human resources department verified he was an employee. I chose to check on him that way, instead of using the superintendent's direct line, but the superintendent checked out with HR, too."

"They must have been very curious why you were so nosy about their employees," Mr. Ishida said.

"I just told them I was from the government." I sighed. "We were talking about Mayumi's transfer of the lacquer to Daigo, who brought it to an auction house. Apparently he gave her a receipt. If we can find that within her possessions, do you think it could be useful?"

"I hardly think her parents would want to present it to anyone." Mr. Ishida shook his head. "This is very bad stuff. We must warn Morioka-san."

"It's a conversation that should be face to face," I said. "I want to go back to Sugihama and find out whether he knows more about the lacquer than he let on to Ishida-san and me."

"How long would this trip be?"

"Train service is back in operation to quite a number of towns in Tohoku. I wouldn't have to wait for a volunteer bus. It could possibly be a one-day trip, or just an overnight."

"I am concerned about your travel. Now that we are thinking about gangsters, the situation seems more dangerous."

"I'll ask Michael to go with me. His work is winding down, anyway."

"Very well. I shall spend the rest of today and tomorrow looking through Mayumi's possessions for a receipt, and also make some calls to learn about the background of Mr. Morioka and the shop he once had in Tokyo."

"That would be great," I said, as his clock chimed on the half hour. "Four thirty already. I need to dash to meet Michael at Shibuya Station."

"Be very careful, Shimura-san."

"I promise not to jaywalk." He knew very well that I didn't always observe Japanese street etiquette.

"I mean be very careful when you return to Sugihama. Especially now that dangerous men may be involved."

The trains were running on time, and the commuter crowd had resumed its normal, gigantic size. Because of this increased human traffic, I had trouble getting to the front of the subway platform so I could get inside a subway car. Then it was moving like quicksand to proceed up the various stairs and out the Shibuya Station's west exit to the bronze version of Hachiko.

When I arrived twenty minutes late, Michael was restlessly pacing.

"I was worried you might not make it," he said, taking me in his arms. When the hello kiss ended, I realized at least two groups of teens were peering at us and tittering. They might have been unsure if the person who looked like Oliver Twist from behind was male or female. They might still not know.

"Sorry to be late," I said.

"It's okay. But after what happened at lunch, I've got serious concerns."

I looked at him in surprise. "I thought you didn't understand much of the conversation—but did Richard translate after you went outside?"

"No, none of us could hear much. But the girl in the black dress made a gesture with her hand that looked like a gang symbol."

"Yes. She was talking about someone who wasn't around." I lowered my voice. "Sorry to put you off a while longer, but we won't have the privacy to talk about it until we reach my aunt's house."

The ride was interminable, but at least it was Michael pressed up against my back and buttocks, and not some stranger. I winked at him as we disembarked.

As we walked uphill in the cool evening, and the crowds faded away, I told him what the girls had said during lunch.

"Of course I'll go with you to Sugihama," Michael said. "But why not just call Morioka?"

"If we can catch Mr. Morioka off guard, we might convince him to give the lacquer back to us, because there's a huge chance he has it. If it's over the phone, he could hide things. You know how my phone was missing for so long, and it turned out it was in his shop? I believed he'd only just found it... but maybe he hadn't."

"Which means he's the likeliest person to be your texting enemy." Michael sighed. "I don't know if it's worse to have the texter be him or someone in the *yakuza*."

"Oh, the *yakuza's* much more dangerous, and I don't think they're likely to be in Tohoku at the moment," I added. "There's also a possibility that Morioka-san is completely innocent of everything, and the Kimura lacquer went to another place holding an auction on the same fateful day."

"Mr. Ishida could look into that," Michael said. "But I still am putting my—our—money on Morioka as being our bad guy."

"But he saved Mr. Ishida's life. That's got to count for something." I felt restless. "Why is all this craziness continuing? I need to leave by Tuesday to get back to work."

"I don't think your aunt's going to like the sound of that."

"She never likes me leaving. So what else is new?"

Aunt Norie was more than annoyed that my limited time in Tokyo and Yokohama would be shortened further by another visit to Tohoku.

"I've been trying to put together a reception for you. A belated wedding reception. How can we have something when you're not here?"

"Obasan, you were at our wedding in Hawaii. There was a reception, remember, with wonderful platters of sushi and flowers around everyone's necks."

"But not every Japanese friend could come. And certainly, not my many friends from the world of flower arranging who are fond of you, and Chika, who will return from Osaka, and some of those people who work at Sendai Limited—"

"You're not thinking of a certain ex-boyfriend from Sendai Limited," I said.

"No, of course not. But I like the chairman of that company very much. For a Japanese wedding, all sorts of important people are invited. It's not just about young people and their friends."

"To do that kind of party right," Michael said, "it takes time. Wouldn't it be better if we returned during Christmas?"

"But there's a unique opportunity now," Aunt Norie pleaded.

"What?" I asked skeptically.

"So many events have been postponed because of earthquake problems. So there are last-minute openings at all kinds of hotels. The Yokohama Grand, that historic hotel with charming water views, has surprising availability. This would be our gift to the two of you."

"How generous! We are truly grateful. May we think about it some more?" Michael said, a properly subtle deflection.

"Rei, surely you want this lovely party as much as your husband does," my aunt said.

I shook my head. "I don't know that I'd be okay with another wedding reception now—or even later. Especially given the troubles of so many people, it seems selfish to hold an event where people will feel pressured to bring a cash gift of thirty- to fifty-thousand yen."

"People give that much at weddings?" Michael looked stunned. "I also wouldn't be comfortable raking in those kinds of amounts."

"Why don't you give any financial gifts to tsunami relief?" Aunt Norie suggested.

"May we give you our answer after the Tohoku trip is finished?" Michael asked. "I'm sure some kind of party to show support for

Tohoku would be welcome. That is, if Rei can get a few extra days off from her job."

My aunt nodded. "I'll just wait. But take the catering menus to study on the train, please."

CHAPTER 31

In Tokyo, I'd washed my body and hair with a whole system of green tea-lemongrass cleansing milk, shampoo, and conditioner. But as we disembarked in Sugihama, having taken a bus from the JR Ichinoseki Station, those pleasant aromas were quickly overpowered by the harsh odor of dead fish.

Michael's face was so motionless that it appeared he'd stopped breathing. My own insides heaved, and I started shallow nose breathing while I got the small gauze face masks out of my backpack and gave him one.

"How far to the volunteer shelter?" Michael asked.

"I have no idea. This bus stop wasn't operational before, so I don't know the area. But don't worry. Akira should be picking us up soon."

When Akira arrived with his truck, he greeted Michael with an enthusiastic bow followed by a firm handshake. Looking confidently into his eyes, Akira said, "I am glad you came along."

"Thanks very much, Rikyo-san." Michael spoke politely, but I knew he was still going to be wary of Akira until we'd resolved some outstanding questions. "I've been here once before, but I didn't know the way to reach the volunteer shelter."

"Yes, it's a bit uphill. Some roads are gone, but I have an idea how to get around it. By the way, please call me Akira, like Rei does. We are the younger generation, *neh?*"

"What are you and your father working on today?" I asked. "I hope getting us wasn't a major interruption."

"We were roofing. Not much fun, but it's necessary," Akira said. "I'm just surprised you're back. I didn't know that I would see you again, since you got the information you needed about me from my boss, right?"

How had he known I'd called human resources? I wondered if Akira had wanted to pick us up so he could figure out what we were still concerned about. I imagined Michael was thinking the same.

"I did get it, thanks," I said.

"My parents would like to see you two this evening for supper. We have a generator that allows for some lamps in the evening. And kerosene heaters for warmth."

"Actually, the circumstances are not good tonight." Michael trotted out the rote turndown a little too quickly to sound sincere.

Akira looked from Michael to me, shaking his head slightly. "It's no trouble for me to drive over and bring you this evening. There is hard work ahead of you. You should have something that is better than miso stew. We have plenty."

"I'm glad to hear it. We truly are looking forward to coming sometime soon." I wanted to soften Michael's rejection. "But my husband is right that we need to spend time checking with the shelter staff about our responsibilities before we make plans."

"Why are you back?" Akira asked.

"I wanted a chance to volunteer," Michael said.

It was an awkward ride, with as many bumps in the conversation as there were in the twisted road. I was sandwiched between Michael and Akira, who was driving as if it were possible to hurry through mud. I stared out the windshield, reversing my thoughts that the cleanup process was going well. Yes, there were plenty of workers here—but where would the mud go, the debris? It seemed as impossible as our own attempt to clean up the rotten end of Mayumi's life.

Mr. Yano was hauling some boxes into the shelter as Akira pulled up. He turned around and recognizing all of us, grinned. "Welcome back!"

"Well, see you," Akira said, his tone suggesting that we had in fact offended him by refusing to come over that evening.

"Bye, Akira-san. Thank you so much for the ride," I called, waving as he drove off, looking straight ahead.

"How was the train journey? My goodness, Rei-san, that is different clothing than we are used to seeing you in," Mr. Yano said in English.

"Michael teased me about it, but I didn't want to dress like a woodsman during the long train ride—I'd overheat," I said. I was actually wearing a Missoni sweater dress with tights and ankle boots—not what anyone would expect to see these days in Sugihama.

"And what about that fine red down jacket you wore last time?"

"It's in the bag for when I really need it. But the weather's so nice today."

"Isn't this what you Americans call sweater weather?"

"It's very good weather," said Michael, who'd already shrugged off his foul-weather anorak and was in fact wearing one of his favorite aged L.L.Bean sweaters. "Yano-san, although my wife and I have some unfinished business in town, I want to help with the cleanup, too. I hope our plans won't be an... imposition."

"Of course not. And I'm sure you could be of help in a seaside town—perhaps with maritime issues. Rei-san told me you were once with the navy."

"Yes, but it was more than ten years ago. I do know some officers working in the area, though. They've come up from Yokosuka to help."

"Well, maybe they can help us. Mayor Hamasaki hopes to move some boats that ran aground back to the water. We are having some trouble connecting with the Japan Maritime Self-Defense Force about this. They are incredibly busy, especially because of Fukushima."

"At least the Reactor Four fire is out," Michael said, and I could see from his relaxed stance leaning against the shelter wall that this was a tremendous relief, despite how much he muttered about continuing risks of radiation. "A few days ago I met a Navy officer who is a liaison to the JMSDF. I'll call her today—how are the phone lines? And can you tell me if any towns nearby have harbors that are still standing?"

As Michael and Yano-san continued discussing the intricacies of moving the landlocked boats, I was suddenly thrown backward by someone grabbing my waist and hips. Regaining my balance,

I turned around and saw that the surprise attack hugger was the small person I'd suspected.

"Rei-san! Your dress is so pretty and zigzaggy. You smell"—Miki inhaled deeply—"of oranges. But why is your long hair gone? I miss it."

"Um, it was a sudden decision. How's your father doing?"

"He's still in the hospital. Remember, you promised you'd visit him?"

"I did promise, didn't I?" And I knew that was where Tom was working and sleeping. If I went to the hospital to see Miki's father, I'd have a chance to catch up with my cousin. "What about tomorrow?"

"A minibus goes to the hospital every day after lunch. Come then," she implored.

"Okay, I will do my best to be on the bus with you. But first, there's some work I need to do in this town."

"I've been working outside, too. When it's not study time, we walk outside and look for toys and other important things. Somebody found my school bag with my stuffed Totoro inside. He was all wet and smelly, though. Like a lot of the stuff we find."

"Are you Miki-chan?" Michael crouched down and spoke in slow English to my young friend.

Miki covered her mouth with her hand and looked at me sideways. She whispered, "Who is that *gaijin*? Does he speak any Japanese?"

"Not as well as she does," Michael answered in Japanese, putting an arm around me. She gasped.

"His name is Michael Hendricks. He is my husband," I said to Miki, who was now laughing quite hard. "I found him in Tokyo and brought him back here."

"Tokyo's a funny place to find a *gaijin*. I would go to America if I wanted one."

Yano-san said, "I know you are happy to meet them, Miki-chan, but right now they must go next door to put away their luggage. I'm sure they will be back for the meal tonight."

"Rei-san, are you cooking again tonight?" Miki asked.

"Probably. Do you think miso stew's on the menu?"

"Yes, I chopped carrots for it earlier. But before we make supper, I'm going back to the shelter to check on my mother. Please come right away. She'll explain about riding to the hospital."

Miki was as firm as if she were my own mother. I smiled and said, "Of course. But first Michael-san and I will go upstairs to leave our bags."

Michael followed me up the temporary staircase to the volunteers' dormitory. After we'd stepped through the window opening, I waved Michael toward the men's side of the space.

"I'm not supposed to go past that line of boxes, but call if you need help," I advised him.

"Rei, just a minute!" As Michael touched my arm, I felt his anxiety.

"Honey, your Japanese is fine. Just tell them you're here to help, and they'll accept you. Really, don't worry."

"I'm not worried about fitting in," Michael whispered. "I'm concerned about all you're agreeing to do. We've got to make finding Morioka-san a priority. You've been talking about cooking, visiting folks in the hospital, and who knows what else is next."

"Morioka's within walking distance. We may still be able to slip out today. But we're part of a group. This means visiting Akira and his parents, plus Miki's father in the hospital, and doing some cleanup with Helping Hands, who are generously letting us sleep here because there's no other place to bunk in town!"

"I don't intend to take advantage of their hospitality. I'm just pleading with you not say yes to anything more."

"Plead a little harder," I said, jokingly motioning toward my boots. When he didn't get on his knees, I sighed and said, "I'll get behind those boxes now and change my clothes. After that, I'd love for you to come along and meet survivors in the shelter. They might be interested to know the real story behind the fire in Fukushima. So little information is in the news. People aren't sure what to believe."

"Okay. I'll drop off my stuff in the guy zone on the other side of that box wall and go back downstairs." Michael's voice was sincere—as were his eyes when he leaned forward to kiss my cheek. Now that so much of my hair was gone, his breath warmed my ear. It was better that he'd be on the men's side; lying chastely next to him at night would be too frustrating.

In the women's sleeping section, I met a few new female volunteers attempting to clean clothes with antiseptic wipes. A stylish girl I remembered seeing in the recent lineup for the bus was flat on her sleeping bag, exhausted, another woman whispered, from shoveling mud.

After I'd changed into jeans, a sweater, and boots, I went downstairs. I waved as I passed Michael, who was talking intently on the phone. From the acronyms he was using, I guessed he had reached a military person. "Go ahead," he mouthed at me, waving his hand. I was disappointed, but if he was this busy, it could mean something positive was happening.

In the survivors' shelter, numbers were diminishing, although Miki's family remained in the same cardboarded area as before.

"Welcome back, Shimura-san," Mrs. Haneda greeted me. "Miki said you might come to say hello. I do like your new hairstyle."

"Well, it's a bit short. But that's easier, isn't it?" I answered, properly deflecting the compliment.

"How clean you look," she gushed. "Is that makeup you're wearing or just the effects of soap?"

"Both, I think. How is your husband's recovery?"

"The infection is healing, but he still needs to remain in a very clean place, which is why he's being kept at the hospital. The girls miss being with him. I remind them how much more fortunate he is than most patients in the hospital."

"How is that? I thought being trapped like that was about the worst story I heard."

"At least he didn't witness others dying. A teenage boy was moved into my husband's ward. He survived hanging on for his life atop the jungle gym, but he saw his friends slip into the wave."

"That's awful." As I spoke, I remembered the playground near Takara Auction House. It had been a school once, somebody had said. "Was he at the playground near the auction house?"

"Yes, because the auction house once was a kindergarten. The playing space remained because the city legislators decided to keep it. Even older students enjoyed meeting each other there."

The playground was where Akira had told me Mayumi had met him when she'd visited Sugihama as a seventeen-year-old. Surely she had passed by this playground when she arrived on March 11 to the auction house.

"Miki's on the other side of the shelter," Mrs. Haneda informed me. "She is near her friend Keiko's family's space. The girls invited her to play with some toys they found outside in the mud—I'm sure the mother had them cleaned."

"It's nice the children are allowed to look for things outside," I said to Mrs. Haneda. "It keeps them active. I heard somebody found Miki's school bag and returned it to her."

"Yes, she was excited to have Totoro back—but not her math book," Mrs. Tanaka added with a laugh.

Miki was in a circle of three girls, all with neatly brushed hair that spoke of the good care they were still receiving amidst chaos. Their heads were bent over what looked like a rough dollhouse they'd made from parts of cardboard boxes. Each girl had a figure in her hand and seemed intent on finding the best place for it in the cardboard home.

"The mouse sleeps downstairs in the kitchen," Miki, always the organizer, said to her companions. "Keiko, you can put the old man upstairs in the *ofuro*. He will have a long bath because he got cold from the tsunami. And Mariko, use your handkerchief to make a bed for the little lady. She's just glad to be back in her own place, where there's peace and quiet."

Play therapy, I thought. A psychiatrist like my father might say that Miki was processing her trauma. But as I bent closer, still unobserved, I found myself stunned at the sight of the mouse Miki was twisting back and forth in her hand.

The mouse was made from wood, exquisitely carved with tiny ears, and a long tail that wrapped around his form. He was a stunningly polished deep gray color; a finish so smooth it looked like lacquer. Very old lacquer.

"Miki," I said, squinting hard at the object in her hand. "May I see your mouse?"

"Of course." She tossed it up to me and I caught it with trembling hands. I ran my fingers over the smooth little carved figurine, which was not a toy. It was an *inro*. Attached was a red silk cord that ran to a clasp shaped like a tiny kitten. This was the lacquer artist's humorous touch: making a mouse *inro* that was too big for the kitten to catch.

But I'd caught the joke—and also the realization—that these two exquisite items might be a piece of lacquer. As I turned the mouse over in my hand, the lacquer seemed to shimmer, and not just from the patina of age. It was a beacon of something that I realized might be the truth.

CHAPTER 32

"**D**id you find more any more pretty toys like this?" I was striving to sound relaxed, when all I wanted to do was jump up and down. After all, Mayumi had saved the lacquer; she'd got it back from wherever Daigo had brought it.

"Yes. In there." Miki pointed to a black leather backpack. "There are all kinds of toys in there. Nothing was wet or dirty. You can play, if you like."

I looked inside the bag and caught my breath. Numerous pieces of shining lacquer: among them a black *netsuke-inro* set decorated with lucky golden cranes, and a red lacquer box with a beautiful lady on it, and another set ornamented with a gold-leaf grasshopper. These were all things I remembered Mr. Ishida mentioning, and more. "I think I know whose toys these are. Oh, this is just wonderful."

"We have to give them back?" whined Miki.

Reaching out to stroke Miki's hair, I said, "I know the owners.

I'm sure they will be very grateful to you for finding their precious treasures. Where was this backpack?"

Miki frowned, still clearly disappointed. "I don't know. I didn't find it. Keiko did."

Keiko looked at me nervously. "We were near the old Family Mart. It was in a pile of stuff outside there."

"Did you dig very far down in the pile?" I asked, looking at the Coach backpack, which appeared rather clean.

"No. We had to climb up to get it. The backpack was right there, lying on top."

"Why don't you play a few more minutes, but carefully?" I wanted to be fair so the girls didn't come to equate telling the truth to adults with automatic loss.

"Oh, there's your *gaijin* husband. I think he's looking for you," Miki said.

"What a beautiful house you've made," Michael said in Japanese when he'd reached us and saw what the girls were doing.

"Yes, but Rei-san says we have to give back the animals who had just moved in." Miki sighed dramatically, and then added, "However, if we make the rooms a little bigger, my Totoro could fit."

"Yes, and my *daruma* doll," Keiko said.

"Don't forget about Pikachu," the third girl chimed in.

As the girls carried on playing, I opened my hand to show Michael the mouse *inro* in it. But his eyes didn't widen until I opened the backpack that was full of even more lacquer pieces still wrapped in tissue.

"Unbelievable," Michael said in English. "Could it be the Kimura family's lacquerware?"

"This is a Coach brand backpack just like the one Mr. Ishida says Mayumi owned, and what's inside fits his description of the lacquer collection. Apparently the girls found it atop a heap of trash."

"Have you checked for anything else in the backpack?"

"Let's do it together."

Michael slipped his hand in and explored. Eventually he came out with a lavender wand-style lip gloss. "A Shiseido brand luminizing lip gloss in a color called Cool. Aside from this, there's nothing."

"I know it was Mayumi's backpack." I lowered my voice and added, "The best part of removing it from a trash heap means we'll never have to negotiate for it with gangsters or Mr. Morioka. For all they know, it was lost in the tsunami."

"That's right," Michael said. "These are lost family possessions that have been found and are being returned."

Miki's friend Keiko was the one who'd picked up the backpack. She was the saddest about giving up the animals and insects. She slumped down, not looking as I carefully rewrapped everything she'd found. I talked to her parents about what was going on, so they didn't think we were stealing.

"Please take it. How wonderful that you know the owners!" Keiko's mother said. "This is a good experience for the children. It will give them the belief that others will bring back their own toys when they are found."

"Here you go, Keiko," Michael said in Japanese. She blinked as he pulled a supersized American Snickers bar out of the pocket of his windbreaker. Then he whipped out the pocketknife he always carried in the front pocket of his jeans and cut it into thirds for the girls.

Not as good as the toy animals, but it sweetened the parting.

An hour later I was in the kitchen, dropping noodles in the stockpot. As service began, I stood over it with a ladle. Dishing out bowl afer bowl of miso-carrot-onion *ramen*, I pondered the incredible luck of Miki's invitation to see the dollhouse. If Michael and I had refused and gone straight to chat with Mr. Morioka, we would have missed the girls playing with the lacquer animals.

After dinner was cleaned up, Michael caught up on his e-mails, and I sat nearby, placing a call to announce the find to Mr. Ishida.

"Are you sure it is the Kimuras' lacquer?" he pressed. "Almost every Japanese household has some lacquer treasures."

I gave him exact descriptions of all the pieces. At the end, I added, "And I know they're very old. There's a patina and clear evidence the pigments are natural, not synthetic."

"That sounds correct. However, I don't know why anyone would put such spectacular antiquities in a trash heap."

"A volunteer must have found the backpack and thrown it on, not knowing what was within," I said. "I asked during the dinner hour if anyone remembered finding a clean Coach backpack and transferring it to the heap, but nobody had."

"In any case, it's great news. The question is what will you do next?"

"My priority is to get the lacquer back to her parents. Michael's already arranged direct transportation through a military contact to their shop in their village, Kinugasa, tomorrow morning. If I'm back in time that afternoon, I'll visit Miki's father in the hospital with her. Michael and I hope to do some volunteer work for Helping Hands the day after that... and then it's back to Tokyo."

"I hope you'll have some time to relax a bit. How many days have you been in Japan?"

I counted backward. "Twelve. I'm really down to the end of my allotted leave. I should go back on Tuesday. My boss is expecting me to come back soon—"

"Yes, you've told me about Mr. Pierce. He sounds like a kind man, though."

"He is. But I don't want to take too much advantage of that kindness."

After one night back on the hard floor, all the restorative therapy of sleeping in real beds was undone. My back ached, and I knew that I was moving like an elderly woman. Michael rubbed my spine as we sat together on a bench outside the shelter. The sparkling morning light showed that yellow asters had sprung up next to the rubble heaps. They hadn't been there last week. Despite the earth's crack-up, it was still shooting out spring flowers.

Michael took his hands off me to look at his watch. "The jeep should be here soon."

"Okay. You know, we haven't talked about what we're going to say to the Kimuras." I put my face in my hands. "Imagine this. You're grieving the loss of a child who'd caused a great upset in the family by stealing its heritage. The treasure comes back. Do you really want to know the specifics about the treasure's return? Or would you rather believe it was your child's final gesture?"

Michael sighed. "I'd never want to hear lies."

"Here's how I plan to do it," I said. "When we get to the shop,

I'll apologize for disturbing them and immediately present the backpack with the lacquer. After they've happily accepted it, I'll tell them it was found on the street in Sugihama. Then I'll say that we visited Mayumi's apartment and removed her possessions to the custody of Mr. Ishida. I'll finish up by saying that we'll mail them home, if they want that. But I don't know what I should say beyond that."

"I don't either."

The jeep came at last; it was a half hour after the time Michael had been promised, and the driver, an American southerner, was flustered. "Sorry, sir, I got stuck behind a supply convoy. But the road to Kinugasa is not that bad. I went past there yesterday. I think we can get there in an hour."

Sir? I mouthed silently at Michael, who shrugged. The soldier's tone made me think he believed Michael was still an officer. With his marine haircut and crisp blue anorak worn over a polo shirt and jeans, he had a kind of bearing that wasn't exactly civilian. I'd gone for the upscale folk-arts shopper look, wearing indigo skinny jeans and a white silk blouse with my green boiled-wool jacket. I'd tied a multicolored *shibori*-patterned silk scarf around my neck. The only thing marring my appearance was the gauze nose-and-mouth mask that I felt was necessary to keep from vomiting at the smells around us.

Calling the road clear was an exaggeration; there was still plenty of waste that the driver cheerfully slalomed around. The young private chatted to Michael about being stuck in mud on three separate occasions earlier in the week. When I asked how he'd got the jeep moving again, he'd laughed and said, "Kitty litter. But now the commissaries are all sold out of it. We'll have to keep our fingers crossed."

Fortunately, as we proceeded inland and uphill, the trash and mud became more sporadic, as well as the dead fish. I took off the mask, put on some lip gloss, and smiled at Michael.

"Isn't it gorgeous?"

We'd moved past the wave's reach and were in the familiar, rolling Tohoku countryside of TV dramas and postcards. The town of Kinugasa was small and charming. A narrow road was lined by small shops on either side, many of them advertising pottery or lacquer. Hamlets like these usually were packed with tourists' cars during the spring sightseeing season. Today there were few cars with out-of-prefecture plates. I guessed that it would be a long time until tourists came back to Tohoku and Fukushima, even to inland towns like this that hadn't been touched by the wave or radiation.

"Kimura Lacquer!" I said, spying the *kanji* characters on a modest brown building a few yards ahead on the right. "This is the right place. "

"Did you say liquor?" the driver joked. "The guys and I could use something."

"Lacquer," I clarified. "Wooden objects painted with a kind of natural shellac. They are really gorgeous."

"Not that this is a shopping trip," Michael said tightly. Probably he didn't want any rumors arising about the misuse of official transportation. We were lucky to have had the ride, especially since we didn't even know if the Kimuras would let us in the door.

Fortunately, the blue *noren* curtain was fluttering over the door, signifying the business was open. I opened the door and went in first, holding Mayumi's backpack. Mrs. Kimura was behind a counter, going through a pile of receipts. Her shoulders were bent and her face drawn and tired-looking.

"Hello? Sorry for disturbing you—" I began.

As if operated by machinery, her head came up and she chirped out a welcome.

She hadn't recognized me with the new hairstyle and city clothes. I said, "We met before in Sugihama."

Now she took off the glasses she'd put on to do the accounting and stared at me. "Are you Shimura-san?"

"Yes. And this is my husband."

"Mr. Shimura?" Her eyes goggled at him. "Truly?"

"My name is Michael Hendricks," Michael answered with a grin in his American-accented Japanese. "My wife enjoys keeping her Japanese family name."

"I don't think my husband wants to see you. It's a difficult time, I'm very sorry—"

"Yes, it is a difficult time. But won't you please look at what we've brought?"

I put the backpack on the counter before her.

"What is this?"

Belatedly I remembered Mayumi had bought the backpack on sale in Tokyo. Her mother must never have seen it. "This is Mayumi's backpack. Some children found it yesterday, and there are some special things inside."

Slowly Mrs. Kimura pulled the zipper. She pulled out the first tissue-wrapped object. "This paper is from our shop." In a palm that was suddenly trembling, she unveiled a tiny grasshopper *inro*.

"This was made by my husband's great-great-grandfather." She looked at me. "Where did you find it?"

"Some little girls playing in Sugihama's business district came across Mayumi's backpack on a pile of rubble. They were so excited, thinking the *netsuke* and *inro* were toys—"

"Yes," she said with a wistful half smile. "Mayumi wanted to play with the *inro* when she was young. I told her no, they were too special. But now, I wish I hadn't."

"We can't fully understand what our possessions mean to others. I think about that often when I work with antiques." I paused. "I'm grateful for the chance to see you again. I apologize to you and your husband for troubling you with the details of Mayumi's death. That was too painful right after learning she was gone."

She shook her head. "Please don't be sorry. We were so rude because we were upset. But I think we can feel peace again, if not today, sometime soon. I'm sure that she meant to bring the lacquer home. It means she never stopped loving our family."

She had given me the answer about what *not* to say. I wouldn't explain that Mayumi preferred her new, adventurous life in Tokyo, and in fact had intended to sell the lacquer so she and her girlfriend could set themselves up. I wouldn't say it, because I had no intention of giving these people sorrow that they didn't need.

"Is your husband here as well? We would like to pay our respects," Michael said.

"Yes, and he will want to thank you. I'll fetch him from the studio. Just a minute, please." And Mrs. Kimura hurried out the door, still holding the grasshopper in her hand.

Mr. Kimura arrived still wearing an apron over heavy canvas work pants. He nodded at Michael and me before going straight to the backpack. Each piece was pulled out, unwrapped, and studied.

At last, he spoke. "Thank you for bringing this. Everything is here. But I would like to say something else."

"Of course, Kimura-san." I was glad that at least he was speaking to us.

"You were correct that she did not die from drowning."

"Oh," I said, completely caught off guard. "Did you learn something new?"

"The death probably came because of a fall. She had bleeding inside her brain."

"Sorry?" Michael said, who'd missed a few words. Quickly I translated for him.

"She had bleeding inside her head," Mr. Kimura repeated. "This is what the policeman who called us said. The likely way to have such bleeding is if the head is impacted—like falling down."

"Did you ask the police to investigate?" I asked.

Mrs. Kimura glanced at her husband, who nodded. Then she spoke. "As you know, the funeral happened three days ago. There was a delay for Mayumi's cremation until yesterday because of so many people requesting such services."

This was a grisly situation I didn't want to ruminate much longer about. I was glad when she continued.

"During the time we were waiting, one of the doctors at the Sendai Community Hospital phoned the police. He said there was some irregularity in our daughter's death report and was willing to make an x-ray. The crematorium staff brought her in the casket. We were too upset to attend, but later the police telephoned and explained the doctor's findings. Apparently the added check showed that she had died by falling. They thought we'd appreciate knowing this."

"I'm sure," I agreed, knowing that Sendai Community Hospital was where Tom was moonlighting.

"I had a new wave of sadness knowing this," Mrs. Kimura said. "For Mayumi to have survived and then hurt herself so badly that she died..."

"We only hope she wasn't in great pain," Mr. Kimura said.

I heard the industrial beep of Michael's cell phone.

"Excuse me," he said. "I've just got word about the boat-moving project. I had to text that I'd be at the right place soon for a meeting."

"Our daughter really liked to text message," Mr. Kimura said. "She found it more convenient than speaking aloud."

"We will be in Japan a few more days," I said. "I'll help Mr. Ishida mail the rest of Mayumi's possessions to you right here. We brought them out of the apartment where she stayed. But unfortunately, there's no phone with it."

"I wouldn't expect that," Mrs. Kimura said. "She surely brought her phone on this trip. But it's a shame not to have it, isn't it?"

"Do you know what I think is a shame?" Mr. Kimura said to his wife.

"No." She looked anxiously at him.

"I wish we had saved the buttons from her coat." Mr. Kimura shook his head. "I was too upset to think of asking for those when she was being prepared for the funeral. They could have become part of our heirloom collection."

"But there are more buttons," I reassured them. "I found a box of them in her closet. You will see them. They're wonderful."

"Oh, that is a great gift," Mr. Kimura said. "We would not have known they still existed if you hadn't gone to her place. We are so grateful. I'm sorry about the other day. I just didn't understand that you cared."

"Yes," I said softly.

"I'm sorry, but we must go now." Michael's voice cut in gently. "It's an issue with our transport. Again, we offer our sincere condolences about your daughter."

"You know, the last year was quite hard for us. Everyone around us thought we had a bad daughter. It was easier to only speak to her about getting the lacquer back. But what we really needed to make things right was—just her."

"Don't leave yet," Mrs. Kimura said, going back to the counter and reaching into a drawer. She came out with a ribbon-wrapped box. "This is for the little girls who found the lacquer collection. It's a group of *kokeshi* dolls. Five of them. They are lacquered, not painted, which is a bit unusual."

"Oh, I'm sure they would be delighted." These sounded like extremely beautiful, high-end dolls that would impress the girls—and their parents.

Mrs. Kimura said, "I would like to give you a gift as well. Do you care for lacquer?"

"Of course, but I don't deserve anything. I only wish I had come here many years ago when I lived in Japan and met you two with your daughter. Maybe at one of those craft shows—that's my kind of thing."

Mrs. Kimura glanced at me, as if assessing my sincerity again, and then reached into a drawer. She leafed through some envelopes and came up with two wallet-sized snapshots. She handed me the two pictures of a smiling Mayumi about fourteen years old. Her hair was braided and she wore a nautical-style black-and-white school uniform. *Before she met Akira,* I thought. When there was still peace at home.

"Are you sure you can spare these sweet pictures?" I asked.

"We have many copies of this school picture," Mrs. Kimura said. "One is for yourself, and the other, for Ishida-san. I want you to know how she was when she was still a little girl."

"She's very lovely. I will treasure this picture, and so will Mr. Ishida."

CHAPTER 33

We didn't say much on the way back. Mr. Kimura really didn't strike me as the one who'd sent threats to my cell phone. And his wife had freely shared information about Mayumi's head injury. It nagged at me, though. While a fall could cause internal bleeding, so could a heavy blow.

But Mayumi's body had been cremated. There was no chance to take anyone's questions further.

Michael asked the driver to take a different road as we approached Sugihama. "See those grounded boats up ahead?" he said to me. "Those are the ones finally getting moved."

"Well, how's that going to happen?"

"A combination of a crane and flatbed truck. The text I received said to look out for a special kind of tow truck with a flatbed attached. The driver will leave me to wait for it to arrive."

"Hmm. I don't like the idea of you hanging here all alone."

"I have to sign for it," Michael said with a shrug. "Don't worry, nobody's stalking me. I'd rather have you return to the shelter now so you can still visit the hospital with the Hanedas."

"But Michael, you only had a couple of granola bars for breakfast, and it's lunchtime. We should have taken the time to get food when we were in the village—"

"I've got plenty of MREs for you to choose from," the driver said, turning around to wink at Michael.

"Fair enough," I said as the jeep halted for Michael's departure. "You take that little foil-wrapped mystery meal. I prefer miso stew."

When the military driver dropped me at the shelter a half hour later, though, I found that lunch was over and done with. The minibus bound for the hospital in Sendai was already filling up. As was becoming my habit, I was the last person to scramble on.

"Sit with us!" Miki demanded, patting the bench next to her and her sister. It was a tight fit as I maneuvered myself into about fourteen inches of space, so I wound up with Chieko on my lap.

"Shimura-san, how lucky that you returned in time to ride with us. Where were you all day?" Mrs. Haneda inquired. She was in the seat behind us with the baby.

"Michael and I returned the lacquer Miki and her friends found. The owners were so grateful to the girls. They also gave them a special gift." I presented the box and let Miki and Chieko open it together. The sisters squealed over the five brilliantly colored dolls and then became busy deciding who would get which one. I handed the smallest one to Mrs. Haneda to save for the baby to enjoy in a few years, and put the remaining two dolls away for Keiko and the other girl who'd been with her when the lacquerware was found.

"*Kokeshi* dolls are very special to this region. Do you know why?" Mrs. Haneda asked.

"They were originally created by carpenters in Tohoku and sold as souvenirs in hot spring towns, right?"

"That's correct. But did you know about the special wood used for the doll's head?"

"No. Isn't it just pine?"

"Actually, it's called *mizuki*: water wood. This is an excellent wood because it resists the flames. So while some people feel a *kokeshi* doll is a charm for having a healthy child, others think it's a way to keep your home safe from fire." She paused. "So, because of these fine gifts, after we move into our next home, we can feel very safe."

Fire was the opposite of water. But there was no talisman that could possibly protect Sugihama from too much water hitting it again. I'd heard of a Japanese coastal town that had been lashed by tsunamis on four occasions spanning just one hundred years. I didn't say anything about my thoughts, but I wasn't sure it was worth settling so close to water again—for the Hanedas, and for everyone else.

The question of Tohoku's future hung with me as we entered Sendai City. Here, it was too far from the ocean for the wave to have come, but the quake's effects on buildings was much more dramatic than it had been in Tokyo. I'd heard about many days in Sendai without electricity and fresh water, and terrible damage to its buildings, so I was relieved that the tall, modern hospital building where we stopped looked relatively unscathed.

Every passenger had someone to visit in the hospital. However, the first stop for most was the restroom, with real toilets enclosed in stalls and fresh water running in sinks. At least, that's what I expected was behind the closed door with a little lady icon. I figured I'd visit the honorable hand-washing place when the line wasn't so long, and use the gap of time while the Hanedas awaited their turns to check in with Tom.

I'd texted Tom on the ride over but heard nothing. So I decided to politely raise the big-shot Tokyo E.R. doctor's name with the information desk attendant.

"I'll page him right now," the receptionist said after I explained that I was his cousin. A few minutes later, Tom emerged hurriedly from the elevator, his white coat worn open over a sweater and jeans.

"Not the way doctors dress at St. Luke's International Hospital, huh?" I teased with a grin. "But where are those great wading boots?"

"Hey, this is a nice surprise," Tom smoothly ignored my ribbing. "I thought you were in Tokyo. Did you ever find Michael?"

"Yes, he's come back to Tohoku with me but is doing his own thing right now."

"And what is your thing, Rei? You've got the look I know. I'm about to get some questions, right?"

"First things first." Quickly, I explained about finding the lacquer and returning it to Mayumi's parents—who'd given me some startling information about their daughter's head injury. "The parents also mentioned a doctor performed an autopsy of Mayumi." I looked hard at Tom. "I can't imagine how that happened."

"I did an informal postmortem examination." Tom was

speaking English, something I guessed he was doing both for privacy and because my knowledge of Japanese medical terminology was limited. "Let's sit down over there, and I'll explain."

As I perched beside him on a vinyl chair in a reception area, Tom's voice remained low. "I made a call to the Sugihama police saying I'd heard about a suspicious death. I asked if I could run some x-rays on the body before cremation. A look at the bones was really all I could do because she was so decomposed."

"I remember," I said, swallowing hard. "It was really generous of you to do the examination. I don't even know how you heard I was concerned about the circumstances of her death."

"Michael had a little information you texted to him, but it was Michiko—I mean, Nurse Tanaka—who really explained what was going on. I felt badly for the young lady. Some others were getting autopsies—so why not her?"

"Tell me everything about the x-rays. What the Kimuras know, they heard from the police, and who knows how the story might have been altered?"

"When I reviewed the film, there was clearly a crushed area in the front of the cranium. Bone shattered and pierced the brain. She would have lost consciousness quickly, but also slowly bled to death."

"Do you think a fall crushed her skull?"

"This is the unclear part. Falls usually cause head injuries to the rear of the skull. Mayumi's head injury was in front, close to the top of her forehead. The splintering was more consistent with contact from a hard object. If she fell, she would only have fallen forward and bumped against something high."

"Mayumi had been found in the room's center, not near a wall,"

I said. Tom was silent, and during this time I thought about Asao and Daigo, the two gangsters that Glock and Eri had mentioned. If they'd confronted her at the auction house and grabbed her outside, they could have knocked her in the head and then left her body wherever they pleased.

Tom's voice interrupted my thoughts. "Now, the second part of my findings. The x-ray also showed a shoulder dislocation—the left shoulder, I believe. This trauma could have been caused by either a fall or a punch."

"When we saw her in the butcher shop, she was curled in a fetal position. Why would anyone curl up after falling down?"

"Someone in pain might do that to try to comfort herself," Tom said. "It seems to suggest being conscious for a while, rather than being knocked out cold."

"How awful for her," I said, imagining it.

"The police didn't contact me about the report, which makes me think they've accepted the idea of a fall. They may have communicated this information to Mayumi's parents. If you'd like, I can call them later, but unfortunately, I've got to return to work."

Shoot. I'd have to delay telling him about the gangsters, a detail that would have raised his eyebrows, to say the least. "Tom, your decision to examine her was really important. I don't know if anything will ever come of it, but thank you so much."

"If I can help, I'll do it. I learned that approach from a younger cousin." Tom gave me a light pat between my shoulders.

I smiled halfheartedly. "I'm on my way to visit a male patient in his thirties called Haneda-san. He was crushed under a vending machine."

"Haneda-san is recovering nicely. It seems that almost all the survivors who've made it to this hospital are extremely tough. I don't know if it's the Tohoku genes or just determination. A teenaged patient in the same room as Mr. Haneda has a similarly incredible survival story about a jungle gym—you should ask him."

Tom gave me a swift goodbye hug just as Miki and her family emerged from the ladies' room. Riding up in the hospital elevator, I realized the teenager Tom had spoken about was the same person Mrs. Haneda had mentioned.

The patients' room was sunny, with its window shades pulled all the way up, a standard procedure in Japanese hospitals. I could barely recognize the good-looking man wearing fresh pajamas and sitting upright in bed as the filthy, gaunt wreck I'd met a little more than a week ago. The girls rushed to surround their father, leaning in to hug and kiss him until Mrs. Haneda lifted up the two older ones to cuddle on either side of his bed.

"You must be Shimura-san," he said, bowing his head toward me. "I heard the lifesaver was coming. Thank you for what you did last week. So many times people walked by and never heard me call for help."

Bowing back, I told him, "But Hachiko was the one who knew you were there. She smelled you and was absolutely set on getting you out."

"This dog deserves a big bone. I'd like to give her one."

"I wish I could have brought her with me," I said. "Unfortunately, she's gone to Tokyo and resumed her old life in Mr. Ishida's shop."

"A dog that goes shopping? That's very funny," Miki giggled, and her parents laughed along.

"I'm so delighted you're doing this well," I said to Mr. Haneda.

"I understand one of my doctors is your relative," Mr. Haneda said. "He says I'll be released soon, as long as there is good temporary housing for me to go straight into."

"My husband can't stay on a shelter floor," Sadako said to me, "and it will be at least another week until trailers are delivered. And then, we have to find furnishings."

"I hear the trailers will be in Sugihama, not too far from my office," Mr. Haneda said.

"But your office is closed for a long time. That would make it easy to stay with your sister in Yokohama, who's offered several times."

Slowly, he shook his head. "But that's inconvenient for her. She has her own children and husband. The place is not large. It's better to stay in Sugihama."

"Yes, Otoochan. Then Butter will come home," Miki said.

"She was just so glad you were alive—and there are jobs there—good schools..."

As Mrs. Haneda began murmuring to her husband, I felt I was becoming an intruder on a very painful, personal scene.

While the parents remained locked in discussion, the daughters had moved on. Chieko and Miki were showing their *kokeshi* dolls to the patient in the other bed. As I walked closer, I saw he was covered in even more bandages than Mr. Haneda, plus casts on all limbs.

"This is our big-boy friend, Masa-kun!" Miki announced when she noticed I'd come over to them. "Please meet Rei-san. She came from Hawaii. She had a really nice dog for a while, but now she's in Tokyo."

"Are you the famous one who survived by holding onto the jungle gym?"

"Yes, that's me." A smile emerged between the bandages. "But I wasn't on the jungle gym for long."

"Really?" I asked, glad that he was interested in talking.

"The wave swung me all around so that I couldn't hold on anymore. I caught hold of a building roof that was floating in the current. Ten hours later I was rescued."

"What an incredible story. A lot of people are talking about it."

He shook his head. "I learned a little too late that staying on the jungle gym wasn't an intelligent idea. My friends didn't make it. All of them drowned."

"I'm so sorry."

"You know, I climbed that jungle gym because I wanted to make a movie on my cell phone. I really thought the town's sea wall was going turn it back."

"When I was watching television in Hawaii, I saw the wave come up over the sea wall," I told him.

"Because we were high, I could see the water coming in. Right then I began thinking of trying to get to the evacuation staircase, but it seemed too late. A girl yelled at us to run with her into the old kindergarten; it's the tallest building on the street. A couple of my friends followed her, but they ran out again and said the door to the upstairs was locked shut and the guy wouldn't let them in. They climbed up the jungle gym to be with me. By that time, the water was coming into the street."

After his words, I felt like all the other sounds in the room had faded. "How old was the girl?"

"She was maybe a little older than us. I hadn't seen her before. She probably came from out of town."

"Was her hair blue?"

"Um—it was a distance, so I couldn't see clearly. I don't think it was black—it was something weird. Do you know her?"

"A little bit. Can you remember which direction that girl went when she came back out of the auction house? Was anyone with her?"

"I really don't know." He lay still, and I sensed how hard he was thinking. "I didn't see her come out. I remember my friends, because they came back to the jungle gym and climbed up. We were all getting nervous."

Mr. Ishida had believed that she left the building for good. Masa was saying otherwise. What was the truth?

"Masa-kun, did you see two men hanging around the shop at all? One man, any man? Someone who didn't run away, but lingered?"

"No. All those auction people drove away right after the earthquake happened, but before the wave."

"That makes sense." I put my fingertips on my temples. My head was aching, very likely because I'd become faint from hunger—and this strange new information.

"Are you feeling all right, Shimura-san?" Mrs. Haneda asked from her chair near her husband's bed.

"I'm getting a headache. I'd better find some aspirin and have a snack. What time will the minibus leave?"'

"We still have thirty minutes. Do you want Miki to help you?" Mrs. Haneda looked concerned.

"No, thanks. I'd rather take care of myself. I'll meet you in the hospital driveway when it's time to go. Goodbye, Masa-kun. Thank you for telling me all that information. I wish you a continuing great recovery—and to you as well, Haneda-san. It could be fun for your family to stay a while in Yokohama. I like that town a lot."

"Are you sure you're all right alone?" Mrs. Haneda called after me, but I was moving too fast to answer.

CHAPTER 34

Back on the main floor, I went to the seating area where I'd met with my cousin and took out my phone to ring Michael. His voice recording sounded distant and formal. I guessed he couldn't answer because he was in the midst of moving the boats.

Just for the record, I left a detailed message starting with Tom's information about Mayumi's injuries, and then Masa's thought that Mayumi had gone in—but not out of—the Takara Auction House. I said that I would be returning soon with the minibus.

As I hung up, I realized the headache had intensified. I needed to eat. Through the hospital's clear glass windows, I saw the red and yellow signage of McDonald's. I wasn't a usual customer, but what else would be instantly available?

I hurried across the street to purchase "Mega Potato," a pound of fried shoestring potatoes, plus a vanilla shake. As bad as it all sounded, I felt the shakiness drain from me. This was the power of fast food. I resolved not to criticize Michael so much for his McDonald's habit. I had forgotten about aspirin, but had just enough time to throw away the meal's paper wrappings, wipe my hands, and get back to the minibus that had returned to the hospital driveway.

"Did you have a bath?" I asked Miki as we boarded. Her hair was sopping wet, and she smelled like soap.

"A shower. We all took turns in the shower of Otoochan's hospital bathroom. The nurses allowed it, even though we aren't staying there."

"*Kizuna,*" I said.

"What?"

It felt odd to explain a Japanese word to a Japanese child. But it had only been spoken widely since the tsunami. "*Kizuna* means connection: the help people give each other, especially when there's serious trouble. Remember when you gave me the rice balls for breakfast? Ishida-san and I wouldn't have had anything to eat that morning if it wasn't for your *kizuna.*"

I thought of Akira and his father rebuilding houses and shops. And of Michael, sending boats run aground back to the sea. But above all, I was remembering Mayumi, who had tried to save not just herself and Mr. Ishida, but some unknown teenage boys on a jungle gym.

"Oh, I understand now," Miki said. "It's like my aunt and uncle wanting us to stay with them in Yokohama. But I'd rather live here."

"Sugihama's wonderful. Yokohama is also a good town with a lot of fun things. I stayed there every summer with my relatives when I was a little girl."

"Yes, that Shimura-sensei who's your cousin told us. The problem is that if we go so far away... how will Butter know where to find us?"

I thought of saying they could have a new dog, but that would be like telling a mother that having a new child would help her work through losing the old one. "Everyone is looking for Butter. His name is on his collar. Either he will be found here or he's found another family who've welcomed him. He could have swum to their house."

"He knows how to swim—but I don't want to, anymore. It was cruel of the ocean to kill people and take away our houses."

"I can understand your feeling." I realized that, since coming, I'd been unable to look at the ocean due to resentment—and fear. I hoped this feeling would fade, because I was eventually headed back to my own coastal home.

As we drew closer to Sugihama, the bus began making familiar, uncomfortable detours around gigantic objects in its path. The bus passed the corner of the street with the auction house, butcher shop, and some other unopened businesses. But the grocery and hardware stores had noren curtains hanging outside and their lights on. This was a great sign. Some of the bus riders, in fact, called out polite requests for the bus driver to please stop for a moment so they could get out and speak to the shop owners and perhaps buy some necessities.

Once the driver stopped, I decided to disembark, as well. I still needed aspirin, and I wanted to visit the nearby street where the girls had said they'd found Mayumi's backpack. I also needed to ascertain whether the Takara Auction House door was in clear view of the jungle gym where Masa had perched. I figured that I could be finished in about a half hour and walk the mile back to the shelter.

I explained my plan to the Hanedas, promising I'd see them at dinner. Then I joined the line to get off.

I hurried ahead of the shoppers, passing the butcher's shop and aiming for the Family Mart. Although the convenience shop was still closed, it was brightly lit within, revealing a group of people scrubbing and shoveling. Outdoors, on the side of the shop, a small rubble pile lay. This was the place where the girls had found Mayumi's backpack. A young woman wearing denim overalls and long, thick rubber gloves was examining each piece from the big pile before placing it onto a new pile. I saw piles for photographs, sodden books and papers, toys, and kitchenware.

I greeted the woman and asked if she'd let me sort through some of the piles.

"Wouldn't you rather come back when you're dressed to work?" She looked skeptically at my outfit.

"Yesterday some girls found a backpack belonging to a young woman called Kimura Mayumi. I've returned to look around because the pack didn't contain Mayumi's cell phone. I thought there might be a chance it was in another place."

"We have a section of phones, but almost all of them are broken because of their hours underwater. Do you know the phone's make and model?"

"I believe it's a later model iPhone inside a case featuring the cartoon character Totoro."

"Better put some gloves on. And please roll up the sleeves of your nice cardigan."

I put on rubber gloves and began examining mobile phones. So many different brands of phone, and even one Totoro case, although it was yellow and housed a Samsung. I kept picking up phones, the gloves growing grimier from all that I touched. I was looking for a clean phone, because it had probably been with Mayumi all along. And the only reason it hadn't been in the backpack—or on Mayumi's body—was because someone had separated it from her.

After I was done, I said goodbye to the woman, who promised to send the phone over to the volunteer shelter in care of Mr. Yano, should it be found. I felt too grubby to go into the Family Mart for aspirin, so I walked back the way I'd come on the busy shopping street.

I stopped in my tracks when I saw the Tanuki Carpentry truck right by Takara Auction House. Akira was unloading a long, plastic-wrapped roll. At the sight of me, he nodded.

I came up to him and spoke in a low, apologetic tone. "Hello, Akira-kun. I'm sorry for not coming over yesterday evening."

"It's okay." His half smile told me he understood.

"What are you working on here?"

Morioka-san wants new carpeting installed into his place. He offered a good price if we could do it now."

"So you can do carpeting as well as carpentry? Is there anything you can't do?"

"This will be my first time doing carpet." He sighed. "There's a lot of important rebuilding work to do around town, so it's a little inconvenient. And those stairs weren't carpeted before, so I'll have to remove trim from the sides and do other things to prepare. But before I forget to say it—Michael-san is looking for you."

"Really! So he's returned from overseeing the boats?"

"Yes. I gave him a ride back to headquarters after the tow left. Those boats are going to a harbor about thirty miles west from here. You should call him. He was concerned that you hadn't come back from the hospital along with the others."

"I tried to call him earlier. I'll do it again."

"Michael-san told me some children found Mayumi's family's lacquer collection. That's really good news for the family, isn't it?"

"Yes, and not just because they had a valuable collection returned," I added, when I saw his cynical expression. "They opened a whole conversation about Mayumi that was really nice."

"Was anything else inside her backpack?"

"Unfortunately, nothing. The phone and wallet were either lost or removed."

"Removed," Akira said with a grimace. "I still think someone killed her."

"Perhaps you're right," I admitted. "A doctor who ran a few x-rays on her body said the upper front of her skull was crushed, and her shoulder was dislocated."

"Really!" Akira's eyes flared with emotion. "But *who* would do that to her? Who could hate like that?"

"Maybe the answer is in her missing phone. I'd like to stop by the playground next to the auction house. She was seen going in by one of the boys on the jungle gym."

"That must be Masa-kun," Akira said. "He's the younger brother of one of my school friends, just starting high school."

"Yes, it is. How observant do you think he is? Some kids that age exaggerate things—"

"Not Masa-kun. He's a good kid, and smart. What did he say about Mayumi?"

"Masa said Mayumi was on the street and tried to encourage all the boys to come up with her inside the auction house to take shelter. Masa stayed outside—I guess he was the group's leading daredevil—but the others went in with her. Masa says his friends came out but wasn't sure if he saw Mayumi do that."

"But if she'd been with Ishida-san and Morioka-san, she would have survived." Akira gave a long, low whistle. "Of course, there's a back door. It's where I went in earlier today when I had to measure. Maybe that's the exit she took."

I said goodbye and walked over to the opposite side of the street, continuing down the block to the playground. Mud had been shoveled and sawdust laid down to give children a path to the swing set and other equipment. Two young boys and a girl were on the swings, laughing and pumping their legs as they soared.

Like many jungle gyms, this one was a dome of criss-crossing iron bars, with the top of the structure about twelve feet off the ground. It had also been scrubbed clean. Climbing up carefully, I found a clear view of the view of the auction house from one direction and the ocean from the other. Would Masa really have stayed facing the auction house?

No. He'd already told me about watching the coast, camera-phone at the ready.

As I turned away from the water to look back at Takara Auction House, I noted the dark water line close to the top of the first-floor windows. This water line showed the height the wave had reached. I remembered how thick the mud was on the ground floor and the depressing sight of so many antiques drenched in dirt. My boots had been heavy with mud; I'd had to remove them before going upstairs.

I saw again those steps made of cedar, the local tree that gave Sugihama its name. They were wide stairs, suitable for at least three or four people to climb at the same time, which made sense for a place that had been designed as a kindergarten.

Was I correctly remembering the staircase? I stared hard at the building, and then began climbing down.

Seconds later, I'd jogged the short distance to the shop. Akira's truck was no longer parked outside. I guessed that he'd dropped off the carpeting roll and moved on to do something else.

More than ever, I needed to speak with Mr. Morioka about whether he'd seen Mayumi and the boys run in and out of the shop. If he were not in, I'd take a quick look at the stairs to satisfy my curiosity about the strange thoughts that were percolating.

A jingle of antique cowbells announced my entrance as I opened the door. Mr. Morioka had improvised a historic alarm. I stood in the auction house threshold, glancing around the well-lit room. A roll of gray carpet stood like a fat, woolly pillar at the bottom of the wide staircase. A thin sheet of paper lay atop a big toolbox next to the carpet. Glancing down, I saw that the cost of the carpet was about $4,000, with labor $3,000. I'd thought contractor prices in Hawaii were high, until I saw this.

The letterhead said TANUKI CARPENTRY, and Mr. Rikyo's signature and *inkan* stamp were at the bottom of the page. Mr. Morioka had also signed and marked with his own *inkan*. Forest and high knoll were the characters for his first name. Every time I saw *kanji* characters I recognized, I felt a brief surge of competency. His first name was even easier: the *kanji* for "big" followed by the kanji for "myself." Read aloud, it started out "Dai."

Daigo. This was the older gangster-type Mayumi had met in Tokyo.

All this time, I'd thought Daigo was someone who'd fenced to a dealer: a gangster middleman to unethical dealers. But now it seemed the other way around. He was a bona fide antiques dealer with mob connections. And since Mayumi hadn't known this, he would have been able to collect double commissions from her on the lacquer.

It was a lot to ponder. However, I couldn't forget what I'd been thinking about while staring at the building's exterior. I turned on the flashlight function of my phone and approached the stairs, sweeping the bright yellow light over the cedar stairs.

The center of each step was a slightly lighter, worn shade than the edges: evidence of all the foot traffic from the kindergarten years. Although the entire staircase had been scrubbed, the bottom ten steps were still discolored from the days that mud had lingered; and the plaster on the wall near these steps was also stained.

The top half of the staircase had never been flooded. It was unmarked, excepting two steps marked by several rusty, reddish brown blots. The previous times I'd been here, I'd had too much on my mind to notice any particular marks on stairs. But I didn't hurry today.

During my years buying and selling antiques, I'd seen all manner of stains on wood. But never blood.

CHAPTER 35

Using my phone's camera, I shot a quick, close picture. I wanted to take another shot at enough distance to make it apparent the bloodstained step was part of Mr. Morioka's staircase.

The door's jingling bells made me think Akira must have returned. I could only imagine his reaction when I told him whose blood marked the stairs.

"Hey, Akira!" I put the phone in my pocket and began hurrying down to meet him. But as I reached the halfway point, I stopped.

It was Daigo Morioka. At first, he gave me the kind of surprised, professional smile one might give a customer. As he saw past my new hairstyle and city clothing, though, that smile dropped.

Acknowledging his recognition, I made a slight half bow. The plan had changed. I needed to evacuate without alerting him that I'd figured out who he really was.

"You are alone," he said. He was dressed ruggedly, in work pants, a down jacket, boots and gloves.

"I'm here with my husband." I put emphasis on the word, trying to make him believe I wasn't in the auction house alone. But my predicament was obvious. If I'd been on the ground floor, I could have rushed for the door. But because Mr. Morioka was blocking the foot of the stairs, there was no way out.

Mr. Morioka narrowed his eyes, looking at me skeptically. "Why are you back? You found the Kimuras' lacquer."

"How did you hear that?"

"Ishida-san rang me with the good news." As he spoke, his gaze shifted to the toolbox near his feet. He bent down, rummaged for a moment, and then came up holding a large hammer.

"You left Mayumi's backpack where it could be noticed. What a kind gesture."

I couldn't take my eyes off the hammer. Morioka was a quick thinker who wasn't afraid to act violently when he had the opportunity. How clever of him to go after me with a hammer already marked with Akira's fingerprints.

"Kindness?" He made a snorting sound. "After Ishida gave me the details of every piece, I realized his knowledge and communication about these goods to other dealers would make the lacquer impossible to sell. And then, there was the problem of you."

"Yes. Because you worried about me, you tampered with my mobile phone."

"A precaution. From the moment you started asking questions, I knew you could be troublesome. You should have just taken Ishida back to Tokyo."

I shrugged, trying to appear calm. "That was not his wish."

"I never realized the connection between them. The stupid girl I'd met in Tokyo phoned me two weeks before, saying she wanted to take back the lacquer. I couldn't, of course; it was going to be a high point of the event."

"It meant a lot of money," I added, looking at his flushed face.

"Money that nobody's getting now," he grumbled. "What a vulgar, noisy kid; she ruined everything."

"Actually, the tsunami ruined everything. And when the sirens blew and she wanted shelter, I don't know how you could have turned her away."

"She tried to drag in a bunch of town teenagers with her. Lots could be stolen with urchins like that lingering on my third floor."

"Did you know those kids died?" I stared at him, and from the way his eyes dropped for a moment, it seemed he might feel guilty. "When the tsunami siren rang, you knew that if Mayumi perished, you'd have the lacquer collection to yourself, if you could get it upstairs in time."

A jingling arose near the door. Someone was coming; hope surged within me.

"Excuse me, mail delivery," a cheerful male voice called out.

"Help," I shouted, but the clanging bells from the door closing drowned out my voice. Mr. Morioka picked up the hammer and advanced up the first step toward me.

"You shouldn't have called out like that."

The moment had come. I pulled out my phone and punched in 110. Glancing down, it was clear to me that the cell network wasn't working. But he didn't know. I said, "Soon, they'll be on their way. And you'll have a second murder charge."

"Don't you understand that there was no murder? I had to push her away from the door. That's all I did."

"You hit the front of her head. Maybe with the same piece of wood you threatened me and Mr. Ishida with, when we surprised you the first time."

From the tightness of his expression, I guessed I was right. "She fell down. I don't know any of the other events. I had one minute to lock that door and get to the third floor. I was shocked to open my door after the waters went down and see that she'd stayed. All I did was move her to a place where she could be collected."

"So you got rid of her."

"Later that night, I rolled her into a carpet that I carried to the butcher shop on the next street. So much was going on that nobody gave me a second look."

I reconsidered my earlier thoughts about escape. If I ran into his second-floor apartment, I could lock the door behind me. I remembered a landline phone on the desk. If the line wasn't functioning, I could raise the window and call out for help to the street.

I made a snap decision. The stairs creaked horribly as I swung around and began running up. At the second-floor entrance, I found the door was locked fast. Damn it. Even if I'd had my tools with me, I would not have had time.

Mr. Morioka was chuckling as he now mounted the stairs at a leisurely pace.

"Forget it," I yelled, sounding tougher than I felt. "You can't get out a body out with all the volunteers around."

"Work stops in the evenings, doesn't it? You know the volunteers' schedule."

Mr. Morioka surged toward me, filling my view. When we were a foot apart, he raised the hammer. As it traveled fast down toward my forehead, I ducked and punched out with braced arms against his belly. He lost his balance, and in an instant, he tripped backward down the stairs.

At the bottom, he lay moaning, his hands cradling his head. I made my way down, my entire body shaking. I leapt over his body, not wanting to risk him catching me by the ankle.

There was no need to do anything more with him. All I wanted was to get out of the dark auction house and into the light.

Across the street, the Tanuki Carpentry van had reappeared. Michael was sitting on the rear bumper. He was drinking a canned coffee with Akira. Seeing the two strong men chatting over their petite cans of coffee—while I'd almost had my brain bashed—was damn annoying.

"Oh, there you are!" Michael greeted me happily. "We were hoping you'd turn up. I didn't know if your phone was on silent mode, or if the cell network is down again."

I shook my head at him. I didn't know where to begin.

"Rei, what is it?" Michael's voice shifted an octave.

"You are clueless," I exploded. "Morioka murdered Mayumi! I was in there, and he trapped me on the stairs and was coming at me with a hammer. I just barely got away, and now I think I might have killed him!"

In that instant, Michael grabbed me to him. I felt his heart pounding against mine.

"Rei, I'm so sorry. I had my suspicions, but I can't believe you were alone with him—"

"Well, if you want to see the results, he's lying at the foot of the stairs."

"What's wrong?" Akira cut in, as if sensing the rapid-fire English passing between us meant a major problem.

"Please contact the police," I said to him in Japanese. "My phone didn't work."

"I'll call these guys in to help." Michael jogged off toward a group of Japanese soldiers shoveling mud.

Akira dialed the police and then handed me the phone. When I'd finished explaining to the dispatcher about the need for both police and an ambulance, I hung up and told Akira about how Daigo Morioka had killed Mayumi. Before I was quite finished, he was running for the building, his face red with anger.

"Don't kill him," I called out, following him. "He's already down!"

But when we opened the front door and looked at the place where Mr. Morioka had been, it was empty.

"He's gone," I explained, not wanting to believe it. "How could he get away so fast?"

"The back door," Akira said. "I brought in the carpet that way—"

As he crossed the floor in swift strides, I followed, hoping we weren't in for some kind of a hammer-throwing, horror-movie surprise.

But Mr. Morioka hadn't the strength for that. He was lying halfway between the inside of the building and the outdoors, his head close to a puddle of vomit. His face was as pinched as a pickled plum.

The skin around one of his eyes had swollen, giving the impression it would soon be black-and-blue. The unbruised eye glared at me. "I should have killed you, too."

"You took Mayumi." Akira ground out the words. The rage on his face made me shiver.

"I didn't take her anywhere," Morioka moaned.

"You told me—"

"He doesn't need to say anything. Look at that." Akira kicked at the edge of Mr. Morioka's boot, so the underside showed. It was rubber, with diagonal tread.

"Too much has happened," Morioka muttered.

Michael and the soldiers arrived at a run. In seconds, they'd surrounded the immobilized criminal. And to my relief, Akira stepped back.

"That bitch hurt me," Morioka whimpered, raising an arm to point at me. "Some bones must be broken."

"Actually, I called to make sure you have police and medical attention." I could not keep the sarcasm out of my voice.

As the police came through the door, the bells jangled hard. I slipped my hand into Michael's, thinking that Mr. Morioka was right about one thing.

Far too much had happened.

It was time to close the investigation; to let the water wash away Daigo Morioka to his final destination.

CHAPTER 36

O n our last day in Tohoku, the sun shone. Michael and I had an early breakfast of granola bars, followed by group calisthenics. Then we all put on gloves and got to work cleaning up the business district.

"I wasn't sure of your strengths before," Mr. Yano said with a smile. "I did not know what you Americans could do. But after yesterday's events, I have confidence."

Ironically, I was tasked with moving furniture stuck in the street and then cleaning it off enough that residents could come through and make claims. Within this category were many antique pieces most likely from Takara Auction House. Nobody wanted to bother with saving anything from that particular business.

The story of Mr. Morioka's savagery had spread through the town. I wasn't sure whether it was soldiers or volunteers or the Rikyos who told, but soon everyone understood that the boys who'd been on the playground had died only because the auction house owner had refused them admittance to the upper floor of his building. And Mayumi's effort to help the boys was described with one word: *kizuna.*

"I always knew that girl had good within her," Akira's mother said. She'd come in the truck with Akira to bring carrot muffins for the volunteers. "I've been thinking of making a doll for the Kimuras that would look just like Mayumi. Do you think that would be all right?"

"That's a lovely idea."

Mrs. Rikyo continued, "But I'm not sure if the doll should have *blue* hair."

"Her parents treasure the memory of her at this age." I reached into my wallet and pulled out the photograph of young Mayumi with braids.

Mrs. Rikyo nodded. "Yes! That is a good picture. She even reminds me a little of my daughter. But a school uniform... isn't that a bit plain?"

"You could ask her parents if they still have any of her childhood dresses for you to cut from," I suggested.

"Or some old kimono silk," Mrs. Rikyo said. "Surely they've saved what she wore to a childhood shrine ceremony. Most *kimekomi* dolls wear kimono."

Akira had been listening quietly, but now he spoke: "The doll should have clothing with the buttons she made."

"Yes," Mrs. Rikyo agreed, after a pause. "I will make a coat to go over the kimono. Do you know about those kimono coats, Shimura-san? They are called *michiyuki.*"

I put the photograph in Akira's hands. "Why don't you keep this? You can make a copy for your mother's use. I have another for Mr. Ishida."

Akira bent his head. I ached for him, as well as for Glock. She, too, had loved Mayumi. I would give her the artist's notebook.

Michael came around the corner from Mr. Yano's office. He waved at me.

"What is it?" I asked.

"I heard the police arrived. They want to talk to you."

"Oh." I expected this would happen, sooner or later. Mr. Morioka had been taken to the hospital. His fate was still up in the air—as was mine, if he decided to press assault charges against me.

"I'll be there, too," Michael's voice was reassuring. "And it turns out one of the mud-shovelers is a lawyer, so he volunteered to support you as well."

"That's probably a good idea, based on my past experiences with Japanese cops."

"I'll back you," Akira said, folding arms across his chest. "I overheard what he said to you about killing when I came upon him yesterday. And he wore those boots to the hospital, didn't he?"

"Well, surely the old evidence of the tracks in the butcher shop is gone by now—"

"Of course it isn't!" Akira said. "I shoveled out the mud in the butcher shop, except for that area, and put cones around so no one else would step there."

Michael gave Akira a thumbs-up. "Are you sure you want to stay in the construction field? There are quite a lot of career possibilities for someone who thinks the way that you do."

Akira put his hand on his mother's arm. "I left my family once. It was a mistake. And the work I do here will nail this town together."

As he finished speaking, his mother smiled. "Akira has our

permission to visit you in Hawaii. Maybe all of us will take a holiday after this is finished."

"Akira, you're a really great guy. One of these days... " I almost added, "*you'll find a wonderful young woman who deserves you*," but I held off, knowing the statement would only make him think of Mayumi. So I finished with: "One of these days, we'll be back to see you and your revitalized town."

Michael and I barely had the time to clean up with wet wipes and knock the mud off our work boots before meeting the police in Mr. Yano's office. Fujita-san, the volunteer lawyer Michael had recruited, had engaged in a preliminary conversation with the police. Mr. Fujita had already reassured me that I wasn't going to be charged with assault. Mr. Fujita hinted that Morioka was already a person of interest to the Tokyo police.

"It will be interesting to hear what they say to us," he whispered to me as the three of us went in and took the usual chairs around a classroom table.

The senior police official, a long-faced man named Kodama, had come from a larger Tohoku town not hit by the tsunami. The other man was a regular constable who introduced himself as Constable Ota. This was the same young policeman I'd approached earlier. At that time, he'd said no coroner was available to perform an autopsy. Now he was attentively taking notes on everything being said.

"Thank you for coming. Tea?" Sgt. Kodama began the meeting as any businessman might, although I wondered where his tea-making office lady could possibly be. In the next moment, I saw

Constable Ota had a little tray containing half a dozen UCC brand cans of green tea. Quite practical.

"Earlier this morning, I spoke with Ishida-san in Tokyo," Sgt. Kodama said. "Apparently he had gathered some information from TADA, the Tokyo Antiques Dealers Association."

"Oh, yes. He was working on that." I wondered when Mr. Ishida had contacted the Sugihama police. I'd called my mentor the previous evening to explain all that had happened. It had been hard to tell the story, because it meant telling Mr. Ishida that he really had heard Mayumi's voice calling out in distress. He'd rung off rather quickly.

"A knowledgeable antiques dealer from TADA told Ishida-san that Morioka was fencing antiques gathered by gangsters. These thugs strong-armed elderly people who couldn't repay their children's debts into giving up jewelry and antiques. The Tokyo police came to the shop and questioned Morioka. Apparently frightened by the investigation, Morioka closed his shop and moved to Tohoku, where nobody knew his reputation."

"Ishida-san thought he might also have chosen Tohoku because he believed there were a lot of people here who might be persuaded to sell old country furniture—but there really isn't that much old furniture in people's homes anymore," Sgt. Kodama continued. "So, because Morioka couldn't create a strong base of antiques shoppers within the Tohoku community, he decided to make the business an auction house to attract dealers from around Japan and overseas."

"Excuse me, but was there a reason that the Tokyo police didn't press charges after visiting him at the shop?" Michael asked politely in Japanese.

"Oh. Your Japanese is very good," Constable Ota said.

Sgt. Kodama shot the junior policeman a look and then answered Michael. "I have asked Tokyo about it. They couldn't charge him because it could not be proven that he knew the provenance of his wares. I think it's also likely the original owners were too frightened to ever admit that *yakuza* were the ones who'd taken their antiques."

"Did you ask Morioka anything specifically about the *yakuza?*" I asked.

Sgt. Kodama nodded. "Yes. He confessed the name of the person who introduced him to Mayumi and also several other names of people who'd provided suspicious goods that he sold. Apparently you made a blind date with one of them at a place called Summer Grass?"

"Not knowingly! The guy tried to get me to leave in his car, and I just barely got away. He gave me a false name, I think—"

"Does the name Hashimoto Asao sound familiar?"

"Yes," I said. Poor Eri. With a client like that, no wonder she was so surly toward the male gender.

Mr. Fujita cleared his throat. "Officers, the fencing of goods is not a very serious criminal charge, is it? I worry that Morioka could receive a wrist-slap, although he's very likely responsible for one woman's death and assault with homicidal intent on my client."

"Yes, fencing does not carry a long term," Sgt. Kodama said with a sigh. "In this case, he didn't commit any kind of crime because he gave up the backpack containing lacquerware to be found by the volunteers."

"But he killed Mayumi." I felt something sharp in my left hand and realized that I'd crushed my coffee can. "His original intention was to have her out of the way so he could sell the lacquer and keep all the profits. He said all this, just before he came at me with the hammer."

"It's complicated," Sgt. Kodama said. "You are saying that he confessed this, but he maintains that he didn't know anyone was still on the other side of the second-floor door he'd locked as a proper precaution against the tsunami. It is one person's word against another's."

"He says the death was accidental." Michael surprised me by speaking up in Japanese. "But the medical report suggests violence, doesn't it? And he didn't leave the body where he discovered it. Strange, isn't it?"

"Morioka won't admit to moving the girl's body," Sgt. Kodama said. "Just as he denies killing her."

"What about the x-ray showing the blow to the head?" I demanded.

"Could be a blow, could be a fall," Sgt. Kodama said.

"Excuse me again, officers, but since you were good enough to consult Ishida-san, I recommend you ask Rikyo Akira what he knows. After all, Morioka contacted his father about a rush job carpeting the stairs." Michael's voice was quiet and pleasant; he was a good counterpoint to me.

"The Rikyo family is well known in this community," Constable Ota said, writing down the name and circling it. "Tanuki Carpentry is leading the rebuilding movement."

"I understand that Japan's new trial system gives family and community members a voice in the courtroom," Michael said. "What an excellent idea!"

"Constable, please call the Rikyos. Mr. and Mrs. Hendricks, good luck with your return to Tokyo and Hawaii. We will contact you by telephone in the unlikely case you're needed for any more information."

I breathed deeply, allowing myself to work through my perpetual frustration at how agile some people were at saying no without needing to use that word. And now I could guess why Daigo Morioka had been so forthcoming about the *yakuza* friend's name. The louder he squealed, the more lenient the law would be.

Sgt. Kodama swiftly drew the interview to a close. While the men were still gathering up their papers, I strode out of the office and then the volunteer shelter. I stood on a bluff, looking down toward the water. That horrible, homicidal water that was no longer a threat to anyone.

Michael joined me about ten minutes later. "Not entirely reassuring, was it?"

"I can't believe Mr. Morioka will get away with this crap *again*."

"I'm sorry. Perhaps they are waiting to see what the National Police will want to do with him, given his *yakuza* connections."

I exhaled hard and stared at the ocean. "I suppose that after Morioka gets out of the hospital, he can just get into witness protection."

"That's doubtful," Michael said. "Japanese society is too closed for people to move easily into new communities with false identities. With an organized crime grudge against him, Morioka will spend the rest of his life looking over his shoulder in fear. That's one of the most psychologically unsettling punishments anyone could suffer."

Perhaps he was right. The tsunami had turned so much upside down. When I thought about all that had happened, the police's reluctance to put a criminal in jail was just another form of collateral damage. Mayumi was just one death among hundreds not yet tallied in the small community.

"You see the big picture," I said to Michael. "You were much more civil with those cops than I was. Now I understand why you like intercultural negotation."

"The secret is not showing emotion on the outside, no matter how strongly you feel. And remember, there's no resolution yet. Akira has evidence to bring to light."

Michael took my hand and squeezed it. I felt the strength flowing from him. And suddenly I understood that although hidden fault lines lay deep below the surfaces of our lives, these lines were only cracks—not canyons. And just like the people of Tohoku, we had a strong enough foundation to keep going.

In early evening, we'd made it to JR Ichinoseki Station for a bullet train back to Tokyo. One of the JMSDF jeeps took us all the way; its driver had been involved in the soft-drink-machine rescue of Mr. Haneda and wanted to know all the details of his medical recovery. A pleasant conversation resulted in a name-card exchange and promises to look out for each other the next time anyone was in Hawaii or Japan.

"I will miss the warmth of Tohoku," I said as we made our way into the station. "Even though it's technically much chillier than Hawaii."

"There's our train," Michael said, sighting down the brightly lit zone where bullet trains were stationed. "Is it early?"

"If it is, I think Japan's getting back to normal," I said. The Shinkansen had pulled up to the platform. Speakers throughout blared a polite message to stand back. Passengers would disembark first; we needed to wait for our turn.

Despite the sadness of saying final goodbyes to our Sugihama friends, I was ready to board the train. I needed the buffer of Tokyo between this passage in my life and the return to Oahu. I hoped for a late night out on the town with Michael, Richard, and Enrique. I wanted to drink tea with my aunt and plan a fundraising reception that would fit both our styles. If I could sneak Michael off for a few hours to a love hotel, that would be the icing on the cake.

I felt someone push at my hip and then circle my waist with strong arms. Miki Haneda grinned up at me. She was wearing clean jeans, and she had a new denim jacket and a shiny backpack featuring Totoro.

"Thank goodness the train is still here," she exclaimed. "The ticket seller was very slow. A real bother!"

It had been hard enough to say goodbye to the little girl and her family the previous evening. Now I was faced with a repeat farewell with a sixty-second time limit.

I glanced in the other direction and saw Akira.

"Relax, Rei-san. Everything is good. Her mother and I managed it together."

"Akira, it's so good to see you, too. It was too short when we said goodbye at the shelter."

"Yes. And you know, just a couple of hours ago the police came to talk to me. I told them about the rush carpeting order and then showed them the footprints from his boots in the butcher shop. They took photographs and samples."

"You convinced them," I said, feeling incredulous.

"It's not just me. Our town has its spirit back. We feel duty to support anyone who's helped us including you, Rei-san. Everyone ate your miso stew and remembers your kindnesses to the Hanedas. People saw you working in mud even earlier today."

His words were embarrassing. "You make me sound a lot more noble than I am. But thanks."

"Tonight, Mayor Hamasaki is addressing the community about the matter. And Morioka's in the hospital. He can't run away."

"I'm so glad about that. Can we talk later? The train's just come in. I should concentrate on Miki." I had kept my eye on the child, who'd been bouncing on her heels and looking around the station with interest while the three adults talked.

"Actually, she's coming with us," Michael said.

"That's very spur of the moment!" I stared at my husband.

"Norie thought it would be fun to host a little girl for a few days, especially since she may be moving to Yokohama for a while."

"I'm going to be a flower girl at your wedding reception!" Miki announced. "And after I get my dress, I will take Hachiko shopping just like I promised her. I brought dog biscuits, in case I need to make friends with her again."

Thoughts of caipirinhas were being replaced by milk and cookies. Hugging the little girl, I said, "I bet that Hachiko's been looking out the shop window every day, waiting for you to come play with her. We'll stop to see her after this train ride."

"Kids and dogs together are great, aren't they?" Michael's blue eyes shot meaningful glances at me right over the smooth top of Miki's head. I raised my eyebrows at him. This was a better conversation to have in Hawaii, on a Friday night in the cottage's backyard, watching the sun set over the Pacific.

"Hey, don't miss your boarding call," Akira said. The station attendants were signaling more vehemently and electronic bells were ringing out warnings. The three of us jumped on just as the doors whooshed closed.

Through the glass, Akira waved wildly until our train was past the platform. Then I turned away from the window. Michael was talking to the confectionary seller with a cart at the far end of the compartment while Miki skipped down the aisle, looking for the correct empty row.

Watching them, I thought about how this was supposed to be the end of a journey. But somehow, it felt like the start of something new.

Acknowledgments

I am grateful to a number of good people for helping bring *The Kizuna Coast* to life. Foremost are my longtime friends Satoshi Mizushima and Koichi Hyogo, who furnished many helpful details about the immediate days following the earthquake. Of course, Sugihama is a fictional Tohoku town hit by the wave, but general details about the volunteer experience were supplied by Masako Tanaka and Jun Sato, Tokyo residents who volunteered many, many weekends in Rikuzen Takata and are living examples of the concept of *kizuna*. Thank you so much for what you did for the people of Tohoku, and how you helped me in my work.

Naomi Hirahara, a dear friend and fellow author who volunteered in Tohoku in 2012, also provided wonderful details about Tohoku. Jennifer Sawyer Fisher was an insightful developmental editor with great ideas, and Barb Goffman a ruthless, accomplished line editor. Before them the early chapters of this book were reviewed by my Minneapolis reading group: Gary Bush, Heidi Skarie, and Stanley Trollip, and two other writer friends, Eden Unger Bowditch and Marcia Talley. Lifetime Honolulu resident Liz Tajima once again was a superb vetter of Hawaii details.

I also thank the readers of my Asiafile newsletter for commenting on early chapters and so many Facebook friends from around the world who cheered on the book's creation. Honest reviews are very helpful to me as an author and also to other book buyers. Please consider leaving a review at Goodreads or anywhere else. If you're a blogger interested in advance reading copies of other books that you'd write about or review, contact me via my web site (sujatamassey.com) for details on joining the reviewers' list.

About the Author

Sujata Massey is the author of many books set in Japan, India, and the United States. She was born in England to parents from India and Germany, but was raised mostly in Saint Paul, Minnesota. Sujata is a graduate of the Johns Hopkins University in Baltimore, Maryland, where she studied in the Writing Seminars department. After university she worked as a features reporter for Baltimore's *Evening Sun* newspaper. Her next adventure was moving to Japan with husband Anthony Massey, where two wonderful years passed by too quickly. As an effort to preserve memories—and try her hand for the first time at fiction—Sujata began writing *The Salaryman's Wife,* the first book in the Rei Shimura series. Rei novels have won the Agatha and Macavity mystery awards and been named finalists for the Edgar, Anthony, and Mary Higgins Clark awards. They're published in fifteen countries so far. The entire Rei series is forthcoming as audiobooks. Currently available in audio are *The Typhoon Lover* (Rei #8) to be followed later this year by *The Kizuna Coast* (Rei #11).

Readers who like international fiction and historical suspense should check out Sujata's books set in early twentieth-century India. *The Sleeping Dictionary* is available as both a novel and audiobook in the US, and is also published as *The City of Palaces* in India, as *L'Amante di Calcutta* in Italy, and as *Yutak Ogretmeni* in Turkey. *The Ayah's Tale* is a novella in paper and e-book.